# HEROES OF THE RANGE

Zane Grey's great western novel NEVADA first introduced Jim Lacy, gunman and near-renegade, who changed his way of life to fight on the side of justice. In BEYOND THE MOGOLLON RIM, Nevada Jim takes up his sixgun once again and hits the trail on a lonely manhunt, with a vengeful outlaw gang lying in wait for him.

Al Slingerland, a trapper so wise in the ways of the redmen that he was known as "The White Indian," made his initial appearance in THE U.P. TRAIL. In THE TRACK OF BLOOD, Slingerland tangles with both Indians and whites, as he protects a beautiful young Indian girl from her attackers.

# ZANE GREY'S NEVADA JIM LACY

# BEYOND THE MOGOLLON RIM

**Romer Zane Grey**

Based on characters created by Zane Grey

*221 pages*
*18 cm*

LEISURE BOOKS ⚮ NEW YORK CITY

A LEISURE BOOK

Published by

Dorchester Publishing Co., Inc.
6 East 39th Street
New York, NY 10016

Printed in the United States of America

# CONTENTS

# BEYOND THE
# MOGOLLON RIM

# I

Hettie Ide tightened her fingers about those of the lean-faced rider at her side in the shadowy depths of the little church. "Nevada," she murmured, "in just two more weeks we will be standing where they are now, and you'll be fumbling for the ring just as awkwardly."

Jim Lacy — the Ides had never gotten around to calling him by his real name, but had continued to use the one they'd tacked on him back in the hell-for-leather, wild-horse-hunting days in the Forlorn River country — shook his head.

"I'm wishing it was right now," Nevada drawled softly. "Waiting until we get to San Diego don't set well with me."

"I've told you I feel the same way. But Mother—"

"Sure, sure. I know how it is, sweetheart."

The droning voice of the Reverend Mr. Kingsley rose higher as he extended his hands, and held them over the heads of Marvie Blaine and Rose Hatt.

"I now pronounce you man and wife."

Marvie, young brother-in-law of Ben Ide, turned to his bride. She wore no veil, no elaborate wedding gown, only a simple white dress hurriedly whipped together by Ben's wife Ina and his sister Hettie. Taking her awkwardly by the shoulders, he planted a kiss on her lips, and drew back, smiling, embarrassed.

"My turn now!" Ben Ide said, stepping up and taking Rose in his arms. "I guess a brother-in-law has the right to be first in line."

The other wedding guests surged forward—Hettie, Ina, Mrs. Ide, Judge Franklidge and his daughter, the Tom Days—all offering congratulations and best wishes. Nevada, never fully at ease at such times, held back until their exuberance had subsided before claiming his moment with the flushed, happy girl.

"Good luck to you, Rose," he said. "Marvie's a fine boy."

"I know he is," she replied, a look of understanding passing between them. Rose Hatt, daughter of the notorious Elam Hatt, sister of the now dead outlaw, Cedar Hatt, marrying into the wealthy Blaine family. It was a big step for her. "I don't deserve such happiness," she said. "But I'll be a good wife—and I'll do the best I can."

"I know you will," Nevada said. "Marvie's lucky, too." He turned to the young bridegroom. "She's yours now. It's up to you to take good care of her."

"Don't worry about that, Nevada," Marvie said. "I'll spend the rest of my life—"

"Forget that her folks weren't as law-abiding as they might have been. It's no fault of hers, so don't ever mention it."

"I won't—you can count on it! I aim to make her the—"

"All right, folks," Ben Ide's voice broke in, overriding the excited talking. "Everybody head for Clem Walter's restaurant. The wedding dinner's there."

10

Nevada felt an arm slip under his, and he grinned down into Hettie's calm gray eyes.

"I'm so happy for them," she said. "There's so much ahead for them. I—I regret all those years we were apart—the ones we lost. I feel—well, cheated."

"We'll make them all up," Nevada said, drifting toward the doorway with the others. We've a lifetime together waiting for us."

Outside, Winthrop's single street lay quiet in the warm spring sun. Somewhere a dog was barking, and the sweet smell of lilacs growing along the front wall of the church filled the air. Marvie and Rose stepped out onto the landing, the others close behind them. Ben Ide pushed to the edge of the porch.

"No need for any of you gentlemen to stop off at Haley's Saloon on the way," he said, grinning broadly. "I've ordered champagne sent to the restaurant. Fact is—"

"Jim!" an urgent voice shouted from across the street. "Jim Lacy!"

Nevada, in the act of handing Hettie down the step, paused and swung quickly about. A familiar figure was coming toward him at a hard run from the passageway that lay between the bank and Mason's Feed Store.

Cash Burridge!

The lean rider hadn't seen Cash, an impulsively reckless friend from the old days in Lineville on the California-Nevada border, since that morning he'd warned him to leave the Mogollon Rim country or get caught in the rustler clean-out he'd undertaken—and successfully completed.

"Get out of here, Jim!" Burridge yelled, waving his arms. "They've come to kill you. Cud Richardson—

11

Ed's brother! He's right behind me."

The shouted words were almost instantly drowned out by a crackling burst of gunfire. Burridge halted in mid-stride and spun half about as bullets thudded into the front of the church.

"Back inside!" Nevada shouted. "Fast, all of you!"

Another burst of gunshot erupted close to the bank. Ben Ide sagged to one knee. Marvie Blaine staggered, clutching at his shoulder as a dull red stain widened about his contracted fingers.

"Get inside!" Nevada yelled again and, seizing Hettie about the waist, hurled her toward the doorway.

Behind him, Franklidge and Tom Day, jolted from their stunned lethargy, began shepherding the women into the chapel. Nevada leapt to Ben's aid. Slipping an arm under the wounded man's shoulder, he lifted him to his feet.

"Come on, pard," he said in a low, unhurried way, "Let's get you inside, where we can fix up that leg."

Ide swore deeply. "Not bad hurt. What in the name of hell is this all about?"

Gunfire rattled a third time. Bullets splintered into the flooring, thudded into the wall, plucked at Lacy's sleeve. But there were fewer shots this time. Down the street voices were shouting—one voice calling for the marshal.

Nevada, grim-faced, laid Ben Ide on the first pew, and wheeled to Tom Day. "Slip out the back way—get the doctor," he urged, his voice strained. "They won't see you."

Hettie clutched at his arm. "Who is it?" she breathed, searching his face with a terrified look in her eyes. "What's it all about?"

12

Nevada shook his head. "I'm not sure. But it is nothing good. I want you to stay right here, and keep others from following me. They'll listen to you if you stay calm."

Her fingers tightened on his arm. "You're not going out there?" she said in a shocked voice.

"I've got to, Hettie. Cash is in a bad way and needs help."

"No—you can't! You're not even wearing your gun!"

Nevada's hand dropped to his hip. He swore silently. Like all the other men in the wedding party, he had put aside his weapon.

"Reckon I can manage," he said, and stepped quickly to the doorway.

The day had begun with promise.

It was to see the wedding of Marvie Blaine, Ina's nineteen-year-old brother, and Rose Hatt, who had come to live with the Ides after Nevada Jim Lacy and other ranchers had cleared the Mogollon country of a ruthless band of outlaws—the Pine Tree gang.

It would all work out well. Ben and Hettie's mother, in failing health for the past year, had been ordered to San Diego where a milder climate would be of benefit. It was decided that the family would escort her to her new home, leaving the ranch in the care of Marvie and Rose, although—as Ben observed to Nevada as they perched on the top rail of a corral awaiting the family he doubted there'd be any large amount of work done by Marvie.

"A man doesn't get married every day," Lacy had replied.

"You and Hettie going to tie the knot, too?" Ben Ide

asked.

"We decided to wait until we get to San Diego. Your mother wants it that way—though it'd be fine with Hettie and me to get the job done right alongside Marvie and Rose."

Ben Ide nodded. "Obliged to you for humoring Mother. She's always talked about a fancy wedding for her only daughter."

"I know that," Nevada drawled, "but I'm getting a mite anxious. Your sister means more to me than life itself."

"I don't have to tell you how much you mean to her," Ben Ide said. "I'm dead certain she's as disappointed as you."

Nevada stared out across the sage-covered flats toward the frowning Mogollon Rim. "We've come a long way since those wild-horse-trapping days on Forlorn River," he mused. "Don't think Hettie's been out of my mind hardly a minute since the trouble here I was falsely accused of being right in the middle of. Kept me on the run, drifting—just trying to forget. Only I never could."

"Where did you go, Nevada?" Ide asked, looking up. "I always intended to ask. We tried to find you, let you know your name had been cleared, and the killers you flushed from cover exposed for what they were."

"Just kept dogging along. I went back to Lineville where I knew folks who figured me for a friend, and didn't mind if I was a gunslinger named Lacy. Worked around there for a spell. Then my heels got to itching and I struck out for Arizona. I showed up at Tom Day's ranch, and he put me on and asked no questions.

"When it came to my name, I sort of held back, not

wanting to mention the one you'd hung on me—
'Nevada'—for fear you and Hettie might hear of it.
And I sure wasn't going to tell him I was Jim Lacy, the
gunman half of the lawmen west of the Missouri were
after.

"But Tom's a real gentleman. He just sort of grinned
at me, and said: 'Well, I'll call you Texas Jack. The
name sort of fits that drawl of yours.' So Texas Jack I
became. Judge Franklidge called me that, too, when I
later on hired out to him." Nevada paused. "Mighty
fine people, those two. One thing I'll always be thankful
for—the kind of friends the Good Lord lined me up
with."

"I'm the one to be grateful," Ben Ide said quietly.
"If you hadn't stepped in, I'd have been strung up as a
horse thief. You and that fast gun of yours."

"That's over and done with. I'm through with being a
fast gun. We've put the Pine Tree rustling bunch out of
business and we can be grateful the law's no longer
interested in me because I had a hand in doing that."

"A hand in it!" Ben Ide echoed. "It was practically
you alone—"

"I'm sure it was Judge Franklidge who set everything
straight," Nevada said, ignoring Ide's protest. "He
probably made them take a real hard look at the
record—at the kind of men I'd gone up against."

"You never were a killer," Ben Ide said. "A gunman,
maybe—a man who uses his weapon when he has no
choice, but always—"

"Hold on," Nevada interrupted, grinning, "you're
making me sound like some kind of a hero—one of
those knights in shining armor I've heard you reading to
little Blaine about."

15

"It's the truth, Nevada. If Franklidge hadn't put the law straight, I'd have seen to it. I owe everything to you, Nevada. After my father disowned me—"

"I told you to forget it. It's all in the past, buried six feet under."

"No," Ben Ide said slowly. "I won't ever forget. None of the Ides will."

"You've done as much for me. You gave me the chance for a new life. You made it possible for me to have the woman I love for a wife."

"It was Hettie's love for you that made it possible," Ben Ide said. "All the wild mustangs we ever trapped at Forlorn River plus California Red couldn't prevent my sister from marrying you! I'd hate to be the one who tried to stop it!"

Jim Lacy's face was sober. "Just the same," he murmured. "I'm grateful to the Ides."

A thousand lonely thoughts lay behind the words—ten thousand haunting memories of empty days and nights, endless trails, dusty, hostile towns, and always the deep yearning in his heart for the girl he'd felt necessary to give up—and forget.

But all that was over with now. Never again would they be apart for long. Today was the marrying time of Marvie and Rose; tomorrow the rest of the family would head for San Diego. Once there, with Mrs. Ide comfortably settled, Hettie and he would be married, and then he could really believe that what he had hardly dared to take seriously during all of the lonely years—a happiness that would remain steadfast until he ceased to draw breath.

"We're ready, Ben!"

It was Ina's voice, coming from the house. Ben and

Nevada descended from the corral rail.

"It didn't take them as long as I figured," Ida said, smiling. "Proves a woman can fancy up in a hurry, if she has a mind to."

Nevada moved toward the two-seated carriage, knowing that Ben Ide would drive the surrey. "Do we swing by Tom Day's for them?" he asked.

Ben Ide shook his head. "Nope. They'll meet us at the church. So will the Franklidges."

Nevada nodded in understanding and swung the matched sorrel team up to the porch where the family had gathered. Ben Ide curved in behind him.

Stepping down, Nevada assisted Hettie into the front seat. Marvie handed Rose onto the rear cushion. Mrs. Ide would ride with Ben and Ina, taking over the back of the surrey with her small grandson.

Circling his team, Jim Lacy glanced at Ide. "All set to go?"

"All set," Ben answered, "You'd better keep those sorrels plenty far ahead of us, or my blacks'll climb right over you!"

"Now, Ben," Mrs. Ide said. "I hope you're not going to do any of that foolish racing, are you?"

"No, Mother," Ide replied, "no racing. I just don't want you to breathe in a lot of dust." He winked broadly at Lacy, and raised the reins.

Nevada, placed his foot on the iron step pad, swung up, and seated himself beside Hettie. She was frowning.

"Something wrong?"

Hettie pointed to the gun on Nevada's hip. "I know you have to carry a gun while you're working the ranch. But to the wedding?"

Nevada grinned sheepishly. "I guess I forgot," he

17

said. "When we get to the church, I'll leave it in the buggy."

## II

Halting just inside the doorway, Nevada cast a quick glance up and down the street. It was deserted now, except for the sprawled figure of Cash Burridge stirring weakly in the dust. Those along the way who had emerged into the open at the first crackling burst of gunfire, had apparently experienced second thoughts as to the danger of exposing themselves, and had wasted no time in vanishing from the scene.

He was sure that the outlaws were somewhere in the shadowy, weed-filled passageways between the buildings on the opposite side of the street. He was equally sure that without a weapon he could do nothing. Even if he had been armed, an attempt to shoot from where he was standing would have been answered by a hail of bullets that would have endangered the others inside the church.

His gaze passed to the buggy parked next to the surrey which Ben Ide had driven. It was a couple of dozen long strides away, but it was a bit nearer than the stricken man, and the gun he'd have on his hip.

Again he felt the touch of Hettie's hand on his arm. She knew him, knew the direct way his mind worked.

"Wait, please," she murmured. "Let the marshal—"

"He can't be in town," Nevada replied, "or he'd have shown up by now. I can't expect another man to do my fighting for me." He paused, frowning. "How about Ben and Marvie? They hurt bad?"

"Marvie's only scratched. A bullet went through

18

Ben's leg, but I don't think it's serious."

"A bullet meant for me," Nevada said bitterly. "I'm bad luch for anybody who's my friend, it seems."

"That's foolish talk!" Hettie replied, almost angrily.

He shook his head, looked down at her. In the dim interior of the church her face was a pale, intent oval, her eyes soft with a glimmer of tears.

"You're going out there, aren't you?"

"I've no choice," Nevada said, and bending swiftly, kissed her on the lips. Then he swung about and plunged through the doorway.

Instantly guns opened up on him. As he raced for the buggy he felt a bullet rip through his sleeve. Others spurted dust around his feet, or buried themselves in the wall of the church behind him. The outlaws were hiding in the passageways, just as he'd thought.

He reached the buggy, and, breathing harshly, halted behind its thin bulk. He'd have little protection there, he knew. Outlaw lead would quickly enough search him out. But he had no intention of remaining so precariously shielded longer than it took him to seize his gun belt, and the heavy .45 hanging from it.

Keeping the high seat of the vehicle in front of him, he reached into the bed and probed about blindly for the weapon. His fingers touched the worn leather of the belt. Quickly he picked it up, drew it to him. Still crouching, coolness moving through him now, he strapped the belt about his waist and lifted the well-oiled weapon from its holster. He was their equal now. He could meet them on even terms.

"Jim—"

The instant Burridge's voice reached him he crouched still lower, peering under the vehicle, and gripping a

19

wheel spoke to steady himself. Cash was moving, struggling to drag himself out of the street.

"Stay put!" Nevada called, taking care to keep his voice from rising to a shout. "I'm coming."

Gathering his legs under him, he spurted suddenly from behind the buggy. The gun flaming in his hand, he headed on the run for the wall of the buildings opposite. The unexpectedness of the move caught the outlaws by surprise, for there was no immediate crackle of answering gunfire.

Without halting he rushed on to the first passageway. Just short of it, he slowed, and at a crouch moved in carefully, reloading his weapon as he did so. Puffs of smoke coming from the weedy corridor earlier had warned him that one or more of the killers was hiding there. Gun ready, he drew a long breath, rose, and lunged into the narrow area. A man was hurrying toward its far end.

"Pull up!" Nevada shouted.

The outlaw wheeled, his gun coming up fast. Lacy fired. The man staggered, flung out his arms and crashed to the ground in a headlong sprawl.

Immediately Nevada moved on to the next passageway, one considerably larger. Behind him he could hear men coming into the street now, ready to back him. He grinned wryly. Someone else always had to take the first step, fire the first bullet. But it was hard to blame them. Most were family men, with dependents—and it really wasn't their fight.

He pulled up. From the rear of the buildings he heard the quick, hard pound of horses moving out. Throwing caution aside, he ducked into the passageway, and legged it for the alley behind the structures. Three riders, bent low over the saddle, were just disappearing into the grove of trees east of the settlement.

Jim Lacy swore softly, and started to turn back for the street. Then abruptly, he halted. A fourth rider, wearing a fringed buckskin jacket and riding a black horse, broke from the far end of the row of buildings, and raced to overtake his friends. One of the gang had been a little slow in getting away.

Nevada brought up his gun, then lowered his arm again. The distance was too great. He stood for a time watching the outlaw fade into the trees, before continuing on to the street.

Now that all danger was gone, a small crowd had gathered around Burridge. Nevada pushed through them, nodding to those he knew, and dropped to his knees beside the wounded man. Slipping an arm under his friend's shoulders, he raised him slightly. There were two broad stains on the man's back. A single, quick glance convinced Nevada that he didn't have much time left.

"Glad—you—made it, Jim," Cash Burridge said slowly.

"Not soon enough," Nevada answered, with an edge of suppressed anger in his voice. "Somebody get the doctor in the church."

"I—I mean—they didn't get you. It's what they're—out to do. Was anybody—in your party hurt?"

"Ben Ide. Marvie Blaine."

"Sorry for them. Glad they didn't hurt you—or your wife."

"We're not married yet, Cash. It was Marvie and Rose Hatt—"

"Little Rose Hatt? Not good for her—if Marvin is hurt bad. Thought it was you—and Hettie."

"We're getting married later, in San Diego. Cash, if you hadn't warned me in time—"

"Owed you—a favor. You gave me a break. Had to—pay back."

"Wasn't necessary. Cash, what's behind this, what's it all about? I didn't quite get what you said before they cut you down."

"It's Cud Richardson. Ed's brother—fro over New Mexico way. Swears he's going to—to get even with you. For killing Ed."

"The old Pine Tree trouble! And I told Ben it was over and done with, a buried part of the past. Cash, it was a fair fight—just between the two of us."

"I know that. But Cud's the kind—who never forgives or forgets. It was his brother you killed and—even coyotes have kinship feelings."

Nevada's thoughts swung briefly to a long-ago moment of violence near the corrals of the Ide ranch. It had been late in the day, near meal time. Several punchers had been there, along with Ed Richardson—known as Clan Dillon then, foreman for Ben Ide, and, unknown to Ben, the secret leader of the vicious Pine Tree rustlers. Face to face they'd shot it out, and Richardson had died, victim of Nevada's deadly bskill.

The dying man's words started coming in a rush, with no pauses between words, as if a sudden realization that the end was near had made Burridge determined, by exerting himself to the utmost, to tell Nevada everything he felt the lean rider should know.

"Cud aims to start up the Pine Tree outfit again. He figures he first has to get rid of you."

Nevada nodded. "Looks like he'll try again then. But thanks to you, it won't be so easy for him now. How did you get mixed up in it?"

"Ran into him an' the bunch riding with him in Mesilla. I knew Cud from Texas. He told me what he was aiming to do. We'd done a few jobs together—in the old days. Reckon he never thought I'd lean toward you.

"He—he wanted me to handle the selling of the beef they'd be rustling. Him and his bunch would drive the herds to Palos Verdes. It would be my job to have a buyer—be the business end of the set-up."

Burridge's voice faded, choked off. He began to cough deeply. Lacy glanced to one of the men standing close by. "Where's that doc?"

"I'm doing fine," Cash mumbled. "Wasn't that much interested—in lining up with Cud. He ain't the kind of man you can turn your back to. Figured I'd—best go along with the deal. Then I learned what he had in mind—bushwhacking you."

"So you rode in here with them."

Burridge nodded. He started to say something, but fell into another violet spasm of coughing. He brushed wearily at his lips.

"You reckon I could have a drink?"

"Somebody get over to Haley's, and bring a bottle," Lacy snapped.

"No need," a man said, stepping forward. "Happens I got a pint here in my pocket."

Nevada held the liquor to the dying man's mouth, and let him drink his fill. Burridge managed an appreciative smile.

"That helps—the pain's getting real bad. We seen

23

you drive in. Cud hid the bunch along the street. Aimed to nail you when—you come out. Said it'd be a joke on you if you never got the chance—to be a bridegroom."

Burridge's words had begun to come haltingly again. His voice was weaker. He reached for the bottle of whiskey and took another long swallow. At that moment Doc Able shouldered his way through the thickening crowd. Kneeling, the doc made a hurried examination, and shook his head.

"Wanted to warn you—earlier," Burridge said. "Couldn't get away—from Cud."

"Warning me cost you your life," Nevada said quietly. "I owe you plenty, Cash."

"You owe me nothing. Was just a favor—I had to pay back."

"You've done that, and more. Is there anything you want me to do, like getting word to somebody who's important to you?"

"Ain't nobody. Just look out for yourself. Cud won't quit—until he's cut you down. He won't—"

Nevada waited for Burridge to finish. The words had come slow, with effort, and were almost inaudible. He bent own in order to hear.

"No use," Doc Able said. "The man's dead."

### III

Nevada Jim Lacy rose slowly, badly shaken and unable to tear his gaze from Cash Burridge's slack features. Cash had changed. Things had evidently not been going well for him. His clothing was worn, faded and the golden mustache he had once taken such vain pride in was unkempt. Only his eyes had remained the same—a

24

bright, intense blue that seemed to pierce a man.

But the eyes of Cash Burridge would never look out upon the world again, and the flashing grin and engaging manner that had so easily won over new acquaintances, often enlisting them in some far-from-honest scheme, was gone forever.

Cash had known that his loyalty would probably cost him his life. He had been fully aware that the moment he yelled his warning, Cud Richardson and his ruthless companions would turn their guns upon him. It hadn't held him back. With all his shortcomings Cash Burridge was a man—one who had not stopped to add up the costs when there was a debt of friendship to be repaid.

"What'll I do with him, Mr. Lacy?"

Nevada, jarred from his reverie, turned to a tall, darkly bearded onlooker who had elbowed his way through the crowd. It was Rufe Daniels, who did undertaking chores in Winthrop, along with his regular profession of barbering.

"He's to get the best funeral you can arrange," Lacy said. "I'll foot the bill."

"Yes, sir. How about the other one?"

Nevada frowned, his gaze passing to the outlaw he had downed. "I'll pay for him, too," he said. "Every man, even a vicious killer, is entitled to a decent burial."

"Yes, sir. I'll do the job up right. When do you want the services held?"

Lacy stared off toward the Mogollon Rim. "Tomorrow, or the next day, whenever you're ready. I doubt if I'll be around."

He turned then, found Hettie standing directly behind him. She was looking up at him, pride showing in her

25

gray eyes. Beyond her, Marvie Blaine and Rose were looking on from the porch of the church. Marvie was standing at their side with a white bandage on the upper part of his arm, but the others were still inside.

Ben's absence sent a tremor of anxiety through Nevada, but he managed to keep his voice level when he asked: "Is Ben hurt worse than you thought, Hettie?"

"He's fine," Hettie replied. "It was just a flesh wound, and won't take long to heal. It's mother. She's terribly upset."

Daniels and three men moved in, lifted the body of Cash Burridge, and placed it on an improvised board stretcher. As they straightened his lax form, his gun fell to the ground. Daniels recovered it hastily and offered it to Nevada.

"Expect you'll want this, Mr. Lacy. He won't be needing it now."

"Bury it with him," Nevada said. "A man's gun belongs with him, no matter what."

Daniels nodded, and with the three others aiding him, headed for his shop. The crowd began to break up, some of the men pausing to compliment Lacy, and slap him on the back.

"You sure potted that owlhoot hiding in the alley," an angular man with mud on his boots and a quid of tobacco in his cheek said. "Bullet took him dead center of the brisket. Real shooting, I call it."

Nevada moved his head woodenly. Men who stayed on the far side of the street when guns opened up could never know how it felt to be dealing out death—the sickness, the hollow, empty feeling it brought, the dead stop to the heart. No matter if he victim deserved to die, the taking of life was a terrible thing not easily erased from memory.

"I wish I'd had my gun, and been out there with you!" Young Marvie Blaine's voice claimed Nevada's attention. "I'll bet the two of us could—"

"Just be damned glad you weren't!" Nevada cut in savagely. "And start praying every day of your life that you're never called on to kill a man."

Marvie's jaw sagged. "But I thought—"

"I know. You're thinking it's a great thing to handle a sixgun—outdraw another man, cut him down! You think there's some kind of glory in it. Well, think again!"

"Nevada," Hettie broke in gently. "Marvie didn't mean—"

"Neither did all those galoots who came by, and thumped me on the back. If you're smart, Marvie, you'll forget you even own a gun."

Young Blaine's features were frozen. He glanced at Rose and then at Hettie. "What did I say wrong?" he asked, perplexed.

Nevada stared at the boy for a moment, then reached out and gripped him by the shoulder, his fingers tightening in a friendly squeeze. "Don't mind me," he said. "It will make sense to you in a few years." Taking Hettie's hand, he moved off toward the buggy.

"Hettie, you know what all this means," he said, as soon as they were beyond earshot of the others.

The girl nodded soberly.

"There'll be no peace, no safety for anyone around here unless I got after Richardson. He won't quit until he gets me—or I get him."

"I know, Nevada."

"What's worse, he's the kind who'll take it out on you and everyone else who's close to me—if he gets the chance."

27

"I understand I hate it—hate it worse than I can say. But with a posse, it won't take long."

"No posse," he said flatly. "It's a job for me alone. If I head out of here with a bunch of men Richardson will lead us on a chase that could last weeks—maybe months. If I got by myself he'll stop, make a stand."

Fear crept into Hettie's eyes, and as quickly vanished. "Of course I'll worry. There's no sense in my pretending I won't. But I know you can take care of yourself."

"Something I learned how to do mighty young," Nevada drawled.

"I know—but I keep thinking there were four of them. And now it will be three to one."

"Five to start with. Four rode away."

"Four to one, then. Couldn't you take at least one man with you? That would make the odds better—and it wouldn't be like a posse."

Nevada shook his head. "It would be asking too much, even if there was somebody around whom I could trust, and depend on—like Ben. It would be no problem getting a posse together. But to ask one man to side me against four killers—well, it just wouldn't be right."

"Ben would go instantly."

"I know that, but he's in no shape for a hard ride."

Nevada glanced toward the porch. Mrs. Ide, assisted by Tom Day, had come out, and Judge Franklidge had lent his arm to Ben. The others had gathered around them, and were looking expectantly toward the surrey and the carriage.

"Appears they're about ready to head for home," Nevada said. "I want to get this straight with you, Hettie."

"It's settled," she replied. "We'll go back to the ranch, and postpone the trip to San Diego until you return."

"No, that's what I want you to understand. You're to go on just as planned. I don't think it's a good idea to keep your mother here any longer than is absolutely necessary."

Hettie faced him. "Tell me the truth, Nevada. Are you afraid Richardson might raid the ranch while you're out searching for him?"

"Possibly. But by going after him, I'll be giving him little reason not to make me his target. It's just that I'd feel better, knowing you were in San Diego. Besides, the doctor told you to take your mother to the coast as soon as you could."

"I know, Nevada, but leaving without you—it doesn't seem right."

"It's right. Just trust me. I'll come to San Diego just as soon as I've handled this chore. Then we'll go right on with the plans we made. One thing I've been sort of holding back from you. I thought we'd go down into Mexico for a honeymoon. It's nice down there, this time of year."

Hettie smiled, and her eyes brightened. "I'd love that. I've never been in Mexico."

"Something else. Figured we could do a little business while we're there. Rancher I've heard of near Mexico City raises a fine breed of horses. Tan color with white man and tail. Thought maybe we could make a deal for a stud and a couple of mares, and get the strain started up here."

"It would be wonderful," Hettie murmured.

"Then we're all squared away. As soon as Ben can

ride comfortably, you will head for San Diego. I'll join you the instant I've made sure Richardson can't sink his fangs in anyone else. Cash died from a rattlesnake bite as surely as if he'd stood in the path of an uncoiling diamond-back. It mustn't happen again."

Hettie Ide shuttered. "I—I don't know. I'm still not sure."

He stared at her. "Not sure of what? Is there something wrong?"

Hettie shook her head. "I don't know what's the matter with me. I had the strangest feeling, as if everything was ending right here, that we'd never see each other again. Oh, Nevada—"

He caught her in his arms, and held her close.

"Now, now, you're letting all this excitement get the best of you. We'll meet again—a lot sooner than you expect. Nothing bad is going to happen to me."

"I wish I could be sure of that."

"You can. My luck's always been good when guns open up unexpectedly. Take today. In all that shooting I wasn't even nicked. Poor Ben and Marvie caught the lead intended for me. It always has been that way. Good thing for me, but a mite hard on my friends."

Hettie laughed in spite of her fears. "All right," she said, "We'll do it your way. And I'll try not to worry."

"Fine," Nevada said, heaving a vast, inward sigh. He'd dreaded telling her of what had to be done. But she had seen his side of it, accepted it as he had felt she would. Taking her by the arm, he helped her into the two-seater.

"We'll explain it to the others when we get to the ranch," he said. "I aim to get an early start in the morning."

# IV

The next day dawned cool and pleasant. Nevada Jim had chosen a tough-bodied little buckskin for a mount, preferring it to the tall, much faster bay gelding that Ben Ide had suggested. Cud Richardson had headed east out of Winthrop into rough, rugged country and Nevada knew it would take a horse with plenty of bottom to stand a grueling chase, in which speed would not be a major factor.

He rode due south in preference to wasting the hours that would have been required if he went first to the settlement and picked up the trail from there. By angling, he could eventually intersect the road a dozen miles or so above the town. Knowing Richardson as he did, he was quite sure that a man of the outlaw's stripe, being certain of pursuit, would be very unlikely to head back for the settlement.

Cud Richardson would want to have all the cards stacked in his favor. He would strive to meet a pursuer on his own ground, and pick his own time for a confrontation. And Nevada was determined to have something to say about the location of the final showdown.

One factor was not good. Richardson and his companions were strangers to him. He would not be able to recognize the outlaw leader if they came face to face, unless of course, Cud bore a strong resemblance to his brother. The only definite identification upon which he could depend was that one of the renegades he'd seen had worn a fringed leather jacket, and a somewhat narrow-brimmed hat.

But he'd find Richardson—or perhaps Richardson would find him. That particular problem did not worry him.

As the sun rose higher, his sense of his grim mission dropped away from him somewhat. This part of his trail led through deep forest, and the shafts of light striking through the tall pine and spruce contrasted vividly with the deep green of the trees. The forest was bathed in an atmosphere at once cool and bright golden, and wild turkey and pheasant flashed as the sun caught them in movement.

The peace that the wilderness always brought to Nevada came upon him as he rode the familiar forest track. He entered a grassy glade, and a startled deer bounded away, an increasingly distant crashing of the undergrowth marking its passage.

The forest gave way to open country then, and his heart lifted as the illimitable space spread out before him—the purple of the sage, the red and yellow of the rocks stretching like a stormy sea lit by a lurid sunset, to the distant mountains. A flight of prairie warblers darted from the trees behind him and shone like whirling dust-motes for an instant in the bright blue air.

Near mid-morning he reached the road out of Winthrop that curved on in twin ruts toward the Mogollon Rim. He halted at once, dropped from the saddle and moved a foot until he found a stretch where the earth was soft. He nodded in grim satisfaction. He had been right. Clearly imprinted in the roadway were the hoof marks of three horses traveling abreast. Only three.

This brought a frown of puzzlement to Nevada's face. He began to search about more closely, and eventually discovered the tracks of the fourth outlaw's mount. The man in the fringed buckskin jacket had apparently not overtaken Richardson and the others—at least, not at that point. It seemed strange, unless the outlaw was deliberately maintaining a distance behind his four companions, the better to keep a lookout on their back trail for pursuers.

Nevada decided that almost had to be the answer. Accordingly, he went back to the saddle, cut off the trail at right angles for a full quarter mile, and then resumed his northward course but on a line paralleling the twin ruts. Anyone looking back now would have seen no one in the roadway.

The sun grew warmer. Nevada loosened his jacket, removed it, and tied it down in its usual place behind the cantle. He had donned the checkered silk scarf he'd worn in years past, associating it vaguely in his mind with good luck. The handmade, scalloped-topped boots and yellow vest had long since worn out, and been replaced with footgear of similar design, and a vest of soft tan broadcloth, heavily corded and frogged to the point of resembling a Mexican *charro* jacket.

Nevada felt confident and in reasonably high spirits. Yet a quiet resentment lay upon him. He'd gone through such time often enough in the past, when he was on the trail of a man he would probably be forced to kill, or who, in turn, would try to kill him. But this was different, somehow.

Responsibility, he guessed it was—responsibility to Hettie on the one hand, and a similar obligation, but not quite the same, to the ranchers, the people of Winthrop, and all those who lived in the area on the other. Everyone was relying upon him to stop Cud

Richardson and the new Pine Tree rustling gang he was assembling before the land was again ravaged by lawlessness.

That covered Ben Ide, Day, Judge Franklidge, and the entire law-abiding community. But it was difficult to place Hettie in quite the same category. True, she must be protected—at the cost of his life, if fate took a cruel turn. But there was more than that involved. Hettie was waiting for him—waiting to become his wife, and help him build a ranch of their own, so that they could make a fine life together.

He'd known she was the woman for him the moment of their first meeting, seven years ago, when he'd teamed with her brother, Ben.

Nevada sighed, and stared out across the long flat—the low hills that built gradually until they became massive mounds of frowning mountains. There was no point in dwelling upon what might have been. Find Cud Richardson, settle with him, and return to Hettie. Then their new life could begin.

Staring out over the purple sagebrush landscape, he considered that. Was it possible for him to settle down, and become a rancher—even with Hettie? Or would the recollections of the past, the years during which he'd drifted aimlessly, never halting for long, prove a barrier too strong to overcome?

A restless spirit is a difficult taskmaster, hard to conquer. There had been times when he'd succeeded in convincing himself that he'd like nothing better than owning a ranch, and becoming a steady family man. But there had been dark moments as well, when a voice deep within him had warned against too great a confidence, had whispered that it could never work, that he'd only break Hettie Ide's heart.

Invariably he had resisted that thought. It could be—it had to be. He was entitled to settle down just as other men did, and enjoy life to the full. He could overcome the recalcitrant trail rider within himself, and make the good dreams come true.

So deep in reverie had Nevada been that the outward signs of the ragged gash were upon him almost before he realized it. Pulling in the buckskin, he raised himself in the stirrups, and looked down into the broken land dotted with round clumps of snakeweed, sand peaked piles of greasewood and patches of saltbush.

Here was the true Arid Zone that had given the Territory its name when the Spanish Conquistadors came. Harsh, unyielding, yet possessing a color and grandeur that more hospitable lands knew not. Far off, the purple hills rimmed the scene, rising up in a frowning, jagged line, dark at that distance even in the bright sun.

Closer to hand, the air shimmered over the sunbaked rocks and sand flats, making the image of all he saw dance and glimmer as if seen through a trembling veil of clearest water. The road curved eastward here, Nevada recalled, and followed the canyon to a point where a crossing could be made, one could press on toward the larger Chevelon Canyon.

On a hunch he swung left, slanted across a long slope and returned to the road. They were stil ahead of him—the fourth rider still trailing his three friends. Just how far behind the man in the fringed jacket might be it was impossible to determine, but Nevada made it a point to use more care now, and watch sharply. Once in the canyon, he knew, they could cut off the trail, and angle back for Mogollon Mesa. There were two or three settlements to be found in that area.

Nevada rode on, once again removing himself from the roadway in order to take a side course. He went down into Wild Cat Canyon with the sun pushing hard at him now, and bringing the first flecks of sweat to the buckskin's hide.

A short while later he reached the flat on the opposite rim. Halting once more, he dismounted. It had been a rough, hot crossing and the gelding needed a few minutes' rest. Leaving the horse to graze on the sparse grass, he climbed to a low knoll and looked ahead.

The next break in the land would be Chevelon Canyon, a deep, wild section where a man, if he so desired, could hide with ease. He doubted that Cud Richardson would do so, however. Most likely he would keep moving until he reached one of the settlements. There he would have matters his own way—might possibly have more members of his gang waiting.

And there was that strain of pride men such as Cud Richardson always possessed. He'd want everyone to see and know that he was the one who had brought down the famous Jim Lacy. To Cud it would be a mark of distinction, an invisible medal to be flaunted proudly in all the towns where he walked.

"Reckon I'll have something to say about that," Nevada murmured. "If he nails my hide to the wall, he'll have earned the right to do it."

Raising his glance to the towering mass in the distance, known as Chevelon Butte, he watched the effortless soaring of a golden eagle silhouetted against the empty blue-steel sky for a few moments. Then he returned to where the buckskin waited, mounted and pressed on. Little more than an hour later he reached the larger canyon. There was but one trail leading down into the broad gouge, and he was compelled to take it. The hoofprints of the outlaws' horses were still visible, but on the yonder side he encountered his first change.

The outlaws had swung from the trail, followed a northwesterly course. Nevada grinned wryly. Richardson was running true to form; he was heading for one of the settlements just as he had anticipated. Men like Cud were all alike, they possessed single-tracked minds, and it was never hard to fathom their intentions.

Some time later Nevada halted at a small stream, to rest the sturdy little buckskin, but also to ease his own muscles. He'd grown soft, he realized, rubbing at his thighs and flexing his shoulders. There had been many days in the past when endless hours in the saddle had been scarcely noticeable. But of late he had been doing most of his traveling in a buckboard or a buggy; come nightfall, he guessed ruefully, he'd be paying for all that easy living.

He spent an hour at the creek, taking the opportunity to brew up a lard tin of coffee which he drank hot and black. He wasn't hungry, however, and ate only a little of the lunch Hettie had prepared, and ignored completely the food supplies he'd stowed in his saddle-bags, in case the chase ran into several days.

The sun was well past midafternoon when he mounted and moved on. Gradually, with the passing miles, the heat dwindled and a coolness began to spread over the land. Freeing his jacket, he drew it on, finding it comfortable. Shortly before darkness he pulled to a stop on a low ridge. Miles ahead, in a pocket formed by two towering upthrusts of granite, lights twinkled. A calmness came upon him, took possession of his nerves, and mind.

Richardson would be waiting for him there. There was no doubt in his mind about that.

## V

Nevada Jim Lacy knew that the road would be watched. Cud Richardson would not permit him to arrive unannounced. Slumped on the saddle, he studied the general lay of the land. he town, whatever its name might be, appeared from the distance to consist of no more than three or four buildings clustered tightly together in a small area as if for mutual support in the hollow of the hills.

A mining settlement, he guessed, although he could think of no ore deposits in that general area. But men sought gold and silver at random, often basing their hopes and expending their labor on a hunch, an ancient legend, or a purportedly authentic map passed down through generations.

Regardless of the town's reason for existence, it was where he would find Richardson, and that was why he had ridden to the ball in the first place. Find and stop him before he could plunge Arizona's Mogollon country into another bloody war between a gang of vicious outlaws and the law-respecting townspeople.

Moving on, Nevada cut wide of the little-used road that led to the glimmering lights. The last of the sun's flare in the west had gone, and a weak quarter-moon, affording little light, made it slow going for the buckskin as he picked his way over the loose rock. For a time they moved downward, coming finally to a broad, sand-floored arroyo. It originated somewhere above the settlement, Nevada surmised, and since it offered better footing for the gelding, he turned into its brushy expanse.

The buckskin plodded on tirelessly, while the wash steadily deepened until finally Nevada saw that he was hemmed in on both sides by ten-foot-high banks. He began to watch for a break that would permit him to climb out, since he was drawing close to the town and had no intention of entering it without first looking it over thoroughly.

A side gully, steep and brush-locked, coming in from his left offered the sought-for opportunity. Dismounting, Nevada took firm hold of the buckskin's saddle and led the way, breaking and kicking aside the brittle undergrowth to make it easier for the horse. He had gotten into the big pine country, he realized, noting the pointed tips that were etched blackly against the dark sky farther on.

Finally he broke out onto a small mesa that ran on to where it fused with the choppy foothills of the mountains to the west. To the right of its termination he again caught the flicker of lights.

Nevada grunted with satisfaction as he stepped back onto the saddle. By following the mesa, he could enter the town from its rear side, and it seemed unlikely that Richardson would expect him to do that. In all probability his sentry would be keeping an eye on the road.

The settlement was about what he'd expect it to be like—five small structures and one large two-story building that probably, in some previous decade, had been someone's fine home. Now it bore a crudely lettered sign with the solitary word SALOON. Two of the second-floor windows showed light. All the rest—at least the ones visible to him—were dark.

The ground floor was a different matter. Light blazed in all of the glassed openings and the feeble moon was sufficiently strong to enable him to make out the shadowy forms of a dozen or more horses at the hitchrack. All of the other buildings were in blackness. There should be houses, too, he thought, homes for those who worked in the stores. Probably they were set farther back, below the slight ridge that lay just beyond the town.

He worked his way in closer, taking care to keep well back in the shadows along the base of the towering mountain. Faint music reached his ears—piano chords rendered fast and loud, and with little regard for accuracy.

The reason for the town's existence came to him then. It stood at one of the crossroads that led to Arizona's former capital city, Prescott, miles to the west. It was not a mining camp or supply point for ranchers or homesteaders. It was simply one of those towns that sprang up to offer rest and relaxation to travelers, and break their tiring journeys, to and from widely separated destinations.

He wondered what the name of the place might be; it was even possible he once had been there, coming into it and passing on by a different road.

He swung the buckskin right, moved slowly away from the mountain until he found himself on the lip of a bluff. Below he could see the meandering course of the arroyo which he had followed earlier. On beyond it he located the trail, barely visible in the pale silver of the night.

Tracking it with his eyes, he saw that it entered the settlement at its south-east corner. That was good. If Richardson's man was watching that approach, he would ignore all others. Wheeling the weary buckskin, he retraced his tracks to the foot of the mountain and pushed on.

He reached the town proper—COOPERSVILLE, a faded sign on the roof of a livery stable informed him—and guided the gelding into the deep shadow behind the saloon. Glancing about he saw a small barn located near the base of the mountain, and angled the buckskin toward it.

Keenly alert, he dismounted, and stood for a full minute, tense, listening. Music started up again within the bulky, two-floored structure. A man shouted and then there was laughter. Nevada could see no one outside, either around the building or in the narrow strip of street that separated the saloon from the remaining structures.

Moving silently, he led the buckskin into the barn, and again paused to listen. There were horses; he could hear the crunching of grain, an occasional stamp of a hoof. No human appeared to be present. Still leading the gelding, he continued down the runway until he came to a side entrance. Ground-reining the buckskin, he pulled the door open, and propped it with an empty keg. An emergency exit was always a handy thing to have at one's disposal.

He guided the gelding into the stall nearest the door, forked a quantity of hay into the manger, and looked around until he found a sack of oats. Dipping out a quart, he added it to the buckskin's meal and then turned to leave. He would have liked to remove his tack from the horse, but decided it would be better to wait until he was sure of his ground. If all went well, he'd return, relieve the buckskin of the bridle and saddle, and permit him to get the complete rest he'd earned.

Removing his spurs, he hooded them over the horn and doubled back to the doorway, again cocking his ear into the cool night. The racket inside the saloon seemed to have increased. Everyone in town would be there, he guessed, along with all those who were making a stopover. Only the sentry delegated by Richardson to watch the road would be elsewhere. Probably he would be some distance away.

He swung his attention to the rear of the looming structure. There was a back door, and a back stairway leading to the upper floor. Ignoring the first, he crossed a narrow strip of ground to the steps. Without hesitation he mounted them quickly.

At the upper door he halted, and placed his ear to the crack along the frame. The noise coming from the lower level was so loud he could not tell whether or not there was anyone beyond the panel. He'd have to gamble on it. Twisting the knob, he opened the door, and stepped inside.

A blast of heated, stale air, heavy with the odor of liquor, sweat and smoke, and throbbing with sound, met him head-on. Closing the warped panel, he stepped up against the wall. He was in a small entry area. Three strides in front of him there appeared to be a hallway running at right angles, and dimly lit by a lamp somewhere farther down.

Quietly, he eased forward until he reached the cross corridor, and paused. The hall was long. Several doors opened off it on both sides. At its south end he could see posts indicating the location of the stairway leading to the lower floor. From there he should be able to see what was happening below as well as all of the saloon's occupants.

Nevada reached for his gun, drew it, and made certain the cylinder was fully loaded. Then, sliding it back into its holster, he turned the corner into the hallway. The click of a door lock brought him up short.

"You lookin' for me, cowboy?"

Lacy turned slowly to face the speaker—a girl. She was not young, but far from old in years. Her hair was a straw-yellow, and there were thick daubs of rouge on her cheeks, and a brighter red heightened the color of her lips. Here eyes were deepset and a discoloration was spreading below the left one. Managing a tired smile, she cocked her head, smoothed the garish red-and-yellow spangled dress she wore and spoke again.

"I said—are you lookin' for me?"

Nevada shook his head, realizing how important it was to be careful and not give away his presence to those below. "Not right now," he said. "I'm hunting a pard of mine. Figured he came up here."

The girl shrugged, pushed at stray wisps hanging from her loosely gathered hair.

"Who is he?"

"Uh-name of Hank. Hank Beeman."

"Never heard of him," the girl said bluntly. She started to move on, then hesitated. "Kate's got some jasper in her room—end of the hall. Maybe that's where your friend is."

"Most likely," Lacy murmured and touched the brim of his hat with a forefinger. "Obliged."

The girl shrugged and waited until he had turned for the distant end of the corridor.

"Best you knock first," she advised. "Kate don't like folks bustin' in on her." She shrugged agian, and continued on toward the stairway.

Nevada walked on slowly, stalling until he was certain she had reached the lower floor. Then, wheeling, he followed her swiftly. If the girl intended to report his presence, the quicker he got out of the hallway, the better.

He halted again, cautiously, at the top of the stairs. He stopped the girl instantly through a thick haze of smoke. She was making her way leisurely among the patrons, and he saw with relief that her brief encounter with him was far from her mind.

He turned his attention to the confusion below, searching the smoke-blurred faces of the men standing at the bar, and those sitting at the tables.

One almost had to be Cud Richardson.

## VI

Nevada's searching glance finally picked up the man in the fringed buckskin coat. Instantly he came to attention. There were four others with him, scattered around a circular table playing cards. He stared intently, endeavoring to penetrate the haze. One of the five could be Cud Richardson. Carefully he examined each shadowed face. After a moment he shrugged, and gave it up. Even if the outlaw chief resembled his brother it would have been impossible to tell from that distance.

But Richardson was there in the crowd. The presence of the man in the fringed jacket assured that.

The piano struck up a tune. A huge woman whose

bulk overflowed the stool upon which she sat had begun to hammer mercilessly at the keys. The girl with whom Nevada had spoken in the hallway emerged from a corner of the room, paused beside the table occupied by the outlaws and spoke to them.

Men began to shout, and after a few moments she smiled and made her way to the piano. Taking up a position at one end, she began to sing, rendering an unrecognizable ballad in a rasping, dry nasal tone that could scarcely be heard above the music and the loud hum of conversation.

Suddenly a table overturned with a crash, and a hoarse voice shouted an oath. Abruptly pandemonium broke loose. A fight began at one of the tables and the music and singing halted abruptly. Chairs skittered across the bare floor, and another table splintered. There was a quick flare of fire as a wall lamp fell with a crash. More yelling arose as three men leapt out from the bar, and began to stamp out the tongues of flame which were now licking hungrily at an overturned table.

Someone dashed a pitcher of water, or perhaps it was beer, on the growing conflagration. Immediately a pillar of dense smoke spiraled upward, fusing with the thick haze clinging to the ceiling. A dozen men joined in the scuffle, cursing and shouting. Three more fist fights started up almost simultaneously. One of the bartenders began to wave madly at the piano player. The music started up again and the girl singer climbed into a chair and resumed her ballad in a voice that rose higher in volume.

Then, gradually, the turmoil began to diminish, and the fighting ceased, except for two cowpunchers who continued to trade blows in the center of the room.

Finally they, too, called a truce, and allowed themselves to be pulled apart by friends, who crowded in and herded them into separate areas. As soon as the tables had been righted and there was no more shooting, Nevada turned his attention again to where the five outlaws had been sitting.

A frown crossed his face. The fringe-jacketed man and another were missing. Swiftly his eyes swept the room. They were nowhere about. At some time during the turmoil they had apparently slipped out the door. He swore impatiently at his own carelessness, and then a disturbing thought occured to him.

Was Cud Richardson aware of his presence? Had the outlaw somehow discovered that he was in the building? How? He'd been careful, had remained well back and out of sight on the small landing at the head of the stairs.

The girl. . .That had to be the answer. She had recognized him for a stranger and Richardson had probably dropped the word that he was expecting the arrival of someone who might attempt to keep his identity concealed by telling some hard-to-believe story.

Again Nevada swore. If his hand had been tipped, it was necessary for him to make his move now, at once. But against whom? Which one was Richardson? The man in the fringed jacket? Or the man who had disappeared with him? Was it one of the three who were sitting at the table? Or could it be someone entirely different?

It irked him to stand in the shadows, prevented from acting by his own lack of knowledge. It was even more galling to be unable to simply walk down into the crowd and confront Cud Richardson, his voice raised in a challenge. That was the way he would have preferred to handle it. But there was too much at stake now. The odds were stacked high against him. Not only was Richardson on his guard against that kind of challenge, he was making sure it wouldn't happen—by having four men at his side. He'd never get the chance to face the outlaw leader alone. He'd simply throw away his life, accomplish nothing—and the Mogollon country would again become the private preserve of the lawless. Yet there must be a way to single out Richardson. There had to be.

The solution came to him suddenly. Women such as Kate would do anything for a price. If he had thought, he probably could have bribed the other girl into pointing the outlaw to him. But it was only now that he was faced with that particular problem.

He glanced back along the dimly-lit hall. Kate's door was still closed. He had no choice except to wait, and take careful stock of the situation. Richardson had three men siding him, there could be no doubt about that—four, if you counted the extra man who'd been at the table. And there could be more. But it was best not to worry about odds at the moment.

It was knowing who the opposition was that mattered —the leader and the riders who actually would be backing his play, and not merely bystanders. He'd try to find that out from Kate, too. He had nothing against walking through the doors of the saloon, and calling Richardson out, provided he had the outlaw's men spotted.

A door-lock clicked, and someone stumbled against the panel, cursing. Nevada turned, and glanced swiftly down the corridor. A cowpuncher, in range clothing and very drunk, was coming from Kate's room. Drawing back into the shadows, Nevada watched the man approach. He was walking unsteadily from side to side, ricocheting off the walls as he made slow progress for the stairs.

He passed Nevada unseeing, reached the steps, and stumbled. But he caught himself in time, and, clinging to the rickety banister, fought his way downward.

Nevada turned and, hurried down the hall. Kate's door was still open. He stepped quickly inside, and closed it. The woman, large, dark-haired, with jet-black eyes was rubbing rouge into her cheeks. She almost ignored Nevada's entrance, merely touched him with a reflected glance through the mirror she was facing.

"I need a drink," she said.

Nevada reached into his pocket for a double-eagle, and flipped it onto the dresser before her. "That'll buy a few," he drawled.

Kate picked up the coin, and turned slowly, a look of bewilderment in her eyes. "What—"

"I need a favor."

"You mean you ain't here to—"

Nevada shook his head. "All I'm after is a favor, a small one. I'm looking for a man. I want you to go downstairs, and put your hand on his shoulder. I'll be watching from the landing."

Kate dropped the gold coin into the crevice of her ample bosom. "Who's this man you're looking for?"

"Cud Richardson."

The woman's eyes widened. "What do you want him for?"

Lacy shook his head. "That gold doesn't entitle you to any details. It happens to be a personal matter. I want

48

you to point out the men siding him, too."

Kate continued to stare at him, her lower lip slack, almost petulant. "You some kind of law officer?"

"No."

The woman remained silent for a moment longer, and then shrugged. "Why not? Cud Richardson's tight-fisted and women like me are just dirt to him. You want me to do it now?"

Nevada nodded. "I'll be at the head of the stairs."

Kate turned, picked up a lace scarf, and clutching it in her hand, walked by Lacy into the hallway. As she passed she gave him a faint smile.

"This ain't going to get me killed, is it?"

"Not you," he replied, and followed her down the corridor.

Reaching the landing, Nevada resumed his position in the darker corner as Kate started down the steps slowly, making her entrance as dramatic as possible. Several heads turned, voices shouted to her.

The saloon had quieted considerably. It was filled now with only the drone of conversation and the occasional scrape of a chair. The piano was silent, and the girl singer sat at one of the tables with several men.

Kate reached the foot of the stairs, and paused on the last step. Casually she looked out over the scatter of patrons, then moved on, swinging her hips. This immediately evoked a few more appreciative shouts from the seated patrons and the dozen men lining the bar. Lacy scarcely heard them. His attention was on the woman's hands. The instant she touched—

Nevada stiffened as the hard, round muzzle of a revolver was jammed with abrupt violence into the small of his back.

"Don't you move, mister," a voice coming from directly behind him ordered quietly. "Lift his iron, Dude."

## VII

Lacy raised his hands slowly. It was sure that it had been the girl, dropping a warning to Cud Richardson when she had paused at the outlaw's table. He was just as quick to realize that a moment after the brawl had started—a fortunate accident or possibly an incident deliberately staged to create confusion—two of the renegades must have slipped out the door, circled the building and entered by the same route he had earlier used.

He felt the lessening of weight at his side as his .45 was yanked from its holster. From the tail of his eye he glimpsed the man standing close to him. It was the one who wore the fringed jacket.

"Now start backing up," the outlaw with the pistol said quietly. "No ruckus—unless you want to have your skull bashed in."

Moving slowly, Nevada began to retreat into the dark hallway. He reached the short passage that led to the outside door and stairway. Dude pushed by him, opened the panel, and held it wide.

"Get going," the other outlaw commanded.

Lacy started for the exist, self-directed anger now pushing at him. *Sure messed this one up*, he thought bitterly. *Reckon I should have taken my chances and waded right in on them*.

He stepped out into the moonlit night, and came face to face with Dude. He was a slightly built, clean-shaven man of about twenty-five. His hat, pushed to the back of his head, revealed sandy, or perhaps, red, hair. In the weak light Nevada could not be certain. Dude's eyes were dark and piercing.

"I'll keep in front of him, Clint," he said, and started down the steps.

"Yeah, you do that," the man with the gun said. "Only don't go getting too close. He's a real stem-winding curly wolf, they tell me."

They reached the foot of the stairway. Nevada halted, uncertainly. Clint jabbed savagely with his gun barrel.

"What the hell you want me to do?" Lacy asked.

"Just keep trailing after Dude. He'll show you."

The outlaw crossed behind the building, turned right at the corner and led the way to the street. Without hesitation, he contined on to a low-roofed structured on the opposite side. At one time it had apparently been a livery barn. Abandoned now, it stood in sagging neglect, doors missing, windows shattered and littered with an accumulation of wind-blown weeds and trash. Through this dismal rubbish patch Dude led the way to a small room at the rear.

"Stand easy," Clint murmured, pressing hard with his weapon. "Dude'll get us a light going."

A match flared in the half-dark. Shortly the dusty cubicle came alive with a yellow glow from a lantern. Clint laid his hand on Nevada's shoulder, and pushed him roughly toward a bench in one corner.

"Make yourself to home, Mr. Lacy. Cud'll be coming along in a few minutes."

Nevada eyed the outlaw coldly. Clint was a big, raw-boned man, wide across the shoulders and with a thick bull neck. Clint had been one of the five at the table but

Nevada's glimpse of the party back in Winthrop had been too fleeting to be sure the big man had been there also.

He shifted his attention to Dude. Clint appeared to regard the younger man with faint contempt, tinged with an amused tolerance. He did seem to have little in common with the hardened outlaw, being cleaner, better dressed and with an air of near-refinement about him. But that was no sure guide as to a man's character, Nevada knew. He'd encountered many a hardened killer who had the looks and mannerisms of a Sunday School teacher. It was what lay beneath the veneer that made the difference. Due was a greenhorn taking lessons from a hardened old-timer, he finally concluded.

Boots thudded on the old stable runway. Clint straightened, looked around. Two men were moving up through the murky light. They reached the door to the small back room, and stepped quickly inside. One was a short, red-faced man, the other tall, dark with pale eyes and a sharp hook for a nose. Nevada was sure that he was Cud Richardson. There was a faint but unmistakable resemblance to his brother Ed.

"Got him, eh?"

Clint grinned, exposing his broad, tobacco-stained teeth. "It was as easy as eatin' apple pie."

Richardson swung his piercing glance to Dude. "Seems you'll do," he said, and stepped nearer to Lacy. He leaned forward, staring intently at Nevada's face, then settled back.

"Had me a hunch I'd know you. Jim Lacy . . . Name rung a bell when I heard it was you that cut Ed down. Made you the big muckety-muck down Mogollon way, I take it."

"Ed got what he asked for," Nevada said coolly. "You're headed down the same road."

Cud Richardson laughed. "That wouldn't surprise me none—only you won't be there when it happens."

"Don't be surprised if I am," Nevada replied.

He was studying the outlaws narrowly, searching for an opportunity, an unguarded moment during which he could make a quick break. Clint had relaxed his vigilance somewhat, but Dude, his arms folded across his chest, was standing off to one side. Nevada was sure any move he attempted would place the man in the fringed buckskin jacket at his back—a fatal mistake for certain.

"What are you aiming to do with him?" Clint asked. "I mean, besides making buzzard bait out of him," He added with a laugh.

"We're taking him out a ways into the hills," Richardson answered.

The outlaw stared. "Now, why the hell should we do that?" he said.

"Cooper don't want any trouble around here. He says people'll get so jittery they won't stop over. We'll just drop Mr. Lacy here down a hole with a couple of rocks on him, and there's no fuss and no questions."

"They didn't pay no mind to that ruckus in the saloon?"

"That was different. Cowpunchers are always blowing off steam, anywhere you go. But killings—that's something else. It could cause the law to come poking around—and I reckon he does make a heap of gold for himself with folks trotting back and forth on their way to the Fort or Prescott.

"Anyway, we're listening to Cooper. I want to keep

53

on his good side. It's smart to have us a place to come to where we can lay low when there's need."

Richardson glanced to Nevada. "Where's your nag?"

Nevada remained silent, considered refusing to answer, and then decided it would serve no good purpose. Any move he might make in an attempt to escape would have to come later and his chances would be better with the buckskin under him, instead of a horse he didn't know or trust.

"I tied my horse in the barn—behind the saloon," he said.

Immediately Dude joined the heavy-set man Richardson had called Drawson, and together they left the stable. Cud watched them for a moment and then moved deeper into the room. Placing his shoulders against a wall, he studied Nevada.

Cud Richardson, Nevada saw, was a harder, tougher customer than Ed Richardson. He lacked his brother's smoothness and polish. Ed had been a handsome man with a knack for making friends, and a winning way with women. There were none of these qualities in Cud Richardson—only a cold ruthlessnes that shone in his eyes, and was evident, as well, in the cruel set of his mouth.

The muted thud of horses' hooves sounded in the runway. Richardson swung about and stared through the opening.

"Here they are," he said. "Let's get moving."

Clint, his gun again ready, reached for Nevada's arm. Nevada jerked his elbow away and stood up. Walking slow, he crossed in front of Richardson, and strode to where Dude was holding the buckskin. Silently, he swung to the saddle.

"He got a rifle?" Cud asked from the shadows.

"We looked," Dawson said shaking his head. "Reckon he only totes a handgun."

"What about them saddlebags. There could be a spare iron in one of them."

"Nothing but grub—and some duds."

"Won't make no difference, anyway," the outlaw chief said. "Here's some rawhide, Dude. Tie his hands behind his back."

The outlaw in the fringed jacket stepped forward, and took the length of leather cord. He glanced up to Nevada.

"You heard him. Hold out your hands."

Nevada shrugged, and did as he was directed. He felt the tough, narrow strips of leather encircle his wrists, and cupped his palms to their fullest.

"None of that!" Dude snapped. "You're not tricking me that way."

Richardson laughed. "What's he up to—trying to get some slack so's he can work himself loose?"

"He's trying," Dude answered, giving the rawhide a sharp jerk, "but he's not having any luck."

Lacy grunted as the cord bit into his flesh and locked his wrists together. Dude worked with the ends of the string briefly, and stepped back.

"That'll hold him," he said.

"All right, mount up," Richardson ordered, moving toward his horse.

"What about some grub?" Dawson asked. "We'll be a while getting this done."

"We'll live," Richardson said. "Anyway, didn't you just say he had some grub in his saddlebags?"

"A little. Ain't hardly enough for all of us."

"We'll stretch it," Cud Richardson said, and swung to the doorway.

Clint fell in behind him. Someone—Dude or Dawson—slapped the buckskin on the rump, prompting him to be next in line, and then those two, riding abreast, followed.

They entered the street, and turned right. The hubbub in Cooper's saloon had not slackened, and the piano was again lending its support to the general din. Up ahead Clint's plaintive voice sounded above the soft *tunk-a-tunk* of the walking horses.

"Sure hate to be leaving—"

Nevada Lacy barely heard. A sharp tingling was racing through his body. He had moved his arms, and felt the cord that bound his wrists give slightly. Dude, obviously inexperienced in such matters, had secured the leather strips with a greenhorn's knot.

## VIII

"What was you saying to do with grub, Dawson?" Clint's voice was a whine. "I'm getting hungrier than a wolf pup with his throat cut." Clint's complaining words faded as Richardson twisted about on his saddle, his face flushed.

"We'd better get something straight, right now. If you want to head back for Cooper's, nobody's stopping you. Only, when you get your gut full, don't come looking for me. Just find yourself some other place to roost."

Clint shook his head. "I'll be staying. All I was saying was that—"

Cud Richardson sighed, and settled himself again on

56

his saddle. Nevada, working carefully to avoid drawing attention from Dude, gradually freed his wrists to the point where he could pull his hands apart when a favorable opportunity presented itself. It would have to come later. At the moment they were crossing a high shoulder with little brush and no trees at all into which he could bolt.

He dug into his memory, endeavored to recall the area. The arroyo was to his right, a good quarter-mile distant. Farther ahead the trail veered closer. The banks of the wash, he thought, were six or seven feet high at that particular point—a dangerous leap for a horse running full speed in the dark. But if any horse could manage it, the tough little buckskin was the one.

But if he made it to the arroyo—then what? Lacy rolled that through his mind. With no weapon he could not fight off pursuit. He could only run—and keep running. To where?

Slowly, refusing to be hurried, he began to shape a plan that would get him out of the desperate situation in which he found himself. It would be fatal to go down the arroyo; for the outlaws would simply race alongside the sandy-floored gash, with their own horses on firmer ground, and pick him off with ease.

Suddenly he remembered the small, brushy wash coming in from the opposite side—the one that he'd used earlier to climb out of the arroyo. If he could make his break below it, and turn back up—which the outlaws would hardly be expecting him to do—he could employ the gully as a means for gaining the other bank. On beyond that lay the mountain with its rocks and dense timber.

But after that?

Nevada stirred restlessly. He'd make that final, important decision when he came to it. First things first. He'd have to manage somehow to break away from the outlaws and gain the comparative safety of the arroyo without stopping a bullet. Assuming he managed that, and the buckskin didn't snap a leg bone in the downward plunge, the problem of finding the gully and gaining the opposite side could wait. He might not even be alive at that stage.

He began to slow the buckskin, doing it imperceptibly, to avoid the watchful scrutiny which Dawson was keeping almost constantly trained on him. There was nothing he could do where Dude was concerned. He'd be trusting wholly on luck there, hoping the greenhorn would be so taken by surprise that his reaction would be slow.

The most important thing at the moment was to pick the proper place for the break. It must be below the side gully—not above it. And he should be as near to it as possible. He couldn't risk a lengthy race with the outlaws above him on solid footing.

He looked ahead. A gnarled cedar tree looked familiar, and a mound of rock also evoked a stir of recognition. They were swinging in nearer to the arroyo. Tension began to build within Nevada. He stirred again, striving to settle his nerves, and glanced warily at Dawson.

The outlaw was now slightly ahead of him, half the length of his horse—a little more, perhaps. He wished the heavy-set man had decided to ride on his left flank rather than on the right. There would then be no one between him and arroyo. No, he decided suddenly. It was better this way. When he made his break, he'd try to drag Dawson off the saddle as he raced by. That would create confusion, and temporarily block the use of one gun. If Dawson had been riding on his left, the big man would be in position to open up instantly.

Dude was the one who could give him the most trouble. Riding behind, he'd be sure to detect the start of an escape attempt instantly, and be in line to bring it to a halt almost immediately. Head down, Nevada stole a backward look. Dude's face was tipped forward. He appeared to be dozing in the saddle.

Lacy could see the edge of the arroyo now, less than twenty yards away. There was little brush in between—a few clumps of sage, large stands of rabbitbush, and a row of snakeweed thriving in the sterile soil, hedgelike, along the rim of the big wash. The gully was above him. He was pleased with what he saw for the position of the growths was in just the right relation to the mountain.

Nevada bunched his muscles, tested his wrists, and made certain the rawhide would fall free when he exerted pressure. The hindquarters of Dawson's horse were now even with the nose of the buckskin. He risked another covert glance at Dude. This outlaw rode as before—head bowed, face slanted as if sleeping. Ahead Clint and Cud Richardson slumped on their saddles as their horses slogged on wearily. They, too, could be catching a few winks of sleep.

It was now—or perhaps never. Once deeper into the hills he'd find no opportunity at all.

Abruptly he jerked his arms apart. Seizing the reins, he jammed his heels into the buckskin's flanks, and swung sharply to the right. The horse responded instantly. With his left hand, Nevada grabbed for Dawson. His fingers caught the collar of the outlaw's jacket, and locked about the fabric. The buckskin's momentum lent strength to Lacy's grip. The startled man yelled, and tried to save himself by clawing for the horn. He missed, and fell heavily to the ground as Nevada rushed off into the pale darkness.

More yells sounded as Richardson and the others realized what was taking place. A gunshot ripped through the night. Two more followed in quick succession. Lacy began to swerve the buckskin from side to side, making good use of the training for roundup work the horse had received.

"Get after him!"

Cud Richardson's voice was an exasperated, infuriated bellow rising above the confusion.

The arroyo was in front of Nevada before he realized it. The buckskin did not hesitate. He simply sailed over the rim, and struck solidly on all fours with bone-jarring force. He went to his knees for an instant, then recovered and staggered on. Lacy cut right, up the broad gash as the horse gathered his balance and regained his forward momentum. Dust arose in a great swirl beneath the animal's clattering hooves.

Nevada squinted into the murky night before him. To the rear the pound of hooves above and directly behind him sounderd uncomfortably close. One of the outlaws had followed him down into the arroyo. He hadn't expected that.

Ten yards—twenty. Where was that side gully? Had he misjudged the distance? Thirty yards. Gunshots were blasting through the night again, but now the bullets were striking behind him. apparently they were shooting blind, not sure of his exact location.

Fifty yards. Clearly he'd made a mistake, waited too

long to make his try. In a matter of minutes the outlaws would overtake him, and have him at their mercy again. He grinned tightly. It was a good try—one that had almost succeeded.

A long, gusty breath of relief came whistling up from his lungs, and out between his lips, making his entire body shake. The gully at last! He veered the buckskin toward it. There's be no time, he realized, to dismount and lead the horse up the rough course again. He'd have to make it, rider and all.

They plunged into the narrow, brush-choked opening. The buckskin faltered, bunched his hindquarters, and then leaped swiftly ahead. His front hooves dug in, caught. He heaved again, stumbled plowed on through the losoe rock and clawing undergrowth.

Abruptly he gained the top, muscles quivering, wheezing for wind. Nevada, crouched low, hammered at his flanks again, and set him rushing for a dense clump of brush a dozen strides distant.

Harsh voices arose from high above, whipped by the wind.

"He's pulled out of here!"

"Where?" Richardson's voice was taut with anger.

"Wash, on the side."

"Well, follow him, damn it! We'll circle, try crossing below."

"I am trying," Clint shouted back. "Blamed jughead's balking. He's afeared to climb—"

Lacy reached the cedars, allowed the buckskin to slacken his dead run. But he did not halt. Keeping the brush between himself and the point where the gully led out of the arroyo, he pushed steadily on for the towering, black mass of the mountain.

He had the jump on Richardson and the others. They would lose a good ten minutes trying to find a place where they could cross over. And Clint would finally be forced to dismount, and lead his balky mount up the steep and treacherous wash.

A decision as to his next move was now urgent. He couldn't turn south to the plains, for that, he knew, would lead him straight into the outlaws. Neither could he get up on the mountain, and lose himself in the thick pines, the oak brush and rock. With no weapon of any sort he could do nothing but lie low for the time being.

A quarter of an hour later he reached the first outcropping of boulders at the foot of the mountain, and began to search for a trail that would lead him to the crest. A sheer wall faced him here. But he rode on, seeking a break, an arroyo, a crevice—even an old game trail. The solid granite slab shining dully in the starlight ran on indefinitely, offering no relief.

Faintly, considerably to the rear, he could hear the thud of oncoming horses. The outlaws had crossed over, and by this time Clint had probably managed to climb out of the gully. All four men would be together. But at least they could not see him, he was certain of that. They would have no way of knowing which way he had chosen to go—back to the arroyo, directly up the center of the small mesa, or into the mountains.

He topped a slight ridge and came to an abrupt halt. A half-mile ahead a scatter of lights broke the darkness of the night. It had to be Coopersville.

Nevada swore softly, scanning the face of the mountain anxiously. Nothing but palisades—steep, vertical cliff walls of solid granite. He was trapped at the base, with no way to go except straight on. The drumming of the oncoming horses was growing louder. Abruptly he came to a decision.

Urging the winded buckskin to a faster lope, he bore directly for the twinkling lights. If he had to make a stand, his chances would be better in the town. And maybe he could figure out some way to get his hands on a gun.

## IX

They saw him as he topped the last ridge at the edge of the settlement, and immediately opened up. The burst of gunfire was deafening, but the bullets fell short. Had they been using rifles, their luck might have been better.

Nevada rode into the town, again from the rear. The barn in which he had earlier stabled the buckskin was to his left. He ignored it, and continued on. It was sure to be the first place the outlaws would look when they started a search for him.

The racket within the saloon had not decreased to any extent. He was grateful for that, for it almost ruled out the likelihood that anyone had heard the gunshots and emerged into the open to see what it was all about. Walking the buckskin, nevada circled the building, came to the street, and crossed. The abandoned barn where he had awaited Cud Richardson was directly in front of him.

Avoiding that weathered structure also, he pushed on, pointing his horse for a dark, brush-filled hollow a short distance beyond. Swiftly he dismounted and tied the horse to a scrub cedar. Then, crouching low, he trotted back to the old barn.

Approaching from the rear this time, he snatched up

an empty crate, climbed upon it, and pulled himself onto the building's roof. The timbers beneath him creaked and groaned in protest as he worked his way forward. But he minimized the danger of their collapsing by keeping close to the wall where the studding could support his weight. Reaching the forward end, he crawled in behind the six-foot-tall false front to wait.

There was no movement in the street below. He turned his eyes to the hitchrack of the saloon, and tried to locate a rifle still in the boot of some rider's saddle. The light was too poor, and he could make out nothing at that distance. Odds were against his finding a weapon, for most punchers, leaving their mounts, took their long guns with them. But he refused to give up all hope in that respect. He'd make a closer inspection as soon as he learned what Richardson intended to do.

Apparently there was another stable somewhere along the short street. There weren't enough horses at the saloon's rack to account for the number of patrons he had seen in the saloon, and there had been only two or three tied up in the barn where he had first left the buckskin. If he failed to find a rifle on one of the saddles in the street, there was nothing to prevent him from locating the other livery stable, and trying his luck there.

He saw movement at that moment—a dark shadow slipping quietly along the side of the saloon. The figure came to the corner of the building, and halted. For a full minute he remained motionless, and then advanced farther into the open.

It was Cud Richardson.

The outlaw chief was alone. That could only mean that the rest of the party had separated, and taken up positions around the edge of the town. Apparently they had decided to work their way in, toward the center, hoping to pocket him. Nevada grinned tightly. It was not pleasant to find himself backed into a corner—with no weapon. But there was one thing in his favor. He was almost sure he knew what they had in mind.

Richardson, walking slowly, almost indolently, but taking care to remain in the shadows, rounded the end of the saloon, and crossed in front of it. He stopped again, this time at the edge of the landing. Leaning back against the wall, protected by the darkness, he simply waited. Lacy could see his head swing back and forth as his eyes maintained a continuous watch along the street.

They knew he was there, somewhere—that he had few choices in the selection of a hiding place. Sooner or later he would be compelled to move, to show himself, and Cud Richardson was clearly determined to finish up the chore he'd undertaken.

"It's not going to be that easy, mister," Lacy murmured into the night.

Dawson and the others might work their way in, and tighten the noose. But they wouldn't find him in it—at least not down where they could see him. But the time would come, he knew, when he'd be forced to do something. And at any moment one of them could stumble on the hidden buckskin.

He had no intention of worrying about that, however —not so long as there were other mounts standing nearby. It wouldn't be the first time he'd been tabbed a horse thief when an emergency had called for borrowing the mount nearest at hand. He could always return, explain an exchange the animal he had taken for his own.

Richardson continued to wait in the darkness fronting the saloon. Piano music, the girl's off-key singing, shouts, laughter, and an occasional crash as a chair or table overturned were the only sounds riding the cool night air.

Once the three missing outlaws reached the street, gathered to report their failure to flush him from hiding, it would be a simple matter to drop back off the roof, make his way to the buckskin and depart. There would be another day, another time when, under more favorable circumstances, he could settle with Cud Richardson.

But no such thought was in Nevada Jim Lacy's mind. The man he sought was here, standing no more than fifty feet away. He'd not pull out until he'd settled up in full.

"Cud?"

The carefully hushed voice came from somewhere below Nevada, and to his right, in the street. Standing absolutely motionless, so as to cause no creaking of the rotting planks beneath him, Nevada listened. There could be little doubt that the owner of the voice was standing in front of the building adjoining the old barn.

"Over here," he heard Richardson reply. "Any sign of him?"

"None."

A moment later the heavy-set, square-shouldered form of Dawson moved into Lacy's line of vision as he crossed over.

"You think he may have kept right on going? He could have taken the road to Prescot, or maybe the Fort?"

"No—get rid of that idea. He's here, just setting

tight. I'd bet on it."

"Funny we can't find that buckskin he was forkin'."

"He's made sure we wouldn't. Lacy's plenty smart."

Another figure appeared, this time along the dust-covered brush at the edge of the street north of the saloon. A tall, gangling shape—Clint. Ignoring all precautions, the outlaw strode into the open, revealing himself fully in the flare of lamplight coming through the saloon's doorway. He halted directly in front of Richardson and Dawson.

"Well, he sure ain't around here nowheres," Clint announced flatly.

There was a short run of silence and then Cud Richardson, his voice thick with disgust, said: "If he is—one thing's dead certain. He sure as hell knows where we are, with you bulling around in the street that way."

"I can't see as it makes any difference," Clint replied. "He ain't here. My guess is he's high-tailed it for home."

"You'd be guessing wrong. Lacy won't run. See the Dude anywhere?"

"Sure ain't, but I reckon he'll be showing up pretty quick. He feels powerful bad about that chewing you done on him."

"He's got more than that coming to him."

"Claims he put that rawhide on good. Lacy must've had a knife tucked up his sleeve or somewheres."

"Maybe. All I know is he got loose—and we're right back where we started from."

Dawson removed his hat, and rubbed at his head. "You going to run Dude off?"

"Ain't made up my mind yet. A jasper like him is

mighty risky to have around. All right, he's trying. But a mistake like he made can hurt like hell. That him coming?''

There was a brief silence, and then Dawson said: "It's him. Over here, Dude."

The outlaw appeared at the edge of the light, the fringe on his jacket swaying gently as he walked. "No luck," he announced.

"Us either," Clint said. "I figure he kept right on going. We'd have spotted that horse of his, is he still around. Place just ain't big enough for a man to plain drop out of sight."

"You could be right," Richardson said suddenly. "Maybe that's what he's done—kept going."

Dawson jerked off his hat again, scrubbed at his head. "I thought you said—"

"Been thinking it over. Maybe this Lacy ain't such big shakes after all. Could be I figured him wrong. Let's go on in and get a drink. Are you ready to eat now, Clint?"

"I sure am!" the tall outlaw said at once.

"All right. Come on then."

A faint smile on his lips, Nevada watched the four men emerge from the shadows, mount the steps to the landing and cross noisily to the saloon's entrance. In single file, they entered, and disappeared into the smoky haze.

Cud Richardson was fooling nobody. Failing to turn up his intended victim by combing the town area, he was making a noisy show of giving up, fully aware that the man he sought was hiding somewhere nearby, watching.

"Obliged to you, Cud, old hoss," Nevada murmured, and worked his way to the back of the roof.

Two could play at the game as well as one.

Reaching the edge, he dropped lightly to the ground. He'd have, he realized, only a few minutes in which to act. Richardson and the others were probably on their way to the rear door of the saloon, and in another moment would be doubling back to the street.

He hesitated, considering the wisdom of looking over the horses at the saloon's hitchrack for a rifle, instead of trying to locate the stable he felt certain was somewhere nearby. But he decided against that. Not only would conducting a search further away involve less of a risk, he would be afforded more time.

Wheeling, Nevada ran along the rear walls of the structures lining that side of the street, listening, testing the still night air for the familiar odor that would indicate the location of a livery barn. He found it at the extreme end of the alley.

The door was open. He slipped inside, and remained for a long moment motionless, getting his bearings in the gloom. Gradually, he was able to make out the vague outlines of five or six horses, all of them occupying separate stalls. He could see the hump of the saddles still on their backs.

Pressing forward, he entered the first compartment. A scabbard—but no rifle. The result was the same in the next. But in the third stall his heart skipped a beat, and the strain and uncertainty under which he'd been laboring became less oppressive and much easier to bear. The stock of a rifle protruded from beneath a dangling stirrup. He jerked it clear, and stepped back.

The gun was an old seven-shot Spencer. Rust scarred the mechanism in places, and the stock was cracked. But the action seemed tight. Hopefully, he checked the next two saddles but found no other weapons. There were no more horses in the stable. The Spencer would have to do. He looked then at the rifle's magazine. It contained five cartridges.

His spirits rising. Nevada returned to the alley, deciding he'd be better off on the opposite side of the street, since that would place him behind the outlaws, and his movements would be less likely to attract their attention. He needed all the advantages he could muster.

Turning, he trotted to the corner of the livery stable, and followed along its south wall until he came to the street. There was no one in sight, but it would be a mistake, he knew, to draw any comfort from that. The outlaws could have returned, and be waiting again, unseen in the shadows.

He'd have to risk it. He still believed his best chances lay on the opposite side. Crouched low, he sprinted across the dusty strip of roadway, and ducked into a deep pool of blackness behind a clump of rabbitbush. No gunshots had challenged him; perhaps Richardson and his crew were still inside.

Nevada, still crouching low, moved forward, toward the corner of the bulky structure. The shadows Richardson had made use of would serve well for his own purpose. He drew near the wall of the building, and paused to study the surrounding area. No one was visible. Moving on, he gained the wall near the center, and began to edge cautiously along its dark bulk.

"Right there, mister! Hold it!" Clint's voice lashed at him from the darkness. "Make a move and I'll blow your head off!"

# X

Nevada Jim Lacy's reaction was instinctive and instantaneous. He bobbed, lunged to one side. Clint's gun smashed through the night as the lean rider hit the ground, went full length, and rolled fast. The outlaw's bullet thudded into the wall of the building. The blast was still echoing through the darkness when Nevada stopped rolling, triggered his weapon and took aim.

The old Spencer bucked in his hands. Clint's jaw fell open and his shoulders jerked as a glistening redness spread across his chest. But reflex action enabled him to press off a second shot as he fell, the bullet digging into the ground at his feet. Lacy continued to hug the ground, striving to keep clear of the light, knowing that the other outlaws would be somewhere near.

"That was Clint! He's found him!"

The shout came from a passageway on the opposite side of the street. Men were pouring out of the saloon now, gathering on the porch, shouting questions. Nevada lay sprawled on his stomach under a small cedar, his eyes sweeping over the ground ahead of him for a glimpse of Dawson, Richardson and Dude. A dark shape moved near the old stable. Richardson, he thought.

Instantly he bounded to his feet and darted into the blackness alongside the saloon. A gun cracked sharply, the sound coming from the opposite end of the street. A breath of hot wind plucked at his arm. Nevada whirled, fired the Spencer from the hip, aiming only at the flash of the outlaw's weapon. Then he raced for the other side of the street.

"There he goes!" someone on the saloon porch yelled.

Gunshots racketed through the night again. Lacy ignored the blasts. It has been Cud Richardson he'd seen near the abandoned stable—and Cud Richardson was the one he wanted. Gaining the darkness just below that building, he pulled up short. If the outlaw leader was hiding somewhere beyond the dilapidated structure it would be foolhardy—suicidal in fact—to approach from the street.

Spinning about, he raced back toward the livery stable where he had obtained the rifle, having decided to circle the line of business houses and come in on Richardson from behind.

Drawing abreast of the stable the figure of a man lying half in the roadway, half in a clump of brush, caught his eye. It was the outlaw who fired at him after he downed Clint. He flung a glance at the sprawled shape. Dude or Dawson?

It was Dawson. Nevada moved silently past the man toward the near corner of the livery barn. He came to that point, plunged suddenly to one side as the unexpected blast of a gun, almost at his heels, rocked the night. He spun about, the older Spencer up and ready.

Dude, revolver in hand, was motioning to him from the doorway of the building. A short distance away Dawson, on his knees was falling forward.

"He was about to pot you from behind," the man in the fringed jacket shouted.

Lacy stared. "You're not—"

Dude shook his head. "Here," he said, pulling Nevada's .45 from his belt and tossing it.

"Expect you're handier with this than you are with that old thunder gun."

Lacy caught the revolver, tossed the Spencer aside. Straightening, he stepped back to the corner of the building.

"Don't know what's going on," he said. "But I'm obliged to you."

"We'll talk about it later," Dude replied. "We both want Richardson. I prefer him alive."

"Don't count on that," Nevada said. "I'll circle the buildings. You—"

"I'll work toward the end of the street," Dude said, cutting him short. "Luck."

Lacy hurried on, checking his gun as he moved, making certain that it was loaded. He was stunned by the change in Dude. Perhaps, he thought, it was all some kind of a trick, and he was being led into a trap. But the cylinder of the .45 was full and the revolver was in perfect working order. Dude would hardly have handed him a loaded gun if they were hoping to bushwhack him.

Dude almost had to be some sort of lawman. He said he wanted Richardson alive, but Cud, Nevada knew, was not the kind to let himself be taken. Dude should have known that, too. But a government lawman, a Deputy United States Marshal perhaps, could have some peculiar ideas. U.S. Marshals had a code no one could talk them into abandoning. They always wanted to capture the man they sought, haul him up before a judge. It was a fine idea. Only it didn't usually work out right. A lot of dead lawmen were proof of that.

Nevada reached the end of the alley and halted in the darkness behind the abandoned barn. He was sure that

Cud would be near, either inside the building, or in the adjacent brush. He considered climbing again onto the roof, but almost instantly rejected the thought. It would be impossible to do so quietly, and the noise created would attract the outlaw, put him at his mercy.

A shadow crossed the passageway alongside the structure. Instantly Lacy hunched low and catfooted his way silently up the weed-littered corridor to the street. Halting, gun ready, he peered around the corner. Stray light from the saloon touched a figure only an arm's length away—a man in a fringed buckskin jacket. Dude again.

In that same instant there was a quick hammer of hooves off to the right. Dude swore violently, having evidently been quick to realize that Richardson was making a run for it.

"It's me behind you," Nevada said, stepping out into the sagging board sidewalk. Further down the street several men had collected around the body of Dawson. Others were bringing the limp form of Clint from where he had fallen near the rear of the saloon.

"Reckon he got away from us," Nevada drawled, eyeing Dude keenly. "You mind telling me now just who you are?"

Dude holstered his weapon, swung about and offered his hand. "Name's Drake. Harlan Drake."

Nevada accepted the man's hand, "I'm Jim Lacy."

"I know," Dude said, smiling. "Fact is, I've heard a lot about you in the last few years."

"Nothing too good, I take it."

"Not all bad, anyway," Drake said. "I know that gun of yours is fast—too fast maybe at times—but that you've made use of it plenty often."

74

"I always had a good reason," Nevada said coolly. "Don't doubt it."

Lacy glanced toward the saloon. The bodies of the outlaws had been carried to the porch and placed side by side for all to see. Suddenly, there was a stir among the onlookers. One of the bartenders came into the open, shouldering his way through the crowd. He stared briefly at the dead men, then motioned impatiently to several others standing close by. At once they stepped forward, lifting the bodies and started around the building with them.

The white-aproned man faced the remaining crowd, said something Nevada couldn't catch and started making an effort to herd his patrons back into the saloon. Several obeyed and the gathering began to thin. About a half a dozen men, ranged along the outer edge of the porch, made no effort to comply. Instead they continued to talk, now and then glancing across the street to Nevada and Harlan Drake.

Lacy considered them absently. "Looks like Richardson's got some friends here who don't exactly like the way things turned out," he said.

"They figure I doublecrossed him," Dude replied. "Makes no difference to me. Expect we ought to get on his trail."

Nevada shook his head. "That would be playing it his way. It's just what he's hoping we'll do. Best we wait for daylight."

Drake frowned. "He'll be plenty far from here by then."

"Not likely. I'm almost sure he's sitting in the dark a couple of miles up the trail right now, just waiting to pick us off when we come riding past. Let him sweat out a wait. Meantime, I'm feeling a bit hollow. Let's get a bite to eat.''

"Saloon's the only place.''

Nevada's shoulders lifted. "So?''

Drake nodded at the men on the landing. "We're not going to be very popular in there.''

Nevada grinned. "I can't recollect ever losing much sleep over something like that.'' Taking a step out into the street, he paused, his expression serious again. "And I can't recollect you answering the rest of my question. What are you—some kind of a lawman?''

Harlan Drake brushed at the stubble of beard beginning to show on his chin. "Not the kind you're thinking of, maybe. I'm with the Pinkerton Agency.''

## XI

Nevada Jim Lacy said nothing for a moment. Finally he murmured, "A detective.''

"In a way. But it would be better to say that I'm a special government agent. Explains the jobs I do more accurately.'' It was Drake's turn to be silent. After a time, he said, "Why? You have something against detectives?''

Nevada laughed. "Not me. Man's got a right to be what he wants to be. But I'll admit it surprised me some. Come on, let's get those vittles.''

Drake fell in beside him, and together they crossed the street. Reaching the saloon landing, they ascended it in silence, Lacy's cool, challenging glance raking the men standing there, stifling any comment. Continuing, they entered the building, which was still clouded with smoke but considerably quieter than before the shooting.

Spotting a table in a far corner that gave them a complete view of the room and both front and rear doors, as well as the stair to the upper floor, Lacy led the way to it. Drawing out a chair for himself, he motioned to Drake to take the one on his left.

A hush settled gradually over the place. Lacy beckoned to one of the bartenders. The man came quickly.

"Yes, sir," he said, centering his attention on Nevada.

"Something to eat. Whatever you've got that's ready."

"Steak. Boiled spuds. Biscuits."

Nevada glanced at Drake. "Suit you?"

"Be fine."

The bartender frowned, fidgeted nervously. "Well, I ain't so sure we got enough for two plates—"

Lacy straightened in his chair slowly. "There'd better be," he said softly. "Maybe you'd like us to go have a look-see for ourselves."

"No need for that! I'll try."

The man bobbed his head, and scurried away. Lacy watched him for a moment, "That Cooper?" he asked.

Drake shook his head. "No, the other bartender standing at the end of the counter's Cooper. They call this one Cary." Drake studied Lacy with a half-smile. "No call for you to stand up for me. I can look out for myself."

"Expect you can. Only I don't like weasels. If he'd come out and said he didn't want to serve you—either one of us—I wouldn't have thought much about it. But squirming around, lying like that—"

"A man in my business runs into that problem a lot of times," Drake said. "You learn to live with it."

77

His eyes shifted to the doorway. The men who had gathered on the porch were just entering. Their faces were set in grim lines and there was a belligerency to their manner. "Looks like it's one of those times," Harlan Drake added dryly.

Nevada watched the group pause to scan the room before moving forward. Folding his arms across his chest, he awaited their arrival.

"Something bothering you gentlemen?" he asked as they came to a stop in front of the table. Getting in the first lick at such times was a way with Nevada, who believed firmly that a strong offense was the best defense.

"Not you, mister," the spokesman for the party said. He was a large, square-shouldered man with a stubble of red beard. "It's that there back-stabber you got setting with you."

Nevada's pistol was suddenly in his hand. Thumb hooked over the hammer, he lazily recrossed his arms again.

"Sure," he drawled. "You go right ahead, speak your piece. Don't mind me."

A long minute of complete silence followed. Then another member spoke up. "We just don't cotton to doublecrossers," he said, looking straight at Dude. "We figured you was a friend of Cud and the men who ride with him. Then you turn around and shoot Dawson dead. We're wanting to know why."

"No business of yours," Drake said evenly.

"Could be, we're making it our business—"

The Pinkerton man shook his head. "My advice to you is forget it."

Nevada nodded approvingly. "That's mighty good

78

advice, gents. I strongly urge you to take it. Now, if you'll step aside I'll be obliged to you. Man's bringing us some grub. We're both a mite on the hungry side—and you know how ornery being hungry can make a man."

The group parted, allowed the bartender, carrying two heaped platters, to reach the table, and place the dishes before Lacy and Drake.

"Coffee," Nevada said. He glanced at Drake. "That all right with you, pard?"

"Fine," Dude replied, a faint smile again tugging at his lips.

The bartender turned away. Nevada laid his .4 alongside his plate, took up his knife and fork and began to eat. Drake also fell to. The red-bearded man and his companions stirred uncertainly. One worked his way to the foreground, his eyes on Nevada.

"Seems I ought to know you—" he began.

Nevada continued with his meal. "That's not surprising. I've met a lot of people I just can't recall to mind straight off."

"Ain't you Jim Lacy the gunslinger?"

"I'm Lacy," Nevada cut in coldly.

A murmur ran though the party, spread across the saloon. And then again there was a hush.

"You two working together?" the red-bearded man asked.

"Could be."

"Then I reckon that makes you what I just said he was—a backshooting doublecrosser!"

Nevada set his fork down very quietly. Slowly he raised his eyes to meet those of the speaker.

"You've got a big mouth to match your size, Red,"

he said with a tinge of sadness in his voice. "It could get you in trouble."

From somewhere in the saloon a voice said: "Let it go, Tom. You don't know how fast he can draw. There ain't another gun—"

"His gun is in plain sight," the red-bearded man snapped. "Maybe he's buffaloin' the rest of you, but he sure ain't me! I'm not scared."

"If you had any sense, you would be," Nevada said. "I figured you for a fool. Otherwise you'd be dead right now, after calling me what you did."

The words seemed to bring courage to the big man instead of serving as a warning. He shrugged his massive shoulders.

"Ain't it like I've always said? Man stands up to such as this pair, and right away they start talking loud—and backing off."

"Ease off, friend," Harlan Drake said. "This man is Jim Lacy—and everything you've heard about him is true, I *know*."

"Only thing I ever heard about him was that he'd killed plenty of men. I'm wondering how—by shooting them when they looked the other way?"

Nevada kept his eyes on the table before him. He was tyring to ignore the man, but his temper was getting out of control. It was nothing new. He'd been through the same situation man times in the past—a man, like the red-bearded giant seeking to prove his own courage, and build a reputation for himself.

There appeared to be a slight difference here, however. The man called Tom evidently thought he was in the right. He could actually be sincere. They were the worst kind—the stupid ones. They usually ended up dead because of poor judgment.

"Move on, Red," Nevada murmured, settling back in his chair. "I don't want any trouble with you."

The bartender appeared at the end of the half circle, a small pot of coffee in one hand, two mugs in the other. He set them on the table, spun about, and hurried back into the hushed crowd.

"Maybe I ain't of a mind to move on," Tom said. "Maybe I would just rather stand here, and—"

Nevada Lacy was on his feet, gun in hand—all in a single, blurred motion. The muzzle of the .45 was suddenly pressing against the red bearded man's throat.

"Listen good," Lacy said in a harsh, dry voice. "I'm not saying it again. Get the hell away from me—and stay away!"

Tom gagged as the barrel dug into his windpipe. Eyes spread wide, he managed to bob his head. "All right," he got out. "I guess—I made a mistake."

"Goes for everybody else," Nevada said, drawing back, and sweeping the remaining men with an angry glance. He then swung his attention to Cooper, still at the end of the bar. "If you don't want somebody hurt in here, keep them backed off."

Cooper started forward, but the group was already breaking up, melting into the crowd. Nevada continued to stand until they had all disappeared. Then he holstered his weapon, sat down, and resumed his eating.

Drake said softly, "I thought for a minute he was a dead man."

"His kind usually end up that way," Nevada said, "Never seem to learn. I guess they plain don't get the chance."

"You gave him some good advice. Let's hope he

81

profits form it.''

Nevada grunted. "Yeah, I'm downright surprising at doing good turns. One thing you'd better understand, however.''

Drake's brows lifted. "What's that?''

You said something about wanting Richardson, alive. I aim to track him down myself, and I give you fair warning I expect it will wind up in a killing.''

## XII

The Pinkerton man looked at Nevada steadily for a moment, his eyes troubled, almost accusing. "Sorry to hear that. I need him alive.''

"It's not that easy,'' Nevada said impatiently. "You don't take a man like Cud Richardson without a fight. And in his kind of fight you either win—or you're dead yourself.''

"It doesn't have to be that way,'' Drake protested. "I figure if you give a man a chance to quit, he'll likely take it. Nobody wants to die.''

"They don't look at it that way. All they're thinking about is staying alive—no matter how. Fact is, I doubt if any of the owlhoots I went up against would have listened to sensible advice. Chances are you'd never live long enough to make them an offer.''

"I've been around a few years,'' Dude said stiffly. "And I'm still breathing.''

"How many gunslingers like Cud Richardson—the tough ones who figured themselves for dead years ago and are living now on borrowed time—have you hauled in alive?''

"Well, I can't say there's been any exactly like him—''

82

"Here's what I'm driving at. Their kind just don't give in. They'll fight you down to the last breath—and if you don't watch them close, they'll kill you after they're dead. Like Dawson. I got careless out there in the street. He almost got me—and would have, if it hadn't been for you. What are you after Cud for?"

"Robbing the United States mail—and murder. Cud and two others were in on it. We got the two. I've been on Richardson's trial ever since—almost a year."

Drake told of how, after the robbery and killings in Kansas, Cud Richardson had vanished from sight, very likely taking refuge in Mexico. About three months ago, the Pinkerton agent had had news of him in Arizona, and had made his own way there.

Posing as a tenderfoot from the East, looking for a quick way to make a lot of money, he had gained Cud Richardson's confidence, and been taken into the gang as a recruit.

The first order of business had been to get rid of Jim Lacy—in revenge for Ed Richardson's slaying, and, more practically, to eliminate the strongest obstacle to the rustler's plans.

"That man who tried to warn you, Cash Burridge," Drake said, "was to take care of the business end of it. The gang would rustle the stock, he'd dispose of it. Was Cash a friend of yours?"

"More of a friend than I knew," Nevada said moodily.

"I liked him," Drake said. "I was around him only short while, but I liked him. He didn't seem to be of the same stripe as Richardson and the others."

"He wasn't. Cash got himself into a few shady deals, but never anything real bad. He was more on the slicker—"

"Confidence men, we call them in our business."

Lacy grinned. "Fits. That was Cash all right." He leaned back, and toyed with the handle of his coffee mug. "How'd you plan to take Cud, with his bunch always around close? You sure couldn't have been loco enough to just walk up to him some day, and tell him you aimed to arrest him."

"Hardly. After I'd finally got myself set with him and the others, I began to look for a way to manage it. Law wanted him real bad, so, that a trial could be held and an example made of him. They figured a show of strength on the part of the Law would have a good effect on other renegades—prove that it was big enough to lay the best of them by the heels."

"It meant taking him alive," Drake went on, after a pause. "Dead he'd be just another outlaw to bury. I had to come up with some long-range scheming. When he got the idea of bushwhacking you in Winthrop, it fitted right in. The town had a marshal and a good jail, something the places we'd been hanging around in—like Cooperville here—didn't have."

"Winthrop's the only town that does in the whole county."

Dude nodded. "Had to have those two things—a lawman and a jail where I could keep Richardson until I could get help to take him back to Kansas. Plan was simple. I'd get Richardson off alone while he was setting up the ambush for you, throw a gun on him, and lock him up before the others knew what was going on. Once he was behind bars I didn't think Dawson and the rest would try hard to break him out."

"You're probably right," Nevada admitted. "They'd figure it was Cud's hard luck, and go on their way. Cash doing what he did must have spoiled the play for you."

"It sure did," Drake said. "Broke it wide open. We got there a little late—or maybe you were early. Anyway, there wasn't time to do things the way Richardson wanted. He was going to scatter the men all along the street. As it was, we'd no more than got off our horses when Cash made a run for that church, yelling at you to look out."

Drake tightened his lips. "After that, there wasn't anything I could do but go along with the way the cards had fallen, and hope for another chance in another town where I could get help."

"One thing bothered me—why did you all pull out? The odds were with you. Why didn't Cud stay and finish what he'd started?"

"He thought the town would come swarming out to help you. He said it would be smart to high-tail it, and let you come looking for him. And that was just what you did."

Nevada nodded. "Cud knew I was playing his game—something I try not to do. But I had no choice, leastwise not until I found him." Nevada paused, added, "Forgot to say I'm obliged to you, too, for leaving that rawhide loose."

"I took a chance on one of them looking the job over," Drake said. "But I guess by then they figured I was all right."

"Did it cause you any trouble with Richardson?"

"Cud had himself a fine time cussing me out, but nothing worse." The Pinkerton man hesitated, then said: "You really think he's waiting for us somewhere up the road north of town? Seems more logical to believe he'd ride on, and try to reach another settlement."

"He'll be waiting," Nevada assured him. "All the cards are on the table. He knows I'm after him, and that you are, too. He's probably trying to figure what your angle is, but he's damned sure you're not the prize tenderfoot you made out. He'll be there, all right."

"I've got to find a way to talk to him."

"Forget it," Nevada broke in roughly. "Your chances of taking him alive are less than ever now."

"I suppose so, but it's still up to me to try." The lawman stopped, faced Lacy squarely. "I'd like to ask a favor of you, Jim. I know I can't persuade you to give up going after him. But I'd like the opportunity of talking to him first. There's just a chance he might be willing to surrender if he knows he'll be riddled with bullets otherwise."

Nevada studied his empty cup. "It fair goes against my grain," he said finally. "But you did me a couple of mighty big favors. I can't say no."

His face was somber as he studied Drake, and he wondered if the Pinkerton man realized that the undertaking he had just given had lengthened the odds aginst them dangerously. But he had given his word now and would play the cards as they came, new rules and all.

## XIII

They rode out of Coopersville shortly after dawn the next morning. The air was brisk and both men sat in their saddles with their hands tucked in their armpits, and reins hanging from the horn, while the horses followed the distinct ruts of the road.

Silence hung between them like a thick blanket, as

each, filled with his own thoughts and turned quiet by the cold, found nothing to say. A half-hour or so later, when the pearl of the eastern sky began to lighten, and change gradually to pale gold shot with fingers of color, the reserve broke.

"You making any guess where he'll be?" Harlan Drake asked, chafing his palms.

Nevada shrugged. "It was mighty cold last night. He could have looked for a shack or cabin to hole up in. He won't be far off the trial, however."

Dude looked ahead, hs eyes following the course of the trail running almost due north through the wooded hills.

"Expect you're right. But I'm still wondering if he didn't keep going.

"And be looking back over his shoulder every minute, knowing we were on his trail? Not Richardson. He'd pick a hiding place, wait and settle things."

They lapsed into silence as the riding grew worse. They were into rough forest, trending generally up, but often descending into precipitous ravines.

Cedar, oak, pinon, and pine surrounded them, giving way from time to time to sandy flats that slowed their horses, as the glare of the early sun, now well up, struck them. Though occasional small streams, limestone out-croppings gleaming from their banks, impeded them, they were grateful for the cooling water, not least the refreshing music of its splashing.

As they rode on, Nevada told Harlan Drake something of he background of Cud Richardson's emnity for him: of how, when working on a ranch in the Mogollon Brakes, he had determined to break up the

Pine Tree rustling outfit which was ruining most of the nearby ranchers, including his old friend Ben Ide.

He had worked his way into to the Pine Tree gang—much as Harlan Drake had done with Cud Richardson's—and soon discovered that Ben Ide's trusted foreman was Ed Richardson, leader of the outlaw band.

"I called him on it," Nevada said, "and that was the end of it."

"You outdrew him."

Nevada shrugged. "As I recollect," he drawled, "the drawing was a tie. I put my bullet where it counted."

"Wouldn't it have been better to disarm him, and turn him over to the law?" Drake asked, staring off into the hills. "Hanging him might have stopped the rustling in the Mogollon country for years to come. The way it turns out, you not only brought another killer into the area, but you got the gang started again."

"Maybe," Nevada said, "but there just wasn't any way to arrest Ed. You could have a Gatling gun trained on him from ten feet away, and he'd still draw and fire. You didn't grow up around men like Cud Richardson— or me. I can see that."

"You mean if you were—" Drake hesitated uncertainly.

"Go on, say it. It won't hurt my feelings any. I was one of the worst when it came to using my gun—or maybe you'd say one of the best since I'm still alive to talk about it. Law was looking for me plenty of times."

"But the men you killed were outlaws—renegades every lawman was after. It made you a sort of lawman yourself, outside the law."

"An excuse-seeking way of putting it," Nevada said drily.

"All right. What I meant to ask was—if you were in Cud Richardson's boots, and two lawmen had you backed up with the odds against you, would you turn down a chance to surrender, and take your chances on a trial? You wouldn't feel that things might still go in your favor, that a judge might sentence you to a long term in prison instead of a hanging? You'd not see a little hope there, knowing you'd be sure to die if you tried to shoot it out?"

"No," Jim Lacy said, "I wouldn't. I'd take my chances with a gun. So will Cud Richardson and all the others like him. You've got a fine idea there. Only this country's not ready for it yet."

"You have to start somewhere—sometime—"

"You've said that before. But if you'll take my advice you won't try beginning with Richardson. You won't—" Nevada broke off abruptly. "Smoke ahead," he said, pointing, and rising slightly in the saddle.

Harlan Drake pulled to a halt, and swung his eyes to the trail, where a pale blue streamer was twisting its way into the cloudless sky.

"You think that's him?"

"It could be a trapper—or a miner," Nevada replied. "It's a little hard to believe it's Cud. He's not fool enough to advertise his presence with a fire."

The pressed on, keeping to the road until they reached the rise beyond which the smoke was rising.

"We'd better split here and keep to the brush until we have a look," Nevada said, pulling away from the ruts.

Drake immediately cut to the opposite side of the road, and together they crossed the ridge. The instant they reached the other side they could see, in a cleared hollow below the crumbling, time-ravaged remainder of a cabin. The roof was half-gone, forming no more than a slanting, lean-to affair with it upper end resting upon the only wall which was still intact. The smoke they had seen from the other side of the bridge was issuing from the stone chimney.

"It must be him," Drake said. "Nobody would be living in that place."

Lacy nodded in agreement. But a strong current of suspicion and dissatisfaction was running through him. He no longer doubted that it was Richardson—but why would a man waiting in ambush build a fire and create smoke that would reveal his hiding place? Something else troubled him. Why hadn't they seen the smoke earlier?

A man bulding a fire for warmth or comfrot would have done so hours ago. Why had he waited until they were fairly close. So near, in fact, where they could not have failed to notice it?

"It has to be a trap," he said aloud. "Cud's got something up his sleeve."

"A sign of some kind is right in line with what we were hoping to find," Drake said, turning to face Nevada straight on. "We'll get nowhere if we're too suspicious. I'll take over from here."

Lacy stared at the Pinkerton man. "If you try riding down there, you'll be making a mistake—perhaps your last one," he warned.

"I don't think so. This is a good time to prove that everything I've been trying to tell you makes sense."

Nevada was silent for a long minute, his eyes again on the cabin. Finally he shrugged. "All right, you're dealing. We'll see how the cards fall. I'll stay in the game as I promised, but I don't like it. What do you want me to do?"

"Stay back in the brush at the edge of the clearing, out of sight. I'll shout when I want you to move in."

"You're not aiming to ride—" Nevada began, and stopped when Drake made a motion wit his hand.

"Not exactly," Dude said, and moved on.

In full view of the shack, he crossed the road to Nevada's side, and angling through the brush, approached the ruined cabin slowly. Reaching the edge of the clearing, he halted.

"Richardson!" he called in a strong, clear voice. "This is Drake—Dude. You in there?"

"I'm here." The outlaw's reply was muffled, and came from somewhere at the rear of the structure.

"I'm a Government lawman. Pinkerton Agency. Jim Lacy's waiting in the brush. You haven't got a chance. I want you to throw your guns down, and come out."

There was no answer. After a time Drake yelled. "You hear me?"

"I hear you. What're you dogging me for?"

"That Kansas train robbery. You come with me and you'll get a fair trial."

"Sure—I'll just bet."

"You have my word on it."

Again their was that dragging silence, broken this time by the outlaw. "You ain't fooling me. I show my head, you'll blow it off."

"No. It won't be like that."

"How do I know?"

"We'll have to trust each other. There's no other way."

Once more there was quiet, once again broken by Cud Richardson.

"I ain't so sure. You crossed me once. It could be

91

you're figuring to do it again. Come on down—we'll do some talking.''

"No!"

The word exploded involuntarily from Jim Lacy's lips as he spurred forward. Richardson was giving nothing; Drake was accepting all the risk.

The Pinkerton man twisted hurriedly on his saddle, and halted Nevada by lifting his hand, palm outward.

"My way—" he said.

Swearing in helpless anger, Lacy pulled up, watched Dude move on, saw him break from the fringe of brush into the open, and head directly for the cabin. He covered half the distance. Two-thirds.

Abruptly the small valley echoed with two quick gunshots. They came not from the cabin but from the trees a short distance to its right. Harlan Drake jolted on his saddle, buckled forward.

Roweling the buckskin, Nevada swept out his gun, and started down the slope on a swerving, erratic course. Richardson had run true to form.

## XIV

The outlaw broke from the trees, reining in his horse so abruptly that the animal reared. The weapon in his hand bucked, puffs of smoke lifting from its muzzle. Nevada, steadying himself as best he could on the plunging buckskin, returned the fire. But accuracy on the part of either man was impossible.

It was clear what Richardson had done. He had allowed Drake to think he was still inside the cabin, but had slipped out after talking to him circled, and waited in the brush until the Pinkerton man was in range. From that side vantage point it had been easy to cut the lawman down.

Suddenly Richardson flinched. Bent low, he wheeled his horse around, and headed for the road that led on into the country beyond the Mogollon Rim. Nevada, dull fury beating at him, triggered another shot at the outlaw. But just as the shot rang out, the buckskin veered to avoid a rotting log, and he knew that the bullet had gone wild.

"Run, damn you!" he grated through clenched teeth. "I'll hunt you down wherever you go!"

Drake lay sprawled beside his black horse when Nevada reached him. Leaving the saddle in a hurried leap, the lean rider hunched beside the lawman. A broad crimson stain had spread across the Pinkerton man's chest. There was a slackness to his features, but his eyes were bright, alert.

"You—figured him right," he murmured. "Should have listened."

"Don't try to talk," Nevada snapped. "I've got to get you to a doctor."

Drake shook his head. "Waste of time. You know I won't make it—same as I know."

Lacy glanced toward the cabin. Someone had bridged two rocks with planks to form a crude bench. Slipping his arms under Drake, he carried him inside, and eased him down on the rough pine boards, feeling it would be warmer and a little more comfortable close to the fire that was still smoldering.

Harlan Drake looked around, his lips twisting in a faint smile. "Not a bad place to die."

"It's a hell of a place!" Lacy said harshly. "And for no good reason."

Drake checked him with a raised hand. "Too late now for regrets. You were right, and I was wrong, but it does no good to hash it over. We've still got a long way to go before we get the respect for law we need. But like I said—we have to make a start."

Drake paused slightly and took a bubbling breath. "Day's gone when one man, like yourself, can be jury, judge and executioner—all rolled into one. Has to be that way. Country will never amount to anything until there's law . . . every place."

Nevada said, "The Pinkertons are about as important to you as anything—I can see that. But I don't know much about them. Sort of a private law force, is that it?"

Harlan Drake nodded. "It's more than that," he said, his voice suddenly stronger, more intense. "The Agency got started about ten years before the was broke out. Pinkerton was a Scotsman, and he opened his first company office in Chicago. Did mostly railroad work.

"Did such a good job that when the trouble between the states started, Washington asked him to set up a Government secret service. It was the Pinkerton agents who smuggled President Lincoln through Baltimore to the Capital right after the trouble at Charleston Harbor that set off the war."

Drake paused, breathing heavily. He brushed at his lips, glanced around. "Could you get me some water? Throat's mighty dry."

Nevada obtained his canteen from the buckskin's saddle, returned and held it to Drake's lips. The lawman took it in his own hands. He showed amazing strength, considering his wound. But to have loaded him on a horse would only have hastened the end, and Nevada knew that the dying man had been right in refusing to let himself be moved.

Lowering the canteen, Drake smiled faintly. "Much better. Where was I? Oh—President Lincoln issued blanket authority to us, gave Pinkerton agents the right to go anywhere in the country, and arrest a man for breaking the law. That's why I was sent here. I was in Pennsylvania on another case. Head office ordered me to Kansas, to get Richardson. I'm ending up in Arizona."

Drake paused, his voice faltering again. "That shooting—Richardson—get away?"

Nevada nodded. "Could be I winged him. But he won't go far. I'll find him. Today, next week, sometime. But I'll find him."

"Know you will—Jim."

Nevada looked more closely at Drake. "Better just lay there, take it easy."

"Why? I feel like talking. And when I shut up this time—it'll be for good."

Drake turned his head and gazed out over the gently rolling hills dark with pines. The sun was well on its way and a warmness was spreading over the land.

Suddenly the change came. Drake was going fast and with his last strength he caught at Jim's arm. His voice was a hoarse mutter: "Take the leather packet inside my shirt. Papers."

Drake made a feeble attempt to brush his eyes, swallowed hard. "Take to Bern Jensen—Prescott, chief agent—tell what happened."

The stillness was suddenly absolute in the decaying shack. Somewhere across the road a meadowlark trilled cheerfully. A man dies, a bird sings, and the world continues to spin through space.

For a long minute Nevada Jim Lacy stared at Harlan Drake's slack features, and then he rose stiffly, angrily. Yes, a man dies. But another man would pay for the dying. That was the way it had to be—the code of retribution, of vengeance.

Grimly, he moved to the edge of the lean-to roof, and stood for a long moment staring up the road. Cud Richardson was out there, somewhere, waiting, no doubt planning another ambush with some slight variation. His mind worked that way.

Like a kill-crazed, hunted animal, he'd run, stop to fight, and failing in his efforts to down the man on his trail, would run again. And thus it would go until he had destroyed his pursuer—or himself. Kill or be killed. That was the rule Cud Richardson lived by—and would die by.

Stepping out into the open, Lacy gathered in the reins of Drake's black, and led him back to the cabin. Bending over, he found the papers that Drake had mentioned, sewed to the fabric at the dead man's shield-type shirt just below the left armpit. Without examining the packet's contents, he thrust it into the inner pocket of his own shirt, and finished loading Drake's body on the black, securing it firmly to the saddle with a double lashing of leather strings.

Mounting his buckskin, Nevada returned to the ridge, and pointed Drake's horse down the road for Coopersville. He slapped the animal smartly on the rump, and sent him trotting for the settlement. The black, he knew, wouldn't stop until he got there—and Cooper would see that Dude was buried. He would have liked to be there for the funeral, but there wasn't time.

Cud Richardson was waiting, and he had no intention

of disappointing the outlaw. Dude would want him to keep that appointment.

## XV

Ahead the trail curved slightly westward on its way to join the Prescott-Fort Apache road. The valley was not wide here, and trees and brush crowded in close on either side, creating an almost channel-like course.

Nevada didn't like it. He was pursuing Richardson on the outlaw's own terms again, and that was the surest way he could think of to get a bullet in the head. He must get off the road as soon as possible, and do his traveling through the trees where he would not be so conspicuous. But he must also stay in the open for a time—long enough for Richardson to see him, and become convinced that he was being followed.

The problem was to decide how far he would have to ride in the open to mislead the outlaw—one mile or ten? Much depended, of course, on how great a lead Richardson had.

Lacy endeavored to put himself in Richardson's position. How would he have figured it? Probably, after shooting down Harlan Drake, and knowing that the lawman was not alone, he had ridden hard for the first few minutes, not certain whether pursuit would be immediate or come later.

Within five miles or less, he would have become fairly sure that no one was on his heels. He would have slowed his place to spare his horse as much as possible, and have started making plans for a second ambush.

Maybe Richardson would spot another deserted cabin, but the outlaw was smart enough to realize he could not work that ruse twice. Most surely he would look for a narrow place in the trail where rocks would provide good self-protection, and take his stand there.

Nevada was sure no hard-pressed man would make a stand in an area similar to the one through which he was now passing. Not if he had any sense. There was too much brush, and vision was limited. Cud would seek open country that would enable him to see an approaching rider for a considerable distance, while he crouched in a well-concealed vantage point.

The trail ran on. Now and then, in mud turned soft by recent showers, Lacy saw the hoof prints of the outlaw's horse. He did not stop to examine them closely, for only the knowledge that Richardson was ahead of him was important while they both remained on the road. Near noon the trees and brush began to think out and the country became broken and rough.

Nevada began to rein in his horse occasionally and sit motionless in the saddle, searching the far distance for signs of movement. He could see nothing but that was understandable. Cud had a full hour's start on him, barring the possibility that he had stopped on the way.

The road slashed across a wide, grass-covered swale, and for a long mile Nevada knew he was visible from all directions to anyone who might be watching.

It was just such a point in the trail which Nevada had been hoping to encounter. In all probability, Richardson had by now seen him and the hunt would take a different turn.

The buckskin, loping tirelessly, crossed the swale; and entered a small grove of stalwart pines that followed a ridge extending down from the higher hills to the west. It would be a good place for an ambush, Nevada thought, probing the dark shadows beneath the trees with a sharp eye. But he reached the grove without incident, and there pulled to a halt.

That Richardson had some specific location along the trail in mind seemed a certainty now. Otherwise, Nevada told himself, the outlaw would have made use of this particular section of the road. And there had been two or three other spots that would have served him almost equally well.

The lean rider glanced at the sun. In three or four hours it would be setting and there was a distinct possibility that Richardson could be stalling, waiting until he had the added advantage of darkness. A hunted man strives to build the odds in his favor.

But permitting the outlaw to grasp the whip handle was far from Nevada's mind. Up to the present moment, he'd been forced to play the game Richardson's way, to let him know that he was being pursued. Now everything would change.

The grove was a good place to make the break. Cutting the buckskin sharp left, he held the horse to a due west course, keeping deep within the trees where his passage would go unseen. Richardson, having seen him enter the dense grove, would be watching the point where the road emerged. When no one appeared, he could hardly fail to conclude the man following him had paused to rest.

For a full hour Nevada pushed on and came finally to the foothills which rose gradually to melt into the high bluffs and ridges of the mountain range proper.

He found a trail after paralleling the base of the ragged formation for a mile and a half and began at once to ascend the steep slope. A few minutes later he broke out onto a small, flinty, roundtop, and continued on.

The road was below him and he knew that he could look down from it by moving to the edge if and when he desired. But that was not an immediate part of his plan. Later when darkness closed in over the land, he would take that look.

Sometime before sunset he reached the crest of a high bluff and halted. Leaving his horse to graze he prowled the edge of the rim—taking care to avoid becoming visible from the valley below—and succeeded in locating a point where he could descend. That fixed in his mind, he doubled back to the buckskin to await total darkness.

He became conscious of hunger and, digging into his saddlebags, pulled out the sandwiches which Hettie had prepared. They were dry and had lost their flavor. But he ate them gratefully and took a long drink of water from his canteen.

The last trace of sunset glow had gone when he finished. Restoring the remainder of the food to the leather pouches, he moved to the rim of the bluff, sprawled out flat, and began a slow, methodical search of the country below.

Darkness all but obscured the road. But a pale glimmer of moonlight made it possible to see it in a few separated places. He could detect no signs of life. There was only the long stillness broken by the occasional bark of a coyote, high up on the slopes behind him.

He did not change position, simply waited, patient, almost sure the moment could come when his search would be rewarded. And eventually it was, two dragging hours later. A tiny red eye sprang to life a short distance from the road—a small camp fire, well hidden, to his right.

A grim smile pulled at Nevada's lips. He'd overshot Richardson and the ambush, and was now behind the outlaw. It was a stroke of luck he hadn't counted on. Establishing the location of the outlaw's camp by noting adjacent landmarks in his mind, he returned to the gelding, took up the reins and led the horse down the steep trial he had discovered.

As soon as he reached the floor of the valley again, he cut sraight across, walking the buckskin to avoid the warning sound which clattering hoofbeats would have made, and in less than three minutes emerged on the road. Halting, he took stock of the landmarks. Richardson would be a mile, perhaps two, below him. He swung right and, holding the gelding on the hardpack of the road, then quietly and with finality, closed in.

Cud Richardson had chosen the location well—a low, rock-strewn hogback through which the trail cut a narrow pass. The outlaw had dropped back a short distance from the gash and built his fire in a deep pocket that would prevent the flames from being seen from the valley to the south.

Standing behind a climp of juniper, Nevada watched Richardson moving about, mistakenly confident that his intended victim was still somewhere below him. His movements were unhampered and Lacy guessed he had not wounded him, even slightly, back at the cabin.

Suddenly a faint stir of movement on the opposite side of the pass caught Nevada's attention. By staring hard he was able to make out the outlaw's horse, tied to a tree and standing unsaddled in the moonlight. And there was something else— a hat perched on a stake near the front of the ridge where it could be seen from the road. Nevada grinned. Richardson had evidently

101

gone to great lengths to fool him. The plan was easy to fathom. The instant his attention was drawn to the decoy that the outlaw, crouching in the rocks fifty feet away, would blast him down in cold blood.

Cud Richardson would have no qualms about shooting him in the back. Yet, to Harlan Drake's way of thinking, for a lawman to meet such a man as Cud with matching coldbloodedness couldn't be more wrong. The law and only the law should deal out the punishment for those vicious men who have no regard for the law.

Maybe Drake was right. Maybe there was no other way to establish law and order, to advance civilization. But Nevada refused to let himself dwell on that as he continued to watch the outlaw. Richardson was boiling up a can of coffee but apparently had no other provisions with him. Every few moments he would move to the ridge, stare off down the road for a time, and then return to his fire. Plainly, he expected his pursuer to appear at any moment.

Removing his spurs, Lacy cut silently to his left and made his way through the brush and rocks until he was slightly above and to the east of Richardson's fire. There, gun in hand, he crept in to a point where he was at the edge of the pale flare cast by the flames.

Richardson was crouched by the fire, absently stirring the coffee with a twig. Nevada knew he had only to rise and speak the outlaw's name to bring Cud whirling about, weapon in hand, for the showdown. He studied the hunched figure of the man for a brief time, and then came to a decision.

*All right, Dude, I'm trying it your way.*

The words formed soundlessly on Nevada Lacy's lips as he rose suddenly and lunged at the outlaw.

# XVI

Three days Later Nevada pulled into Prescott, a black stubble covering his cheeks and chin, sweat clinging to his clothing, Cud Richardson's horse trailing behind him at the end of a short rope.

The outlaw himself was slumped on the saddle, morose and somber with his hands tied behind his back and his legs linked together with rope stretched taut under his horse's belly.

Both riders bore witness to the changes which could be brought about in a man's physical appearance by no more than a minute of harsh violence on the trail. A long red gash lay across Nevada's forehead. Cud Richardson's eyes were swollen, his mouth crushed, nose slightly askew. He was a thoroughly beaten and cowed man.

He had wheeled that night by the fire, just as Lacy lunged. The two had come together in a bone-crackling collision. Nevada's rock-hard fists smashed into Cud's jaw as they sprawled, and the outlaw had countered, using his sixgun as a club.

Nevada had jerked away. The barrel of the weapon had grazed and left its mark, but had done no more. A flurry of punishing blows to Cud Richardson's head— and the man had given up, raising both hands as a gesture of total surrender.

Oblivious to the curious standing/passersby, Nevada made his way into the business center of the settlement halting finally before a small, narrow building which bore the neatly lettered sign *THE PINKERTON AGENCY* on the window.

Pulling in to the hitchrack, Nevada looped the buckskin's reins over the rail, and turned to anchor Richardson's mount more securely alongside. A man appeared in the office doorway, and stared wonderingly at the operation. From farther down the street a tall individual wearing a star was approaching at a fast walk.

Satisfied that the outlaw's horse could not jerk free, Nevada faced the man in the doorway. "You Jensen?" he asked.

The graying man, his pin-point blue eyes veiled with reserve, nodded. "That's me."

Lacy gestured toward the outlaw. "Here's a little present for you," he said. "Name's Cud Richardson."

"Richardson!" Jensen echoed.

"I brought him in for a friend of mine—Harlan Drake."

"Ah-h-h," Jensen said in a sighing voice. "I see."

"What's going on here, Bern?"

It was the tall lawman who had approached with just about the fastest and longest strides Nevada had ever seen. The Pinkerton agent pointed to the outlaw. "He's Cud Richardson, Tom. Wanted for murder, robbing the U.S. mail and a few other things. Tuck him away good. I'll bring the papers over in a few minutes."

The deputy freed Richardson's horse, moved back up the street. Bern Jensen studied Nevada for a few moments, then stepped back into his office.

"Like to know what happened, Mr.—"

"Name's Lacy. Jim Lacy."

Surprise again sharpened the Pinkerton man's eyes. But he recovered quickly, smiled, and waited for Nevada to enter.

"Is Drake dead?" he asked, as if sensing the truth in

104

Nevada's grim manner and slight reluctance to meet his gaze.

Nevada nodded, noting at that point the empty sleeve on Jensen's right side.

"Sit down," Jensen said, pointing to a chair. "Naturally—I'd like all of the details."

Nevada sat down on the padded cushion gratefully, and reaching inside his shirt, removed the packet of folded papers he'd taken from Drake and handed them to the lawman's superior.

"He asked me to give you this."

Jensen examined the creased sheets idly. "Was Cud Richardson the man who got him?"

"That's right. Place called Coopersville—or near it."

"I'm eternally grateful to you for finishing the job for him."

"It was what I started out to do—get Richardson, only it was for myself. We sort of joined forces." Nevada looked off into the street. "Dude would have been alive right nw if he'd listened to reason."

"Dude?" questioned Jensen.

"That's what Richardson and his bunch called Drake. He'd worked himself in as a member of Cud's outfit. He had it strong in his head to take Richardson alive—let the law punish him, it was the only way, he said—the only *right* way."

"You don't agree with that?"

"Not a hundred per cent. I figure it's all right to give a man the chance to quit. But you've got to know who you're talking to, and be ready to make your own move if it's a doublecross."

Bern Jensen nodded. "Exactly the way I feel about it. A man has to use good judgment—keep remembering

105

you can't trust a killer very far."

Nevada frowned. "I thought I understood from Drake it was your company that wanted it that way."

"We do—if it's possible. We feel it's better for the courts to do the punishing. But with Harlan Drake it meant more than that. In fact, it was almost an obsession with him. He insisted every outlaw should be given a chance to surrender. I warned him several times he was sticking too close to the letter of the idea, that he was stretching things too far, and that it might get him killed someday."

"It did," Nevada said slowly. "But it works, if you handle it right. Richardson was all set to fill me full of holes when I went after him—and I had plenty of reason to cut him down when I caught up with him. But I tried it Dude's way. Only—I went about it real careful, knowing that Cud Richardson was the type who would kill me in a minute."

Jensen was plucking at his chin, his face wreathed in a deep frown. "You mean Drake was killed by Richardson, and then you went out after him, and brought him in?"

"It was what had to be done, and I sort of felt—well, that I owed it to Dude to finish the job."

Bern Jensen crossed to where Nevada was sitting. "I'd like to shake your hand, Jim Lacy. You did a fine thing, and made a right thorough job of it."

"Fine? I don't know about that," Nevada said slowly. "But the thing was, it had to be done, and I was the man who had to do it."

Both men were silent for a moment, thinking of the dead—the outlaws, and the lawman who had gambled his life in his masquerade as an outlaw. But there was a

106

lightness in Jim Lacy's heart, too. For the first time in what seemed a year, though it had been, in reality, only a few days, the people and country he loved best were free from the threat of criminal savagery. And he was free, too; free to return to Hettie and to take up their new life, a life interrupted before it had really started.

And it was about time he was on his way to Hettie! Nevada Jim Lacy swung into the saddle, gave a bid farewell wave to Bern Jensen, and rode out of Prescott . . . bound for home.

# THE
# TRACK OF BLOOD

# I

A fluffy cloud puff obscuring the full moon scudded past, urged on by a cool breeze off the northern Colorado mountains to the west.

In the silver light, the riders could be seen clearly. There were about fifty of them, superb horsemen controlling their barebacked ponies with strong knees and rope hackamores.

Naked torsos gleamed with bear grease; eagle feathers stuck from braided hair. The streaked war paint gave the faces of Sioux warriors a terrifying expression. The savages wore deerskin leggings, tassels hanging from their moccasin heels. Most carried bows and quivers of arrows, the usual long knife for scalping and close fighting, a coup stick with which a brave could count coup on an enemy in combat.

They bunched around their chief on a low rise overlooking a small settlement which lay across a little river winding down from the heights. No lights showed; the inhabitants were asleep.

Whites were crowding into this lovely country; ranchers, hoemen, tradesmen, miners. The Union Pacific had joined the great continent, and Cheyenne, in Wyoming Territory, a station on the railroad, lay a few hours ride to the north.

Many Teton Dakotas were large men, but the leader of this band was a tall, striking figure. His massive breast carried the scars of the sun dance, powerful muscles rippling in his mighty arms. He had a proud eagle beak—the broad face of the Sioux, streaked with war paint.

The Indians spoke in their guttural tongue.

"Here we wait," ordered the big chief. "If any warrior goes ahead of me in battle, or makes a loud sound before I give the word, I will cut out his liver and eat it."

No brave challenged this, they knew Flint Heart would do as he threatened, for they had seen him carry this out on an overeager youth who had rushed into the fight prematurely during a raid on a Crow village the previous autumn.

Two horsemen pushed slowly from a nearby spruce grove.

"Flint Heart!" called one softly.

"I am here," replied the chief. He turned his mount and went to face the pair. "*Hou, cola*," he greeted "Hello, friend."

His massed warriors waited as Flint Heart talked with the whites, who wore war bonnets and were disguised as savages, but were not Indians. They were "Gray Men," as the Sioux called renegades who masqueraded to hide their evil deeds.

"Talk English," said the white fellow who had hailed Flint Heart.

"Where are the guns?" demanded Flint Heart.

"You'll get 'em. Ammo, too. First listen. Take no prisoners. Leave no witnesses."

"Young women are good for the Sioux," argued Flint Heart.

112

"No. Spare none, kill girls, children, savvy? We got coal oil for you. Burn every house. Spare nothing."

"*Hou*. It is good. Give us the guns and the burning oil." Flint Heart's dark eyes had a bloodred glow in them.

The big-boned, lean white man's leather creaked as he pulled the rein of his black stallion, turning back toward the spruce grove. His companion followed, and Flint Heart, braves slowly trailing their chief, moved after the two Gray Men.

It was inky among the trees, and the lean fellow said, "Light that bull's-eye, Joe." He swung from his saddle, tied his rein to a low branch.

Flint Heart and Joe Cordell got down. The latter struck a match and in the rays of the little flame, Cordell's curly hair could be seen under the Indian headdress. He was younger, slimmer than his friend, who ordered:

"Keep the beam turned this way so it don't show in the town."

"Okay, Pate."

Joe Cordell raised the slide, adjusted the wick as he touched the match to it, and the yellowish light showed the bundles of repeating carbines, boxes of ammunition, a dozen small cans of oil. Also, there were plugs of tobacco, a roll of gingham cloth, a box of beads and other trinkets prized by the savages.

These items were the price the Gray Men were paying for the death massacre.

Pate's cheekbones were high as Flint Heart's; he was bronzed by sun and wind, and a crisp mustache grew under his long nose. One pale-blue eye fluttered a bit as he spoke to the Sioux chief.

"You sure you can handle your braves?" he

113

demanded.

"They are all warriors. They are young and eager for brave deeds to prove themselves. The Sioux hate all *wasichus*. They are ready to kill."

"Don't look at me like that," growled Pate. "Ain't I white? One move outa any of you and I'll show you who can kill, savvy?" Pate spoke icily.

"Friend. Yes, you are a friend of the Indian. We look on such as you as brothers."

"Keep it in mind. And young Joe Cordell here is the boss's son, and if you want more guns and trinkets, you'll do what we tell you."

Flint Heart nodded. He stared greedily at the fine carbines and ammunition, at the goods which would please any squaw.

Joe Cordell set the lantern on the smooth, brown-needled earth, assisting Pate as he began passing the weapons to Flint Heart. The chief armed his braves; the Indians quickly loaded, caressing their new guns. The Sioux never had enough rifles and ammunition. One older Indian grunted something as he accepted his weapon, and Pate asked, "What'd he say?"

"He wants burning water," replied the chief.

"Nothing doing. Not till you finish this job. I don't wany any drunk Injuns ravin' around."

Flint Heart nodded. "We leave the other goods here till we are done." He turned, giving orders to his followers, who started to their mustangs, carbines in hand.

Below, the hamlet slept in the night, unaware of the horrible fate in store. There were about a dozen buildings, one a store with a livery stable at the side, the rest cabins, all constructed from timber cut in the nearby mountains.

The two Gray Men, putting out the lantern, led their mounts to the edge of the spruce grove and stood, reins in hand, watching Flint Heart and his Sioux warriors move down the slope and stealthily fan out through the village.

Joe Cordell said, "I reckon they'll do it, George." There was a little quaver in his young voice which Pate didn't miss.

"You got to harden yourself more, boy. You travel with me a while and you'll learn. Your pop and me can tell you plenty and teach you what's what. Dog eat dog, every man for himself. That's what we say. Why worry about a few stupid cusses?"

"Well, let's get on home."

"No. Hold on. You watch. It'll be good for you."

There was cold steel in George Pate's cruel tones. "I've seen plenty men die in front of my own guns and so's your pop. While we were in Leavenworth together we watched others get it from cold steel. You got to learn, I tell you. Wesleyville's a stumblin' block. Your old man and me got big plans and we don't aim to let a handful like those below stand in our way."

Flint Heart was most efficient. He'd led many raids on isolated cabins and tiny settlements as the Sioux savagely fought the white invaders of their hereditary hunting grounds.

Their *Pa Sapa*, the sacred Black Hills, had been taken from them despite the solemn treaties and promises made by the pale faces. The buffalo was being slaughtered, the iron roads—the white man's rail-roads—were being inexorably thrust into the great wilderness. The Union Pacific had joined the East and West, in 1869, and already there was another, called the Northern Pacific, stabbing into the heart of the

Dakotas. And small branch lines were being surveyed, crisscrossing and uniting the main ones.

A shiver, almost a shudder, passed through young Cordell. He was not yet as hardened to murder and horror.

The gunny gripped his arm.

"Hold on," Pate growled. "Watch!"

The peace of the Spring night was suddenly shattered by bloodcurdling war cries of the Sioux. Yellow flames quickly licked up around the bases of the log cabins, around the larger store.

A gun shot rang out, then a spattering volley. High-pitched screams of women joined hoarse shouts of men, awakened by the attack. From the rise on which they stood, the two Gray Men saw figures running from the buildings, already burning hungrily with the oil thrown on the pine and spruce walls.

As the whites rushed outside to escape the choking smoke and heat, Indians shot them down, shouting in triumph at each victim who crashed in the dirt street. Women, children, were riddled with carbine lead. A few males got off a few retaliatory volleys, but they were against the yellowish-red light of the fires, the attackers in the semi-darkness beyond. Three females carrying children in arms fell in the road. There was no mercy.

Flint Heart was carrying out Pate's orders.

The two on the rise could hear the increasing crackling of the licking flames consuming the structures of the settlement.

Now there were no more outcries from the victims; they were dead, men, women, children. . .

The bronzed figures of the Sioux could be seen as braves hurried from corpse to corpse, lifting scalps, raising them high as they whooped in victory.

116

Joe Cordell gasped, turning away from the horror below. Several Indians were driving off some horses they had run from stables and corrals; others were picking up weapons dropped by the whites, searching them for loot.

Pate remarked in a satisfied voice, "They done a good job."

Joe Cordell began to retch. Pate laughed, said, "Here, take a swig, brace up." He held out a flask.

Cordell downed a long pull, then said apologetically, "This—well, this ain't like downin' some hombre you're mad at."

"It had to be done," replied Pate, in a practical voice. "Forget it. C'mon, let's ride home. You can see that little blonde filly Penny tomorrow. Think how rich you'll be! Why, she'll fall over for you, boy." Pate laughed coarsely.

Young Cordell had drunk several ounces of burning liquor. He turned to pick up his handsome pinto's rein, swung into the saddle. "Dammit, George, my horse started limpin' a while back. This paint horse is the finest money can buy and I don't like ridin' anything else."

"Probably picked up a little pebble. You can have a new shoe put on when we get back"

George Pate led off, glancing back over a hunched shoulder as they rode away. The ghastly massacre seemed to fascinate and please him.

"Yeah," he said satisfiedly, "that Flint Heart's a good boy. I'll use him again, when I need a job done."

They skirted south of what had been Wesleyville, hitting a trck which led through rising, wooded hills from which jagged rocks thrust serrated formations.

And they heard the long, mournful howl of a lobo

117

wolf in the beautiful night.

## II

Al Slingerland rode easily along the trail winding near the crystal-clear mountain stream.

The early morning air was bracing with the aromatic odor of conifers, which dominated the slopes. In meadows alders grew and cottonwoods lined the creek; in season, there were wild grapes, raspberries, bear cherries, gooseberries, currants, buffalo berries, the pink flowers marking the rattlesnake root. Wild turnips were good eating, too, for Nature's bounty furnished the knowing man with many fine things.

Tall and raw-boned, Slingerland had no spare suet on him; his sinews were whipcords and his muscles were hard as steel. In one huge hand he held the rein controlling his handsome bay stallion; his piercing gray eyes missed not the slightest sign in range of his vision.

In the boot rode a long-range hunting rifle, a Sharps Creedmore which could bring down big game, while he also had a carbine, a Colt revolver, and the indispensable long knife, sharpened to razor edge.

He had breakfasted at dawn in his log cabin, set on a pleasant rise by the little river. This wild valley was his home. He had built the place himself and furnished it comfortably. An expert trapper, he could earn more than enough to satsify his needs. All along the eastern slopes of the Rockies game was still plentiful, though it was threatened by the encroaching whites who pushed into the land of the Tetons, the mighty Western Sioux.

Slingerland didn't fear the Indians. They were his friends; he spoke their tongue and was versed in the universal sign language. As a youth he had lived with the Oglala Sioux, hunted and caroused with them, as had other trappers and mountain men. The savages would not harm a comrade.

On a lead-rope behind the bay trudged a long-eared, sleek mule, the packs on his sturdy back holding traps and other gear.

Jays, squirrels, butterfies abounded in this lovely valley. But like the Indian, Slingerland killed nothing save what was required for food, and for pelts which he sold to earn his living. He wore soft buckskin, with a coonskin hat on his thick hair. A beard protected his bronzed cheeks from sun and icy winds. Contented with his lonely life, he could take care of himself.

But he wasn't a hermit who disliked other humans. His nature was open, expansive, and he was always glad to help anyone in distress. He often thought of Warren Neale, the young engineer he'd assisted when Neale was helping lay out the U.P. Trail, the Union Pacific Railroad which had joined East and West. When he'd met Neale, Slingerland had been living in a wild Wyoming Territory valley, but other settlers had spoiled the hunting there, so he'd moved south into the northeast quadrant of Colorado.

Neale had opened a consulting engineering firm in Cheyenne. The nation was now railroad-minded. The Northern Pacific would pierce the very heart of the Sioux's traditional hunting grounds. So naturally the Indians were infuriated and were ready to fight to the death.

Connecting and branch lines were being laid or planned all through the land, so Neale had plenty of work. He and his pretty wife, Allie Lee, sole survivor of an Indian attack on an east-bound wagon train, lived with their two small children in a spacious home south of Cheyenne, which, like so many new settlements, was growing by leaps and bounds.

But Al Slingerland felt as the Indians did. The rapid expansion of civilization saddened him. How much longer would a trapper be able to operate? The forests were being systematically destroyed. The hordes of bears, elk, deer, martens and minks, skunks and foxes, beaver, and, most vital to the savages, the bison, which furnished them with food, shelter, and clothing, were being killed off with the same ruthless abandon by white hunters.

The bay stallion snorted, ripped his sleek hide, and Slingerland alerted instantly. The horse had told him something, and his keen gray eyes swept every inch around. He glimpsed a small paint horse, with a rope hackamore, as the mustang showed for a moment as it retreated up the slope, covered with balsams. He knew it was an Indian pony.

Where was the Indian? He made sure his carbine was loose in its socket by his hip. Then he decided to dismount, and swung a long leg off, fastening the bay's rein to a handy limb and pulling the light rifle out.

It was something he must check. While the Indians were his friends, there were bad ones, sometimes outcasts, or it might be a member of some tribe which didn't know who the tall trapper was.

Carbine in one hand, he flitted along the trail. He paused several times to listen intently. Birds trilled to the new dawn, the creek murmured over a rocky stretch not far away.

He came on fresh, unshod hoof tracks, no doubt left by the paint pony. To his left, toward the river, was a dense thicket, and several stalks of grass at one side were slowly coming back into position after having been crushed down. Nor did he miss a small twig, broken off low on one of the bushes. Somebody had just crept off the path at this point.

Slingerland threw a cartridge into his carbine. If a brave was crouched in there, waiting for him, the savage might kill without warning.

"*Hou, cola,*" he said softly, tentatively.

There was no reply. As he squatted, listening, watching, a sudden raucous scolding began, jays in a dither at being disturbed, closer to the creek. Jays were constantly scolding, but the pitch told Slingerland's trained ear the birds were alarmed about an intruder.

This was all he needed. He moved that way.

He found her huddled beside a huge gray boulder on the bank.

Light glinted from the butcher knife in her left hand. She wore soft, bleached doeskin on her slender body. Dark braids hung over her swelling bosoms, telling him she was a maiden. He could guess that, anyone; she must have just gone through the Sioux ceremony making her a woman, ready for marriage. Her full cheeks were smooth save for a dark bruise on one. Large, long-lashed eyes, fearful, wide open, watched him.

Slingerland almost gasped at her loveliness.

"*Wasichu!*" The Indian girl was terrified, and she raised her knife to defend herself.

She kept her right arm bent up, pressed to her side.

He leaned forward to put down his carbine. She misinterpreted this, thinking he was reaching for her, and with a faint cry, slashed at him with her knife. He caught her wrist so the point only ripped his shirt. He disarmed her easiy and stepped back, speaking in Sioux.

"I'm your friend, the Indians' friend, Slingerland,

the trapper. I have lived with your people. I won't harm you. Let me help you."

Her breast was heaving. She dropped her eyes and he saw tears, unusual in an Indian.

Finally she began to talk, her voice low and musical. She was an Oglala, as he'd believed.

The English equivalent of her name was Mountain Flower. She'd run away. Though she was a good rider, she had fainted. And her pony had thrown her off. Next, she found she was lying on the ground. When she heard someone coming, she'd crawled off to hide.

"I won't hurt you, Flower," he said again, gently. "What's wrong with your right arm? Is it broken?"

Flower shook her head; she kept the arm crooked up.

When he touched it, she tried not to wince. He couldn't be sure about her injury without a closer examination. "My cabin's not far off. There I'll fix your hurt."

He held out his hand but when she tried to get up, she fell back. She was in a state of shock.

The fact he spoke her tongue, the look in the big trapper's eyes, his kind manner, had reassured her. When he stopped to pick her up, she put her left arm around his neck, relaxing against him.

He felt a sudden, deep emotion, the thrill of a strong man for a young, lovely female, soft and womanly, most desirable.

Slingerland spoke soothingly as he carried her back to his horse. He set her up befor ehim, swung aboard, and turned the bay. The mule trailed along as they moved toward his camp.

The cabin had two rooms, with a porch where the trapper might sit, enjoying the view across the beaver pond below. High racks, out of reach of wolves, coyotes and other predators, were strung with drying pelts and meats. There was an open shed where his two horses and the mule could shelter, though usually they preferred to stay outside. His second mount, a chestnut gelding, whinnied and started toward him.

Mountain Flower now seemed to trust him fully. Again she put her arm around his neck as he carried her into his home, and once more, the man felt her soft body against his. He found she was looking up at him, studying his face, but when he smiled at her, she dropped her pretty eyes.

The main room was comfortably furnished; he'd fashioned benches, tables and other conveniences; animal skins served as rugs. Through an open door could be seen the second chamber, filled with trappings and other gear, a gun rack, a stove and cooking utensils, a frame where hung spare clothing, boots beneath it.

He set Flower down on his bed. Rawhide strips stretched between the pine-limb sides held a mattress stuffed with fragrant mountain hay, and soft furs were laid on top, making a most comfortable couch.

"I'll fetch you a drink, Flower. Then I'll heat up some coffee and broth. You look piqued."

He was aware of her large, dark eyes following him as he went about his tasks.

She drank gratefully of cool water he brought her. Then he lit tinder and kindling in the stove and set the coffee pot and a pan of bear-meat soup, with pieces of liver in it, to warm over the fire.

Returning to Mountain Flower, he pulled up a low stool, and sat before her. "Now we must see about your arm. I'll be careful."

If he removed her deerskin blouse, her full bosoms would be exposed; and she was a modest girl, he could tell that. The sleeves were side, in Sioux fashion, so he fetched a pair of scissors and carefully cut off the right one at the shoulder. Now he could see her pretty arm; it was discolored.

But it looked in line, and he began to check the bones with long, gentle fingers, seeking a possible break. This hurt but she didn't wince or whimper. An Indian woman could withstand pain.

"I don't believe any bones are cracked, Flower. It's a strain, a terrible wrench."

Again, as he looked into her sweet face, she dropped her long lashes. She'd been studying him again.

Slingerland rose and went into the kitchen. The coffee and soup were bubbling hot. He poured two mugs of coffee, and ladled out the broth into a bowl. He put a horn spoon in the bowl, and carried it to her, with a mug of steaming coffee, set it on the stool so she could easily reach it.

When he returned with his own drink, she was sipping the soup. He sat on a chair, enjoying his coffee, while the girl ate. He was glad to see her finish her meal, and then her coffee. And she kept covertly glancing at the big trapper.

"When you're well, Flower," he said, "I'll take you back to your village."

But at this, she looked alarmed, and shook her head.

This puzzled him. He'd believed the girl had been hurt in a fall. But he began to wonder about it. His curiosity aroused, he asked, "Why don't you want to go back to your tribe?"

He had to repeat the question but finally she told him. A chief, one of her people, had struck her in the face and brutally twisted her arm.

This surprised Slingerland, for a Sioux seldom struck

a squaw, no matter what the provocation. Their women were honored as keepers of the tepees, owners of the lodge and all within it save for the man's weapons of war. The children belonged to the mother, and if a wife so wished, she might turn her husband out, refuse to serve him any longer.

Patiently he led her on, learning her unhappy story. The suitor who desired her had slain two rivals and seized their ponies and other valuables, using them to buy her, according to Sioux custom, since a daughter's duty was to bring wealth to her father, and Mountain Flower was his only child.

Her mother had died when she was born, her father was elderly and ill with the white man's coughing sickness, and when Flint Heart had paid him for Flower, her father had gone to the hospital on the reservation to see the medicine man there.

Flint Heart had already had two wives. One he had killed, for he had an evil temper. Flower feared him; he was cruel as well very powerful, the leader of many young, reckless braves belonging to his warrior society, his *akacita*.

So Flower had run away into the forest as soon as her father left. But the chief who had bought her found her, struck her and beat her. He'd thrown her into his lodge with his other wife, an older squaw, to guard her. Before he lay with her, though, Flint Heart said he must go on a raid with his men, but would return. And when he had ridden off, Flower had mustered enough strength to slip out under the back of the tepee, while the squaw slept. She'd snatched a tethered pony and fled.

"Flint Heart, yes, I know him. He has a cruel name. I promise he will never hurt you again, Flower."

As they spoke on, he found she was a niece of Black Buffalo Woman, who carried power in her hands as she was related to Red Cloud. Al Slingerland knew Black Buffalo Woman had been sold to a Sioux named No Water, though she was the true love of Crazy Horse, paladin of the Tetons and the greatest warrier in tribal lore. His Indian name was Tasunke Witko.

The Sun was yellow as the trapper went out, unsaddled the stud, relieved the mule of the packs and turned both loose. He gave up his work that day so he could stay near Flower. If Flint Heart came along, Slingerland meant to protect her. Her pony had turned off and he'd brought her here on his bay, so there was no track of her mustang to his camp. Still, he would take no chances.

He looked through the doorway. Flower lay on his bed, her injured arm across her body, long lashes on her cheeks. She'd ridden all night and was exhausted. Now she slept, breathing easily.

He spent the morning around his home, checking pelts and traps, but kept his rifle handy.

When the sun was overhead he went inside and fixed another meal of meat, biscuits with wild honey, and coffee. As he carried this in, Flower opened her eyes and sat up. This time she looked fully at the man, a smile touching her soft face. He gave her a plate and mug, serving her.

Slingerland was astonished at how he felt.

He'd always lived alone. But now someone was by him, someone he felt strong attraction for, and suddenly he realized how lonely he'd been. A rare contentment swept over him as he watched the pretty girl.

And he knew that the Sioux were right when they said

it was bad for a man to be alone, without a mate.

The day passed swiftly. Sometimes, as he worked, he would glance over and see Flower standing in the doorway, watching him, and he'd smile and wave, and she would wave back. And again, during the evening meal, he experienced that wonderful contentment, the joy of looking at Flower.

That night he stretched on a pad at the barred door, his guns by him, ready for possible trouble. Flower lay quietly on his bed. He didn't fall asleep at once, for he was excited, and thoughts raced through his head. If Flower would marry him—

Up at dawn, Slingerland found the girl awake, and she rose, going toward the kitchen. Her hurt arm was at her side, so she could straighten it.

"Let me see," he said. He examined it, and now was sure it wasn't broken. "It'll get well in a few days," he told her. "Be careful of it."

She insisted on helping fix breakfast, using her left hand. They sat down together, and now she would smile whenever he looked at her.

After they'd eaten, he decided to get fresh water form the brook and picked up two pails, unbarred the door and went out into the crisp, cool morning air.

As he looked all around, as was his habit, he saw a pall of black smoke hanging in the sky to the northeast.

He knew every foot of the surrounding land and could place the smoke. It was over Wesleyville, a small settlement where he sometimes went for supplies, to sell his pelts, and for a bit of human company.

The smoke wasn't billowing up as if just generated. Wesleyville lay south of the usual Tetan range, but, desperate from the crowding of the whites, the bison and other game rapidly being wiped out, the Indians

127

had to cover more ground to find food.

The savages seldom fought after sundown. Evil spirits were abroad in the darkness, but there were practical reasons, too.

Falling dew softened bowstrings so arrows wouldn't fly true and a wet moccasin was easily penetrated by a thorn or sharp stone.

He had friends in Wesleyville and he felt worried. He didn't want to leave Flower, but there might be people who needed help. He fetched the fresh water and joined Flower.

"There is trouble in Wesleyville. I must go there. Wait. I'll come back. You have food and I'll leave you a gun. You can catch the chestnut horse or the mule but it will be best if you keep out of sight so Flint Heart can't find you. Hide if anyone approaches. You must be here when I return. Do you promise?"

She nodded, and he said, "I'll teach you to speak English, Flower. Say, 'Yes, Al.' That's my white man's name, Al."

Earnestly, she formed the words, her small, even teeth showing as she spoke: "Ye-ess, Al-al!"

"Good!" He patted her and rose, taking his guns; there was another carbine and belt of ammunition he left with Flower.

He waved to her at the doorway and she waved back.

Saddling the powerful bay stallion, Slingerland set off on the trail over the ridge which would lead him into the north-south valley in which Wesleyville stood.

A song was in his heart as he thought of the Indian girl. It was good to think of her in his home, that she'd be waiting for him when he returned.

# III

Slingerland pushed the bay stallion across the shallows at the creek ford; the water flecked off the horse's legs as he reached the east bank.

The valley was unusual for the area. It ran for many miles generally in a north-south direction and was comparatively level, from Cheyenne on down the line. East and west, sharp-crested mountain ridges, steep slopes clothed in conifers, hemmed it in.

As the bay came up to the wagon road, Slingerland could take in what had been Wesleyvile, and he stifled a gasp of horror, though he had looked upon massacre scenes before. There was not one building left standing; all were smoldering ruins, just a few walls still upright. Even the stables and sheds had been fired. In the main street lay several longish objects and Slingerland knew exactly what they were: the scalped corpses of men, women, even some children.

A hound bayed mournfully somewhere past the blackened wrecks of homes, and as the trapper rode slowly along, a huge mastiff, standing by the twisted figure of what had been his master, bared his teeth, snarling as the stranger approached. But the dog didn't attack; he was simply guarding the remains of the man he had loved, and Slingerland passed without disturbing him. Raucous cries of vultures sounded; stray chickens scratched in the dirt, cows and a few mules grazed in nearby fields. Stray cats slunk uneasily through the ruins.

He glanced at another man's body; the face had collapsed when he'd been scalped. The shirt was bloody, and the victim had pulled on a pair of Levi's when he'd run outside at the night alarm. His trained eye noted the crisscrossing marks of unshod hoofs in softer spots, and he knew many Indians had been there.

There were few better trackers in the West than Al Slingerland. He had lived with the Sioux and could read sign with the savage's expert eye, as well as with that of a hunter and white trailer.

He swung off northwest as the welter of tracks came together near the river bank; now there were shod hoofs, too; the raiders had run off the horses found in the settlement. He splashed across the creek to the west side, easily picked up the trail. Without even dismounting, he decided the Indians had attacked around midnight and after wiping out the settlement, made off northwest with the stolen horses and whatever loot they might have picked up.

With Mountain Flower, the Sioux girl, in mind, he recalled what she'd told him: Flint Heart had hurried off with his warrior band, which had given her a chance to escape. He couldn't swear to it, but chances were the giant Sioux chief had led the raid.

He pulled up and started back, slowly; there was much to be done in Wesleyville's ruins. On the other side of the wide, cut-up trail, his alert, keen eye noticed something else. This was a second set of tracks, pointing toward the town, and he followed it; probably this was the way the savages had approached.

But soon he discovered they'd turned off, toward a spruce grove. He stopped the big stallion. Maybe the band had lurked in there until the time came to strike. Then his roving glance was diverted by the sheen of sunlight on a bit of metal, and he started toward the grove. The Indians had paused here. Now he grew very alert

130

because he saw two sets of shod hoofs, coming to join the large group. They'd stopped, evidently for a parley, then the shod hoofs and some of the others had entered the grove.

Slingerland dismounted, dropped rein, and began to range about like a hunting dog seeking a scent.

The sun had glinted from a carbine cartridge, carelessly dropped there. Farther in, under the spruces, he came upon the spot where they'd got off their horses. He found a burnt match end in the needles, some indentations where he thought heavy objects had been set down. Slingerland squatted down, minutely examining every foot of the brown-needled ground.

There were a number of moccasin prints, but what most interested him were the high-heel dents; two men in riding boots had met the Indians. Several round marks gave him pause; he finally lay down and sniffed at them. Even with the aromatic scent of the needles he detected the faint odor of coal oil; there had been gallon cans of this set down.

"Huh!" He grunted aloud, pushed back his cap.

He never jumped to conclusions. He picked up his rein and began slowly moving toward the river. The shod hoofs led back that way, but didn't go into the settlement. No, the two on these horses must have sat their saddles for a time, perhaps watching, while the Sioux had crossed and struck in the night.

The needles in the grove and thick grass hadn't clearly retained marks. It wasn't until he reached the softer earth of the river bank that he found what he was hunting. The left forehoof of one horse had a shoe on it which had a slight crack on one side.

He was facing the smoking remains of Wesleyville now, and as he was about to remount and try to pick up the sign of the two who'd been riding animals with shod hoofs, he sighed a saddle brown horse and a second one, a dun, with a lead-rope attached to the brown's horn. They'd been cut off from his range of vision when he'd started through the town because of a blackened house wall.

So he crossed the stream and headed that way. Closer, he noted the long, metal-footed legs of a tripod he recognized as a surveyor's transit in the bulky packs on the dun.

Warren Neale had had such equipment. When he came to the waiting animals, he saw the man huddled on a flat rock near the smoking ruins of the cabin. A woman, scalped, lay dead nearby and not far off were the bodies of two males.

"Hello," sang out Slingerland, but the man on the rock did not even look up.

The trapper dismounted and went to him. The warm breeze caught his flared nostrils, on it the sickening stench of burned flesh, wood, other smoldering things.

"Howdy," he said again.

The man had his face in his hands; he was either sobbing or retching, slim body drawn up in a knot. He wore whipcord pants and high-laced boots, a gray flannel shirt; his hair was auburn under the Army Stetson.

"Mister, who are you?" began Slingerland, reaching down, touching the young fellow's hunched shoulder.

At this, the other looked up, brown eyes dazed; his smooth cheeks and even features were convulsed with grief. "Lee! By golly. It's Lee Davis," cried Slingerland.

Lee Davis shook his head. After a time he said weakly, "My parents—and my only brother—"

132

Slingerland understood. This had been Lee's home. The dead, scarcely recognizable as they had been scalped and partially burned, were the youth's father, mother and elder brother Hal. The trapper was aware Lee had been away at school for two years, that Warren Neale, the engineer who'd helped build the Union Pacific, a close friend of Slingerland's, had taken a fancy to the bright Lee and given the lad money so he could study surveying and other engineering subjects.

Slingerland knelt, put an arm across Davis's shoulders.

"Take it easy, boy. I know it's awful. The Sioux struck last night. Your folks are gone, and you'll have to accept it. Pull yourself together. You'll have to be a man, pick yourself up and keep goin'."

He had a small flask of brandy in a pocket, and passed it to Lee. "Take a swig. It'll brace you. No sense sittin' like this.'

Lee's hand shook violently as he downed a gulp. Slingerland helped him rise and led him to the road. If he could start Davis talking, it might snap him out of his daze. "When'd you get back, Lee? Have you seen Warren Neale? That your rig?"

Davis gulped, but replied. "I reported to Mr. Neale—he gave me a job—survey, branch line—came to see my folks, and—"

"I savvy," nodded Slingerland, as Lee Davis broke off. "It's mighty hard but you're a good fellow. Now, there's lots to be done here. We better ride to Cordell City. We'll need help."

Davis glanced at the flapping buzzards.

"All right," agreed the trapper. We'll plant your people first."

They found two shovels in a partially burned shed out

133

back and set about the unhappy task.

By the time the sun was overhead, the two men, the pack horse coming behind, had crossed the rough trail over the mountain between the long north-south valley where Wesleyville had stood and the next town, Cordell City. From the heights they could see a magnificent sweep, a winding river, high peaks thrusting to an azure sky.

And below stood Cordell City, much larger than Wesleyville. The river was wide and clear, furnishing unlimited water. Cottonwoods and alders lined the banks, though this growth was kept cut near town. The panorama was pleasing, Main Street with stores and saloons, hotels and restaurants, a spacious plaza with a statue marking a watering fountain and a loop of railroad track hanging from a frame, a sledgehammer by it, so fire alarms could be sounded. Smaller streets right-angled from Main, which bounded the square, the river just beyond. Private homes, smaller establishments, stables, barns and corrals showed. Curls of smoke issued from stone chimneys, as women prepared the noonday meal.

"Doc Cordell did a fine job layin' out this town," said Slingerland. "Most as good as Brigham Young did for Salt Lake City. Now, there's a farsighted hombre if ever there was one!"

Davis was still stricken but was recovering his poise.

"Jake Cordell is *it* here," he agreed. "This is his burg. He owns the Colorado Queen, biggest palace this side of Cheyenne, the best hotel."

"Not to mention the gun shop, handiest livery and top store! What Doc says goes. For an ex-con, he's come up in the world."

"They say he did ten years for armed robbery when

he was younger.''

"He did, but he's reformed, and it paid off. He hit it lucky here, settlers flockin' in for land and minin'. But between you'n me, I ain't too fond of Doc. He's too smooth, maybe oily. And I sure don't cotton to that strongarm gunny, George Pate. Cordell met Pate in prison. You must know Doc's son, Joe. He's about your age.''

"Yeah, I know Joe. He's got a mean temper. We tangled a couple of times when we were kids.''

They made rapid time downhill and headed for the closer of the two wide, railed bridges spanning the swift river.

The shale-covered track they'd been following held few impressions, and Slingerland was in a hurry. But as they reached the stream level, they came to softer under-footing, and Slingerland slowed, his gray eyes flicking this way and that.

"Hold on a jiffy, Lee,'' he said; and swung off the bay, squatted and studied the ground.

"What's up?'' inquired Davis.

"Nothin'.''

The trapper remounted and they pushed on, the thick planks of the bridge rumbling under the horses' weight.

Slingerland wasn't the sort who went off half-cocked. He kept his hunches to himself till he was sure of what he said.

But he'd found the imprint of a left forehoof with a slight crack on its side.

## IV

The buildings were chiefly of wood. There was plenty of timber in the surrounding mountains, and Doc

Cordell's sawmill, powered by a race from the river, did a thriving business.

Slingerland made no attempt to pick up the cracked-shoe print, for there were hundreds of crisscrossing tracks in town as well as wheel marks of buggies and wagons. He knew the trail left by the two riders was many hours old, made during the night. It was impossible to examine the hoofs of every animal, some in corrals or stables, and besides, the unknown men who had rendezvoused with the Indians might have passed on through the settlement.

Most of the structures had been painted neatly. Homes had vegetable and flower gardens, with chicken coops and sheds or stables for horses, cows and goats. Barns held hay cut from the hills, while the feed store stocked oats, barley, wheat and seeds. Both men knew this also belonged to Jake Cordell.

"Yep," said Slingerland, "Cordell owns this burg, even the Law."

Davis knew what he meant. "There goes Stu now, headed for the Queen, Cordell's place."

"He gets free red-eye there. Stu Barrington does what Doc says. 'Course, with George Pate on deck, you won't see any real trouble here. Doc's all for law and order now, and has ordered Pate to plug any cuss who pulls a gun. He had Stu deputize Pate, so there ain't much work for the marshal, except to light the lanterns and sweep out the calaboose once a month. Say, that's a mighty pretty daughter he has!"

His eyes, narrowed to the bright light, flicked to Davis, and he knew he'd made a hit by the way the young fellow reacted. "Yes, that Penny's a beauty," went on Al Slingerland glibly. "Good girl, too, keeps house for her dad and sees to him since her ma died. A shame Stu's a drunkard. Penny deserves better."

Men and women were on the wooden walks and around the stores. Wagons and buggies, saddle animals waited in the street; two cowboys were watering their mustangs at the big stone trough at one side of the square. A stream flowed into this by gravity from a higher elevation upriver, and spilling over, found its way through a narrow ditch back to the creek.

Cordell's Colorado Queen occupied a central position facing the wide plaza, with a magnificent view of the western mountains.

Its veranda was long, built of heavy pine, and there were two sets of batwings, side entries as well. A large sign over the center of the porch roof proclaimed, *The Colorado Queen, Jake Cordell, Prop.*" And another advertised *Finest Brandies and Liquors, Cigars, Dancing, Rooms*.

Davis and the trapper hooked rein over the continuous rail which kept horses from encroaching on the sidewalk, and stepping to the veranda, pushed through the nearer batwings. A smell of damp sawdust, whiskey, and tobacco smoke greeted them.

On the right was a long bar, large mirrors behind it with an array of bottles, glasses, boxes of cigars and plug tobacco. Two bartenders were on duty. Marshall Barrington was draining a tumbler of whiskey. He was stocky, vest loose over a flannel shirt, tucked into leather pants, half boots with runover heels, a sand-hued Stetson shoved back on his head. He was about fifty but drink was showing its effect. His unshaven jaws sagged and his nose was swollen, crisscrossed by tiny broken blood vessels. His deepset eyes were darkly underlined, his hair shot with white streaks. Seeing the newcomers in the mirror, he raised a fat hand but didn't turn around.

Several other men bellied to the bar. Damp sawdust had been freshly sprinkled. The hanging oil lamps and cuspidors were polished brass. A piano stood against the wall by a dance floor ringed with tables, but it was too early for the saloon girls to be one call. A free-lunch counter was laden with slabs of roast beef, hams, cheeses and breads, pickles, pretzels and other goodies.

The walls were sanded hardwoods, the chair, tables and such appointments the best that could be imported via the Union Pacific. Cheyenne was a station on the U.P., and within wagon haul of Cordell City, though there were steep mountains between. Past the dance space was a section dedicated to games of fhance: roulette, bird cage, dice, poker and monte tables, while in the rear were private rooms.

A lean man who had been dealing cold stud hands at a table got up and shoved back his chair. Large-boned shoulders pushed out his black silk shirt. His face was craggy, cheekbones high, long legs in dark pants tucked into halfboots decorated with the red lone star of Texas. His hair gleamed with pomade. A .45 Colt revolver rode in an oiled, open holster at one bony hip; the smooth-grained walnut stock and polished metal showed it was meticulously kept, a professional's weapon. He yawned, set his straight-brimmed black hat on his head, and sauntered toward the bar.

"Howdy, Slingerland. Howdy, Davis. Ain't seen either of you for a coon's age." His eyes were pale-blue, icy, a gun-fighter's orbs.

"Hello, Pate," nodded Slingerland. "Lee just got home from school. He's doin' a surveyin' job for Warren Neale."

138

"I hear a branch line's to be run from Cheyenne to Denver."

"Sure, Lee's on that. When he stopped to see his folks in Wesleyville, he found the settlement wiped out. Sioux, from the sign. His father, mother and brother scalped, dead, and not one sould left alive in the town."

"No!" Pate cleared his throat and the pale eyes shifted off the trapper's. "Cussed redskins are on the prod. Wipe 'em out, I say."

"We're here to see Doc. Men are needed over there."

"He's in back, eatin' dinner. C'mon."

Pate led them through a hall to a spacious salon. Two figures sat at a table laden with viands. One was slim, with curly hair, about Lee Davis's age; the other was about 45 and heavier. The latter was Jake "Doc" Cordell.

"Come in, gents," cried Cordell. "Siddown, have a bite."

Pate and the visitors took chairs. The boss of Cordell City beamed at his guests. His belly pushed out an expensive fawn-skin vest crossed by a thick gold watch chain from which hung an elk's-tooth fob. The hair on his large head was thinning and he kept it brushed across his pate to hide his balding. He was smooth-shaven; large ears stuck out, and the pointed nose was an acquisitive one over his tight-lipped mouth. The jaw was stubborn.

Al Slingerland and Lee Davis were hungry and helped themselves to the platters Cordell pushed at them, urging them to stoke up. Slingerland knew Doc Cordell had spent time in Leavenworth, but many others had come West for a new start. If a fellow behaved himself, the past would be forgotten.

"A horrible thing has happened, Mr. Cordell," began Davis. He'd taken a drink and begun to eat, but his mind was filled with the terrible tragedy. He described what he'd found in his home town.

"Why, that's awful, awful!" Doc Cordell acted appalled. "You ever hear the like, Pate? The whole settlement wiped out!"

"Mighty bad, Chief," agreed Pate. One pale eye fluttered.

"We need a crew to hustle over, bury the bodies and clean up Doc," said Slingerland. "The coyotes and wolves'll be in at dark."

"Right. I'll send a gang over pronto. See to it, George, and make sure they got plenty of shovels and all for the job."

Pate nodded, rose, glided soundlessly off.

Slingerland was watching Cordell's muddy eyes, seamed by crow's-feet at the corners.

Joe Cordell hadn't said a word except to mutter a greeting when they came in. When Slingerland glanced suddenly at him, Joe Cordell looked down at his plate. The trapper had a queer sensation. Nothing he could define; it was just a vague, uneasy feeling.

Doc Cordell was saying, "Look, Al, why don't you sell your pelts to me?"

"Well, Wesleyville was closer, and then, old Ed Turner and I were pards a good many years. But Ed's done in; his place was burned to ashes last night. I saw his scalped body when I rode by."

"Fetch 'em here. I'll pay you top prices."

"Maybe I will, at that." Slingerland knew Doc Cordell would have given more than Turner, who had had only a small turnover, but he'd never cottoned to Doc Cordell. He'd take his pelts to Cheyenne, though it

140

was much farther away than Cordell City. However, he saw no use in making an enemy of Cordell over this, at the moment.

"Reckon I'll step outside for a breath," said Joe Cordell, and as he rose, Slingerland saw a bandage on his left hand.

"Hurt your paw, Joe?" he asked.

"He ain't learned yet not to pick up a hot horseshoe," said Doc Cordell, a hint of sarcasm in his deep voice.

Joe Cordell said nothing but went out. Doc Cordell passed around cigars and lit one for himself.

"Warren Neale sent you off to college, Lee," he remarked. "You aim to work for him?"

"He already is," said Slingerland. "Lee's surveyin' the line from the U.P. south to Denver."

Cordell's broad face wreathed in a grin. "Why, that's great, son! Glad to hear it. You ought to run through this town. The territory's growin' fast, with stockmen, grangers, miners and all. Cordell City would be an ideal point for a station and railroad shops, too. We're ready to accommodate as many as come along."

Lee Davis's clear eyes fixed Cordell. "It would be, sir, but for the mountains hemmin' it in. The grades would be too steep, and far too many. Besides that, there are bottomless quicksands in the rivers just where we'd need to cross. I know all this terrain, which is one reason Mr. Neale picked me for the job."

Cordell stopped smiling, "Shucks, a top engineer like you could beat such small obstacles, Lee."

"They ain't so small. Mr. Neale knows that. You see, that valley Wesleyville is—was in—is unusual. It runs north-south for almost fifty miles and Mr. Neale aimed to locate the shops there, in my old town."

141

"But Wesleyville's done for, wiped out, boy."

Lee Davis shook his head. "I'll have to see what Mr. Neale says."

"You do that. And be sure to tell him I'll give the railroad free land for their shops."

Cordell was insistent, pressing, and Davis said uneasily. "I'm upset on account of my folks, Mr. Cordell. I'll think it over. Right now I am to see Penny Barrington."

"Sure, sure." Cordell smiled. "You're a fine boy, Lee, I always said so. Penny's growed up lately; she's a beauty. My Joe's chasin' her himself! Well, we'll talk more later. Don't you leave town without seein' me again."

"I won't. And thanks."

Slingerland and Davis went out to the sunlit main way. A bunch of riders were heading west across the lower ridge, leading pack animals with shovels, picks and other gear on them. This would be the crew on its way to the grisly task of cleaning up Wesleyville. Slingerland didn't see George Pate among them but there were several others he knew.

"I aim to buy something for Penny, Al."

"Good idea." Flower was on the trapper's mind, and he decided to pick up gifts that might please her.

Mounting, they rode over to Cordell's general store, Davis' pack horse bobbing behind. Inside, Davis bought a *Godey's Lady's Book*, a necklace, a box of sweets. "Al, if Penny asks me, I'll stay for supper. Maybe I'll spend the night in town. I told Doc Cordell I'd talk more with him 'fore I left. Tomorrow I'll head back to Cheyenne from here and see how the route looks. I know a lot more than I used to and will check it all out."

142

"*Bueno*, Lee. Long as you're okay, I'll mosey on home."

He hadn't mentioned Flower to Davis or to anyone else. It was safer to keep such information to himself.

Lee Davis thanked him deeply, and took his leave. Slingerland watched from a window as Davis mounted and rode off toward the north end of town, the pack horse trotting behind.

Slingerland spent some time in the emporium, choosing items he thought Flower would enjoy, a swatch of bright cloth, a small sewing kit, pretty beads he knew Indian girls fancied.

## V

Stu Barrington's small cabin stood off by itself; the paint on the walls was peeling. There was a garden, probably planted by Penny. Chickens clucked in a pen; the stable door sagged on leather hinges, wide open. The marshal would have ridden to work.

Davis secured his horses to a post near the rear stoop. He could hear a woman singing in the kitchen. Taking his packages, he rapped on the back door. Penny Barrington opened up, and stared up at him for a moment; she cried, "Oh, Lee! Come in." There was a lilt of delight in her voice.

"Penny, I can't tell you how happy I am to see you!" he told her.

As a virile young male would, Lee Davis couldn't help appraising the lovely girl. She took off her apron, smoothing back her golden hair, pinned on her trim head. She had matured since Davis had last seen her, and as all said, she was a beauty, brown eyes sparkling, full red lips inviting, swelling bosoms pushing out her

143

blouse.

"Sit down, Lee. I'll fetch you a bite."

"I ate at Cordell's. I'd rather sit and look at you."

She dropped her eyes, but smiled, apparently pleased. "Well, shall we go into the parlor?"

"Let's stay here, it's homey. I fetched these for you." He pushed the parcels toward her.

She exclaimed with pleasure over the gifts. "You shouldn't have spent so much, Lee."

"I've a good job, surveyin' for Warren Neale."

They sat together and he told her about Wesleyville. Tears sprang to her eyes and impulsively she patted his hand. "I'm sorry Lee. This is terrible for you." She watched him anxiously.

"It hit me mighty hard. But the hope of seeing you held me up, Penny. I got your letters."

"I've kept every one you wrote me, Lee."

Davis seized her hand; he pushed on faster than he might have, had he not been away so long. Over and over, he'd thought of what he would do when he returned to her.

"Penny, I worked mighty hard at school. There were other girls but I never saw one like you. You been in my mind day and night. I love you. Will you marry me?" He almost blurted it out, he'd rehearsed it so often.

And then she was in his arms, and he was kissing her soft lips, pressing her body tightly to him.

After a time, he felt in his pocket and brought out the ring. "I bought it in Cheyenne, Penny. It ain't as big a diamond as you deserve, but later I'll get you another."

She smiled, holding out her left hand, and he sipped the ring on her finger; she gazed at it delightedly. "It's beautiful, Lee!"

The time flew magically by as the two lovers planned

144

for their future together. "I'm worried about my father, Lee. I take care of him, you know. And he won't quit drinking. I must tell you this, that Joe Cordell has asked me to marry him, again and again. He just won't take no for an answer. Be careful of him, will you? He has a hot temper."

"I know that, Penny. I'm not afraid of him, though."

"Joe will make Doc fire my Dad when he hears you and I are engaged, I'm sure. Joe says if he can't have me, nobody else can, either. He's a lot tougher than he used to be, Lee. He hangs around with that awful George Pate, I—I don't know what my father will do if he loses his job."

Davis took her in his arms, saying, "My work means we'll travel a lot, Penny. We'll live in Cheyenne till this branch line is finished; then Mr. Neale may send me way off, and I'll sure take you with me. But I promise your dad will be taken care of; I can afford to pay his expenses somewhere."

This was a great relief to her. Later, she asked him to stay for supper, when Barrington would be home and they would break the news.

"I sure will, Penny. Now, I promised to see Doc Cordell again before I left town. But I won't be gone long."

"You go ahead, then, but hurry back. Dad killed a chicken this morning and I need to pluck it and get things ready."

After leaving the store with the things he'd bought for Flower, Al Slingerland rode his bay stallion to the livery near the Queen. Nest to it was a blacksmith's, and the sound of a hammer clanging on iron came from the forge.

The bay needed a rubdown, and a grain feed, before starting the run back across the mountain. Slingerland unsaddled him and removed the blanket pad, examining the animal's sleek back carefully, as was his wont. There was a slight rub and he smeared some dope on it to keep it from getting any worse. He paid fifty cents for a nose-bag of oats, and while the bay was eating, stepped over to the open door of the smithy.

As he stepped in, the familiar odor of smoking hoofs, seared as the hot shoes were pressed home, greeted his nostrils. A hammer clanged. The blacksmith, torso naked except for the leather protective apron, was driving fresh nails into a shoe he'd just set on the rear hoof of a draft horse.

The man was a friend. For a time, the blacksmith had tried trapping before he'd gone to work for Doc Cordell. He was a burly fellow, with a wiry black beard and tousled hair, great muscles standing out in his arms.

He had nails in his mouth so he nodded at Slingerland. The trapper waved back, and looked around as he waited. There was a small heap of discarded horseshoes nearby, and Slingerland, who seldom missed small details, glanced at them idly.

He suddenly became interested, and stooping, picked up a shoe which had a bad crack on one side. The split was wider than that in the left forehoof he'd come on close to Wesleyville and again on the river bank outside Cordell City. But it was in the same place. There was a pebbled wedged in the crak; that would have caused the metal to keep on splitting when the horse's weight was on it, as the hard little stone worked farther and farther in.

Slingerland waited, with a purpose now. In a few

146

minutes Vince Farley, the blacksmith, finished the docile draft animal and tied him near the front door to wait fo rhis owner to claim him. He wiped sweat from his brow with the hairy back of his brawny arm and grinned through is beard as he came to shake hands with Slingerland.

"You old so-and-so!" he swore affectionately. "What fetches you over this way? Ain't seen you for a year."

"I been busy, Vince. I just rode over today with Lee Davis. You heard about Wesleyville, I reckon."

Farley had. The news had spread quickly through town. He shifted his cud and spat a brown stream of tobacco juice at a corner, swearing a blue streak as he vented his opinion of the Sioux.

Slingerland held up the cracked shoe and asked casually, "Horse go lame?"

"Sure it went lame! I don't think much of a man who stays on a horse when it begins limpin'." Farley cursed again. "Lucky the sprain ain't bad. In a week or two, if that gelding's rested, he'll be good as new. Doc's young whelp is stupid; danged if he didn't grab holt of a shoe while it was still smokin'!"

Slingerland didn't have to ask questions, for Farley was telling him what he wanted to know. "You mean Joe Cordell?"

"Sure. He thinks he's Gawdamighty 'cause his pop's top dog here. Well, I told Doc he spoiled Joe, rotten-spoiled, that's what!" Joe Cordell had irritated Farley and he was letting off steam. "So he busts in 'fore I even had my fire up and orders me to hustle and take care of that pet pinto of his'n. He don't like to ride anything else. Told him to keep his pants on, and he give me lip, said he'd have his old man discharge me!"

147

"Early this mornin', eh? He must've been out last night."

"Yeah. Chasin' some female, I reckon. He's been after Stu's daughter, but that don't stop him from buzzin' around other gals like a fly after honey. So when I warned him not to use the pinto till the leg was sound, he called me a liar. I near took my sledge to him! But finally he said he'd let the pore critter rest up."

"Was Joe out alone last night?"

"Dunno. But I think he was with George Pate. The young jackass follers that gunny around like a cussed hound dawg."

Farley hadn't the slightest idea of what grave information he'd given Slingerland, who showed no sign of his inner thoughts as he tossed the cracked shoe back onto the pile. After telling the blacksmith about what luck he'd had in trapping, Slingerland took leave of his friend.

The fact that Joe Cordell, and probably George Pate, had been the two who'd armed the Indians outside Wesleyville, was a soul-chilling, horrible thing. Slingerland felt he must think it over most carefully before taking any action. He couldn't make any accusation on the slight clue he'd uncovered. It was his word against young Cordell's and Pate's, and the trapper knew he'd never get out of Cordell City alive if he even hinted at his suspicions. The motive certainly wasn't clear to him as to why the pair might have done such a ghastly thing which had resulted in the death of many men, women and children and left Wesleyville a smoking ruins.

Bearded face set, keen gray eyes slitted, he strolled back to the livery and called the wrangler.

"I won't be ridin' out for a while, Billy. Turn my

horse into the corral and pitch in some hay." He stowed the presents for Flower in his blanket roll, leaving it with his saddle gear, and went into the main street.

People were around, at the stores; a few dedicated drinkers were in the saloons. Slingerland took a chair at the end of the Queen's long veranda and filled his pipe, lit up, leaned back, his mind busy with what he'd uncovered. He could hardly go to Cordell with such deadly accusations against Doc's only son.

He was puzzled. While Joe Cordell was mean of temper and unpredictable, why should he arm a band of savages and egg them on to wipe out Wesleyville? Then he recalled that George Pate had probably been along; the Texas killer would think nothing of instigating such a massacre if there was profit in it for him. Suffering and death for others wouldn't bother Pate.

Yet Pate was Doc Cordell's chief of staff. Would he carry out such a grave enterprise without Cordell's consent?

Slingerland shook his head. He was up against the same problem: why would Doc Cordell want Wesleyville obliterated?

His brown study was interrupted as Lee Davis rode up on his brown gelding and got down at the Queen. He didn't have the dun and his gear with him. Seeing Slingerland, he hurried to him, crying, "Al, congratulate me! Penny says she'll marry me!"

"Great," said Al, slapping him on the back.

"I'm goin' in to see Doc Cordell as I promised. Then I'll have supper with Penny. I left my pack horse at her place."

Slingerland was relieved to see the youth cheerier, after the awful shock Lee had experienced. He watched Davis enter the Queen, and then resumed his seat,

149

sucking on a cold pipe.

An hour later, the surveyor emerged. Davis almost ran to his horse, and he jumped aboard without touching the stirrup. He didn't seem even to see Slingerland, and the trapper thought his face was set, red with some inner emotion. Lee Davis rode swiftly away.

Davis was out of sight when the batwings down the porch banged open and Joe Cordell catapulted out. Doc's son looked infuriated, also, as had Lee Davis. He was flushed, and his lips writhed as he cursed. Apparently he didn't notice Slingerland hunched in a chair down the veranda, but stepped into the gutter, staring in the direction Lee Davis had taken. His fists were clenched and he was breathing hard.

Finally he swung, muttering to himself. He scowled at the trapper but gave no sign of recognition as he went back inside.

Interested in this exhibition, Slingerland rose and peeked over the nearer batwings. Joe Cordell was at the bar and began talking animatedly with Stu Barrington. The marshal heard him out, then shrugged and spread his hands in the classic gesture of impotence. This disgusted Joe Cordell, who waved the officer off, looking as though he'd whiffed a rotten fish. Cordell crossed the big saloon to a table where George Pate sat, playing solitaire.

Intrigued, Slingerland watched. Pate listened to Joe Cordell who was obviously making an impassioned plea. The gun boss shook his head, but as Joe Cordell argued on, Pate finally seemed to agree, for he nodded. Joe Cordell sat down beside his mentor, and for several minutes the pair spoke earnestly together. Then the younger Cordell left Pate and disappeared through a corridor to the rear of the big structure, where he had his quarters. Pate resumed his game.

Slingerland strode down the long porch and entered the other batwings which were nearer the bar. He shuffled up beside Barrington. "Howdy, Stu, glad to see you."

Barrington turned bleary, worried eyes on him.

"Howdy, Al," he said, dispiritedly, and downed a swig of redeye.

A bartender came up and Slingerland ordered a beer. "Say, Joe Cordell looks peaked. You reckon the whippersnapper's sick?"

The marshal slowly shook his head. "Well, no, not exactly. But he just now heard my Penny aims to hitch up with Lee Davis. What can I do? I can't stop her. She's got a mind of her own, like her maw had. Scolds me all the time 'cause I take a snifter or two, till I wonder who wears the pants in my own home!"

The marshal was aggrieved, but was afraid of losing his job. Joe Cordell might prevail on his father to fire Barrington, and Stu was voicing his anxiety.

"See," he continued, "Joe's been stuck on Penny a long while but she won't have him. I've begged her to take him, but she says she'd rather be dead. I'm done for, I reckon. If Doc takes away my badge, I'll starve." He was wallowing in his misery. Pouring another three fingers, he tossed it off at a gulp.

Lee Davis must have told Jake Cordell of his engagement to Penny. After the young surveyor had left, the father had passed on the tidings to his son.

Joe Cordell's violent temper was notorious. He considered himself the crown prince of the Cordell empire, and he wasn't used to being balked.

And Joe Cordell had enlisted George Pate in the deal.

Much as Slingerland yearned to get back to Mountain

Flower, he couldn't leave Davis in the lurch. He could only conclude that Joe Cordell, infuriated at losing Penny, had talked George Pate into some plan to get rid of Lee.

And if, as Slingerland suspected, the two had sparked the Wesleyville massacre, one more killing would mean nothing to them. The hot-tempered Joe Cordell would revel in his rival's death.

## VI

So Slingerland hung around, trying to make himself inconspicuous, until dark. Marshall Barrington touched off the street lanterns with a taper attached to a long stick and then rode off home to supper.

The town picked up steam. The day's work done, men flocked to the Queen. Music could be heard. Saloon girls and dealers, other employes had come on duty. Saddle horses and buggies crowded the hitch rails. Stores had been shuttered for the night. A cool west wind sprang up, blowing over the river from the mountains, and myriad insects piped in the brush along the stream; moths and smaller flying things circled thickly around the yellow lights hanging from their posts beside the street.

Slingerland was devoted to Warren Neale and his wife, Allie, whom he'd helped so much in the U.P. Trail, when Neale had solved knotty engineering problems for the transcontinental road. And Lee Davis was Neale's protege. Besides this, the kind-hearted trapper liked the young surveyor, and was sorry for him because of the terrible tragedy which had struck him when the Davis family had been killed in Wesleyville.

Yet there was more to it, something bigger than Lee's

personal fate. Slingerland had grown convinced that George Pate would not have armed the Sioux and set them upon Wesleyville without Doc Cordell's consent. He felt compelled to check this out.

He kept peeking in over the batwings at Pate, who stood at the lower end of the long bar. Joe Cordell wasn't in sight but he was probably eating dinner in back with his father. The way Joe had acted up that afternoon, after Davis had left the Queen, forced Slingerland to believe he'd enlisted George Pate in some scheme to dispose of his rival for Penny's hand. Pate had agreed to whatever it was Joe Cordell had suggested.

It was time to make ready. Slingerland's long legs took him quickly back to the corral in which his bay stallion was penned. The horse scented his friend, whinned and trotted to the gate. Slingerland led him out, closed the barrier so other animals couldn't follow.

There were lanterns around, and some light from the rear windows. The trapper belted on the blanket, and setting his high-pronged saddle, tightened the cinches carefully. Due to the presents he'd bought for Flower, the roll was a bit bulky but wouldn't bother him in riding. As was his habit, he checked his carbine and the heavy Creedmore, made sure his Colt was loaded, that his long shining knife was in its sheath at his hip. Leaving the rifles in their boots, he led the bay off behind a barn, tethering him in dense shadow.

Returning to his watch, he waited around. Pate was still at the bar. Slingerland had an Indian's patience. At last, this was rewarded as Joe Cordell came from the back of the roomy building and skirted the dance floor.

Joe Cordell joined George Pate, who signaled. Two men in cowboy garb got up from a table and slouched

153

over. Slinglerland knew one, Lew Ince, as a tough who rode for Pate; the second would be a new member of the Texan's killer gang.

Pate led the way to a rear corridor, trailed by Joe Cordell and the two gunnies.

Convinced his diagnosis had been correct, Slingerland loped back to Tin Can Alley. A brass lantern burned over the Queen's rear exit.

Crouched in shadow, the trapper watched the quartet emerge and cross the alley to the stable. Music and voices from the front of the Colorado Queen came to him, but he could hear the four talking together as they saddled up.

They brought out their mounts, got aboard and started off, swinging through a lane to the plaza.

Slingerland took his time. He knew exactly where they were headed. He picked up Reddy, his bay stud, and let the four have a long start so they wouldn't see him as he trailed.

He hit the north road. Dust still hung in the air, raised by the riders ahead. Cabins along the way were lighted, families in them enjoying the evening meal.

He soon left the beaten track and made a wide circle. There, from a rise, he watched the four horsemen dismount well out from Stu Barrington's little house. One man stayed behind, holding the mounts. Slingerland glimpsed three stealthy figures flitting to the rear of Barrington's. The moon was up and there was enough light to glint on the barrels of their carbines.

He untied his bandanna and knotted it around the bay's snout, so his pet wouldn't sound off. Reddy would sometimes whinny to him if left for a time.

In Barrington's back yard was a post with a flickering lantern hanging from it, and the kitchen windows were lighted. A saddled horse waited by the rear stoop.

Before long the stocky marshal came forth and mounted his plug. Barrington rode off, headed back for the center of town and the Colorado Queen, where he would hang around and drink until late in the night.

Tethered outside the stable were Lee Davis's brown and the dun pack horse. Davis had unsaddled them, relieving them of their loads as they waited; he would have watered and fed them before going into the cabin.

Slingerland went way around and tethered the bay in darkness near a pine grove. He left the heavy Sharps, but took his repeating carbine with extra loads he shoved into his pockets. Stealthy and silent as a stalking Indian, he kept low, always in shadow, and approached the Barrington yard.

A thick spruce grew several yards out from the perimeter of light cast by the post lantern. Slingerland bellied the last stretch of its protective cover, and flattened out, the carbine laid in front of him.

The armed trio had also hidden themselves. With inexhaustible patience, Al Slingerland watched. Again this paid off. Men waiting under such conditions would shift slightly to ease cramped muscles, or from boredom. He finally caught a faint glint on the far side of the yard; that would mark one. In a few minutes, a second moved a bit, and at last, the third. Now Slingerland had all three positions marked in his mind.

They evidently didn't believe Lee Davis would remain here overnight.

And they were right about this. About an hour after Barrington had left, the kitchen door opened. Slingerland saw Penny's feminine figure, and Lee's taller one. Davis kissed her, held her for a time, and the girl stood in the lighted doorway, watching as her sweetheart

155

started outside, meaning to pick up his horses. Slingerland figured Davis would ride north, in the moonlight, for a time, then camp on his way back to Cheyenne, where he would report to Warren Neale.

But the trapper no longer watched Davis and the doorway, where Penny stood. He raised his carbine, a cartridge in its breech, ready to fire. And a breath later, he caught the telltale glint as one of the three threw his rifle into position, then a second and a third—

Slingerland opened fire, aiming at the points he'd spotted. His carbine crackled, once, twice, three times, as he moved his accurate rifle. Somebody over there screeched; a gun flamed from the brush but Slingerland could tell by the flash it was high, thrown off as he dusted them, peppering them as fast as he could shoot.

Penny screamed, and Lee Davis, frozen for an instant in his tracks, turned and ran back inside, slamming the door.

A high-pitched wail sounded. "I'm hit—I'm hit—my face—" Slingerland thought it was Joe Cordell's voice.

As he ceased firing and rapidly reloaded, a hoarse order rang out from the ambushers' spot.

"Hustle, get on back, you fools!" That must be Pate, Slingerland decided.

They were running for it. Slingerland glimpsed three figures, one staggering, the other pair close together; maybe a wounded man was being supported by another. Slingerland let them go. They reached their horses and climbed aboard, and he heard the beat of hoofs as the four, including the holder, retreated back to town.

When he was sure they were gone, Slingerland loped to the kitchen door. "Lee—Penny!" he called, softly but urgently. "It's Al Slingerland. Open up, pronto."

After a moment the door was unbolted and pulled

156

back a few inches; Davis peeked out. "That you, Al?"

"Sure." He shoved inside. Penny stood, eyes wide, frightened, a hand on her sweetheart's arm.

They watched the trapper's bearded face as he said grimly, "Get away fast as you can. Take Penny with you if you want to see her again, Lee. Pate and Joe Cordell just tried to drygulch you."

"I was afraid something like this would happen," Penny said to Slingerland. "Joe's made threats."

"This is Doc Cordell's town. He'll cover his son."

Davis seemed hesitant. "But it's dark, Al, and Penny can't very well—"

Slingerland broke in, "There's no time to talk, Lee. George Pate won't give up so easy. He'll be back in a jiffy with a big enough crew to do the job. I know that Texas gunny!"

"What should we do?" asked the girl.

"You grab a few things you need, Penny. Lee, leave your gear. Penny can ride your pack horse."

"I—I have only one saddle. I don't see how Penny can—"

"There's an old one of father's in the stable," the girl said quickly. "I'll get ready."

"Good girl," said Slingerland. Sometimes, he thought, a woman saw things quicker than a man did.

"I'll put on Levis, and ride astride. I'll be there by the time you've saddled up." The girl turned and ran into the other room.

"Hustle, Lee. Pate'll be back and this time we can't beat him off. He's got a dozen gunnies workin' for him."

The two men hurried outside, and Al Slingerland found the old saddle on a wooden peg inside the stable. Davis had his brown gelding ready, and the two cinched

157

Barrington's worn saddle on the dun. The pack horse wasn't made for speed; he was sturdy but no runner.

Penny ran out, carrying a small bundle, and Davis helped her mount; the tight Levis accentuated her rounded feminine thighs.

"Listen, Lee! Now, you can't go through town, they'll spot you sure. Hit the track north, this side of the river. You savvy this country. When you reach Beaver Ford, five miles upstream, cross there and go over the mountain, and get on the Cheyenne road in the Wesleyville valley. Neale and Allie'll shelter you. Do like I say. Don't turn off course."

"Ain't you coming?" asked Davis.

"Never mind me. I'll take care of myself. Ride fast as you can and don't stop 'less you have to."

Slingerland watched the lovers start for the wagon road winding northward. The moon was rising, well up over the brooding heights.

When he was sure the two were on their way, Al Slingerland hurried into the house, loped to the parlor and bolted the front door. Back in the kitchen, he turned the lamp down but left it burning, shot the bolt on the kitchen door and eased out a side window, shutting it after him. He trotted to the point where he'd left his horse.

He shoved his carbine into its boot and removed the bandanna muzzle; the bay stallion sniffed and nuzzled his big hand. Swinging a long leg over his mount, he rode off but pulled up after a short run, and turned to wait on a wooded rise from which he could look back and watch Barrington's.

Cordell City's glow dominated the south sky as he sat his saddle in the darkness. It wasn't long befor ehe saw his conclusion verified. Horsemen's figures showed, hurrying from town, sifting around Barrington's house. From this distance, he couldn't tell exactly how many there were, and was unable to identify individuals, but he was sure George Pate was the leader, and the other were his gunslingers.

A faint grin touched his bearded lips as he observed the stealthy, careful approach as Pate threw a death cordon around the place. Pate was taking no chances this time; the Texas killer knew very well he'd been made a jackass of, and such a man had his pride. It was an evil pride, perhaps, with the overweening ego of a notorious gun boss.

Slingerland patted his handsome bay's neck.

"Look at 'em, Reddy," he murmured, chuckling. "It's perfect! That is, if there was anybody inside!"

The bay rippled his hide; he liked it when the trapper talked to him.

Pate had left the mounts back in shadow. Afoot, the armed stalkers flitted around, trying the doors, finding them locked.

Slingerland had figured on this. It would give Lee Davis and Penny a few minutes start on their desperate night run. The trapper was aware that Pate's string of horses consisted only of the fastest, best mounts available. Davis' pack horse, even his riding critter, couldn't outdistance such runners. The bay stallion was probably superior to them, but that was a question only a race could settle.

Noises came from town, strains of music, a whoopee now and again as some over-exhilarated drunk sounded off, dimmed by distance.

Next there was an interval; Slingerland figured they were consulting with Pate on what to do, as the entrances were bolted. He knew that they'd finally get in

159

through a window; that was obvious. Pate would also check the point from which Slingerland had fired his shots; the flashes of the carbine would have marked the spruce for that.

He allowed a few more minutes; they'd search the house carefully, hoping to root out Davis and Penny.

Failing to find them, Pate would make sure Davis's horses were gone, too. Then he'd start after them, aware they could have gone only one way, northward. Had they passed through the settlement, they'd have been seen, and rugged mountains loomed to the west and east, impassable to riders and difficult even for a man afoot. Only a few steep paths could be used to cross over to the long valley in which Wesleyville had stood.

Slingerland did not underestimate George Pate. He was well aware the Texas was a master tracker, as trained and keen as Slingerland and most Indians were.

Feeling he'd stayed there long enough, he rode down the slope and sat his saddle at the edge of the road, silver moonlight slanting down on the rutted way.

To the west lay the deep, swift river, the serrated black shapes of cottonwoods and brush outlining its course. Across it was a high, rocky ridge. Familiar with the terrain, for he'd hunted and trapped all through it, he was aware that not far above Beaver Ford the vale came to an abrupt end, a mountain blocking off the route to Cheyenne. The wagon road climbed it by switchbacks, a slow, difficult feat, while the river cut through a deep gorge with perpendicular granite walls, then, on the other flank, in a dip between heights, the stream widened in a swale abounding with quicksand. To cross the swamp a corduroy road of rocks and great tree trunks had been laid over which sturdy freight

160

wagons and horses could maneuver.

He drew his carbine, making sure a cartridge was in the firing chamber, eased one leg up, staring intently at the moonlit road.

He heard them before he saw them. Swinging the bay, he trotted to a bend where the track veered with the winding river's course. Again he pulled up. They were coming fast, for Pate would be sure the fugitives were ahead, though he wasn't aware Slingerland was in between.

Here they came, two-by-two, low over the withers of their swift mustangs, ready for a fast run and certain of success.

He raised the carbine and threw two shots close to the van. The leaders, hearing the vicious whine of the bullets, jerked hard on their resins, turning off into the brush. Moments later a mass volley ripped the space where they'd noted the rifle flashes, but Slingerland was galloping toward the next turn.

But they wouldn't know he'd shifted, and would work around to make sure the drygulcher wasn't still there. So he'd gained a few more minutes for Penny and Lee.

When they finally came out they moved slower and more carefully, in a single file, a man out front with carbine at the ready. Slingerland let go, a couple, but did not linger, for they were on the prod and instantly replied.

It was expert delaying tactics. Of course, there was always a chance one of the blind bullets would find either Slingerland or the bay, in which case that would spell the end for the trapper and no doubt for Lee Davis and his sweetheart.

# VII

Slingerland bedeviled them for five miles but George Pate doggedly hung on.

The road was now close to the river and he heard the low sound of rapids. Beaver Ford was an upthrust of hard rock where the stream shallowed and widened. There were quicksands at either side, and he put the bay carefully into the hock-deep, swift current. A wooded mountain loomed over there but he could make out the break marking the west gap and kept the stallion directed toward it.

Davis and Penny must have come this way had they obeyed his directions, as he was sure they would. He knew this trail over the mountain wall wasn't as easy as the one he and Davis had followed from Wesleyville to Cordell City; wheeled vehicles couldn't negotiate it, and it was hard even for horses or mules, slow going.

He started up the narrow, shale-strewn path, the stallion straining at the grade, pebbles sliding under his digging hoofs. When he'd made enough headway, he dismounted and stood, rein in hand, looking down at the moonlit crossing.

Before long, the pursuers began splashing over; and as the next fifty yards was unusually steep, Al Slingerland led his horse. Pausing, listening, he heard them coming, stones rattling down as they were disturbed. He couldn't see much now but fired several shots back blindly to give them pause.

He was near the summit when the trail passed between two brutal granite shoulders which almost closed it in. He led the bay through the gap, and tethered him to a stubby spruce. Taking his carbine, he returned to the gap and crouched at one side, listening, watching.

After a while the first one arrived, a dark blob against the sky. The gunny was leading his mustang, straining up the slope. Slingerland opened fire, and the man uttered a high-pitched shriek and fell down. The others behind him began shouting, hurriedly throwing lead at him. The metal slugs spattered against the stones, breaking off bits that sounded like hail.

He knew they'd have a tough time working around behind him, even on foot. Still, it could be done, and Pate would try.

Then he had an idea. There were some large, roundish boulders close at hand, poised on the shale. He couldn't possibly lift them, but by putting his shoulders to a couple, managed to start them rolling. They were stopped short by the narrow slot, and he pushed down as many as he could, forming a crude barrier, blocking the trail.

Eventually, Pate's boys would clear the way, but that would take an hour, anyhow; they wouldn't keep coming without their horses.

He led the stallion over the summit, hit leather, and started down the western slope into the next valley, sure he'd gained the time Davis and Penny needed to escape.

From a low rise, the exhausted Lee Davis and Penny Barrington looked ahead over the endless, dusty plain on which Cheyenne stood. The sun had risen an hour before and was beginning to heat the air.

Davis glanced at his sweetheart. During the hard, frightening night ride, the young woman hadn't uttered a word of complaint. He could see she was suffering,

163

that she was completely drained. Lather had dried on the horses and the animals were almost completely played out.

"We'll be at Warren Neale's in half an hour, Penny. Hold on."

She tried to smile at him. Her face was drawn, caked with fine dust, her hair matted to her head.

North of the U.P. tracks, a wood-burning locomotive with a brass bell stack puffed toward Cheyenne station, drawing a long string of freight and cattle cars. Cheyenne really owed its existence now to the railroad; it was said to be a God-forsaken, God-forgotten place. Uneven lines of frame houses and shanties, some painted a glaring white, other unpainted, sheltered the permanent population of some 5000 souls. Some of these "souls" were white enough but many were evil, for the scum of advancing civilization had flocked in, rowdies and desperadoes. Stabbings and shoots were a commonplace. A vigilante committee had been organized recently to try and stem the violence. Several outlaws had been strung up.

Few homes had gardens or even trees by them; huge rubbish heaps, some as high as the buildings, were everywhere. In the distance a cattle herd was being held on the outskirts of the town, and there were numerous freight wagons. Far off, three peaks like immense teeth thrust to the sky.

Neale's ranch stood on the southern edge of the city. It was built of mountain timber, chinked logs, with two stone chimneys. There was a stable, beyond this a hay barn for the few cattle and horses the engineer kept. Allie had chickens and geese, a milch cow. Neal had his office in his home; he was very busy now with his work.

Smoke came from the kitchen chimney. The couple

164

had two children, a girl about three, a baby boy starting to toddle.

As the bedraggled pair rode slowly up, Warren Neale waved at them from his low front veranda; he'd stepped out for a breath of air before breakfast. Lee Davis slid from his sweated saddle, turned to lift Penny down, and Neale came toward them, staring at them, keen eyes questioning.

A New Englander of poor family, Neale had come West as an eager young fellow, wild for adventure, intrigued by the engineering problems of the U.P. Trail. His face was bronzed by sun and wind. He was just under six feet, built like a wedge; though not heavy, he'd taken on a few pounds with the years and a few lines in his brown showed how deeply he took his work to heart.

"Lee!" he cried, shaking hands. "What's wrong?" He glanced inquiringly at Penny.

"Mr. Neale, this is my fiancee, Penny Barrington, from Cordell City. She—I, too—well, we're both frazzled. We've had to ride all night to escape. We'd never have got clear if Al Slingerland hadn't saved us."

Neale saw the straits the two were in. "Tell me all about it later, Lee. Now, come in, and Allie will give you breakfast. It's about ready. I'll have a man see to your horses."

He put a fathering arm around Davis' shoulders, and smiled at Penny, escorting them into the house and through to the roomy kitchen. Allie had just set a large pot of coffee on the table, and there were fried eggs and bacon, biscuits and syrup. The baby was in a high chair, banging on the tray with a spoon. The little girl, who had her mother's large, violet eyes, sat demurely at the table.

Allie Neale was slight, with rich chestnut hair. She had been the sole survivor of a Sioux attack on a wagon train before Neale had met her and later married her. But had it not been for Al Slingerland's help, Allie and Neale would have lost each other forever.

Allie greeted Lee Davis and Penny; she could see what straits the girl was in, and quickly led her off so Penny could wash up, catch her breath. Neale poured coffee for Davis and himself and they sat down together, Lee Davis giving a quick account of the massacre at his home, how Wesleyville had been destroyed, of the events in Cordell City.

"Mr. Neale, Doc Cordell's determined the branch line be run through his town. He wants the shops located there, too. He offered me a big bribe if I'd recommend this, but I can't. The grades over the mountains, the swamps and quicksands, would bankrupt the company."

Warren Neale frowned as he nodded. "I know that. I've been through there, Lee, and I'd never okay such a route. I meant to use Wesleyville. Since it's gone, we'll have to think up an alternative, but Cordell City is entirely unsatisfactory."

Allie fetched Penny back into the kitchen. She'd loaned the girl a fresh pink gown, and Penny had washed up, fixed her hair. Tired as Lee Davis and his sweetheart were, they needed food and drink first of all, and both ate heartily as Allie pressed them to fill up.

Once they'd eaten, the two younger people couldn't keep their eyes open. Allie led Penny to a bedroom where she could turn in, while Neale, who had ordered his hired man to take care of the horses, showed Davis where to sleep . . . .

Slingerland, in the meantime, had swung south,

166

picking up speed on the good road which led past Wesleyville. He made a detour when he neared the site, believing Cordell's crew would still be there, cleaning up. Crossing the river, he threaded through forest trails toward his valley home. He'd been gone longer than he'd expected.

He was most eager to see Flower again, recapture the enchanting magic of her presence.

"I'll marry her if she'll have me, Reddy," he told the stallion, and the bay flicked his ears.

The moon was high, offering plenty of light for a rider who knew the territory as well as Slingerland did. He was planning what he'd say to the Sioux girl as he crossed the divide and swung down along the path to his cabin.

Dawn wasn't far off. There was a west wind, and as Al Slingerland rode on, the creek on his left hand, a worrisome odor suddenly struck his nostrils. It was a smell of burning, not clean smoke from a wood fire which Flower might have going in the fireplace, but more like what he'd whiffed around Wesleyville, though it had been stronger there.

He slowed, and a troubled emotion clutched at him; he loosened his carbine in its boot. A moment later the bay gave him warning, snuffling, jerking his head to veer off. This was more than enough for such a man as Slingerland. He drew up, got down, muzzled Reddy, and tied him off in a pine grove. Carbine in one big hand, he began his approach, not a direct one, but a stealthy, studied circling so as to reach the camp from the far side.

He made scarcely a sound as he flitted from tree to tree, bush to bush, pausing to listen. Once on the west edge of his clearing, he crouched beside a clump of wild raspberry shrubs.

Moonlight bathed the cleared space. There was a black mass where his cabin had stood. The fire was nearly out but faint curls of smoke still rose slowly from the ruins. The shed had been razed, too. He heard the piping of frogs form the beaver pond, the incessant chirp of innumerable insects. Far off, a lobo wolf howled mournfully.

Slingerland was not a man to panic easily but as he thought of Flower, he felt as though a knife had been thrust into his vitals. Flint Heart must have tracked her, recaptured her! Generous to a fault, slow to anger, his strong hands tightened on his rifle. If he ever got them on Flint Heart's throat—

As the pounding blood eased a bit and his heart steadied its beat, he caught a "thud-thud" nearby, knew it was a horse stamping as it stood in the woods. He was on the point of creeping toward this, but the infinite patience he'd acquired from the Indians, his long experience as a top scout, stopped him. He would wait until there was enough daylight so he could make his maneuver properly.

If Flint Heart and his hotheads had burned his camp, the chief would have left two or three warriors to kill him when he returned home. That was the way of the Sioux.

So he waited, difficult as it was. At last the gray dawn came over the beautiful land.

He'd heard the first mustang twice, and knew about where the Indian pony would be tethered; and he'd caught faint wounds beyond, that of a second animal. So there would be two watching for him, at least.

Now he began his stalk. Inch by inch, never making even a faint noise, Slingerland bellied along. The

Indians wouldn't be far from their mounts. The daylight have overcome the moon's glow, stabbing into the shadowed forest. He lay flat, peeping through a narrow gap in the brush, seeing the dark outline of a horse.

After a long, painful study, he realized that what looked like a log lying on the needled earth was a man. The Sioux would have his mustang's rope attached to his ankle or wrist as he slept.

Slingerland carefully laid his carbine down, soundlessly. He had his Colt, and he drew his long, razor-sharp skinning knife.

He started across the several yards of open space toward the Sioux; he'd finish the Indian silently, then deal with the other one. The brave he was watching hadn't stirred.

He was almost upon his enemy when faint noises stopped him; he had to glance back. A large jackrabbit came hopping through the forest aisle. The animal's labored movements showed he was almost run out, close to the end, and a short way behind, Al Slingerland saw two small fiery red dots, knew they were a weasel's eyes. The snaky, low predator, intent on his prey, seemed like a shadow, and with a great bound, the weasel leaped, catching the rabbit's neck in his sharp death grip. The rabbit gave one last, high-pitched scream as he fell.

And the Sioux suddenly sat up, alerted by the sound.

There was only one thing to do, for Slingerland was in the open. Knife raised, the trapper launched himself at the Indian.

The weasel dropped his catch and scooted off into the bushes.

Slingerland could see his opponent clearly now. The Sioux wore a single eagle feather in his black hair, bound with a snake band. He was naked to the waist, deerskin leggings on his strong legs. The black eyes gleamed as he saw the white man upon him; he had to disengage the rope holding his startled mustang, which had jerked back as Al Slingerland attacked.

But he managed to kick up and knock the descending knife out of line. An instant later Slingerland was on top of him, the sinewy Sioux getting his strong arms into play. He had hold of Slingerland's wrist, fighting for his life, seeking to keep the deadly point from slashing into his belly. The savage had a knife in his belt and a repeating carbine lay close by, but he had no time to snatch at his weapons.

The struggle was silent, the only sounds the breathing of the two fighting men.

Slingerland sat astride of the Sioux, holding him down; slowly but surely, he was breaking the Indian's grip, and then—

Al Slingerland would never have lived long in this land had he not been possessed of survival instincts as strong as that of an Indian. He'd known there was a second savage nearby, and suddenly he ripped his wrist from the Sioux he held, and rolled frantically off across the needles in the small clearing.

The Sioux hadn't been expecting this, so Slingerland broke clear. The man he'd had down sat up, just in time to catch an arrow through his breast.

The second Sioux had heard the sounds, stolen around, aimed to kill the white man.

He was kneeling there, and as Slingerland pulled his Colt, the Indian had whipped another arrow from his quiver and fitted it to his bow. An Indian could send them as fast as a gun could fire. The bow was already well-bent as Slingerland fired, once, twice.

170

The second arrow flew from the string but drilled into the earth a yard in front of the trapper, who was curled on his left side.

Without a sound, the Sioux let go of his bow and fell over, two .45 slugs in his black-haired, feathered head.

Slingerland wasted no time. There might be more where these came from.

He crawled a long time. Neither Sioux had moved; the man he'd shot lay on his back, while the first leaned half against a tree, the feathered end of the shaft sticking from his breast.

The eastern sky was a glorious red, the daylight full.

Slingerland padded around and retrieved his carbine. Checking carefully, he found no more sign of his enemies. To be sure, he had a look at the two bodies; the Sioux were dead. He removed the rope halter from the mustangs; the second stood not far off in the forest. The doughty ponies were nervous; this was a white man, and they didn't like it. He let them go free.

Finally he went to the creek and washed up, drank heavily. Hustling back, he took the bandanna off the bay's nose, mounted and rode close to the clearing, where the wreckage of his home smoldered.

The mule and his chestnut gelding weren't around. He hadn't expected to find them. The Indians would have taken them. He cast about, and in several soft spots, found numerous moccasin tracks. One was extra large.

"Flint Heart," he muttered aloud. His Sioux rival was almost as big as the great Minneconjou chief, Touch the Clouds, who was seven feet tall, and a close comrade of Crazy Horse. Flint Heart, the trapper knew, was a Hunkpapa, as was Sitting Bull, and also Gall, the field general of the tribal branch.

171

Slingerland had some jerked meat in his saddlebags, a couple of hardtack biscuits. With water, he made a meal of this. He had no appetite but he knew he would need all the strength he could muster.

The sun had turned golden as he rode off west of his valley trail. Before long, he passed the spot where he'd found Flower, and his heart turned leaden as he imagined Flint Heart having his way with the pretty girl. He ground his teeth, but tried to cool off. He'd need to be in full command of himself for what he meant to do.

He rode fast through the warming morning, climbing out of the beautiful valley, veering northwest with the sign. He'd lived with the Indians and knew how they left pointers to show friends the route to a camping ground. Two small bird legbones arranged in a V turned him onto a winding trail; next, he came on a small cairn and took the direction this indicated. And in midafternoon he rode into the Sioux village on the bank of a mountain stream.

The wigwams were properly arranged according to protocol; the pony herd gazed in a meadow. A pack of mongrels challenged him. They snarled but didn't bark; barking dogs might betray a camp to enemies, and a noisy canine didn't live long. Puppy stew was a favorite Indian delicacy.

Some squaws worked with awl and sinews, making moccasins; younger ones, faces vermilioned, beaded bands hanging from braids, brushed flies off sleeping papooses. Long-legged naked boys played along the brook, while old men sat in little circles, smoking red willow bark or tobacco. Cooking fires were banked by the lodges.

Slingerland's approach had been open, deliberate; he was known to the Sioux as a friend and comrade.

A frantic bray rang out and the trapper's mule, Longears, came running to greet his beloved leader, the bay stud. Reddy was twitching and sniffing uneasily; he didn't like the smell of the savages. Slingerland didn't see his chestnut; the gelding would have joined him had he been nearby and could do so.

A slim warrior emerged from a lodge. He was short for a Sioux brave, his hair and complexion lighter than average. A single eagle drooped from his fur-wrapped braids; behind one ear was a small red hawk, behind the other a pebble, his "medicine."

Slingerland dismounted, holdng his rein.

"Tasunke Witko," he said, respectfully saluting Crazy Horse, the mighty Sioux paladin, who came to welcome the guest.

Al Slingerland alerted as a large Indian came around a tepee, but then saw it was Touch the Clouds, the Minneconjou, who was seven feet tall. He was one of Crazy Horse's closes comrades. The Minneconjou chief's poweful breast showed scars of the sundance, where the rawhide thongs had ripped through flesh and tendons.

Slingerland spoke in Sioux to Crazy Horse. "Tasunke Witko, my brother. Is the Hunkpapa Flint Heart in this village?"

"No. But he will return. When, I can't say."

Slingerland greeted Touch the Clouds, and the three entered Crazy Horse's lodge, the Minneconjou ducking low as he came inside. Black Shawl, Crazy Horse's faithful squaw, was there. She had known, before Crazy Horse had married her, she was second in his heart to Black Buffalo Woman, his earlier love. But she was happy to serve him because he was such a great chief and defender of her people.

173

Black Shawl bought the guest spoon, the horn of a large mountain sheep containing soup and pieces of meat. She also set before them other viands, an antelope haunch, flat cakes she had baked. The three men squatted in the center of the lodge, and Crazy Horse offered a bit of food to the earth, to the sky, and to the four great directions, according to ritual, before they began to eat.

When they had finished their meal, the silent squaw brought the pipes for smoking.

Al Slingerland would wait. He would learn where Flower was, and he would be there when Flint Heart rode in.

## VIII

Doc Cordell fumed in his chair behind the table, glowering at his son and his partner, George Pate.

"You're fools!" he snarled, "tryin' to drygulch Lee Davis. I need him. You've wrecked the cussed deal."

Pate reddened; he hadn't shaved for two days and black bristles stuck from his smudged cheeks. Deep lines around the cruel mouth and crow's-feet at his eye corners showed how exhausted he was.

"How was I to savvy that, Jake?" he snapped back, temper flaring. "You should've told me. Your whelp here begged me to get rid of Davis. Joe's got the hots for that Penny wench."

"To hell with that. One girl's good as another. I'd just promised Davis I'd see he got rich if he'd rout that branch line through here. You know what that'd mean. A railroad, probably their shops, would draw thousands of new settlers. What with the business and land we own, we'd rake in millions! But if the tracks are laid

174

through the next valley, folks 'll desert us like rats, and Cordell City'll be a ghost town. It's happened again and again. That's why Wesleyville had to be destroyed. With it gone, the railroad would have to come here instead."

The Texas gunslinger shrugged. He was worn out, in a murderous fury. "Jake, you asked me to help Joe, didn't you, teach him and try to make a real man of him. It ain't been easy. So far I haven't even been able to teach the fool to keep his head down!"

There was an ugly but superficial bullet burn, scabbing over, the length of Joe Cordell's cheek. He was sullen, pouting; his father had been jawing him constantly since the fiasco at Barrington's place.

"How's Lew Ince?" asked Pate.

"Still livin' but he won't be much use any more. Slug caught him through the hip." Doc Cordell lit a cigar, blew out a puff of blue smoke. "I doubt if Lee Davis 'll be of help to us now, not after what happened. We'll have to figger what to do next. I don't aim to lose everything I got here."

Jake Cordell was the brains of the partnership. Pate the brawn. Pate was saying, "Trailed 'em to Bever Ford, but this cuss hung back and slowed us. Then, he blocked us on the mountain. Davis is back in Cheyenne with Warren Neale, safe and sound."

"Young Lee didn't stop you, though?"

"No, sir. I savvy just who it was, that white Indian, Slingerland! They tell me hung around here all day. It was Slingerland wounded Ince and Joe, and bedeviled us on the route that night. And if I ever killed man, so help me, I'll kill Slingerland. Slow, if I can. I know plenty Indian tricks to drag it out." In his rage, saliva drooled from Pate's lips, and he raved curses.

"Pop, I didn't understand—" began Joe Cordell.

"Dry up," snapped his father. "From here on, you do as I tell you and try to learn some sense."

"Did the boys come back from Wesleyvile yet?" asked Pate.

"Yeah, this afternoon. They buried the bodies and cleaned up some."

Pate yawned, swore again. "I ain't had any shuteye for two days. I'm goin' to turn in."

"All right. Now, George, there's only one thing we can do. Lee Davis didn't cotton to takin' a bribe, and Warren Neale's a stiffneck, too, so we probably couldn't make a deal with 'em. We'll have to get rid of Neale. I got political influence, and I'll pay to have another engineer outfit appointed to build that branch line, one I control."

Weary as he was, Pate was interested. "How you aim to dump Neale?"

"Neale lives south of Cheyenne. You savvy where his ranch stands. Contact Flint Heart and his braves. We'll use all our men, too, fix 'em up like Indians. You lead the attack, surprise Neale at night. And you know what's got to be done." Doc Cordell stared at his outlaw pard.

"Yeah, I know what to do!" Pate ground his teeth. "Maybe I can trap Davis and even Slingerland at Neale's. That'll be a pleasure!"

"You can make it look like another Sioux raid. They been strikin' far and wide."

"*Bueno*. Neale's wife is mighty pretty, the Indians 'll have a good time with her, and they can have that Penny female, too. We can't leave any witnesses. George, don't listen to anything Joe says."

Pate shrugged, stood up. "Suits me, fine. I'll get some shuteye and then we can lay out all the details."

176

The sun had warmed the beautiful wilderness.

In the Sioux village, Al Slingerland had bided his time, not asking direct questions, but steering the talk into channels from which he might discover what he needed to find out.

He learned that neither Crazy Horse nor Touch the Clouds had a high opinion of Flint Heart, though Flint Heart was a Sioux and couldn't be interfered with unless it was a strictly personal matter.

As for the warriors who followed Flint Heart like coyotes after rotten meat, said Crazy Horse, puffing at his short-stemmed pipe, they were hot-blooded young fools. "I do not like to lead such into battle, for they are hard to control and apt to strike before I give the signal. Yes, they have spoiled more than one trap by shooting too soon, killing a few when many might have been taken."

Slingerland knew Crazy Horse to be a master at decoy. The brilliant Oglala had engineered the Fort Fetterman massacre and other skillful engagements against both white and red foes.

"Flint Heart himself is a fool," said Touch the Clouds, blowing out bluish smoke. "It was he who shot the two Crow scouts leading the white soldiers into the clever pitfall arranged by my friend Crazy Horse, so we slew but seven instead of all. And I do not like men who beat their squaws. Had Flint Heart's wife, the one whose neck he broke in one of his rages, been my relative, he would have answered for it."

"*Hoye!*" agreed Crazy Horse. "But, like the Mountain Flower, she had no men to protect her. A runner just brought word that Flower's father will die. The white man's medicine cannot help him."

Burning with desire to know where Mountain Flower

was, Al at last found out when Touch the Clouds casually remarked, "I do not blame the girl for running away as she did. I hope Flint Heart never lays hands on her again. But he is a most skillful tracker, and where could such a woman go that Flint Heart cannot find her?"

Both chiefs glanced at the trapper with as much curiosity as was polite toward an honored guest. Slingerland had already guessed they were aware Flint Heart had tracked Flower to the cabin and had burned it in fury when he failed to recapture her.

He was relieved as he realized she must have escaped. This would explain what had happened to his chestnut gelding. Flower had heard or seen Flint Heart's band approaching and ridden off into the forest. He didn't mention the two braves he'd left dead near the ruins of his home; they were Flint Heart's men, but still they were Sioux.

The quiet, efficient Black Shawl had fastened back the tepee flaps, and Touch the Clouds, who was facing the entry, gave a snort. "Here comes Red Antelope, Flint Heart's heel-dog. Look at his pony! He has ridden another good horse to death."

Slingerland glanced over a hunched shoulder. A wide-bodied Sioux, eagle father drooped over his braids, face streaked with paint, naked torso caked with sweated dust, hopped off a heaving pinto just as the handsome animal collapsed. Without a backward glance, Red Antelope went to the creek, where he put down his weapons and then stretched on his belly to drink deeply of cold, clear water.

A dozen more braves straggled in from the north woods; they were weary, horses showing the effects of hard riding. Their squaws hurried over to take care of

178

the ponies and gear, as their men drank from the brook, then stalked toward their tepees, worn out, hungry. They were lithe young Sioux for the most part; each had bow and quiver, a new repeating carbine, and ever one carried the usual long knife in his rawhide belt.

"*Pagh!*" exclaimed Touch the Clouds suddenly. "Here comes that mighty killer of women!"

Slingerland swung so he could see more of the clearing. A huge Sioux, who was almost the size of Touch the Clouds, came riding in on a powerful, lathered black stallion, a white man's horse he'd undoubtedly stolen in a raid. The stud's chest was heaving, and he stepped slowly, pushed to the limit.

The trapper could see the sundance scars on Flint Heart's barrel breast; the chief was naked to the waist, a feather in his black hair, deerskin leggings and moccasins, a snake belt holding a Colt revolver and his knife. He had bow-and-arrows, a fine carbine as well. The eagle-nosed, painted face was a fierce one.

And Slingerland's heart fell, for on a lead-rope behind the black stallion came his chestnut gelding, also scratched and sweated, head drooped. On the chestnut's back Flower clung to the mane. She almost lay over the withers, so completely exhausted she couldn't raise her head. Then Slingerland saw her wrists were tightly fastened, though she could use her hands to grip the chestnut's thick mane. He rose and stepped outside. Flower's face was stained, her cheeks were mottled, and Al Slingerland thought the marks were fresh bruises, for he could make out a long, bloody welt on one side.

Now, Crazy Horse emerged and stood just behind the trapper; a moment later, the towering Minneconjou joined them.

An almost insane fury seized upon Al Slingerland. It

179

was plain Flint Heart had been abusing the girl again, after capturing her. It had been a long, hard search before they'd managed to overtake her.

Flint Heart slipped from his horse's back, stepped to the chestnut's lathered, heaving side. Reached up, he roughly pulled Flower from the gelding and cut the cords on her wrists. He shoved her toward his lodge and she went down on her knees, saving herself from falling over by using her right hand. The sprain had evidently improved since Slingerland had first found her, though as she glanced back, her face was contorted with pain. But she did not cry out.

Flint Heart shouted angrily, calling her the worst of names. His first squaw, an older, heavier woman, waited at the entrance to the lodge, and reaching out, helped Flower inside.

All the Indians in the village watched this display, stoical faces never changing expression. If Flower had any close male relatives there, none dared defend her. They knew Flint Heart would kill them if interfered with.

Flint Heart went over to the creek, laid down his weapons, and washed the sweated grime from his powerful torso. His hotheads, most of them young braves, only a few as yet displaying the sundance scars, ultimate test of a warrior's ability to withstand torture, followed their savage leader's example, cleaning up after the long, hard chase engaged in as they combed the forests for the runaway.

Now Flint Heart took a long drink of the cool crystal-clear water.

Refreshed, he rose to pick up his weapons and go to his lodge.

As he turned, he found his path blocked by the tall

steel-muscled figure of Al Slingerland, huge hands at his lean hips.

## IX

Flint heart was evidently surprised the trapper would dare come here, even more that Slingerland challenged him.

Slingerland figured Flint Heart had tracked Flower to the cabin, that she'd ridden off when she saw the band coming. So he'd destroyed the camp in his frustrated rage and left two tough killers to drygulch Al Slingerland when the trapper rode home.

"Go away, white-man spy," he said in guttural Sioux. "You are a *wasichu*, the Indian's enemy. I would kill you here but will wait for I don't wish to soil our village with your foul blood."

Slingerland answered coldly, deliberately, "Yes, Flint Heart, I will go. Gladly, since it makes me vomit to look on such as you. I will go—but my squaw must go with me!"

Flint Heart started, taken aback by the trapper's claim. He said, "The Mountain Flower is not your squaw. She is my property. I have bought her."

"I will give you what you paid her father. But I tell you, she is my woman, surely. She slept the night with me and freely gave herself to me. And the Teton law says that a wife may leave one husband for another if she chooses, provided she is a virtuous woman."

There was a low murmur of agreement from older Sioux behind Slingerland but he didn't turn, for he was watching Fint Heart's burning, furious eyes carefully. The chief held his carbine and bow and might attack at any instant.

"You are a liar, like all white men," growled Flint Heart.

Slingerland had lied when he'd claimed Flower had been his. But it was the only way he might save her from Flint Heart.

"Ask her, then," he replied coolly. "Ask the Mountain Flower if she is not my woman."

Flint Heart glanced toward his nearby lodge; in the V of the entrance, Flower squatted, listening, watching.

"Is what the white trapper says the truth?" he shouted at her.

The girl came out and stood, facing the village. Young and old, squaws, children, intently watched, listened.

"Yes," cried Flower. "Yes, I am his woman. I have never been yours, Flint Heart, and I will kill myself before I would!"

A murmur went through the interested gathering.

As Flint Heart's followers saw their chief facing the tall trapper, they had seized their weapons and strolled over to back him up. From the corner of his eye, Slingerland saw the towering figure of Touch the Clouds, who held a war axe in one mighty paw, and by him, Crazy Horse, fingering a razor-sharp knife. Several other Oglalas, who rode behind Crazy Horse, and a group of Minneconjou braves who had come to visit the Indian village with Touch the Clouds, had approached and waited silently, guns, bows and knives ready.

Flower's confession stunned Flint Heart but soon he recovered himself. "Then you must die, Slingerland. After that, I'll decide what to do with this faithless squaw. Perhaps I'll turn her over to my warriors for their pleasure, for she has dared defy the mightiest chief of the Dakotas."

"*Pagh!*" That was Touch the Clouds making the derisive sound as Flint Heart boasted of his prowess. "Someone who is talking has perhaps forgotten such as Tasunke Witko, Pizi, and possibly even a tall Minneconjou Sioux!"

But Crazy Horse was not so impulsive and always he had the good of his people at heart.

"It is not good for Sioux to fight Sioux," he declared. "This I do not like."

Never taking his eyes off Flint heart, Slingerland took a step back. He threw off his coonskin hat, unbuckled his gunbelt and dropped it with the heavy colt in its oiled holster. Removing his deerskin blouse, he stood naked to the waist, on his feet soft, laced moccasins.

Slowly, he drew his razor-sharp long skinning knife and raised it high over his bared head as he called Flint Heart the most insulting epithets known to the Sioux tongue.

An excited muttering came from the spectators. Knowing the customs of the Tetons, Slingerland had issued a personal challenge to Flint Heart. And in the tradition, this made it a man-to-man duel. Flint Heart knew this, as did all present.

"This *is* good," announced Crazy Horse loudly. "For it would be wrong that many die because two blood brothers do not agree."

The fascinated audience waited with bated breath.

Flint Heart's followers were heavily armed, ready to back up their chief.

But Touch the Clouds gripped a war axe in one large hand, idly swinging it, while Crazy Horse had a pistol and knife in his belt. A clot of Minneconjous, who had come here to visit along with Touch the Clouds, strolled over, waiting by their chief. There were older, seasoned Oglalas and Hunkpapas, warriors who rode always behind Crazy Horse.

In a general melee, Flint Heart's band would surely be defeated.

Acting as referee and *akicita* leader, those chosen to keep proper order in camp or in battle, Crazy Horse again spoke:

"I have said it is not good for Dakota to fight Dakota. So only these two enemies may take part in this struggle. It is our custom and must not be forgotten. Now, if either of these men turns away, refusing to continue, he is a coward and the squaws shall drive him from our tribe forever!"

The Oglala glanced around; none challenged him.

Flint Heart grunted. His black eyes shone with fire, his hand tight on his carbine. But he knew if he tried to use the rifle, he would be killed even though he slew his foe, the trapper. So he handed his carbine and bow, his belt with the revolver in it, to Red Antelope, keeping only his knife.

Crazy Horse motioned others to stand back so as to allow the antagonists plenty of space in which to maneuver. A silence fell as Slingerland and Flint Heart, long blades glinting, sized up one another.

The Hunkpapa outweighed the white man by fifty pounds. The great muscles in his arms and body were like steel bands, and all present knew that few could match him with the knife. Both men held their blades for slashing rather than for stabbing, flat in the palm of the hand, the needle-sharp point slightly raised.

It was Flint Heart who made the first move; he feinted left, and Slingerland easily avoided the quick movement, fast as a striking snake. He could see Flint

Heart was trying him out, to discover just how skillful and experienced Slingerland might be.

The Hunkpapa's set, savage face never changed expression as he watched the trapper's narrowed gray eyes. He tried again to the right, and once more Slingerland countered; this time, the trapper, expecting the move, sliced Flint Heart's left forearm, drawing a little blood, but the Indian took no notice of the superficial wound.

But from this and the way Slingerland handled himself, the white man's expert footwork, Flint Heart knew he was fighting a master, perhaps as good as himself. His deadly look did not flicker as he prepared for a difficult contest.

Slingerland, too, had no doubt he would be fortunate if he managed to defeat Flint Heart. Carefully, hoping the Indian wouldn't realize the trick, he slowly tried to switch position so that the sunlight, slanting in through the higher trees, would shine in the savage's eyes. But this nearly cost him a serious wound for Flint Heart knew exactly what he was doing and took advantage of it by crouching, whirling, his knife cutting through Slingerland's right trouser leg and gashing the flesh.

The tall, lean trapper felt blood flowing down into his laced moccasin but paid no heed to this.

Flint Heart, having found his enemy experienced, took no unnecessary chances. He had the Indian's patience, inexhaustible and calculating. And despite his training, Slingerland was a white man, and could not match this, though he knew a rash move might mean his death. As the minutes passed, the time seemed to drag out to Al Slingerland; he was eager, and his anxiety about Flower's fate was ever in the back of his alert mind.

185

His right moccasin sloshed now with his own blood. There was too much. His wound was bleeding more freely than he'd expected. If he lost too much, he would lose strength.

Determinedly, the trapper sought to force the right. Flint Heart was behaving as though he might be chary of closing, seeming to back off as Slingerland pushed in. The trapper decided, too, the Indian was slowing down; maybe he was weary from the long, hard search for Flower.

So Slingerland made his play. His concealed thrust was a deadly one and as he drove in, for a breath he felt triumphant, feeling he had won.

Too late, he realized that Flint Heart had decoyed him. The lithe Hunkpapa fell off, with a cougar's agility, and his knife cut deep into Slingerland's right side, the blood spurting from the terrible wound, several ribs showing white as the flesh was violently torn from over them.

Slingerland fell; with a howl of victory, Flint Heart leaped to his feet, lunging in on the white man for the kill, the gory blade driving straight for the trapper's heart.

Slingerland's right side was paralyzed; his hand, gripping the knife, would not answer his bidding. He knew he was dead, his head spun, and he was blacking out.

His confused thoughts flashed through his brain with kaleidoscopic speed. And the picture of Flower in Flint Heart's arms so horrified him that he made one final, incredibly desperate move. He didn't know how he'd managed it but he'd switched his knife to his left hand and he found the strength to hold it straight up.

Flint Heart saw it but he couldn't stop; all his great

weight and power had concentrated in ths final lunge. The dark eyes widened and the warwhoop of victory, issuing from his open mouth, died in his throat. Impelled by his own muscles, he tried to turn in midair but it was too late.

There was a sickening crunch as Slingerland's point ripped in the Hunkpapa's belly just at the soft, vital spot below the sternum, the Indian's final attempt to save himself causing the blade to turn and tear a frightful, wide gash which opened him up from one side to the other.

And the same frantic twist made his knife, plunging down, veer from its course and miss the kill, though the weapon sliced a chunk of flesh from Slingerland's thigh.

The heavy Indian lay, quivering, atop the long, lean body of his opponent.

But Al Slingerland was unaware of this. Flint Heart's weight had knocked out what little breath he had had left, and the world went black for the trapper.

## X

Slingerland awoke to a strange world. He head was spinning and he was unable to move either his arms or his legs.

When he breathed, it hurt.

For a time, colored lights played incessantly before his burning eyes. He tried to speak but no sound came from his throat.

After while, he grew aware of a strange odor. It was even an effort to think, and it was some time before he remembered what the aroma was; he'd smelled it when he'd lived with the Indians years ago. The old healing women, the medicine men, mixed revolting, stinking

187

poultices with which wounds were bound, an that was it.

It was too much trouble to do anything so he closed his eyes again and slept, deeply, without dreaming at all, lying on his back.

When he came to again, his head felt clearer and the pounding in his brain had diminished somewhat.

Too, he could see better. A pang went through him as he turned his head a bit.

He was lying on a bearskin, a blanket over him. At his side, he suddenly saw Mountain Flower, squatting by him. She dipped a cloth in a pail, wrung it out, and gently applied the cool rag to his hot face.

"Flower!" He thought he'd spoken aloud but it was only a whisper.

Her small hand touched his cheek.

"Al-al!" she murmured, as he had taught her, "Ye-ess, Al-al!"

His smile cracked his dry, parched lips. She held a tin cup of water to his lips so he could drink a bit.

The she rose.

"Don't—don't go," he whispered.

But she only called, in Sioux, from the tepee entry, for now he was in a lodge, the pine poles holding the hides, the opening in the top center where smoke could issue from the fire in the middle.

Flower came back to him and sat down. A medicine man appeared, entering the wigwam. His face was streaked with special paint, and he wore two buffalo horns sticking straight out from his forehead. In one hand he held a stick with large rattlesnake tails attached to it; when he shook this, it sounded like several of the deadly reptiles giving warning.

In the other, he gripped a three-pronged wand with

188

stuffed baby beaver on one tine, a dried animal heart on the second, an antelope's ears on the last. Long black hair hung down the shaman's back, the hair from a grizzly, and attached to it were bear teeth.

He knelt beside Slingerland and using the rattle and waving the special wand, began his incantations, glancing up at the home of the Great Spirit, then at the patient, then at the earth and in turn to the four great directions, north, south, east and west.

When the treatment was finished, the medicine man took his leave, and an ancient crone entered, carrying a steaming pot. The stink grew almost unbearable; she had heated the mixture of healing herbs and roots. Assisted by Flower, the Sioux squaw, her face deeply etched with innumerable wrinkles, began changing the trapper's dressings. This hurt; he evidently had four wounds, but it was the one in his right side that was by far the most serious, and he lost consciousness when the pads were removed from it . . . .

Next, Slingerland found Flower was holding his head in her soft lap. She had a cup of warm animal broth and was speaking to him in Sioux, telling him he must drink. He managed to swallow the liquid; it felt good in his stomach, which didn't reject it.

"Flint Heart?" he murmured.

"He is dead. Flint Heart died on your knife, Al-al."

Slingerland shook his head; he couldn't recall the end of the duel, or how he'd somehow managed to kill his deadly enemy.

He heard sounds not far away, the sounds of an Indian village. "Where are we?"

"Crazy Horse had a lodge set up on the far side of the creek. This was for you to lie in so I could take care of you and you would not be disturbed."

He thought this over, and drank more broth as she offered it. "How long?"

She held up one hand, fingers and thumb extended. "Five days!" he gasped.

Yes, Slingerland knew he was badly hurt. He had no desire to get up, even if he'd been able. And he had fever, he could tell that.

"Crazy Horse—is he here?"

Flower shook her head. "He rode with Touch the Clouds but said he would return. He left Oglala braves to watch so none may harm you, and warned Red Antelope he himself would deal with any who did so. And I am always at your side."

She patted her skinning knife. Nearby were Slingerland's guns and ammunition belts, while his pack and saddle lay at the rear of the lodge.

"Your horses are with the herd," she added.

His Indian friends had done everything possible for him, and he felt the deepest gratitude. And while he had lain like dead with the fever, probably raving at times, Flower must have attended to his bodily functions, cleaning him and nursing him as a mother would a sick child.

Then he remembered. "Will you bring my pack?"

She brought the roll and opened it as he asked. "The presents are for you, Flower."

She trilled with pleasure, holding up the bright cloth, trying on the necklace, examining the sewing kit, looking at the scissors, the silver thimble, the packet of needles and colored threads.

"You are the most beautiful woman I have ever seen, Flower."

At this, the color mounted in her rounded cheeks, and she dropped her long lashes modestly.

"I love you," he said gently. "If I grow well again, will you be my wife?"

Taking his big hand in hers, she looked straight into his eyes as she nodded.

He inquired what had happened after he'd left her at his camp. She had rested through the day, she said, and next morning had found her arm so much better, she'd used the awl and rawhide for mending leather to sew back the sleeve on her blouse. She made no fire, for the smoke might have been seen from far, and she dreaded Flint Heart. Even among the Indians, who could follow sign with magical skill, Flint Heart was acknowledged as a master tracker.

As the sun rose higher, so did her uneasiness increase. She'd slipped out and lassoed the chestnut gelding. She put a rope hackamore on the horse, a thick blanket on his back; taking a canteen of water and hardtack, she rode up to the north rim of the valley and hid in a dense spruce forest. Staking her mount, she slept on the soft bed of needles, wrapped in the blanket.

Awake at dawn, and watching, she saw, far below, the stealthy approach of Flint Heart and his band. Not finding her, they set fire to the buildings, and Flint Heart himself picked up the chestnut's rail. The gelding's hoofs were shod and this would make it more difficult for her to elude her pursuers.

She rode over the divide and into the next dip, seeking rock or shale areas where no marks might be left. Finally she lost herself in the wilderness mountains.

But Flint Heart was not to be shaken off, and eventually had located her hiding place, beaten her and tied her hands, brought her back.

That night Flower nestled by her man, the blanket covering them and her warm, soft body against his to

191

keep him from chilling in his sleep. Weak as he was, Slingerland felt intense joy; once he kissed her cheek, and she put her arms about him. She had given herself to him, without question, and he knew she would be his forever.

For two more days, the fever held. The healing woman left dressings off his wounds save for the bad one in his side, which was very grave. Flint Heart had come close to killing him. The Hunkpapa's blade had caused internal damage and must have cut nerves and muscles, for Slingerland had little control over his right side.

When he would ask the ancient healing woman how long he must lie there, she would only shake her head impatiently, and the medicine man came daily, making incantations.

When the fever subsided, his appetite returned. Flower fed him thick soups, venison and beat meat, Indian bread. She seldom left his side, but her squaw friends would bring her berries and roots, Nature's fruits, and give them to her.

She described the end of his hand-to-hand combat with Flint Heart, acting out parts of it, so he could visualize what had happened. At his lasp gasp, he'd somehow managed a final great effort and so had slain his opponent.

And Crazy Horse, with Touch the Clouds, had prevented Flint Heart's warriors from taking revenge by killing the white man.

"Now Red Antelope is their chief," Flower told him. "He is cruel, imitating Flint Heart, bad to his squaws, though he isn't the war leader Flint Heart was. Crazy Horse told Red Antelope not to come near you and not to say to anyone you are here. And Red Antelope fears Tasunke Witko.''

When the sun was warm, she would raise the tepee sides so Slingerland could see out. Ponies whinnied and stamped, small boys shouted as they played.

There was a sound at the lodge entry and Slingerland saw a young squaw, face painted with vermilion, and her braids tied with red ribbons. She was attractive, about Flower's age. She wore a copper bracelet and a necklace of vari-hued beads, while her deerskin blouse had the wide sleeves of Sioux women. Flower went out and joined her, and for a time, the man heard their voices, though he couldn't distinguish what they were saying.

Squaws knew everything that went on around a village, and they loved to gossip just as much as their white sisters.

Soon Flower returned, kneeling by him; her friend had brought some roots and ripe berries.

"She is Pretty Swan, Red Antelope's second squaw," she exclaimed. "We are the same age and played together when younger. She doesn't love her husband very much, for sometimes he is like Flint Heart."

Slingerland felt better, in a way, but still couldn't move freely. Flower would prop him up sometimes, but his side stayed numb, and when he tried to rise and walk, he would fall back with a groan. For an active, outdoor man, lying idle was sheer torture. Only the fact that Flower was always with him, waiting on his every need, made it bearable. And he knew he really loved her from the close intimacy they shared. It was far stronger than simple physical attraction.

Pretty Swan came daily to bring small gifts and chat

with Flower, and one afternoon, when her friend had left, Flower told the trapper there was excitement in the village. "The man who pays for killing has sent word he is coming to see Flint Heart. He doesn't know Flint Heart is dead, and Red Antelope says he will deal with him instead."

"The man who pays for killing?" repeated Slingerland.

After some questioning, he realized it was George Pate, Doc Cordell's gun boss. He had been to the village before, to see Flint Heart, and Flower had seen him from a distance. With him had been a second *wasichu*, a younger one, not so powerful, and Slingerland decided this had been Joe Cordell.

Pursuing this line, he learned that Flint Heart had led out some fifty hotheads one day—this was the day he had first caught Flower when she'd run off, and had said he was going on a raid but would return.

The time coincided with the destruction of Wesleyville, and Slingerland pressed for details. Flower did not know the name of the village but Flint Heart's braves and Red Angelope, had boasted of their great victory over the whites, laughing at how the men had rushed forth in their night clothes only to be shot down by the carbines furnished the Sioux by the one who had paid them, and describing in detail how the women had screamed and tried to protect their children, before they were scalped.

The man who paid for killing said none, not even the small ones, should be left alive. The great fire had been most satisfying, too, and the triumphant raiders, who had lost not even one man and with but two slightly wounded by stray bullets, had ridden into the village with the bloody scalps flying from their war lances

There had been a great dance and feast that night, Pretty Swan had informed Flower, who had not been present, since she'd escaped and then been rescued when Slingerland had found her.

Lying almost helpless, the trapper thought this all over. It was plain that Pate had bribed Flint Heart to level Wesleyville and kill all its inhabitants. And now Pate was again coming to the Sioux encampment.

He knew George Pate was not only a ruthless killer but a shrewd one, not easily tricked, and he wondered if Pate might have guessed who it was who'd held him off when he'd tried to overtake Lee Davis and Penny Barrington. He figured he himself would have surely decided it could only have been such an expert as himself. He would have been seen, hanging around town, and he'd talked with Vince Farley; without meaning to harm a friend. Farley would have told Pate Slingerland had been asking questions, and the gun-linger would draw the right conclusions.

Crazy Horse had had the lodge set up on the other side of the creek, away from the main village, but if Pate found the trapper was here, he might come for his revenge. He told Flower this, and she seemed worried, but then said, "Crazy Horse ordered Red Antelope and I not to tell you are here."

But he had her move his bed to a point from which he could look out and watch the approach; then he asked her to fetch his rifles and Colt. She helped him clean them and he checked them carefully, putting in fresh loads, making sure they were ready for action.

If Pate came for him, it would be at a high cost to the gunslinger, Slingerland promised himself grimly. He could work his rifles and the revolver, in spite of his wound and the weakness, use his left hand if he had to, to shoot at close range.

Maybe Pate was riding here just to hunt him down He asked Flower if she would see Pretty Swan, and tel her friend, who was Red Antelope's squaw, to listen a much as she could and then quickly as possible le Flower know what the white man wanted.

Next morning, word flashed through the village tha the man who paid for killing was riding in.

Slingerland had Flower lower the tepee sides, jus leaving a gap in the entrance so he could see across th brook to the village.

She squatted beside him and they watched.

Three whites rode slowly in from the trail, escorted b several young warriors, who had taken part in th Wesleyville raid. Red Antelope stepped forth to gree them, and the visitors got down. From a distance Slingerland recognized Pate, in his black hat, dark shir and gun rig. Joe Cordell wasn't along this time, bu there were two other toughs that he knew were gunnie in Pate's gang.

Slingerland held his carbine in his left hand observing the scene across the creek. After a time, Pa and Red Antelope entered the latter's lodge; and soo bluish smoke issuing from the open flap gold they wer smoking pipes as they parleyed together. Pretty Swa and Red Antelope's first squaw were serving the men

Pate's gunnies squatted in the shade, sharing tobacc with some of the braves, talking in sign with them.

The trapper made ready as George Pate final emerged from Red Antelope's tepee. But Pate didn even glance across the stream. He nodded and shoc hands with Red Antelope, and mounting, rode back t way he'd come in, followed by his comrades.

An hour later, Pretty Swan slipped to the lodge a

spoke for some minutes with Flower.

Flower seemed relieved when she returned to Slingerland.

"Red Antelope didn't dare speak of you, but Pretty Swan says the man who pays for killing said he'd stopped and seen your camp had been destroyed. He believes you are dead, probably slain when Flint Heart struck your home. And Red Antelope let him think this, for it seemed to make no difference, to the Sioux, anyway. The *wasichu* hadn't known Flint Heart was dead, but Red Antelope said he'd died during another raid. So the man who pays for killing hired Red Antelope to bring fifty warriors to Bubbling Spring three days from today."

"Do you know why?"

"Pretty Swan says it is to kill more whites and to burn a ranch, near the place they called Cheyenne, after our blood brothers."

Bubbling Spring, Slingerland was well aware, was about five miles south of Cheyenne. It was not far from the valley road, some distance above the site of Wesleyville.

"Did Pretty Swan say who these whites are who must be slain?"

"No. The braves will kill the males but may take the women for their pleasure, and any horses at the ranch. The man who pays for killing will direct the raid and has over a score of Gray Men, whites disguised as Indians, who will take part to make sure all is done as he wishes. There are enough Gray Men to crush this ranch without Sioux to help, but he wishes warriors to be present, too."

Slingerland digested this uneasily. Pate wanted savages along, so blame would be placed on them.

Otherwise clever lawmen might realize outlaw whites had struck. Finally he said, "When you can, find Pretty Swan and ask if she knows who is to die in this raid on the ranch."

After a time, Flower left him. And without realizing at first what he was doing, Slingerland found he was moving his right arm and leg a bit. He tried again, carefully, and hope sprang in his heart. Volition had returned to his muscles. The terrible injury was healing!

Flower came back. She shook her head; Indians seldom used whites' names, strange to their tongue. They usually referred to individuals by descriptive phases. General George Crook, was "Three Stars," while the bitter foe of the Cheyennes, George Custer, was "Yellow Hair." But as the girl told what Pretty Swan had said, he caught something which gave him a violent shock: "The raid will be at the home of the *wasichu* who builds the iron roads which split the Indians' land," Mountain Flower told the trapper.

Warren Neale! The engineer's ranch lay a short ride north of Bubbling Spring. Lee Davis and Penny Barrington had gone there.

And so Pate, with Red Antelope's killer pack and the gunnies decked out as savages, would slaughter Neale and other males, capture Allie and Penny, the Neale children. Knowing Pate's ruthless nature, Slingerland decided Cordell's gun boss had enough killers of his own and would do the job whether the Sioux took part or not.

# XI

Late that afternoon the medicine man again made incantations over his patient. Slingerland was sitting patient. Singerland was sitting up. He nodded to Mountain Flower, who hovered anxiously by as he rose to his feet. He'd have fallen had she not caught his arm. The change in circulation made his head spin, and he was weak, but he was determined. With the Indian girl at his elbow, he walked slowly from the lodge into the sunshine.

The medicine man was elated. He began howling, for all to see how he had healed the one who had been dying but was now cured, thanks to his powers. He demanded more payment. Slingerland had given away all he could spare from his packs but he found a few coins in a pocket.

The medicine man knew exactly what he would do with them; he would drill holes in the metal discs and add them to his necklace.

The ancient healing woman squatted nearby, shaking her head. She still kept a dressing on that side wound and Slingerland had grown accustomed to the foul odor of the herbs.

Shrill whinnies and a bray rang out. Slingerland's stud, the mule and the chestnut gelding came trotting along, and he greeted them with pats and reassuring words.

There was a stir across the creek. Crazy Horse, Touch the Clouds and a dozen warriors appeared. Squaws hurried to take the ponies as the lithe men jumped down.

More Indians came in driving a bunch of horses stolen from whites; some had fresh scalps waving from their lances, though Crazy Horse's sacred medicine forbade that he keep trophies. The Oglala would give away whatever he captured.

"Pizi," said Flower, awe in her voice.

Slingerland knew Pizi was Chief Gall, the war chief of the Hunkpapa Sioux, noted as brave among the brave. He recognized the tall, powerful figure as Gall slipped off his paint pony, rifle in hand, arrows and bow strapped to his bronzed, strong back, hair braided with ribbon, an eagle feather drooped to one side.

While Crazy Horse and Sitting Bull were spiritual as well as military leaders, Gall was entirely practical and was a great field general.

Red Antelope and the young Hunkpapas greeted Gall with tribal acclaim. After they had washed themselves at the stream, the raiders gathered around a central fire to eat, talk, and many of the braves danced around, describing their great fea.- during the foray.

Al Slingerland was glad to return to his soft bed of furs in the tepee. The walking had exhausted him. Flower fixed food and hot drink for him; then, when both had eaten, he asked her to cross the creek and learn the news brought by Crazy Horse, Gall and the rest.

Darkness fell over the village; through the open flap of the lodge, Slingerland watched the dancing red flames of the great fire, and he heard the whooping, the loud voices of the painted Indians dancing about the center of the clearing.

After some time, Flower returned. Crazy Horse and Gall had been raiding the whites' Holy Road many miles to the north. They had killed some walking soldiers, burned wagons and houses, stolen horses and other things. And Gall had brought word that Sitting Bull said because the whites had stolen *Pa Sapa*, the sacred Black Hills of the Sioux, the Dakotas would congregate at new rendezvous to conduct their annual religious and tribal ceremonies. They would all join together on the eastern slopes of the Big Horn mountains, farther west

So, this village must soon start moving to another site. The hunters had brought in plenty of game but it was growing scarce in the vicinity, and it was the habit of the Teton's to wander about, for better forage, easier food supplies, and sanitary reasons.

"We will fashion a travois so you can ride easily," said Flower brightly, touching her husband's hand.

"Maybe I'll be able to fork a horse soon," said Slingerland.

This worried Flower. The healing woman had said jolting might reopen the terrible wound in his side.

Dancing and feasting went on far into the night. Flower fell asleep by the tall trapper, soft and warm against him. According to Indian law, they were married; she had moved into his lodge.

Slingerland lay awake for hours, hearing the shouts and music across the creek. He must decide what to do, for it was plain to him that Doc Cordell intended to kill all who opposed him.

As long as Cordell and Pate were on the warpath, Warren Neale, Lee Davis, and their loved ones would be in imminent danger of death. And the trapper figured Pate would kill him at the first opportunity, when he found Slingerland was alive!

He must warn Neale. But how? He couldn't ride yet; a few steps had been almost too much for him. And Pate, with Red Antelope's reckless band, would soon attack Neale's home.

At last, a nebulous idea formed in his mind. He wasn't sure whether or not it would be feasible, but he must try. Then he slept, but uneasily, starting alert now and again.

Flower rose quietly at sunrise, moving about silently, preparing his breakfast. When he roused, he spoke to

201

her, and she came to him, smiling at him. He held out his hand and she knelt by him, kissing his lips as he drew her closer, the way he liked in the white man's way.

The sunshine penetrated the mountain camp, warming the chill air, drying the frosted dew. The squaws grew busy at their many tasks, and groups of men talked together, smoking their pipes.

Later, when Flower helped him up, he found he was stronger, able to walk about for a while, his woman by his elbow. And he asked Flower to cross the brook and speak to Crazy Horse for him.

"Bring Tasunke Witko and Pizi here to me," he said.

Before noon, Crazy Horse, Touch the Clouds and Gall came into the lodge. It was a great honor to have such guests and Flower bustled about, serving them.

Crazy Horse looked at his white brother, and essayed a jest:

"Yes, you are really a paleface," he said, grim lips relaxing for a moment, and Touch the Clouds agreed, "Hoye!" Gall, too, seemed amused. For the confinement, the suffering, showed their effects in Slingerland's drawn features, chalking under his tan.

The three chiefs listened to Slingerland's plan.

Finally, Crazy Horse said, "*Hou*!" Yes, it was good.

"But Red Antelope," said Slingerland. "He has promised to meet the Gray Men at Bubbling Spring with fifty or more Hunkpapas."

Gall spoke then. "We will see whether the Hunkpapas would rather ride with Red Antelope than with Pizi!"

Touch the Clouds grinned, nodded. "The coyote flees when the lion approaches!"

Details were discussed. There was little time, for the Gray Men and Red Antelope would strike soon. The warriors would make ready the following day and start off, for they must travel on hidden trails through the rugged mountains so they wouldn't be seen, and sleep, rest at the rendezvous in order to be fresh for the raid on Warren Neale's.

That afternoon, Slingerland asked Flower to rope his bay stallion and bring the stud to the lodge. She looked alarmed at this; it wasn't a squaw's place to argue with her husband, but she feared he would be hurt if he rode.

But Slingerland was adamant, and finally Flower went off to find the bay.

She rode the big animal back and tied him outside the tepee; then she saddled him and helped Slingerland to his side. It was an effort, but the tall trapper mounted. It felt good to be in the saddle again. Slingerland drew in a deep breath of the cool, aromatic air, as he spoke soothingly to the bay. Reddy had grown accustomed to the Indian odors and the pony herd in his stay near the encampment. He whisked his long tail, showing he was glad to see his human friend.

Flower stood outside the lodge, anxiously watching as Al Slingerland moved off at a walk, and rode slowly up the creek until he came to a shallows. He set the bay across, and worked back into the village proper. The jogging hurt his side but it wasn't severe.

Up the way he saw a congregation of warriors. They were declaiming, some of them, while the rest listened. Gall was there, Red Antelope, Grazy Horse, Touch the Clouds, and others Slingerland knew.

He drew near enough so he could hear what they were saying, sitting his saddle.

Red Antelope's face was sullen. He was pointing at one young brave after another, those who had followed Flint Heart in the Wesleyville massacre, saying they must make ready to ride with him.

But Gall raised his hand.

"Who would follow Pizi?" he said in a loud voice. "I will see there are scalps and guns and horses, plenty of glory for the Hunkpapas. This I promise. Those who would go with Pizi rather than with Red Antelope will step to my side."

Now Crazy Horse pushed in. "I will be beside Pizi on this raid," he announced. And Touch the Clouds, too, agreed.

Two tall warriors moved over to Gall; then several more, and finally, Red Antelope stood alone.

Fury burned in Red Antelope's dark eyes; he dropped a hand to his knife, glaring at Gall, who coldly outstared him..

Then, Red Antelope turned and went inside his tepee. A chief was no longer a chief when he had no followers.

Gall and Crazy Horse, the towering Touch the Clouds, seemed vastly amused. "Make ready," ordered Gall. "Bring weapons and your fastest ponies. Tell your squaws to fill parfleches with food for the trip." He swung, going off toward the lodge where he slept.

Slingerland walked Reddy nearer to Crazy Horse.

"I, too, will follow you," he said in Sioux.

The Oglala looked up at him; then he nodded. It was his white friend's decision, and Crazy Horse considered it was the best way for a man to die, if he must, in battle. What else was there?

## XII

It was a hard run for Al Slingerland. Every jolt hurt his side, and he felt weak. Yet the wound hadn't broken open, for he felt no blood seeping from the tight bandage the healing woman had put on before he left the village.

He left his heavy Creedmore with Mountain Flower but had his carbine and plenty of ammunitioin, as well as his Colt revolver and long knife. Crazy Horse, Touch the Clouds, Gall and the braves following them were also heavily armed.

Crazy Horse had several seasoned, veteran Oglala warriors sifting ahead as scouts for the main party.

"I do not trust the hotheads who ride with Flint Heart." he told the trapper. "They will spoil the ambush if they're not held back."

Pizi, Chief Gall, was in command of the young ones. And Gall was a master of decoy, just as Crazy Horse was. If anyone could control the youthful Hunkpapas, Gall could do it. He was a revered war leader.

They had ridden at good speed through the night, under the moon, winding on animal trails over the wooden mountains.

Two of Crazy Horse's scouts hooted as they reached a wagon road and they pulled up. The scouts reported all clear, and they formed a long, snakelike single file as they shoved north on the shadowed side of the route. Slingerland knew exactly where they were; several familiar needle spires on the right marked the range along the route to Cheyenne. Wesleyville lay miles south, and Bubbling Spring was close at hand.

The going was easier on the beaten track. They swung off it, along a path, and soon saw the glint of the pools, catching the low, soothing sound of water gurgling from the great boulders. The scouts were already in the clearing and had watered their ponies, then led them back, leaving them hidden in the trees nearby.

Slingerland grunted and cursed as he dismounted. He

was stiff, and he fought against the weakness. He let the bay stallion drink, and the Indians saw to their mounts, they lay flat on their lean bellies and refeshed themselves.

Bubbling Spring was a favorite resting spot for wayfarers. A high precipice loomed, black in the night. At its base was a jumble of huge rocks fallen from above. Melt from mountain snows and ice formations fed the spring, never failing in droughts. There was a large pool, where otters, muskrats and water birds loved to play. A brook was formed here and not far below was a beaver dam. The willow-branch domes of the busy animals' homes showing on the surface of the pond. The stream meandered off through the forest, finally finding its way into Crow Creek.

Now the masterful Crazy Horse prepared the ambush. Gall concealed the Hunkpapas in a semicircle around the ponds; strict orders were issued that no warrior must open fire until he gave the word. Slingerland donned a Sioux buffalo-horn headdress, streaking daubs of war paint on his upper cheeks and fastened a dark bandana around his neck, so he could quickly pull it up and hide his beard. He was glad to rest, and ate from the parfleches with the others as they waited.

Frogs, night birds, splashings of animals could be heard, and a wolf howled in the distance. There was a sound of brush crackling and a small herd of antelope came to the west edge of the pool to drink; the hidden, silent savaged did not startle them.

And at last, Crazy Horse's watching sentinels stole in, whispering the *wasichus* were coming.

Crazy Horse and Gall rose; Touch the Clouds, several warriors behind him, stood to the rear of the two leaders, while Slingerland adjusted his mask and waited behind the towering Minneconjou.

They could hear the white men coming long before they reached the rendezvous on the east side of Bubbling Spring.

Slingerland, peeking past Touch the Clouds, saw the dark shapes of horsemen. They wore Indian headdresses and their faces gleamed in the faint light with paint they had donned as a disguise. These were Gray Men, killers who robbed and slew, their crimes laid to the savages.

The riders pulled up in a bunch; Slingerland figured there were a score of them. Their rifle barrels glinted in the faint light.

"Red Antelope!" a man in front called softly. "*Hou, cola!*"

Pizi stepped forward.

"Here," he said. Gall could speak some English.

A match flared, and in its yellow light Slingerland recognized George Pate, sitting a big black. Pate wore an Indian disguise, but the trapper knew him at once, the shape of his torso, and his eyes. Cordell's gun boss touched the match to a bull's-eye wick, adjusted it and opened the slide a bit.

The beam fixed on the powerful Hunkpapa chief. "Say, you ain't Red Antelope! I savvy you, Gall. Seen you before!"

Gall spoke smoothly, using some English, filling out with sign: "Red Antelope—pony fall—must lie in tepee —squaw and medicine man—Red Antelope tell Pizi— meet *wasichu*—"

Pate hesitated; then he growled, "Where're your braves? All men at the ranch must die—you can have the women and horses, savvy?"

"Warriors near, we kill," promised Gall.

"If you don't, we'll do the job. I got plenty for it. It's

207

gettin' late. We better hustle."

"Guns!" Gall demanded.

Pate turned to a disguised man on a gray by his side. "Joe, get back and tell Dan Wain to bring up the rifles and ammo."

Slingerland decided the assistant was Joe Cordell, fixed up as an Indian. Joe Cordell pulled rein and started to the rear. Evidently Pate had a small pack train near the road, with the weapons for the Sioux.

And now, before Chief Gall gave the signal, for he wished to draw all into the carefully planned trap, shrill warwhoops rang out, and carbines began flaming. Hotblooded young warriors leaped up from their hiding places, yelling and shooting as they rushed upon the massed horsemen.

"It's a trap—a trap!" bawled George Pate, whipping up his repeating carbine. "Back—get back!"

He swung his rifle, aiming at Gall. It belched fire and smoke but Pizi had accurately and coolly beaten Pate to it, and the gunny's bullet shrieked past the chief's ear as he put two slugs into George Pate. The black stallion reared, snorting, trumpeting in fright; several supple braves rushed in, bodies gleaming with grease and paint. Strong hands pulled the white man from his saddle, knives flashed. Pate was slashed to pieces and a Sioux lifted his scalp, another seized the black's bridle so the fine animal couldn't run off.

The glade rang with war whoops and exploding guns. "*Hoka hey, hoka hey*!" howled the warriors as they hurled themselves on the Gray Men. Colts flamed and several Sioux were wounded, but the struggle lasted only a brief minute.

Slingerland had started in, with Touch the Clouds, and Crazy Horse, disgusted because, again, the young

208

braves had jumped ahead of his signal.

"Hurry, or the packs will be lost!" cried Crazy Horse, rushing past the savage melee. The hotheads, eager for personal glory, were lifting scalps, snatching up weapons, stripping and mutilating the whites. Wounded horses gave unearthly screams, kicking as they lay, blood seeping into Bubbling Spring.

Several of Pate's men had been to the rear, guarding the pack horses; and when they realized what was happening, had turned and ridden back to the road. Some dropped the lines but others had tied them to their saddles and the laden animals followed behind.

Slingerland couldn't keep up with his swift Indian friends; his breath came in gasps and he was weak. Crazy Horse shot two fleeing Gray Men out of their saddles, for above all, he wanted to secure the rifles and ammunition, roped on the pack animals.

Slingerland stopped; he could run no farther. He went slowly back, avoiding the horrible melee as savages shrieked in triumph, hacking the wounded and dead, waving bloody scalps, dancing and counting their coups, boasting of their bravery.

A quick fire had been started with oil from Pate's lantern and dry brush, flames licking high, lighting the awful scene. The sickening, acrid smell of blood came to the tall trapper's flared nostrils as he found his bay stud, mounted, and started for the highway.

By nature, Al Slingerland was kind, and enjoyed helping others. He respected decent men, no matter what their color. The savagery of the Indians was frightful, but he had seen whites who excelled them in cruelty. He knew the redmen were making a desperate, hopeless last stand. Their lands, their way of life, were nearly lost to them, and they were cheated and starved by the Indian agents, looked upon as animals by most white settlers.

At the road, he found that Crazy Horse and his trusted Oglalas had caught most of the pack animals, cases of rifles, ammunition and other goods on them with which Pate had expected to bribe the Sioux to wipe out Neale.

"How many got away?" Slingerland asked the chief.

"Seven or eight," replied Crazy Horse. "We would have had all if the fool young men had obeyed me. Now we must hurry, for the alarm will be given and horse soldiers come after us."

Yes, thought Slingerland, and some who had escaped would ride hard to Cordell City, report the fiasco to Doc Cordell. And Cordell, wealthy and powerful, would swiftly and easily gather together a new band of killers. Knowing Cordell, he realized Neale, Davis, and he himself would never be safe while Cordell was free to strike.

But he was exhausted. The wound had sapped him, the hard ride here taken what little strength he'd recovered while Flower nursed him. He spoke with Crazy Horse.

"I must go to Cheyenne, to my friend," he said. "I can ride no longer, and the iron-road builder's isn't far from here. Will you tell Flower I'll come for her very soon?"

"Yes, I will tell her," promised the chief.

"If the village moves, I'll follow. But Flower and I will soon begin to live in white-man ways, Crazy Horse. She is my wife."

"It is good." The great Sioux's eyes gleamed in the faint light. "For the Indians cannot fight much longer, my brother. Already many have given up and gone to

210

the reservations. In a few years, the Sioux will be like children, at the *wasichu's* mercy, whipped and cheated like dogs. This I know, and so does Sitting Bull and Gall, but we would die like men, killed in battle, rather than live like old women.''

Slingerland shook his friend's hand. "I'll never take up arms against my red brothers. Perhaps one day we'll meet again.''

"Perhaps.''

Crazy Horse ordered no pursuit of the handful who had eluded his trap, for he wished to escape with the precious arms and ammunition.

Slingerland rode off north, toward Cheyenne, with dawn at hand. His head spun and blood seeped from his bandaged side.

The night soon gave way to grayness, then fuller light. As a matter of habit, Slingerland's piercing, shrewd eyes scanned the ground ahead as he moved, and bay stallion easy under him on the road. And soon, able to make out details, he saw marks of shod hoofs, knew the sign was fresh. A rider was not far ahead of him. Noting some dark spots in the lighter dirt of the track, he dismounted to examine one, stooping and feeling the earth with sensitive fingers. The stains were wet.

"One of 'em came this way, Reddy," he told the cud. "He's bleedin!''

So he grew very cautious, glancing this way and that. He hadn't made more than a mile from Bubbling Spring when he ripped rein, turning the bay off. A heavy bullet shrieked over his head.

He pulled his horse into the thick growth along the highway, tied to a branch, and with his carbine cocked and ready, stole through the brush. Pausing to listen, he heard a horse snort, a few yards ahead. Inching on, soundlessly, he crouched and studied the gray stallion, a magnificent mount, standing in a small open space. A man lay there, on his side, a Colt in his left hand, his horse's rein looped to his arm. He was staring with wide, pain-wracked and frightened eyes toward the road, his revolver cocked and ready to fire.

Slingerland recognized him; it was Joe Cordell. Carbine raised and aimed, the trapper jumped in close behind him.

"Drop it!" he snapped.

Joe Cordell let go of the pistol. He looked around and began to bawl. "Don't—don't shoot me. Please don't scalp me. My father 'll pay you a big ransom—oh, have mercy!" He began blubbering in an ecstasy of fear.

Slingerland realized he still wore the Indian headdress; to Joe Cordell he looked like a savage. "It's me Al Slingerland, Joe. I won't kill you." He kept a bead on Cordell as he removed his disguise.

Joe Cordell sobbed like a baby. I'm dyin', Al, dyin' Get me to a doctor, for God's sake!"

Slingerland stepped in and kicked the Colt out of reach, then knelt by young Cordell. He'd caught a bull in the back as he had fled from Bubbling Spring. Pa had sent him to bring up the packs, and when the attack had begun, Joe Cordell had run for it, heading for Cheyenne.

The trapper carefully cut away Cordell's shirt, soaked with blood. The slug had entered under his right shoulderblade, ranging up, but hadn't emerged; it was still in there. The trapper fashioned a rough bandage from the shirttails, and lifted Cordell, who cried out agony as he was hoisted to his saddle.

"Hold on," said Slingerland. "I'll take you in and get you a sawbone."

He led the gray to the road, picked up Reddy, and mounted, rode toward Cheyenne in the cool dawn. He used a bandanna to wipe the war paint from his face, and took his coonskin hat from a saddlebag, setting in on his head.

The sun was up and it was breakfast time as he rode into Neale's.

## XIII

Warren Neale, Lee Davis, Allie and Penny had greeted their old friend with open arms, fed him and given him warm drinks.

Joe Cordell had sipped a little water but was coughing blood, and kept insisting he was dying. Slingerland and Neale had stood by him as he lay on a cot in a side bedroom. Slingerland bent over slightly.

"You were were Pate when the Sioux wiped out Wesleyville, Joe," said the trapper sternly. "I can swear to it, for I traced your horse back to Cordell City. There was a cracked shoe on your animal, and the blacksmith can identify it."

"I—I didn't do anything that night," Joe wailed. He was very weak, almost delirious with pain and fear. "Pate hired Flint Heart and his braves. My father told him to—"

"It's a Federal offense to encourage Indians to attack whites," broke in Neale angrily. "Your father will go back to prison."

"It wasn't my idea," moaned the youth. "My—my side's killin' me. Ain't that doctor ever comin'?"

"I sent a man in right away; he should be here any minute," Neale said. "Al, you need attention, too. Your wound's bleeding."

213

The trapper and engineer returned to the kitchen. Allie, Lee Davis and Penny, who had been married shortly after reaching the ranch, were there, and sitting down with them, Slingerland gave a quick account of all that had happened, and how he had married Mountain Flower.

"I'll have the Federal marshal in Cheyenne make out a warrant for Doc Cordell's arrest," declared Neale. "He deserves to swing."

"Sure he does. But you better hurry," Slingerland advised. "Some of Pate's gunnies escaped Crazy Horse's trap and they'll warn Jake. He can easy collect another gang and he won't quit easy. Long as Doc's loose, we're all in danger, includin' me. Joe Cordell will do anything to save his own hide, even turn in his father."

The doctor came riding in with Neale's courier. The physician had been a Civil War surgeon and was expert on gunshot wounds. The trapper insisted he take care of Joe Cordell first, and the sawbones worked on the youth for over an hour.

He came into the kitchen, and Allie poured himself a mug of hot coffee.

"Will he pull out of it?" asked Slingerland.

The stocky, bearded doctor shrugged. "I think he'll live. But he'll never be the same again, gentlemen. I got the bullet out. It looks like a carbine slug though it hit bones and is badly mashed. Did a lot of damage in there, and his arm will be almost useless."

He drank gratefully of the warm coffee. "I gave him plenty of opium, so he'll rest and sleep a while, anyhow. But he'll suffer a good deal for days. I'll leave something here for him."

Later, the doctor carefully examined Slingerland's wound. "By George, sir, I don't know how you came out of this so well! The fresh bleeding is superficial. In time, you'll recover entirely. The knife slashed your liver, maybe, and other vital organs, but that Indian medicine man did a fine job, good or better'n most white surgeons."

"I guess it was the old squaw, the healing woman, as they call her," said Slingerland. "Her poultices must've worked."

The doctor picked up the old bandage which had been on Al's wound and sniffed at it. Then he nodded. "Yes. I wish I could get some of their secret prescriptions. They've learned a great deal from nature, some of 'em."

Later on his great bay stud, Al Slingerland led the way into Cordell City. Behind him rode Warren Neale, Lee Davis, Federal Marshal Ed Thomkins of Cheyenne with a large posse he had sworn in.

A satisfying sleep, hearty meals, fresh dressings on his wound, had braced Slingerland, though he hadn't entirely recovered from the severe hurt dealt him by Flint Heart. Neale had begged him to stay and rest at the ranch, but the trapper was determined to help capture Doc Cordell. He'd scouted ahead, approaching the settlement so they wouldn't be noticed until they were near the Colorado Queen, Cordell's headquarters.

The morning sun bathed the plaza and buildings in warm yellow light. Wagons and saddle animals waited in front of the busy stores, women in bustled dresses and sunbonnets, small children tagging along, were doing their shopping, oldsters whittled on benches near the square, and men in range clothing moved to and fro.

Slingerland eased past the rear of the structures at the north end, and rode through Tin Can Alley. He heard the clang of Vince Farley's hammer as he neared the blacksmith's forge. Near the back entry to the Colorado Queen, he dismounted, and leading Reddy between two stables, tied the stallion to a post ring. Neale, David and Thomkins, with the hard-bitter possemen, drew up nearby and secured their mounts.

Colt and knife in his belt, the tall, bearded trapper, coonskin cap cocked on his head, walked with swift, long strides toward Cordell's lair, his friends hurrying after him.

As he stepped through the doorway, eyes adjusting to the dimmer light of the long passageway to the front of the saloon, a harsh voice suddenly challenged: "Hold on there! Where you think you're goin'—" The man broke off with a voilent curse.

Slingerland dropped fast, hunkering to the wall as he whipped out his Colt. He could see the figure down the hall, a tough in cowboy garb, a sawed-off shotgun in his h ands. And the fellow was raising the weapon, evidently recognizing Slingerland.

The shotgun boomed, the explosion echoing in the aisle. But its load slashed splinters from the pine floor, for Slingerland had thrown one a breath ahead, and the shotgunner was doubling up as his finger squeezed trigger.

Warren Neale, pistol in hand, Marshal Thomkins, young Lee Davis, and the posse members crowded through. "Al—are you hit?" cried Neale.

"No. C'mon. Cordell must've been expectin' us!"

He loped to the closed door which he knew led into Cordell's private quarters, and raising the latch, kicked it open, but then drew back. He could see in now, and quickly checked the room.

"Who's that? What's the shootin'?" called a com manding voice.

Now Slingerland saw Jake Cordell. The boss sat behind a long table, facing the entrance. He was in his shirtsleeves, blue garters holding up his cuffs, which had diamond-studded gold links in them. The thick watch chain, elk's-tooth fob hanging from it, gleamed over his fancy vest, and his think hair was pomaded across his large head, bit ears reddened. The stubborn jaw was thrust out.

Slingerland couldn't tell whether Doc Cordell was armed or not; the fat, hairy hands rested easily on the table top, but he might have a gun in his lap, hidden by the table.

Warren Neale and Marshal Thomkins entered, and Lee Davis, the posse members, bunching behind the leaders.

"I have a warrent, Cordell," announced Thomkins gravely. "You're under arrest."

Cordell blinked mildly. "What are the charges, sir?"

"Yoiu instigated and armed a band of Sioux Indians to destroy the village of Wesleyville. Men, women, children, all were massacred."

Cordell gave an incredulous laugh. "Why, that's loco! I can produce dozens of witness who'll swear I never left here that night!"

"I don't doubt it. But that doesn't relieve you of the blame. It's a Federal offense to furnish the savages with guns and egg them on to attack our citizens."

"That may be, but what's it got to do with me?" Doc Cordell almost beamed, and didn't seem at all alarmed. "I'd like to see you prove such a ridiculous accusation in a court of law, Thomkins!"

"Your agent, George Pate, carried rifles and ammunition to the Indians and in your name ordered them

217

to strike and wipe out all people in Wesleyville," said Thomkins coolly. "We have a written and sworn deposition clinchin' it."

"What goes on here?" demanded a gruff voice.

Stu Barrington, the fat town marshal, pushed through, entering the room.

"Mr. Barrington!" cried Lee Davis. "Penny is fine. We were married in Cheyenne. We are—"

Barrington scowled at Davis.

"You abducted my daughter," he growled.

"She's of age, and she went willingly. She and I want you to come live with u. Penny's worried about you."

Lee Davis held out his hand. Barrington seemed shaken; he looked down, but then he shook hands with his new son-in-law. "Well, I guess it's all right, Lee. You're a good boy."

Barrington waddled over to his master, the boss of Cordell City. "What's up, Mr. Cordell? Anything I can do to help?"

The diversion had stopped Thomkins as he accused Cordell. Now he said, for Barrington's benefit. "Cordell had George Pate arm the Sioux and sick 'em on Wesleyville, Stu. He's my prisoner."

"Tell 'em I was here that night, Barrington," ordered Doc.

"Sure he was," said Barrington earnestly. "Never left town."

"He's still guilty. He ordered Pate to do the dirty work."

Barrington shook his head, bewildered. "But, why would he do such a thing?"

Warren Neale stepped forward, said severely, "I'll tell you why. Cordell was determined to have the new branch railroad come through his town. It would have meant a great fortune for him. But the route's impossible; he tried to bribe Davis to recommend it, but no honest engineer could do so. Slingerland'll tell you Cordell sent Pate to pay the Sioux to kill me, hopin' he could make a deal with the new engineers who took over the job!''

"This is a lot of twaddle, Stu," said Doc Cordell.

Barrington stood close to his boss. He shook his head.

Slingerland noticed that Cordell had taken his hands off the table top and sat pushed back in his chair. He glared furiously at Warren Neale.

"You have no proof," Cordell declared.

Thomkins spoke again: "I told you we have a sworn deposition against you, Cordell."

"Sworn by whom?" demanded Cordell.

"By your own son, Joe. He's badly wounded, but he'll live, and will testify against you, just as he's signed the statement puttin' the blame on you!"

Cordell stared violently, for the first time, a spasm of alarm crossed his set face. "You—" He paused, then began cursing Warren Neale with intense bitterness. "You're responsible, Neale! You'd ruin my town, take away everything I built up! Your cussed branch line would draw settlers away from here, damn your heart and soul—"

"Don't—" gasped Stu Barrington.

And Slingerland suddenly realized the depth of Cordell's hate for Warren Neale.

Doc Cordell had a heavy revolver in his lap, had had it there all the time, and when he'd dropped his hands, had gripped it, ready for action. Cordell hadn't known his son was a prisoner, hadn't guessed Joe would turn against him. But now he knew, knew he was doomed.

219

Slingerland acted with blinding speed, Colt jumping to his steady hand, hammer spur back under a long thumb.

But Cordell had a clear bead on Neale as he threw up his revolver, taking aim at the engineer.

Warren Neale would have died then and there had not Barrington, with surprising agility for such a stout man, thrown himself at Cordell, snatching at Doc's gun.

Slingerland fired, but his shot was a second-fraction later than Cordell's.

But Stu Barrington was between Neale and Doc's weapon, and Cordell's slug drove into his breast.

Pistol raised, Slingerland jumped over.

But his first bullet had struck home. Doc Cordell slumped in his chair. His eyes were already glazing and his arm dropped, the revolver clattering on the floor. A bluish-red hole had appeared in his forehead over the left eye. Slingerland's lead had pierced his brain.

With a sharp cry, Lee Davis started toward Barrington, who had collapsed close by his former master. A door in the back of the big room was flung open and a man with a Colt in hand jumped in; behind him were several more toughs. Evidently Cordell had had them waiting there.

"What the—" growled the leader, but stopped as he took in the scene.

Thomkins raised his pistol. "Back, you," he ordered.

The armed posse surged in, and the gunnies saw the law badges, Doc Cordell dead in his chair. Silently, they backed off.

Slingerland pouched his Colt, stepping beside Lee Davis, who knelt by his father-in-law.

"Dad, how bad is it?" he gasped.

Stu Barrington turned tortured eyes to Lee's face, lips

220

twisting in a fleeting smile. He whispered, "Penny—tell her I love her—" He shuddered as he died.

Slingerland touched Lee's shoulder. "Tell Penny her dad was a real man! Warren, he saved your life."

Neale nodded. "And thanks to you, Al, we're all safe now!"

An hour later, Al Slingerland set Reddy, his powerful bay, across the river bridge, hitting the trail over the mountain.

A joyful song welled in his stout heart. He was hurrying back to his true love, pretty Mountain Flower.

# The World's Greatest Western Writer

# ZANE GREY

Classic tales of action and adventure
set in the Old West
and penned with blistering authority
by America's Master Story Teller

THE BUFFALO HUNTER. Rugged, dangerous men and the
beasts they hunted to the point of extinction.

_____2599-X                              $2.75 US/$3.75 CAN

SPIRIT OF THE BORDER. The settlers were doomed unless a
few grizzled veterans of the Indian Wars, scalphunters as
mean and vicious as the renegades, could stop them.

_____2564-7                              $2.75 US/$3.75 CAN

THE RUSTLERS OF PECOS COUNTY. Although out-
numbered a thousand to one, the Texas Rangers were the
last chance the settlers had. It had to be enough.

_____2498-5                              $2.75 US/$3.50 CAN

THE LAST RANGER. The classic frontier tale of a brutal Indian fighter and a shrewd beauty who struggled to make a
heaven of the hell on earth they pioneered.

_____2447-0                              $2.95 US/$3.75 CAN

THE LAST TRAIL. White renegades stir up the hostile Indian
tribes surrounding the little settlement of Fort Henry.

_____2636-8                              $2.95 US/$3.95 CAN

# DOUBLE-BARREL WESTERNS
## Twice the Action—
## Twice the Adventure—
## Only a Fraction of the Price!

**Two Complete and unabridged novels in each book!**

**The Sure-Fire Kid** and **Wildcats of Tonto Basin**
by Nelson Nye.

_____2474-8                                  $3.95 US/$4.95 CAN

**Gunslick Mountain** and **Born to Trouble**
by Nelson Nye.

_____2497-7                                  $3.95 US/$4.95 CAN

**The Bushwackers** and **Ride the Wild Country**
by Lee Floren.

_____2610-4                                  $3.95 US/$4.95 CAN

# PONY SOLDIERS

They were a dirty, undisciplined rabble, but they were the only chance a thousand settlers had to see another sunrise. Killing was their profession and they took pride in their work—they were too fierce to live, too damn mean to die.

_____2620-1     #5: SIOUX SHOWDOWN
                       $2.75 US/$3.75 CAN

_____2598-1     #4: CHEYENNE BLOOD STORM
                       $2.75US/$3.75CAN

_____2565-5     #3: COMANCHE MOON
                       $2.75US/$3.75CAN

_____2541-8     #2: COMANCHE MASSACRE
                       $2.75US/$3.75CAN

_____2518-3     #1:  SLAUGHTER AT BUFFALO
                       CREEK   $2.75US/$3.75CAN

Wann immer es mir möglich war, hatte ich vom Oktob[er]
[4]0 an Tagebuch geführt. Armselige Notizen oft. Viele ging[en]
[verl]oren. Am achten Mai 1945 schrieb ich ein Gedicht. »D[ie]
[Bä]ume der Armut.« Ich dachte zurück an die Jahre in Rußlan[d]
[und] die Birken am Wege.

## KARL IBACH
## Tag der Befreiung

[D]en achten Mai 1945 erlebte ich als deutscher Kriegsgefanger
[(v]ojna plenni) in dem sowjetischen Kriegsgefangenenlag[er]
[M]ariupol am Asowschen Meer (Ukraine). Wie kam ich –
[Na]zigegner der ersten Stunde – in sowjetische Kriegsgefang[en]-
[sch]aft? Ein merkwürdiges Schicksal – zuerst unter Hitler hint[er]
[Sta]cheldraht, nun unter Stalin hinter Stacheldraht. Einige V[or]-
[be]merkungen sind wohl unerläßlich.
[S]chon dem Aufkommen des Nationalsozialismus hatte i[ch]
[mi]ch kämpferisch widersetzt. Das beglichen die Nazis, als s[ie]
[an] die Macht gekommen waren, indem sie mich 1933 in poli[ti]-
[sch]e Schutzhaft nahmen und in eines der ersten – damals sog[e]-
[nan]nten »wilden« – Konzentrationslager verschleppten. Do[rt]
[wa]r ich mit achtzehn Jahren der jüngste Schutzhäftling.
Nach einiger Zeit wegen meiner Jugend entlassen, nahm i[ch]
[de]n Kampf gegen das nationalsozialistische Unrechtsregim[e]
[wi]eder auf und schloß mich einer aktiven Widerstandsgruppe a[n]
[Im] Feuer der Gestapo-Verfolgungen wurde ich 1936 erneut ve[r]-
[haf]tet und wegen »Vorbereitung zum Hochverrat« – so hieß da[s]
[da]mals – zu acht Jahren Strafhaft verurteilt. Obwohl dadurc[h]
[»we]hrunwürdig«, kam ich 1943 – kurz vor Beendigung meine[r]
[H]aftzeit – direkt aus der Haft zu der bekannten und berüchtigte[n]
[Be]währungseinheit 999 (Ausbildungslager Heuberg in Baden).
[D]er Einsatz mit dem VII. Bataillon/999 erfolgte 1944 in Grie-
[ch]enland. Wir kamen damit in den Strudel des Zusammen-
[bru]chs der Südostbalkanfront und zuerst in bulgarische und

len. Ich hatte ein Ziel, und dieses Ziel versprach trügerisch einen Anfang im vertrauten Kreis.

Das war der Stand der Dinge auf den Rheinwiesen bei Rema-
gen im Mai 1945. Die Erschütterung, die mich im Jahr darauf traf
bei der Entdeckung der Wahrheit, ging an die Wurzel. Ich mußte
akzeptieren, daß der Wahnsinn des Krieges, von Hitler entfes-
selt, bis zum Schluß auf seiner verbrecherischen Logik beharrte.

Er hat mich verändert. Gewalt widert mich an, erst recht die
politisch motivierte, unter welchem Banner auch immer. Mör-
derische Dummheit nährt sich aus Vorurteil und Verhetzung.
Politik nach dem Inferno des Zweiten Weltkrieges muß deshalb
vor allem dies leisten: immer wieder Aufklärung und Verständigung, Verständigung über das Wirkliche.

## HEINZ WERNER HÜBNER
## Die Bäume der Armut

Ich weiß nicht mehr, was für ein Wochentag der achte Mai 1945
war; ich weiß nur, daß die Deutsche Wehrmacht in Nordwestdeutschland, in Dänemark und in Norwegen schon drei Tage
vorher kapituliert hatte. Vermutlich auch bedingungslos. Am
fünften Mai also wurde ich in Rendsburg Führer einer »Gene-
sendenkompanie«, so hieß das damals. Es waren Verwundete
aus allen Truppenteilen, also aus Heer, Marine und Luftwaffe,
die schon wieder laufen konnten und die ich nun auf Befehl
eines englischen Offiziers in das Auffanglager nach Neumünster überführen sollte. Ich habe diesen Auftrag nur zur Hälfte
erfüllt. In Nortorf, auf dem halben Wege zwischen Rendsburg
und Neumünster, übergab ich die Kompanie einem Feldwebel,
und als Genesender mit einem Steckschuß im Bein, die Wunde
eiterte, lief ich auf Nebenwegen nach Süden.

Nicht die englischen Truppen waren die Gefahr, sondern die
aus den Arbeitslagern befreiten russischen und polnischen
Kriegsgefangenen, die – zum Teil marodierend – durch die

Dörfer Schleswig-Holsteins zogen. Betrunken viele. Ehema-lige französische Kriegsgefangene versuchten, oft nicht ohne Erfolg, die Ordnung aufrechtzuerhalten. Ich strebte zurück in mein Lazarett, ein Schulhaus in einem Dorf nahe Hamburg, das ich am 23. April verlassen hatte. In Schleswig und Rendsburg hoffte ich, als die Engländer bei Lauenburg an der Elbe standen und man nachts das Donnern der Geschütze hörte, Kameraden meiner Artillerieabteilung zu treffen, die möglicherweise ebenso wie ich Ende März verwundet aus Ostpreußen – mit Schiffen über die Ostsee – herausgekommen waren.

Aber ich traf keinen. Die überlebt hatten, kamen erst zehn Jahre später aus russischer Kriegsgefangenschaft zurück. Das Dorf, dem ich zustrebte, war von Rendsburg 104 Kilometer entfernt. So exakt wußte ich das damals nicht, als ich es, auf Feldwegen humpelnd, zu erreichen versuchte. Neun Jahre spä-ter bin ich denselben Weg mit einem VW gefahren; der Tacho-meter zeigte 103,6 Kilometer. In dem Dorf wohnte eine Tante von mir und im Haus daneben ein Mädchen, mit dem ich schon im Sandkasten gespielt hatte. Soweit die Vorgeschichte.

Der achte Mai. Vom Lazarett im Schulhaus, in das ich 24 Stunden zuvor vom Oberarzt wieder aufgenommen worden war, bis zum Haus meiner Tante waren es dreihundert Meter. Die mächtigen Linden, die die schmale Straße säumten, filter-ten das Sonnenlicht in helles Grün. Selbst die Schatten waren Licht. Ein Morgen aus blauem und grünem Glas.

Mein Onkel war Soldat und vermißt. Meine Tante weinte, wenn man sie ansprach, sie weinte, wenn sie einen englischen Soldaten sah, wenn Nachbarn sie trösten wollten, und sie weinte, wenn Tasso, der Hund, bellte, denn früher hatte er nur gebellt, wenn mein Onkel aus dem Büro nach Hause kam. Sagte meine Tante.

Hinter dem Haus gab es einen großen Garten mit alten Obst-bäumen, mit einer sich an Staketen rankenden Brombeerhecke. Unter den schwarzen Blättern des letzten Herbstes leuchteten weiß die aufbrechenden Triebe. Zartes Laub von Jasmin und eine Weißdornhecke. Die Kirschbäume blühten. Irgendwann,

es muß gegen Mittag gewesen sein, kamen die N[...] und sagten, der Krieg sei nun überall zu Ende. Sie [...] Radio gehört. An Japan dachte niemand. Das wa[...] Meine Tante weinte.

Ich saß im Garten auf einer Bank und vor einer[...] mein vermißter Onkel gezimmert hatte. Der Hund [...] die Füße. Die Frau eines Lehrers weinte auch. »E[...] mehr verdunkeln«, sagte sie. Eine andere meinte, [...] alle Englisch lernen müßten. Und eine dritte erin[...] Führer, der das alles so sicherlich nicht gewollt h[...] widersprach.

Später kam ein Kamerad aus dem Lazarett. Wi[...] an und zuckten mit den Schultern. Zu Hause war [...] sien. Frau und eine dreijährige Tochter. Der letz[...] Frau war vom Dezember. »Ich bin sicher, daß sie le[...] er. »Ihr Bruder lebt in Thüringen.« Mit meinen Elte[...] hatte ich zuletzt Weihnachten aus Ostpreußen tele[...] Sowjetarmee war nur zwei Kilometer entfernt.

Meine Tante legte eine Leinendecke auf den G[...] eine Nachbarsfrau brachte Tassen; es roch nach Boh[...] Gehortet, aufgespart für einen solchen Tag, sagte ei[...] saßen um den Tisch, aßen Schoka-Kola aus Blech[...] und redeten, ich weiß nicht, worüber. Dann kam [...] nem weißen Kleid, das Mädchen, mit dem ich im S[...] gesessen hatte. Sie lachte. Ich weiß nicht, weshalb [...] aber ich habe ihr Lachen bis heute nicht vergessen[...] kühl. Thesi ging als letzte. Sie küßte mich und flog [...]

Der Krieg ist zu Ende. Viereinhalb Jahre Soldat. G[...] Zeit, verlorene Zeit? – Was ist am Tage danach? – [...] die Zukunft dachte? – Ich weiß es nicht. Mir wur[...] wußt, daß ich nicht mehr auf das Geräusch pfeifend[...] ten, singender Bomben, belfernder Maschinengewe[...] ten haben würde. Und in Erdlöchern würde ich a[...] mehr schlafen und wachen müssen. Die eiternde V[...] Bein, der Steckschuß – das würde heilen wie die and[...] wundungen in den Jahren davor.

danach in sowjetische Kriegsgefangenschaft. So befand ich mich seit Anfang 1944 mit vielen Schicksalskameraden im Lager Mariupol, wo wir schwerste Aufräumungsarbeiten leisten mußten. In der Nähe des Lagers lag das riesige Asow-Stahlwerk, das bei dem Rückzug der deutschen Wehrmacht vollkommen zerstört worden war. In dem undurchdringlichen Dschungel aus Betontrümmern und Eisengeflecht mußten wir mühsam versuchen, etwas Ordnung zu schaffen.

Am achten Mai waren wir wieder wie üblich zu schwerer Arbeit ausgerückt. Wir spürten, daß etwas in der Luft lag. Schon in den Tagen zuvor hatten sich die Vermutungen, Gerüchte und Hoffnungen auf ein baldiges Kriegsende verdichtet. An diesem Tag nun hörten wir Zurufe der sowjetischen Wachmannschaften: »Wojna [Krieg] kaputt!« und »Gitler kaputt!«. Die Russen artikulierten »Gitler« statt »Hitler«, weil ihnen das »H« am Anfang eines Wortes in ihrer Sprache fremd ist. Nach der Rückkehr von der Arbeit erfuhren wir dann am Abend im Lager über Lautsprecher der sowjetischen Lagerleitung die volle Tatsache der bedingungslosen Kapitulation: Frieden! Ende der Hitler-Tyrannei!

Jeder deutsche Wehrmachtsangehörige trug auf der rechten Brustseite des Uniformrocks das Hoheitszeichen mit Adler und Hakenkreuz. Mit vielen anderen Kameraden hatte ich das verhaßte Zeichen schon in der ersten Stunde der Kriegsgefangenschaft mit einem Gefühl tiefer Befriedigung von meinem Uniformrock entfernt. Aber am achten Mai 1945 lief doch noch eine Anzahl von Kameraden mit dem Hakenkreuzabzeichen im Lager herum, was merkwürdigerweise auch von den Russen geduldet wurde. Ich besorgte mir eine alte Rasierklinge und trat freundlich an die Kameraden heran, die noch das Hakenkreuz trugen. Niemand wehrte sich dagegen. Manche waren apathisch und gelähmt. Viele kamen mir freudig entgegen. Sie hatten die Abtrennung vorher deshalb nicht gewagt, weil es noch immer Nazifanatiker im Lager gab. Nach unseren Bemühungen konnten wir am Abend des achten Mai feststellen, daß das Lager »hakenkreuzfrei« war.

Diesen historischen Tag, durch den die endgültige Nieder-
lage brauner Barbarei und der Befreiung der Menschheit von
der Geißel des Nazismus beschlossen wurde, feierten wir im
Kreis der Gleichgesinnten. Für uns war es nicht der Tag der
Kapitulation und der Niederlage. Für uns war es der Tag der
Befreiung vom Nazijoch.

Mit Inbrunst und Tränen in den Augen sangen wir das alte
Lied der Arbeiterbewegung:

>>Brüder, zur Sonne, zur Freiheit!
Brüder, zum Lichte empor!
Hell aus dem dunklen Vergangenen
leuchtet die Zukunft hervor!<<

WERNER KIESSLING
## Wechselbad

Die neunte Armee unter General Wenck war mit ihren Panzer-
spitzen vor Jüterbog hängengeblieben. Berlin war endgültig
verloren. Das XXXXVIII. Panzerkorps, dem ich mit meiner
Kampfgruppe angehörte, brauchte nicht nachzurücken. Seine
Einheiten zogen sich aus Richtung Torgau mit dem Rücken an
die Elbe zurück. Bei Ferchland-Genthin, zwischen Burg und
Jerichow, alles Gerät zurücklassend, setzten wir mit Flößen auf
das Westufer über. Als ich mit dem letzten Floß auf der Mitte
des Stromes war, kamen die ersten Russen ans Ufer. Aber –
wir konnten uns ja bei den Amerikanern vor den Sowjets sicher
fühlen. Dachten wir. Wer nördlich bei Tangermünde über die
intakte Brücke zu den Engländern gehen konnte, hatte mehr
Glück.

Meine fünf Kompanien und eine Artillerieabteilung lagerten
sich auf einer Wiese, weiträumig von Posten umstellt. Nachts
bellte ab und zu ein Schuß auf. Ich hatte meine Soldaten gebeten, nicht unnötig noch Gesundheit und Leben aufs Spiel zu
setzen, wir seien ja jetzt auf der richtigen Seite.

Am Morgen versammelte ein amerikanischer Captain alle deutschen Offiziere um sich und bot uns an, alle körperlich Schwachen und Versehrten auszusuchen, die anderen kämen zum Arbeitseinsatz. Wohin? Wir würden erst nach Süden marschieren und dann verladen werden. Richtung Westen. Ruhrgebiet. Einsatz in den Gruben.

Ich suchte eine große Anzahl »Schwache« aus, stellte alle Rote-Kreuz-Schwestern dazu, die sich uns anvertraut hatten. Lastwagen nahmen sie auf. Wir winkten ihnen nach. Sie fuhren nach Westen und blieben dort. Ich erfuhr es fünf Jahre später.

In geordneten Einheiten marschierten wir anderen singend nach Süden, um nach wenigen Kilometern von einem deutschen Obersten zwischen amerikanischen Offizieren in einem entgegenkommenden Jeep zugerufen zu bekommen, mit Singen aufzuhören – es ginge »rüber«. Ich erstarrte, marschierte an der Spitze meiner Einheit stumm weiter. Links und rechts – alle fünzig Meter versetzt – saßen plötzlich Amerikaner mit MPs. Wir liefen Spalier. Ein Dorf kam in Sicht – Kaaden. Inmitten der Ortschaft rechts eine größere Gruppe deutscher Offiziere, um General Wenck geschart. Ein Oberleutnant stürzte auf mich zu. Ich erkannte ihn sofort, hatte ihn in der Ersatzabteilung eine Zeitlang in meiner Kompanie. »Hauptmann Kießling!« rief er entsetzt. (Später erfuhr ich, daß er ein Neffe von General Wenck und zuletzt der Kommandant seiner Panzerbefehlsstaffel war.) »Es geht auf die andere Seite!« rief ich zurück. »Rabatz!« schrie ein baumlanger Hauptmann. Sofort fuhren die Amerikaner mit vorgehaltenen Gewehren dazwischen.

Es ging rüber. Nach dem Dorf wurden wir in einen Hügelwall geführt, der mit schweren Maschinengewehren Richtung Elbe gespickt war. Auf der Höhe sahen wir die Bescherung. Die Elbwiesen bis zum Ufer voller Gefangener, auf der Elbe drei große Lastkähne, Breitseite an Breitseite, vollbehangen mit Trauben von Landsern, die nach drüben gezogen wurden. Am Ostufer ertönte eine Quetschkommode, grölten russische Soldaten, erkannten wir hochdekorierte Sowjetoffiziere mit viel Gold. Auf unserer Seite lagen Tausende und harrten ihres

Schicksals. Ein Grab war ausgeschaufelt, daneben lag ein Kamerad, der den Freitod vorgezogen hatte. Der »Rabatz«-Hauptmann jagte in einem Kraftfahrzeug heran, sprang herunter, erkannte mich – hatte Wort gehalten aus ehrlicher Gesinnung, wollte sich überzeugen – und fuhr in die Falle.

Ich erwartete auf dem Ostufer den Genickschuß. Die Propaganda saß uns allen zu tief in den Knochen. Aber es kam anders. Wir wurden freudig begrüßt, Offiziere gaben uns die Hand, russische Begleitposten nahmen uns die Feldflaschen ab – aha, dachten wir, es geht los! – und gaben sie uns, mit Wasser an einem Dorfbrunnen rasch gefüllt, aufgeregt lachend zurück. War das ein Wechselbad! Eine Welt brach hinter uns zusammen, und vor uns tat sich das große Niemandsland auf.

In endlosen Kolonnen wurden wir in Richtung Brandenburg getrieben, beiderseits dichter Hochwald, durch den die Russen, wie wir von zurückkehrenden Geflüchteten erfuhren, Schneisen geschlagen hatten, die pausenlos von berittenen Patrouillen kontrolliert wurden. Immer wieder peitschten Schüsse auf. Auch die, die über die Elbe zurückschwimmen wollten, wurden zu Hunderten von den rasch errichteten Wachtürmen aus abgeschossen. Kein Fisch durfte wagen, die Wasserfläche zu bewegen – schon ratterten die Maschinengewehre.

Nach zwei Tagen Fußmarsch nahm uns ein Sammellager bei den Arado-Werken in Brandenburg auf, von wo die Transporte über Frankfurt/Oder in die russische Endlosigkeit führten. 1,2 Millionen Kameraden kamen von dort nicht mehr zurück.

KARL KLASEN

## Ohnmächtig vor Schwäche

Am achten Mai 1945 befand ich mich in einem amerikanischen Gefangenenlager in der Nähe von Cham (Bayern). Von einem Ausbildungslehrgang bei Pilsen waren wir, eine Gruppe von etwa zehn Mann, meistens im Range eines Wachtmeisters, gegen Ende April nach Donaueschingen abgestellt worden. Den Weg dorthin hatten wir bis zur deutsch-tschechischen Grenze sehr schnell und gemeinsam zurückgelegt und uns dann verstreut, um irgendwo möglichst unerkannt das bevorstehende Ende des Krieges zu erwarten. Zusammen mit einem Kameraden, einem Landwirt, hatte ich in einer Försterei Unterschlupf gefunden. Dort wurden wir aber von den vorrückenden amerikanischen Truppen festgenommen und in das Lager bei Cham eingeliefert. Hier saßen wir gemeinsam am achten Mai. Das Lager bestand aus einer großen umzäunten Wiese, wo etwa viertausend Mann unter freiem Himmel lebten. Da wir beide Nichtraucher waren, hatten wir gegen unsere Zigaretten zwei Bretter eingetauscht, mit denen wir uns im Wiesengrund kleine Löcher gegraben hatten. In die setzten wir unsere Füße, wenn wir auf den Brettern saßen. So hatten wir es etwas bequemer und konnten uns, wenn es am Tage oder nachts regnete – was in dem Jahr häufig geschah –, mit unseren Zeltplanen zudecken, so daß wir zumindest trocken die Zeit verbringen konnten.

Die Verpflegung erfolgte dadurch, daß wir in der ersten Zeit alle zwei Tage unter starker militärischer Bewachung aus dem Lager hinausgetrieben wurden und dann beim Wiedereintritt jeder für zwei Tage eine Schwarzblechdose Corned beef aus deutschen Heeresbeständen erhielten. Mein im praktischen Leben mir weit überlegener bäuerlicher Kamerad war sehr dafür, daß wir uns unsere karge Mahlzeit fürsorglich und magenverträglich einteilten. Wieder gegen Opferung einiger Zigaretten erstanden wir eine leere Konservendose und etwas Brennholz, holten uns aus dem Lagerbrunnen Wasser, teilten den Inhalt jeder Dose in drei Teile und kochten uns hieraus eine Suppe.

Da die Fettaugen oben schwammen und damit keiner bevorzugt wurde, löffelten wir immer abwechselnd zu jeder Mahlzeit die Suppe aus. Weil diese rein fleischliche Verpflegung längere Zeit anhielt, hatten wir, da wir sie als warme Suppe genossen, keine Magenbeschwerden im Gegensatz zu manch anderem Kameraden. Trotzdem war es eine sehr unzureichende Ernährung.

Als wir am achten Mai wieder zum Essenfassen hinausgetrieben wurden – es war ein sonniger Tag – und wir gerade in langer Schlange an einem Bauernhof außerhalb des Lagers standen, wurde ich vor Schwäche ohnmächtig. Die amerikanischen Wachsoldaten gestatteten, daß mein Freund mich abseits von der Gruppe auf dem Bauernhof hinlegte und bei mir blieb. Als ich nach kurzer Zeit wieder die Augen aufschlug, bedeutete mein Freund mir sehr energisch, sie sofort wieder zu schließen, weil er inzwischen entdeckt hatte, daß in der Nähe Kartoffeln lagerten und sich dort auch ein Stoß Brennholz befand. Er flüsterte mir zu, daß meine Ohnmacht so lange dauern müsse, bis er Gelegenheit gefunden hätte, davon etwas für uns mitzunehmen. Da ich gegen längeres Liegen gar nichts einzuwenden hatte, folgte ich sofort seinem Wunsch, und es gelang ihm dann auch, drei schöne Kartoffeln und ein Stück Brennholz einzustecken. So hatten wir am Tage der deutschen Kapitulation für unsere Verhältnisse eine vorzügliche Suppe nicht nur aus Fleisch, sondern auch noch mit Kartoffeln. Auch brauchten wir mit Holz an diesem Tag nicht zu sparen.

Wir sind dann aus dem Lager in den ersten Junitagen entlassen worden. Dessen Zustände verbesserten sich kaum, nachdem unsere amerikanischen Bewachungsmannschaften alle Wertgegenstände, die wir noch bei uns trugen, für sich einkassiert hatten. Hätte uns damals jemand vorausgesagt, welches schöne und erfüllte Leben uns in unserem geschlagenen Deutschland bevorstehen würde, wir hätten das allenfalls für eine Geschichte aus Tausendundeiner Nacht gehalten.

NORBERT KLOTEN
## Der Anblick der Amerikaner ließ aufatmen

Das Schlimmste lag hinter uns. Wir, das waren sechs Fahnenjunkergefreite, Jahrgang 1926, Versprengte eines Bataillons von Offiziersanwärtern der Luftwaffe, dann in Kampfanzüge von

Fallschirmjägern gesteckt, denen wohl auch zugeordnet, zumindest von Fallschirmjägerkadern mehr als rüden Stils befehligt. Genaueres war uns nach der Verlegung aus der Kriegsschule in Bug auf Rügen nie gesagt worden.

Der Tag war schön, die Gegend, in der man uns wie viele Tausende Gefangener abgeladen hatte – am sechsten Mai, oder war es schon am fünften gewesen? Damals zählten weniger die Kalendertage als das Erlebte –, nicht minder. In kürzester Zeit hatten sie sich über ein riesiges Gelände südlich von Eutin mit Weiden, Waldflecken und auch Wasserflächen inmitten einer sanft hügeligen Landschaft verteilt, ohne jede erkennbare Ordnung, doch allenthalben vom simplen Wunsch, auch das zu überstehen, angetrieben. Manche, noch vom Schrecken des Ausgestandenen oder auch von Erkrankungen, besonders des Magens und des Darms, gezeichnet, verharrten in Apathie; die anderen aber, zumeist im Gruppenverbund oder gar als Angehörige mehr oder weniger geschlossener Einheiten, fackelten nicht lange mit den üblichen Vorkehrungen wie dem Aufstellen von Zelten und dem Ausheben von Latrinengruben, dem Sichten des verbliebenen Proviants und was auch immer.

Zu den Beati possidentes gehörten wir nicht, sondern zu den vielen, die gerade Zeltplane, Brotbeutel, vielleicht noch Kochgeschirr und Löffel hinübergerettet hatten und sich jetzt hohläugig und hohlwangig, schlapp nach notdürftig verbrachten Nächten mit Regengüssen mehr schlecht als recht einzurichten versuchten. Vielleicht deswegen, möglicherweise aber auch eines noch immer im ganzen properen Eindruckes wegen war eine zwar geschrumpfte, doch im ganzen intakte und im Vergleich zu uns geradezu königlich ausgerüstete Flakkompanie bereit, uns am Rande anzugliedern und auch ein wenig am Eßbaren teilhaben zu lassen. Irgendwie war durchgesickert, daß Einheiten zu hundert oder zweihundert Köpfen zu bilden seien. Uns selbst stand allerdings der Kopf weniger nach solchen Nachrichten als nach dem Nötigsten.

Auch das wenig konturierte Gerücht von der Kapitulation, das sich seinen Weg durch das Lager so bahnte wie alle Gerüchte, berührte mich im Grunde wenig. Der Krieg war für mich aus – definitiv, seit wir ein paar Tage zuvor als Teil eines riesigen Trecks geschlagener Heeresteile und Flüchtlinge, aber auch erbärmlich anzusehender, trotzdem hier und da Drohgebärden wagender KZ-Häftlinge und Kriegsgefangener der Deutschen Wehrmacht bei Schwerin noch vor dem Zugriff der Russen das schmale Niemandsland – ein Wäldchen – hinüber zu den Amerikanern mit Hängen und Würgen hinter uns bringen konnten. Daß der Krieg am Ende verloren sein würde, war für mich wie für manch andere in meinem Gesichtsfeld seit langem Erwartung und schließlich Gewißheit gewesen. Schon als Luftwaffenhelfer im Hydrierwerk Wesseling – neben dem Gymnasialunterricht ein harter Dienst – hatten wir BBC gehört und danach unsere Frontkarte ausgesteckt. Für mich war also der dritte Mai – vielleicht auch schon der zweite – das entscheidende Datum, nicht der siebte; an diesem vollzog Großadmiral Dönitz nur den unvermeidbaren Akt eines Nachlaßverwalters, der allein noch auszuhändigen hat.

Bis Schwerin aber war für unsere kleine Gruppe, für mich nicht weniger als für meine Gefährten, das ganze Trachten einzig auf ein Ziel ausgerichtet: nicht in die Hände der Russen zu fallen, sondern irgendwie den Weg gen Westen zu finden. An jedem Abend hatten wir uns nach unserer Absprengung als Vorposten nordöstlich Berlins (Hohenzollern-Finow-Kanal) bewußt mit voller Bewaffnung bei den jeweiligen Ortskommandierenden mit simuliertem Marschbefehl (eben nach Schwerin) so zackig wie möglich gemeldet, um nach karger Verköstigung hastig zusammengestellten Verbänden zugewiesen zu werden. Nachts setzten wir uns bei erster Gelegenheit wieder ab, in das Chaos der zurückflutenden Massen eintauchend. Die erlebten Szenen haben bis heute nichts von ihrem Schrecken verloren. Aus dem Zusammenprall der alliierten Heeresgruppen von Ost und West erwuchs ein Inferno, in dem jeder sein Heil suchte, nicht wenige auch schießend und plündernd.

Erst der Anblick der Amerikaner ließ aufatmen, ließ das Gefühl sich ausbreiten, davongekommen zu sein. Am Kapitulationstag hatte sich dieses Gefühl schon verfestigt. Geblieben war aber die unterschwellige Angst, vielleicht doch noch den Russen ausgeliefert zu werden. Das Lager schwirrte auch von Gerüchten aller Art. So war es nur gut, daß es mir mehr um praktische Dinge gehen mußte, um ein einfaches Zelt aus durchlöcherten Planen, ein wenig zu beißen und etwas Orientierung in der Unordnung um mich herum, auch bedrückten mich erste Anzeichen einer Erkrankung an Ruhr. Gewiß, die Schrecken des Krieges waren ausgestanden, und doch wurde die unendliche Entspannung aller Sinne streckenweise von der Sorge überlagert, nicht durchhalten zu können, vielleicht lange in Gefangenschaft sein zu müssen. Im tiefsten Innern überwog aber wie eigentlich in meiner ganzen Militärzeit Zuversicht; im Lager war mir Gott näher als jemals zuvor und vielleicht auch nachher. Irgendwie, so spürte ich, würde ich durchkommen und Eltern und Bruder wiedersehen, vielleicht sogar das Studium erneut aufnehmen können.

## Shmuel Krakowski
## Theresienstadt

Auch an diesem Tag wachte ich mit demselben Gefühl auf wie am Tag davor und an all den anderen Tagen – ich hatte wahnsinnigen Hunger. Wir lagen alle auf dem nackten Boden, Gefangene in einem Gefängnis innerhalb eines viel größeren Gefängniskomplexes. Vor zwei Wochen waren wir hier angekommen. Mit dem Todeszug von Rehmsdorf, einem Lager, das ebenfalls zu der Buchenwalder Anlage gehörte. Wir waren mehr als viertausend jüdische Konzentrationslagerhäftlinge, als sie uns in jenen ersten Apriltagen aus Rehmsdorf herausholten. Nur fünfhundert von uns erreichten die tschechische Stadt Terezin, die von den Nazis in ein jüdisches Getto mit dem Namen Theresienstadt umgewandelt worden war. All die anderen waren unterwegs gestorben oder waren umgebracht worden. Unter denen, die zugrunde gegangen waren, befanden sich auch einige meiner besten Freunde aus der Zeit unserer Untergrundtätigkeit in der Jugendorganisation im Getto von Lodz: Rysiek Podlaki, Abramek Kociolek und Srulek Krajkowski.

Nun hatte man uns in Theresienstadt in einem riesen Gebäude – genannt die »Hamburger Kaserne« – eingeschlossen. Diejenigen draußen vor den Toren, die Gefangenen, die Theresienstadt bewohnten, waren besser dran als wir. Sie konnten sich auf den wenigen Straßen des Gettos einigermaßen frei bewegen.

Wir wußten, daß das Dritte Reich zusammengebrochen war und daß unsere Befreiung eine Sache von Tagen, wenn nicht von Stunden war. Doch für die Menschen hier, die nach so vielen Jahren der Hungersnot und der Strapazen der Todesmärsche erschöpft waren, schienen diese Stunden des Wartens auf die Befreier zu lang zu dauern. Jede Stunde glich einer Ewigkeit. Viele von uns lagen schon in Agonie. Auch einer meiner besten Freunde, Lutek Nachtstern. Es bestand kein Zweifel darüber, daß für diese Menschen die Befreiung zu spät kam. Für all die anderen war diese Zeit des Wartens zu einem tragischen Wettrennen geworden, auf dessen Ende wir alle gespannt warteten: Was würde eher eintreten, die Befreiung oder der Tod durch Hungersnot?

Ich kann mich nicht mehr erinnern, wer von uns an jenem Morgen zum Fenster hinausschaute. Ich kann mich nur noch an einen Freudenschrei erinnern: »Jungs, die Russen sind da!« Die Befreiung hatte auch uns erreicht.

Mit vielen anderen zusammen beschloß ich, nach draußen zu gehen und unsere Befreier zu begrüßen. Aber viele von uns waren nicht mehr in der Lage, sich zu bewegen. Sie waren zu schwach, um noch aufzustehen. Ihnen blieb nichts anderes übrig, als zu liegen und zu warten in der Hoffnung, daß die Befreier Nahrung bringen und die ärztliche Versorgung organisieren würden.

Das Tor der »Hamburger Kaserne« war immer noch geschlossen. Ein tschechischer Polizist stand draußen und versuchte, uns zu überreden, drinnen zu bleiben. Er sagte, wir seien eine epidemische Gefahr für die Menschen außerhalb des Lagers. Doch weiter in Gefangenschaft zu bleiben, auch nach der Befreiung, schien uns schierer Unsinn zu sein. Wir widersetzten uns und stürmten das Tor. Der tschechische Polizist gab auf und verschwand.

Wir alle strömten bis auf die Straße außerhalb des Gettos. Dort sahen wir Panzer der Roten Armee, einen militärischen Versorgungstreck und einige russische Soldaten, die auf Fahrrädern eine unendlich lange Kolonne deutscher Kriegsgefangener begleiteten. Deutschland war geschlagen. Wir sahen es mit eigenen Augen. Der Tag, auf den wir so lange gewartet hatten, war da. Weil wir alle sehr hungrig waren, fragten wir die Russen als erstes, ob sie uns nicht etwas geben könnten. Die Soldaten waren außergewöhnlich freundlich, doch auch sie hatten nicht viel zu bieten. Die einzigen Nahrungsmittel, die sie in ihrem Versorgungszug hatten, waren Zucker und gepökelter Schinken.

Ich begnügte mich mit Zucker, konnte mich noch ganz genau erinnern an die ersten Tage in der »Hamburger Kaserne«, als ein Arzt – auch ein Gefangener – uns gewarnt und ermahnt hatte, vorsichtig mit dem Essen zu sein, wenn der Tag der Befreiung kommen sollte, da wir allzulange unter permanenter Hungersnot gelitten hatten. So aß ich Zucker, jetzt löffelweise. Vielleicht hat gerade das mich damals gestärkt und sogar mein Leben gerettet. Es war ein herrliches Gefühl, das ich in den letzten fünf Jahren fast vergessen hatte. Ich konnte wieder essen, soviel ich wollte, und ich wußte, ich würde nie wieder hungern.

Man sagte uns, daß sich deutsche Soldaten in der Umgebung verborgen hielten und daß sie versuchten, bis zum Einbruch der Nacht in ihren Verstecken zu bleiben, um so im Schutze der Dunkelheit zu entkommen. Man bat uns, den russischen Soldaten zu helfen, die Gegend zu durchkämmen und die Deutschen zu finden. Wir waren mehr als glücklich, dies tun zu können. Wir begannen, einzeln zerstreut ein bewaldetes Gebiet, das uns nur wenig bekannt war, zu durchsuchen.

Nach nicht allzulanger Zeit stellte ich fest, daß weder rechts noch links von mir meine Freunde zu sehen waren. Ich fühlte mich ziemlich verlassen in dieser unbekannten Gegend. Plötzlich kam mir hinter den Bäumen ein großer und dicker deutscher Soldat entgegen. Angst überkam mich, denn ich hatte keine Waffe. Was nun, wenn er mich erschießt? Sollte ich jetzt, einige Stunden nach der Befreiung, sterben? Glücklicherweise nahm der Deutsche die Arme hoch. Ich konnte erkennen, daß er mehr Angst hatte als ich. Sein ganzer Körper zitterte. Wie ein Besessener schrie er fortwährend: »Hitler kaputt. Ich war kein Nazi! Hitler kaputt. Ich war kein Nazi.« Ich nahm ihn bis zur Straße mit. Einige meiner ehemaligen Mitgefangenen kamen auch aus dem Wald heraus und führten »ihre Deutschen« vor. Sie alle versuchten, uns laut und hektisch zu überzeugen, daß sie nie Nazis gewesen waren. Sie hätten Hitler schon immer gehaßt.

Die gefangenen Soldaten schienen sich mehr vor uns zu fürchten als vor den Russen. Ich ahnte den Grund: Die Nazis wußten, daß wir, die Überlebenden, die Geschichte ihrer Barbarei der ganzen Welt erzählen würden.

Am Nachmittag fühlte ich mich sehr müde, und da ich keine andere Bleibe hatte, entschloß ich, nach Theresienstadt in die »Hamburger Kaserne« zurückzugehen, zumal ich auch nach meinen dort gebliebenen Freunden sehen wollte.

Als ich die Straße entlangging, erreichten mich zwei uniformierte Männer auf Fahrrädern. Auf den ersten Blick konnte ich ihre Uniformen nicht identifizieren. Deutsche, an die wir uns in den letzten sechs Kriegsjahren auf tragische Weise so gewöhnt hatten, waren es nicht, auch keine russischen Uniformen. Nach einiger Zeit erkannte ich, daß die Männer Uniformen der polnischen Armee trugen, die ich seit dem verhängnisvollen September 1939 nicht mehr gesehen hatte.

»Polnische Armee?« fragte ich die Männer.

»Ja!« kam die Antwort, und sie stellten sich vor. Sie waren beide Juden, Offiziere des polnischen Panzerkorps, das bis an jenem Tag einige dreißig Kilometer von diesem Ort entfernt gekämpft hatte. Man hatte ihnen gesagt, daß unweit ein Konzentrationslager mit jüdischen Gefangenen wäre, und die beiden wollten ihre befreiten Brüder sehen. Ich sagte ihnen, daß ich einer dieser Befreiten war, und bot sogleich an, ihnen den Weg zu zeigen.

Wir erreichten nach kurzer Zeit Theresienstadt und betraten die erste Baracke. Hier befanden sich Frauen, die meisten aus Polen und Ungarn, Gefangene, die ähnlich wie ich mit den Todeszügen aus anderen Konzentrationslagern hierhergebracht worden waren. Unbeschreiblich war die Freude dieser Frauen, als sie die beiden Offiziere sahen. »Unsere Brüder! Jüdische Offiziere! Endlich, endlich haben wir euch bei uns!« Und dann – die vielen Hände, welche die Hände der beiden Offiziere suchten, die Umarmungen, die vielen, vielen Freudentränen!

Die beiden Offiziere wollten wissen, woher die Frauen kamen und all die Einzelheiten ihrer Leidenswege durch die Gettos und Konzentrationslager. Und die Frauen, eine nach der anderen, erzählten über ihre unglaublichen Erfahrungen mit den Nazis. So grausam diese Geschichten auch waren, wurden sie immer wieder durch Ausbrüche großen Glücks unterbrochen, des Glücks, dasein zu können und in Sicherheit zu sein, mit jüdischen Offizieren zu sprechen, wohl wissend, daß es kein Nazideutschland mehr gibt und auch nie wieder geben würde.

Irgendwann fragte dann eine Frau die beiden Offiziere nach deren Geschichte, die Geschichte zweier Soldaten im Krieg. Doch dann änderte sich die gelassene, fröhliche Stimmung fast plötzlich. Trauer und Betroffenheit machten sich breit. Der Leutnant erzählte uns, daß er aus Wilna stammte und daß man ihn in die Rote Armee eingezogen hatte. Er hatte an Kämpfen teilgenommen, darunter auch in Stalingrad, wo er verwundet worden war. Nach seiner Genesung hatte man ihn zur neu ins Leben gerufenen polnischen Armee einberufen. So war es ihnen gelungen, die Deutschen zu schlagen und sie stetig mehr und mehr westwärts zu verdrängen. Doch nicht gering war ihre Betroffenheit, als sie feststellen mußten, daß sich überall in den befreiten Gebieten keine Juden mehr befanden. Die Deutschen hatten eine ganze Nation, unsere Nation, umgebracht.

Als der Leutnant Polen erreicht hatte, bat er um einen kurzen Urlaub, um seinen Geburtsort Wilna zu besuchen. »Ich habe nur Steine, meine Steine, gesehen; die vertrauten Häuser und Straßen, doch keinen der Menschen, die früher dort lebten«, erzählte uns der Offizier. Die einzigen überlebenden Juden im befreiten Lublin waren diejenigen, die als Soldaten in der russischen und der polnischen Armee gekämpft hatten, und noch einige jüdische Partisanen, die es nun wagten, aus den Wäldern herauszukommen. Auf ihren Märschen durch Polen, durch Hunderte von Dörfern und Städten, fanden sie nur die Vernichtungsstätten und die Massengräber. Theresienstadt war der erste Ort, wo sie so vielen Juden noch begegnet sind, Tausenden von Juden, denen es gelungen war, dem Naziregime zu entkommen.

So mußten auch wir erfahren, daß unser Schicksal viel schlimmer war, als wir erwartet hätten, denn obwohl wir eine ganze Menge gesehen und das Schlimmste erfahren hatten, hatten wir dennoch die Hoffnung nicht aufgegeben, hatten wir weiterhin unsere Träume bewahrt. In all den Tagen, an denen wir ums Überleben gekämpft hatten, Tag um Tag, Stunde um Stunde, hatten wir keine Zeit gehabt, uns über das ungeheuerliche Ausmaß unserer Tragödie die Gedanken zu machen, diese zu erfassen. Jetzt aber wurde uns alles mit einemmal schmerzhaft klar. Draußen gab es keine Familien mehr, die auf uns warteten. Und es gab auch keine eigenen Häuser mehr, in die wir zurückkehren konnten. Für uns war der Sieg zu spät gekommen, viel zu spät.

WERNER KRUSCHE
## Waffen abgeben!

Ich habe kein Kriegstagebuch geführt. Aber ein paar Erinnerungen von damals sind geblieben. Natürlich weiß ich noch, daß ich den achten Mai 1945 in der Flakkaserne in Rendsburg erlebte.

Ich hatte nach meiner schweren Verwundung das Theologiestudium in Leipzig aufnehmen und hintereinander drei Semester dort studieren können. Als Studienurlauber. Die Zeit zwischen den Semestern verbrachte ich bei einem Ersatztruppenteil. Nach Ende des dritten Semesters ging es nach Wittenberg (am letzten Vorlesungstag – es war wohl der 28. Februar – hatte eine Bombe das Institutsgebäude getroffen und den Hörsaal weggerissen, in dem wir zehn Minuten vorher – beim Beginn des Fliegeralarms – noch gesessen hatten).

In Wittenberg hieß es eines Tages – es muß Mitte oder Ende März gewesen sein –, die nicht mehr kriegsdienstverwendungsfähigen Offiziere sollten sich absetzen und eine andere Flakkaserne aufsuchen. Ich machte mich daraufhin mit einem beinamputierten Leutnant auf den Weg in Richtung Norden. Ziel war Wismar. Ich weiß noch, wie er richtiggehend zornig wurde – er war sonst eigentlich ein ganz freundlicher Mensch –, als ich ihm unterwegs sagte, nun sei der Krieg bald zu Ende; sonst hätte man uns nicht so einfach weggehen lassen. Er war fest überzeugt, daß der »Führer« noch eine Wunderwaffe habe, die bisher nur noch nicht eingesetzt worden sei, weil sie von einer so schrecklichen Vernichtungskraft sei. Das war im März 1945!

In Wismar überlegte ich mir, ob ich nicht versuchen sollte, in Rostock noch ein bißchen zu studieren. Unsere Truppen hielten immerhin noch ihre Stellungen an der Oder. Mein Antrag auf Studienurlaub wurde genehmigt. Ich trampte also mit meinem Rucksack – mehr Gepäck hatte ich nicht – nach Rostock. Der Superintendent besorgte mir ein Zimmerchen im Martha-Stift. Dann meldete ich mich bei dem Dekan, Professor Quell. Ich war seit zwei Semestern der erste Student, der sich an der theologischen Fakultät immatrikulieren lassen wollte. Theologie war damals nicht gefragt. »Eine Schwalbe, die den Frühling ankündigt«, scherzte Spectabilis.

Ich besuchte noch zwei weitere Professoren (Büchsel und Jepsen) und sagte ihnen, welche Vorlesungen ich gern bei ihnen hören würde. Aber das Ganze dauerte nur eine reichliche Woche. Dann hieß es, die Rote Armee sei im Anmarsch. Die Bevölkerung flüchtete aus Angst vor möglichen Kampfhandlungen. Irgendein Wehrmachtswagen nahm mich mit. Wenn die englischen Tiefflieger kamen und in den Flüchtlingsstrom hineinschossen, sprangen wir von dem Wagen und warfen uns flach auf den Acker. Von Wismar ging es dann weiter nach Rendsburg, nachdem wir uns in einem Wehrmachtsmagazin noch mit allerlei eingedeckt hatten (ich zum Beispiel mit einer Felljacke – man konnte ja nicht wissen . . .).

Die Flakkaserne in Rendsburg war überfüllt. Aus Dänemark und Norwegen waren Hunderte von Luftwaffenhelferinnen gekommen. Es war ein buntes Treiben. Es war Frühling geworden. Das Kasernengelände war von sonnenbadenden Gestalten männlicher und weiblicher Ausgabe besät.

Wir warteten auf das Ende des Krieges und lebten in den Tag hinein. Was dann kommen und aus uns werden würde, wollten wir nicht wissen. Gedanken darüber schoben wir weg. Ich entsinne mich jedenfalls nicht, damals irgendwelche Zukunftsängste ausgestanden oder trüben Gedanken nachgehangen zu haben. In der langen Lazarettzeit war das anders gewesen. Jetzt empfanden wir es als eine Erleichterung, daß endlich bald Schluß sein würde. Nachdem wir so viel durchgestanden hatten, würden wir die totale Kapitulation mit all ihren Folgen schon auch noch irgendwie überstehen.

Ich möchte jetzt nicht nachträglich irgendwelche tiefsinnigen Gedanken erfinden, die ich damals eigentlich hätte haben müssen. Ob es das allgemeine Laisser-faire, Laisser-aller oder eben doch das Vertrauen in Gottes väterliche Barmherzigkeit war, die mich damals innerlich bestimmt haben mögen, vermag ich heute nicht mehr zu sagen. Ich hatte, nachdem die schwere Verwundung überstanden war, gelobt, mein Leben, das ich für eine so schlechte Sache eingesetzt hatte, nun für die beste Sache einzusetzen, die es gibt – für die Sache Jesu Christi. Vielleicht war es das, was mich gelassen machte. Ich weiß es nicht.

Wir lebten in dem umzäunten Gelände der Kaserne wie auf

einer Insel. In Erinnerung geblieben ist mir, daß ich eines Nachts zum Kommandeur gerufen wurde und von ihm den Befehl erhielt, sofort in die umliegenden Dörfer zu fahren und alle dort einquartierten Wehrmachtseinheiten aufzufordern, noch in der Nacht diese Dörfer zu räumen. Großadmiral Dönitz habe bestimmte Operationen gegen die Engländer vor; es werde vermutlich zu Kampfhandlungen kommen. Darum sollten alle Luftwaffenhelferinnen die Kasernen verlassen und Quartier in diesen Dörfern beziehen, die dem Feind als »Fraueninseln« bekanntgemacht werden sollten.

Die Landser bepackten schimpfend ihre Fahrzeuge, und am Morgen kamen dann tatsächlich die uniformierten Mädchen zu Hunderten angerückt. Ich war auf einmal Oberbefehlshaber einer Frauenschwadron geworden! In dieser Eigenschaft quartierte ich mich in einem evangelischen Pfarrhaus ein. Dort gab es ein Klavier und einen Notenband mit Schubert-Liedern. Aber auch dieses Glück dauerte nur wenige Tage. Dann ging's zurück in die Kaserne.

Die Kapitulation erlebten wir so: Am achten Mai hing am Kaserneneingang ein Schild mit der Aufschrift: »In RAF Control.« Damit waren wir zu englischen Kriegsgefangenen geworden. Es war sehr harmlos. Noch am Vormittag hieß es: »Waffen abgeben!« Ich montierte also meine Pistole ab (ich hatte sie nur einmal gebraucht – im Polenfeldzug, um einem Hund, dem sie die Hinterbeine abgefahren hatten und der schrecklich winselte, den Gnadenschuß zu geben). Ich erinnere mich nicht, diese »Entwaffnung« irgendwie demütigend empfunden zu haben, zumal sie nicht einmal von einem »Tommy« vorgenommen wurde. Was hatten wir schon noch an Ehre zu verlieren? Ich habe jedenfalls seitdem keinerlei Lust mehr verspürt, noch einmal eine Waffe in die Hand zu nehmen. –

Als wir Tage vor der Kapitulation uns über die feige Art ausgelassen hatten, in der der Führer sich der Verantwortung entzogen hatte, war uns einer in die Parade gefahren: Wir sollten uns schämen, so zu reden. Der bat mich nun, ihm einen Wehrpaß mit einem anderen Namen auszufertigen. Aber das habe ich ihm abgeschlagen; ich dachte: Soll er doch für das geradestehen, was er nicht nur – wie wir alle – mitgemacht, sondern was er auch noch gutgeheißen hatte! Im Grunde hätte ich ihm ruhig seine Bitte erfüllen können. Nur wenige Jahre nach der Kapitulation brauchte man die Deutschen wieder. Von einer deutschen Schuld war keine Rede mehr, und Leute wie dieser waren wieder gefragt.

## Hermann Kunst
## Finsternis – nicht finster ist bei Dir

Man kann sich über das eigene Erleben des achten Mai 1945 für einen Leser nur verstehbar äußern, wenn man mindestens andeutet, wie man die Jahre von 1933 bis 1945 unter der nationalsozialistischen Herrschaft erlebt hat. Ich war in Herford ein Pastor der Bekennenden Kirche. Ich gehörte nicht zu den »Helden und Heiligen«. Wie viele Hunderte meiner Amtsbrüder erfuhr ich Haussuchungen, Verfahren wegen politischer Aufhetzung, Verhöre bei der Geheimen Staatspolizei, wobei das Brüllen der Verhörenden und die Drohungen schlimm waren, und Bestrafungen. Die ständige Bespitzelung, das Abhören der Telefongespräche und die Kontrolle der Post waren nur einige Zeichen der quälenden Unfreiheit, in der man Tag für Tag seinen Dienst tun mußte. Kein Zweifel seit der Einverleibung der Tschechoslowakei im März 1939, daß der Krieg von uns planvoll vorbereitet und angezettelt wurde. Spätestens seit Stalingrad und unserer Kriegserklärung an Amerika war mir die bevorstehende militärische und politische Niederlage gewiß.

In Memel erlebte ich zum letztenmal die Einkesselung durch die Russen. Auf der Kurischen Nehrung konnte meine Einheit fliehen und der Gefangennahme entgehen. Am achten Mai war ich als Pfarrer in einem großen Kriegslazarett in Hage in Ostfriesland. Nach dem Selbstmord Hitlers waren zwar die Niederlage und das Ende des Krieges unzweifelhaft, aber noch war die Drohung der Erschießung bei defätistischen Äußerungen so wirksam, daß sich jeder vor der offenen Rede im Kameradenkreise hütete. Dann kam endlich die Nachricht von der totalen Kapitulation an allen Fronten.

Es gab in den letzten Tagen vorher zwar einige Kameraden, mit denen man in behutsamer Offenheit sprechen konnte. Aber das Abendbrot am achten Mai verlief schweigend. Wie mechanisch geschah der Dienst an den Verwundeten. Noch hatten die Kanadier nicht das Kommando übernommen, aber über allem, was wir sagten und taten, lag eine wortlose Lähmung. So unfaßbar es erscheint – bis zuletzt hatten einige nationalsozialistische Kameraden mit einer spektakulären Wendung gerechnet.

Gegen zwanzig Uhr ging ich aus meiner Baracke auf eine benachbarte Wiese. Dort stand ein Flugzeug, mit dem ein Pilot geflüchtet war. Der Abend wurde zu einer Station meines Lebens. Meine Erinnerung ist präzise.

Selbstredend liefen die Gedanken zuerst zu meiner Frau und meinen fünf Kindern. Sie waren evakuiert. Lange hatte ich nichts von ihnen gehört. Aber ich ging davon aus, daß ich sie wiedersehen würde. Der Dank dafür war sehr groß. Aber es regte sich kein strahlendglückliches Empfinden.

Sofort wurde die Frage wach, ob mein Überleben nicht gezeichnet sei von Schuld. Gewiß, ich hatte in den verflossenen Jahren nur ein bescheidenes Amt wie viele tausend andere. Aber hätte ich getan, was ich hätte tun müssen, gehörte ich mit Sicherheit nicht zu den Überlebenden. Als ich 1938 nach der »Kristallnacht« von der Entheiligung und Zerstörung der Synagoge in Herford hörte, sah ich aus meinem Fenster auf meine Kirche. Würde Gott in seinem Gericht unsere Altäre und Kanzeln verwüsten, veröden lassen, weil wir schweigend und tatenlos die Verwüstung der Stätten der Verehrung Gottes unserer jüdischen Mitbürger hinnahmen? War es ausreichend gewesen, in der Predigt und in den Gesprächen zu sagen: »Irrt euch nicht, Gott läßt sich nicht spotten. Was der Mensch sät, wird er ernten«? Nein, es war nicht genug. Was sollte ich anders tun als beten: »Gott, sei mir gnädig nach Deiner Güte und tilge meine Sünden nach Deiner großen Barmherzigkeit!« War es ein billiges Gelübde, niemals mehr zu schweigen, wenn die Menschenrechte gebeugt und mit Füßen getreten würden?

Aber – was sollte ich eigentlich in den kommenden Tagen und Wochen predigen? Was sollte ich meinen Kameraden im Gespräch sagen? Auf gar keinen Fall schien mir erlaubt, zu schnell zu sagen: »Bei Ihm ist die Vergebung, daß man Ihn fürchte.« So gewiß dies die einzige Hoffnung für den Weg vor uns war – das Gebet um Vergebung setzt das Bekenntnis der Sünde voraus. Bekenntnis der Sünde nicht allgemein, sondern konkret! Waren meine Kameraden pauschal schuldig vor Gott, vor allem die jungen Soldaten, die ehemals begeisterten Hitlerjungen, denen ihre Welt zusammengebrochen war, die nichts als das Soldatenhandwerk gelernt hatten und sich nun zukunftslos sehen mußten? Ich wußte keine Antwort. Meine Hoffnung war, daß das Bekenntnis der eigenen Schuld Gemeinschaft stiften könnte.

Es war dunkel geworden. Mein Auge fiel auf das Dorf. Der erste Abend, an dem kein Alarm, kein Fliegerangriff mehr zu befürchten war. Aber es war kein einziges nicht verdunkeltes Zimmer zu sehen. Keine Spur von Jubel über die endlich neu geschenkte Freiheit und das Ende von Kriegsangst! Was hatten wir zu erwarten? Durch meine Ämter wußte ich etwas mehr als meine Mitbürger von den Greueln in den Konzentrationslagern. Die Zerstörung der Häuser und Arbeitsplätze war zwar fürchterlich, aber wir konnten wiederaufbauen in der Gewißheit, daß ein heute wiederaufgebautes Haus nicht morgen erneut vernichtet werden würde. Die vor uns liegenden Jahre würden hart und bettelarm sein. Wie würde jedoch die gesamte Welt aufschreien, wenn die Fotos der Untaten der nationalsozialistischen Herrschaft durch die Zeitungen und Wochenschauen gehen würden? Ob nun selber etwas mehr oder etwas weniger schuldig – die Verantwortung für alles, was geschehen war, lag auf meiner Generation. Einen befleckten Namen für das Land unserer Väter würden wir unseren Kindern und Enkeln hinterlassen.

Es war im Dorf und im Lazarettgelände totenstill. Um 23 Uhr ging ich in meine Baracke, die erste Tür rechts. Ich zog mich aus und legte mich auf mein Feldbett. Ich habe gebetet um die Kraft des Glaubens: »Finsternis nicht finster ist bei Dir«, bis mich der Schlaf übermannte.

## Hermann Langbein
## Wie ich das Ende erlebte

Der elfte April ist mein zweiter Geburtstag. Im Jahr 1945 bin ich an diesem Tag auf dem Güterbahnhof von Salzwedel aus einem Häftlingstransport geflohen.

Vier Tage vorher sind die Häftlinge des Außenlagers des KZs Neuengamme, Fallersleben, in Viehwaggons verladen worden. Mehr stehend als fahrend brauchte dieser Zug – einer der unzähligen Evakuierungszüge von KZ-Häftlingen in diesen letzten Wochen des »Dritten Reiches« – für eine Strecke von kaum viel mehr als 50 Kilometern so lang. Auf dem Güterbahnhof standen wir schon viele Stunden. Chaos ringsum. Mehrere Garnituren von Lastwaggons neben unseren. Die SSler, die uns zu bewachen hatten, plünderten Lebensmittel aus herrenlosen Zügen. Damit sie diese nicht selbst zu ihrem Personenwaggon schleppen mußten, öffneten sie den Viehwaggon, in welchem die deutschen Häftlinge – weniger eng zusammengepfercht als die vielen Ausländer – eingeschlossen waren. »Tragt uns diese Sachen in unseren Waggon. Für euch könnt ihr auch etwas nehmen.« Alle liefen, aßen im Gehen, schleppten. Mein bayerischer Freund Hans Biederer und ich nützten diese Möglichkeit zu einer Flucht, die wir schon vorbereitet hatten; Österreicher galten ja in den Lagern als Deutsche, daher war ich auch in dem geöffneten Waggon.

Als ich unter Zuggarnituren durchgekrochen war und auf Hans wartete, stand plötzlich ein SS-Mann vor mir: »Was machst du da?« herrschte er mich an. »Dort gibt's Zigarren!«

sagte ich statt einer Antwort und zeigte auf einen Waggon, aus dem gerade Zigarrenkisten endlos herausgeschleppt wurden. Der SS-Mann drehte sich um und lief dorthin. Es war das letzte Mal, daß mir Gefahr von seiten der SS drohte. Lagererfahrung hat mir eingegeben, so zu reagieren.

Nach Überschreiten der Gleise gingen wir über eine Wiese. In meiner Erinnerung war sie sehr groß. Wir durften nicht laufen, um keinen Verdacht zu erregen. Dann gab's Fliegeralarm, alles rannte kopflos umher und wir mitten dazwischen schnell in einen Wald. Dort blieben wir in der Nacht. Am nächsten Morgen sahen wir schon eine Kolonne amerikanischer Panzer. Wir waren frei. Wir winkten den Amerikanern zu, sie winkten zurück. Wir schlugen die Richtung ein, aus der sie kamen. In Gifhorn verlangten wir vom Bürgermeister Verpflegung und einen Schlafplatz. Das war meine erste Nacht in einem Bett nach sieben Jahren.

Als Hitler am zwölften März 1938 seine Truppen nach Österreich einmarschieren ließ, habe ich meine Heimat verlassen. Damals haben nicht nur viele Hunderttausende ihm zugejubelt, einige Zehntausende wurden verhaftet oder sind geflohen. Über die Schweiz und Paris ging ich nach Spanien.

Dort mußte sich die junge Republik gegen eine Gruppe faschistischer Generäle wehren, deren Putsch sich dank der massiven Unterstützung durch Mussolini und Hitler zu einem blutigen Bürgerkrieg entwickelt hatte. Aus vielen Ländern kamen Menschen der Republik zu Hilfe. Es bildeten sich Internationale Brigaden. In diese reihte ich mich ein. Der Krieg ging verloren, die Waffen der anderen waren stärker. Wer nicht in seine Heimat zurückkonnte, wurde nach Überschreiten der französischen Grenze im Februar 1939 in südfranzösischen Lagern interniert. Als Frankreich von Hitler besiegt wurde, kam eine Gruppe österreichischer Spanienkämpfer nach Dachau. Von dort wurde ich nach Auschwitz überstellt. Die zwei Jahre, die ich in diesem größten Vernichtungslager des Nationalsozialismus gefangen war, haben mich – wie wohl jeden, der dort sein mußte und überleben konnte – geprägt. Im August 1944 wurde ich mit Polen und Russen in ein Außenlager des KZs Neuengamme überstellt. Als dieses ausgebombt wurde, kam ich ins Stammlager, von dort in ein anderes Außenlager bei Lerbeck, das am ersten April 1945 nach Fallersleben evakuiert wurde. Das war – knapp skizziert, mein Weg durch die sieben Jahre, die für jeden Österreicher meiner Generation eine Probe bedeuteten.

Wir baten einen amerikanischen Offizier in Gifhorn, uns eine Möglichkeit zu beschaffen, damit wir unserer Heimat näher kommen. Er bedauerte. Seine Truppe hatte Befehl, auf ihren Fahrzeugen keine Zivilisten mitzunehmen. Aber er schrieb einen Zettel, daß wir Flüchtlinge aus einem KZ seien und man uns zu unterstützen habe.

So gingen wir weiter, Richtung Hannover. Dort quartierte mich ein englischer Offizier in einer Villa ein: »Diesem Mann ist das beste Zimmer zur Verfügung zu stellen!« befahl er den erschreckten Bewohnern. In Hannover erlitt ich meine erste Enttäuschung: Ich bat die Engländer um eine Schreibmaschine und schrieb meine Erlebnisse in den Konzentrationslagern nieder. Als ich sie dem Offizier übergab, bedankte er sich und sperrte das Manuskript ungelesen in seinen Schreibtisch. Auch in den folgenden Tagen kam er nicht auf seinen Inhalt zu sprechen. Später mußte ich erfahren, daß die Kunde von dem, was in Auschwitz geschehen war, ganz allgemein nicht interessierte.

Am vierten Mai eröffnete mir der Offizier, daß für den Aufbau einer Verwaltung in Hannover verläßliche Antinazis gesucht wurden und ich vorgesehen war, dort mitzuarbeiten. Am nächsten Morgen machte ich mich mit einem Fahrrad auf den Weg; ich wollte nicht in Hannover hängenbleiben, ich wollte so schnell wie nur möglich nach Hause. Das Rad gaben mir belgische Kriegsgefangene, die es Deutschen abgenommen hatten.

Die Straßen waren leer. Nur Amifahrzeuge rasten hin und wieder vorbei. Offenbar genügten die Lautsprecherdurchsagen, daß Zivilisten ein Begehen der Straßen verboten sei. Ich wurde niemals kontrolliert.

In Halle, das von Amerikanern befreit war, erfuhr ich von der endgültigen Kapitulation des nationalsozialistischen Regimes. Die Hoffnung auf einen Sieg der Alliierten hatte ich nie ganz aufgegeben. Nach Stalingrad, dem Sturz Mussolinis, dem Vormarsch der russischen Truppen, der Landung in der Normandie blieb für mich nur die Frage offen, ob ich den sich immer deutlicher abzeichnenden Sieg erleben werde.

Nun hatte ich die Zerschlagung des Nationalsozialismus erlebt. Ich konnte mich deswegen nicht so freuen, wie ich es mir früher vorgestellt hatte. Eigentlich war ich leer. Das Wiederfinden der Natur, der Geruch der Wälder, der herrlich weiche Moosboden in den ersten Tagen nach der Flucht, all das löste starke Gefühle aus. Gesprächen mit Deutschen wich ich aus, so wie sie mir auswichen, wenn ich auf der Fahrt einem Bürgermeister den Zettel der Amerikaner zeigte und Quartier und Essen forderte. Nur der Bürgermeister von Marktredwitz kam mir als Mensch entgegen: Er bat mich zu Tisch, bereitete mir ein Bad, fragte mich behutsam, und ich spürte Gefühl; er war neu als Bürgermeister eingesetzt, die anderen waren noch die alten Nazibürgermeister.

Als ich nach Passau die österreichische Grenze mit meinem Fahrrad überschritt – ein Amifahrzeug nahm mich auf einer Behelfsbrücke über den Inn mit –, fing in mir etwas zu singen an. Statt der weißen Fahnen der Kapitulation winkten rotweißrote Fahnen. In der Nacht vom 17. zum 18. Mai war ich in Wien; war zu Hause.

Immer wieder habe ich nach Bekannten gefragt, die damals auch in dem Transport waren, aus dem ich in Salzwedel geflohen war; stets vergebens. Ich fürchte, daß sie so wie viele Häftlinge von Neuengamme und dessen Außenlagern auf die Schiffe verfrachtet worden sind, die am dritten Mai in die Lübecker Bucht hinauszufahren Befehl erhielten, ohne daß sie als Häftlings- oder Krankentransport gekennzeichnet waren, und die – wie zu erwarten – von englischen Fliegern bombardiert wurden. Tausende sind dabei zugrunde gegangen, die böse Jahre der KZ-Haft überlebt hatten. Dönitz, der damals an der Spitze der Regierung stand, hat diesen letzten Massenmord an Häftlingen zugelassen. Seine Macht reichte damals noch bis Hamburg und Lübeck.

Das waren meine ersten tastenden, unsicheren Schritte in ein normales Leben. Eine Überlebende von Auschwitz hat die Ernüchterung, die viele von uns durchmachten, in die Worte gekleidet: »Wir kamen aus der Hölle und glaubten, jetzt kommen wir in den Himmel. Das war jedoch eine Täuschung.«

Es brauchte seine Zeit, bis ich mich damit abfand, daß nach Auschwitz die Menschheit keineswegs so bereit war, aus dem, was dort hatte geschehen können, ihre Folgerungen zu ziehen, wie ich es mir in den kurzen Augenblicken vorgestellt hatte, in denen ich im Schatten der Krematorien und Gaskammern an ein Leben nachher zu denken wagte.

<br>

DIETER LATTMANN
## Mein Kriegsende

Es ist nicht dieser eine Tag, an dem der Krieg zu Ende war. In meiner Erinnerung sind es mehrere Tage, und sie hängen zusammen wie Einstellungen in einem Filmstreifen. Als am achten Mai 1945 in Deutschland fast alle Waffen schwiegen und nur noch versprengte Amokläufer des »Tausendjährigen« Reichs auf einen Feind schossen, der von manchen Deutschen als Befreier begrüßt wurde, war trotz allen Siegestaumels der Alliierten mein vorherrschender Eindruck die plötzliche Stille. Es waren keine Flugzeuge mehr in der Luft. Nirgends krachte es, die Menschen gingen ungewiß durch den Waffenstillstand, aber sie atmeten auf. Man sprach mit dem anderen nur das Nötigste. Ruhe herrschte, das Schweigen dröhnte in meinem Kopf.

Mir ist, als wären wir auch fast lautlos in die Gefangenschaft marschiert. Engländer beorderten uns von Flensburg in die Gegend von Heide in Holstein – ein Stück transportierte uns die Bahn in Güterwagen. Wochenlang vorher hatte auf der Marine-kriegsschule in den Kasernen Mürwik und Glücksburg das Gerücht vorgeherrscht, die Fähnriche sollten diesen äußersten Winkel des Reichs bis zum letzten Mann verteidigen, ein Bollwerk sollte er werden wie einst Alcázar. Zum Glück ergaben wir uns dann kampflos, der Krieg war aus.

Die ersten Tage vergingen in der Stille, so tauchen sie in meinem Gedächtnis auf, wie ein Stummfilm, Bilder, keine Worte. Nur einmal wurde es schrill und laut, das war wie ein Taumel. Daran erinnere ich mich wie an eine Verletzung des Friedens.

In unserem Lager gab es ein paar Birken und einen Brunnen. Es war ein Areal zwischen Weidezäunen, und wir wurden nicht allzu scharf bewacht. Anfangs wurden wir überhaupt nicht verpflegt, ich raufte mir junges Grün von den Zweigen und kaute es lange, bevor ich es hinunterschluckte. Eines Tages fand einer von uns in der Scheune, in der wir untergekommen waren, mehrere Kisten unter dem Stroh. Wir machten uns sofort daran und staunten, was zum Vorschein kam: große weiße Zigarettenschachteln mit Hakenkreuzflaggen darauf. In anderen Kisten steckten haufenweise Flaschen, französischer Cognac und Champagner. Die Zigarettenmarke hieß wahrhaftig »Sieg«, die waren wohl für den Endsieg produziert, als irgendwelche Leute noch daran glaubten. Vielleicht hatte sich ein Proviantmeister das alles da versteckt.

Wir haben geteilt, es gab ein Fest. Jeder in der Scheune bekam eine Drittelflasche Cognac und einen halben Schampus. Es dauerte nicht lange, bis wir in dem Schober wie verrückt umeinander tanzten. Jetzt schrien alle durcheinander. Ein paar fingen an und warfen Flaschen gegen die Scheunenwand, das Glas platzte auseinander, und zwischen Scherben verspritzte auch noch Champagner. Es war, als wäre Tobsucht ausgebrochen, und alle rauchten »Sieg«. Schließlich drehte sich die Scheune um mich, alles kreiste. Ich habe nur noch gedacht: Du mußt dich hinlegen. Also packte ich mich auf mein Strohbündel und sah, bevor mir die Augen zufielen, noch die springenden Gestalten. Als ich am nächsten Morgen zu mir kam, hatte mir einer den Tabaksbeutel und die alte Pfeife aus dem Seesack unter dem

Kopf weggeklaut. Damals begannen wir zu sagen: »Kameraden sind Lumpen.«

Die meisten lagen noch wie ohnmächtig um mich herum. Es war wieder ruhig. Ich trat hinaus auf die Koppel und sah den Frühnebel. Die Sonne griff durch die Schwaden und ließ den Tau in den Wiesen glitzern. In der Ferne läutete eine Kirchenglocke. Ich stand da und spürte, wie die Stille zurückkehrte, und auf einmal brauchte ich sie dringend. Ich war neunzehn und ahnte, daß ich bisher fast alles falsch gemacht hatte. Ich wollte anfangen zu ordnen, was einer wie ich ordnen konnte. In meiner Erinnerung ist das Kriegsende die Stille und das Staunen, daß ich noch lebte.

<br>

EUGEN LODERER

## Kriegsende in Kopenhagen

Den Tag der Kapitulation der deutschen Wehrmachtsverbände am achten Mai 1945 erlebte ich im Kriegshafen der dänischen Hauptstadt Kopenhagen. Um dieses bedeutende Ereignis zu beschreiben, möchte ich kurz darstellen, wie ich nach Kopenhagen kam, in ein Land, das 1945 schon seit Jahren von der Deutschen Wehrmacht besetzt war und das außerhalb der Fronten lag, an denen bis zum Tage der Kapitulation gekämpft wurde.

Am achten Mai 1945 war ich bereits fünf Jahre Angehöriger der Wehrmacht und hatte den Krieg ohne Unterbrechung in Belgien, den Niederlanden, in Frankreich, Polen, Ostpreußen und in Dänemark erleben müssen.

Im Mai 1944 war ich zu einem Obersteuermannslehrgang nach Gotenhafen versetzt worden. So entging ich der wenige Wochen später beginnenden alliierten Invasion an der französischen Kanalküste, die das Ende des Krieges beschleunigte. Nach erfolgreichem Abschluß des Lehrgangs war eine Versetzung zur Ausbildungsabteilung für U-Boote nach Danzig vorgesehen. Zu diesem Zeitpunkt, Ende 1944, standen die russischen Truppen bereits in Ostpreußen, was die Auflösung dieser Ausbildungsabteilung zur Folge hatte. Ich verhehle nicht, daß mich dies mit großer Genugtuung erfüllte, weil ich absolut keinen Drang verspürte, vor dem nahen Kriegsende noch auf einem der U-Boote Dienst zu tun, die wir damals »fahrende Särge« nannten.

So hatte ich mit einigen Soldaten meiner Einheit das große Glück, im Februar 1945 nach Dänemark versetzt zu werden.

Wir wurden dem Hafenkommandanten in Kopenhagen unterstellt. Ausgehungert kamen wir dort an. Im Kriegshafen wurden wir auf einem außer Dienst gestellten Passagierdampfer untergebracht. Es war relativ angenehm. Junge Rekruten und ältere Soldaten, die wie Volkssturmmänner ausschauten, waren von den kämpfenden Fronten nach Kopenhagen verschlagen worden. Unsere Aufgabe war es, die aus Ostpreußen im Hafen von Kopenhagen ankommenden Schiffe, vollgestopft mit Flüchtlingen, zu entladen. Auf diesen Schiffen herrschte ein chaotisches Durcheinander. Bereits verstorbene alte Menschen, Todkranke, verwundete Soldaten, Frauen und Kinder holten wir aus den riesigen Schiffsleibern. Eltern suchten ihre umherirrenden Kinder und umgekehrt. Es gab gespenstische Szenen. Großdeutschland, wie es die Nazis nannten, war in Auflösung begriffen. Alles, was noch einigermaßen gehen konnte, sammelte sich in diesem Hafenbecken: Soldaten aller Wehrmachtsteile, Angehörige der Wehrmachtsverwaltungen, Flüchtlinge und dänisches Hafenpersonal.

Trotz dieses trostlosen Zustandes glaubten Fanatiker immer noch an den Endsieg der Deutschen in diesem schrecklichen Krieg. Von dem Einsatz der deutschen Raketenwaffen V1 und V2 versprachen sie sich die große Wende. Zu diesen Unbelehrbaren zählte ein junger Oberleutnant, mein unmittelbarer Vorgesetzter, der bisher nur in Ausbildungsabteilungen tätig gewesen war und nicht wußte, wie der Krieg an der Front wirklich aussah. Er schwärmte vom Führer und wollte in dieser Situation – kurz vor dem Zusammenbruch – den jungen und alten

Soldaten noch beibringen, wie man mit einer Tellermine »feindliche Panzer knackt« – so seine Ausdrucksweise. Es war ein Irrsinn angesichts der damaligen Lage: Die Russen standen vor den Toren Berlins, und die westlichen Alliierten hatten längst den Rhein überschritten. Seine ständig wiederholte Rede war: »Wenn ich an der Front wäre, gäbe es nur zwei Möglichkeiten: Entweder hätte ich längst das Ritterkreuz oder ein Stück Eisen im eigenen Kreuz.«

Eines Tages zeigte ich ihm in einer stillen Stunde meine Kriegsverletzungen und meinte, die letztere der von ihm aufgezeigten Möglichkeiten wäre wohl die wahrscheinlichere.

Die Gerüchte über die Lage an den Fronten waren verwirrend. Die deutschen Wehrmachtsberichte waren zwar noch immer optimistisch, die wahre Situation jedoch war trostlos. Man hörte nur noch von »erfolgreichen Absatzbewegungen«. Was daran erfolgreich sein sollte im militärischen Sinne, war nicht zu erkennen, und so konnten mich diese Meldungen nicht zum Optimismus veranlassen. Ende April, Anfang Mai wurde die Haltung der dänischen Zivilbevölkerung gegenüber den deutschen Soldaten immer bedrohlicher. Bei Ausgängen in die Stadt verließen wir den Hafen nur in Trupps und stets bewaffnet. Wir versuchten, uns selbst zu versorgen, denn die Verpflegung war sehr schlecht, ja dem Zusammenbruch nahe. Eine geschlossene militärische Einheit gab es längst nicht mehr. Alles, was sich im Hafenbecken aufhielt, lebte auf eigene Faust – in Schuppen, Lagerräumen und auf Schiffen, die im Hafen ankerten.

Alle lebten durcheinander und doch miteinander einem ungewissen Schicksal entgegen. Kein Tag ohne bange Fragen: »Was wird mit den Menschen hier passieren, wenn der Krieg zu Ende ist?«, und: »Was wird alles noch passieren, bis es endlich soweit ist?« Man konnte sich nach bald sechs Jahren Krieg kaum noch eine Vorstellung davon machen, was Frieden und was normales Leben ist.

Am Vorabend des achten Mai 1945 wurde es im Hafen sehr gefährlich, nachdem aus einem fahrenden Vorortzug ins Hafenbecken geschossen worden war. Ein Passieren des Hafentores war zu riskant, denn niemand wußte, wie deutsche Soldaten in dieser zugespitzten Situation draußen behandelt würden.

Am achten Mai kam dann die Nachricht von der Kapitulation der deutschen Wehrmachtsverbände an allen Frontabschnitten. Das von mir lang ersehnte Ereignis erschien kaum glaubhaft. Für viele befreiend, aber auch für viele bedrückend war auch die Nachricht, daß Adolf Hitler bei den Kämpfen in Berlin gefallen sei und daß er verfügt habe, Großadmiral Dönitz solle seine Nachfolge antreten. Ich empfand es als blanken Hohn und Zynismus, den Deutschen jetzt noch klarmachen zu wollen, daß es eine Fortsetzung der Politik des Dritten Reiches – und sei es auch nur in Ansätzen – geben könne. Dem totalen Krieg konnte doch nur die totale Kapitulation folgen, und so war es dann auch.

Laute Kommandos in englischer Sprache rissen uns in der folgenden Nacht aus dem Schlaf, sofern man infolge der Ereignisse von Schlaf überhaupt sprechen konnte. Im angrenzenden Hafenbecken hatten englische Kriegsschiffe festgemacht: Kreuzer, Zerstörer und Torpedoboote. Britische Marinesoldaten hatten auf der Mole – sie war fast so breit wie eine Straße – Posten bezogen. Nach Anbruch des Tages mußten die deutschen Einheiten ihre Waffen ablegen. Vielen dämmerte erst jetzt die wahre Situation: Hitler war tot, die Wehrmacht hatte kapituliert, der Krieg war zu Ende. Vieles, was man vorher verdrängt hatte, kehrte unaufhaltsam in das Bewußtsein zurück. Man konnte jetzt endlich frei über das Verhängnis der deutschen Politik, des Dritten Reiches reden, und ohne großes Zutun fanden sich Menschen zusammen, die ähnlich dachten und fühlten. Was man bei dem einen oder anderen bisher nur vermutet hatte, wurde jetzt bestätigt. Trotz aller noch vorhandenen Ungewißheit, wie es weitergehen würde, überkam alle, die den Krieg schon immer verabscheut hatten oder sich mittlerweile seiner furchtbaren Folgen bewußt geworden waren, das Hochgefühl: Der Krieg ist zu Ende.

Es gab aber auch bei vielen jungen Menschen traurige Gesichter, vor allem bei Offizieren, die sich für eine Karriere beim

Militär entschieden hatten. Alle Orden, Titel und Ehrenzeichen waren plötzlich nichts mehr wert. Ihre Stimmung war depressiv. Die Befehlsgewalt war in ein Nichts zerronnen.

Nach kurzer Zeit ereilte die Kriegsgefangenen im Hafen der Befehl, sich in Kompaniestärke zum Abmarsch fertigzumachen. Es war vorgesehen, die deutschen Truppen nach Deutschland in Marsch zu setzen. Die erste Kompanie rückte bereits am anderen Tag in aller Frühe ab. Stunden später kam sie völlig aufgelöst wieder zurück: Sie waren von dänischen Freiheitskämpfern angegriffen worden, so daß die britischen Wachmannschaften die Umkehr befahlen.

Mein Drang war, so schnell als möglich nach Hause zu kommen. Ein Fluchtversuch durch ein fremdes Land ohne Geld und Zivilkleidung schien mir nicht ratsam. Wieder halfen Gespräche mit besonnenen und gleichgesinnten Menschen, keine riskanten Schritte zu tun. Die dänischen Behörden legten wohl gesteigerten Wert darauf, die deutschen Truppen alsbald loszuwerden. Die Entscheidung der Briten kam rasch: Alle mußten sich mit ihren kümmerlichen Habseligkeiten am Liegeplatz des deutschen Kreuzers »Nürnberg« einfinden, der im Hafen festlag. Auf dem Kriegsschiff wurden die Verschlüsse der Kanonen ausgebaut, die vorhandene Munition wurde von Bord geschafft. Alle Gefangenen mußten auf dieses deutsche Kriegsschiff, mit ihnen kam ein britisches Prisenkommando an Bord. Im englischen Geleit ging es schnellstens in Richtung Deutschland. Es war eine Fahrt ins Ungewisse, die zielloseste in meinem Leben. Tränenden Auges dachte ich in dieser Nacht an meine verlorene Jugend, von der Ungewißheit geplagt, ob das Zuhause noch stehe, ob Eltern, Frau und Kinder noch am Leben sind.

In Wilhelmshaven legte der Transport an. Wir betraten deutschen Boden. Das Gelände war von kanadischen Besatzungstruppen weiträumig umstellt. Maschinengewehre richteten sich auf die gefangenen deutschen Soldaten. Man schrieb das Datum meines 25. Geburtstages, als wir von Wilhelmshaven nach Pedderwardergroden marschierten, um dort in einem Barackenlager untergebracht zu werden. Primitive Holzhütten ohne Mobiliar, bis vor kurzer Zeit von polnischen und russischen Zwangsarbeitern belegt, waren jetzt unser Zuhause. Nach drei Monaten, kurz bevor viele deutsche Kriegsgefangene zum Wiederaufbau nach Frankreich und in die französischen Bergwerke gebracht wurden, wurde ich in Wilhelmshaven aus der Kriegsgefangenschaft entlassen. Mit den Entlassungspapieren in der Tasche, die eine Voraussetzung für den Bezug von Lebensmittelkarten waren, bestiegen wir erleichtert einen Güterzug. Die Fahrt nach Stuttgart im Güterzug dauerte fast zwei Tage. In Stuttgart endete der Transport. Ende August 1945 war ich endlich zu Hause. Es begann ein neuer Lebensabschnitt.

FRANZ D. LUCAS

## Wo und wie ich den Tag erlebte

La Paz, in einem Talkessel am Fuße des schneebedeckten Illimani gelegen, 3600 Meter über dem Meeresspiegel, Sitz der Regierung der Republik Bolivien. Die dünne und trockene Luft schafft eine einzigartige Klarheit und Transparenz der Atmosphäre. Der achte Mai 1945 war ein wunderschöner Wintertag. Keine Wolke am Himmel. Früh schon strahlte die Sonne. Sorgfältig hatte ich die Tageszeitungen mit den sich überstürzenden Nachrichten studiert. Ich nahm Hut und Mantel und ging aus meiner Wohnung in der Avenida 6 de Agosto bergauf in Richtung Stadtzentrum. Doch wie war ich nach Bolivien gekommen? Zehnter November 1938. An jenem Tage erhielt ich vom Rektor der Universität Königsberg einen Brief mit dem Ersuchen, »im Interesse meiner eigenen Sicherheit bis auf weiteres den Vorlesungen fernzubleiben«.

Damit kam mein kurzes Studium der Orientalistik zu einem dramatischen Ende. Ich war damals gerade siebzehneinhalb Jahre alt. Frühzeitig hatte ich mein Abitur bestanden und zu studieren begonnen. Dabei war bemerkenswert, daß ich 1938 noch an einer deutschen Universität zugelassen wurde. Meine

Anträge bei anderen Universitäten waren samt und sonders abgelehnt worden. Nur Königsberg hatte mir einen Platz angeboten. Aber nach dem neunten November war auch da ein Verbleiben ausgeschlossen.

Ich fuhr mit dem Zug nach Glogau. Dort fand ich meine Eltern – sonst immer freundlich, ruhig und ausgeglichen – im Zustand beträchtlicher Erregung und Enttäuschung. Unsere Wohnung, Möbel, Bilder, Manuskripte waren zertrümmert worden, die klassisch-schöne Glogauer Synagoge, an der mein Vater viele Jahre als Rabbiner amtierte, ein Opfer der Flammen und viele Freunde und Bekannte ins Konzentrationslager abgeschleppt.

In Berlin sah ich mich unverzüglich nach einem Visum um. Praktisch alle Länder hatten die Tore geschlossen. Nur die Republik Bolivien genehmigte noch Einreisebewilligungen. Es darf hier dankbar gesagt werden: Bolivien hat damals 15000 Menschen das Leben gerettet.

Am zehnten Dezember 1938 verließ ich Deutschland. Mit einem Billett nach Bolivien – und zehn Reichsmark in bar – einem unbekannten Schicksal entgegen. Meine Eltern sah ich am Anhalter Bahnhof in Berlin zum letztenmal. Es war eine aufregende Reise. In Marseille bestieg ich das italienische Dampfschiff »Virgilio«, das nach vierwöchiger Fahrt in Mollendo, Peru, ankerte. Auch die Eisenbahnfahrt von Mollendo nach La Paz brachte neuartige und unerwartete Eindrücke. Kann man ermessen, was es für einen jungen Menschen bedeutet, kaum dem Kindesalter entwachsen, wenn er plötzlich seine Heimat, das Land, in dem seine Vorfahren seit Jahrhunderten gelebt hatten, verlassen muß? Nein, es war nicht die wirtschaftliche und soziale Ungewißheit, das Abenteuer, das Risiko. Das alles wäre eine verständliche Exkursion, behaftet sogar mit der Attraktion des Ungewöhnlichen und Interessanten und womöglich des Aussichtsreichen. Aber hier war alles anders. Jahrelang waren wir geächtet, eingeschüchtert und lächerlich gemacht, als Untermenschen und Scheusale denunziert worden. So wurde das Vertrauen in sich selbst und die Menschheit erniedrigt und die Konfusion der Begriffe – Mystifikation von alldem, was gut und edel in der Wertstufung des Menschen ist – provoziert. Nietzsche hat recht, wenn er ausruft: »Weh dem, der keine Heimat hat!« Solches belastete den frommen Wunsch, im fernen Andenland zu vergessen und ein neues Leben zu beginnen.

In La Paz trat ich in die Dienste einer bedeutenden internationalen Metall- und Bergwerksfirma, die ihren Schwerpunkt in Bolivien hatte und von dem in Biblis in Hessen gebürtigen Mauricio Hochschild aufgebaut worden war. Es war ein großer Kontrast: Königsberg und La Paz, Studium der Orientalistik und Erzhandel, sorgsam behütetes Elternhaus und Alleinsein in einem fremden Land. Eines Tages zitierte mich die Deutsche Botschaft in La Paz, um mir mitzuteilen, daß ich die deutsche Staatsangehörigkeit verloren hätte und mein Paß ungültig sei. Ich war staatenlos.

Die Bolivianer, ein stolzes und freiheitsliebendes Volk, haben Erfahrung mit politischer Konvulsion, Revolution und Exil. Wir Immigranten wurden mit Sympathie aufgenommen. Allerdings litt Bolivien unter den Folgen der Weltwirtschaftskrise und des Chacokrieges. Das Land, viermal so groß wie die Bundesrepublik, zählte damals weniger als drei Millionen Einwohner, die sich meist recht mühsam ernährten. Die Wohnungs- und Verkehrsverhältnisse waren rückständig. Die massive jüdische Einwanderung aus Deutschland, für die keine Vorbereitung getroffen war, brachte für Bolivien viele positive Entwicklungen, aber auch eine Reihe von Problemen. Da machte sich – systematisch organisiert und von Naziagenten finanziert – ein bis dahin unbekannter Antisemitismus bemerkbar. Die von den Einwanderern verursachten Probleme wurden übertrieben. Agitation fand zeitweise bei einflußreichen Parlamentariern und einem Teil der Presse Gehör.

Diese Entwicklung hatte für meine Eltern tragische Konsequenzen. Ich hatte nämlich bald nach meiner Ankunft Visa für sie beantragt, die auch genehmigt wurden. Unter dem Eindruck der sich entwickelnden antisemitischen Strömung wurden aber die Visaerteilungen suspendiert und bereits erteilte Visa für ungültig erklärt. Zusammen mit dem inzwischen beginnenden Krieg vereitelte das die Rettung meiner Eltern. Unendlich bescheiden und anspruchslos, hatten meine Eltern nie gedrängt. Sie hatten an das Edle im Menschen geglaubt und selbst noch unter den mißlichsten Umständen Gutes entdecken können. Sie hatten darauf gebaut, daß der nationalsozialistische Staat unter dem Gewicht seiner eigenen Taten bald verschwinden müsse. Auch hatte mein Vater noch im Jahre 1940 neue Pflichten an der Hochschule für die Wissenschaft des Judentums in Berlin übernommen, und oftmals sagte er zu Freunden, daß es seine Pflicht sei, auszuharren und anderen Menschen zu helfen.

Die Frage der Sympathie und Antipathie zu Deutschland wurde innerhalb der bolivianischen Parteien und immens komplizierten politischen Situation zu einem gewichtigen Element. Nur so können widersprüchliche Entwicklungen erklärt werden. Das ehemals große Ansehen, das Deutschland genoß, sank damals mehr und mehr. Der deutsche Botschafter Wendler wurde ausgewiesen. Kurze Zeit nach Pearl Harbor brach Bolivien die diplomatischen Beziehungen zu Deutschland ab. Im April 1943 erklärte es Deutschland den Krieg. Über die immer grausameren Maßnahmen, die gegen die Juden in Europa geplant und in Durchführung waren, sickerten sporadisch fürchterliche Nachrichten durch. Es war schwer, das alles zu verstehen. Selbst eine Veranstaltung wie diejenige, die am zehnten November 1942 auf Veranlassung der jüdischen Gemeinde im Sucre Palace Hotel in La Paz stattfand, zu einer Zeit also, als die schlimmsten Aktionen der »Endlösung« in vollem Gange waren, konnte nicht den Eindruck der ganzen, unmenschlichen Realität vermitteln. In der Gedenkrede sprach Hans Baer von seinem Vater, der am neunten November 1938 eingekerkert und ermordet worden war, während der Sohn von der Gestapo gegen Gebührenzahlung die Urne erwerben mußte. Dann ergriff der spanische Freiheitskämpfer und Philanthrop Vicente Burgaleta das Wort, und schließlich sprach der nordamerikanische Botschafter, der forderte, daß die barbarischen Verbrechen, die die Nationalsozialisten begingen, allen Nationen der

Erde die Pflicht auferlegten, vereint gegen diese Feinde der Menschlichkeit, der Sittlichkeit und des Rechts mit allen zu Gebote stehenden Mitteln zu Felde zu ziehen. Zu dieser Zeit hatte also der Leidensweg der Juden und der anderen vom Nationalsozialismus Verfolgten die Aufmerksamkeit und Entschlossenheit maßgeblicher Kreise erregt.

Mit jungen Jahren hatte ich schon viel erlebt. Meine Position in der Bergwerksfirma war befriedigend, aber ich trauerte meinem unterbrochenen Hochschulstudium nach und einem geordneten, bürgerlichen Leben im europäischen Kulturkreis, wie es einst programmiert gewesen war. Natürlich wußte ich zu schätzen, was es bedeutete, in Freiheit in Bolivien leben zu dürfen, zu einer Zeit, wo so viele Menschen leiden mußten. Bolivien wurde meine zweite Heimat. Aber mir wurde auch klar, daß Heimat viel mehr ist als ein Fleck umgrenzter Erde, etwas, was schwerlich einen Plural zuläßt, daß die Menschen, die statt eines Vaterlands zwei beanspruchen, in Wirklichkeit nicht wissen, wohin sie gehören. Grillparzer spricht treffend von zwei Fremden und keiner Heimat.

Meine Tante Dina Lucas aus Marburg war am achten September 1942 nach Maly Trostinec deportiert worden, meine Eltern am 17. Dezember 1942 nach Theresienstadt, wo mein Vater am 13. September 1943 gestorben ist. Meine Mutter wurde von Theresienstadt mit dem letzten Transport am zwölften Oktober 1944 nach Auschwitz verschleppt. Ich wußte von alledem damals nichts und wartete sehnsüchtig auf ein Lebenszeichen.

Im Dezember 1944 entschloß ich mich, meine Position in der Firma Hochschild aufzugeben. Ich mietete im Edificio Iglesias ein Büro und bereitete zusammen mit H. Zwissler ein eigenes Unternehmen vor, das am zehnten August 1945 gegründet wurde. Vor allen Dingen wollte ich frei, unabhängig und ungebunden sein. Das Ende des Krieges, das Ende des Hitler-Regimes würde neue Hoffnungen, neue Möglichkeiten vermitteln. Würde ich bald auf den alten Kontinent zurückkehren? Würde ich meine Eltern bald wiedersehen? Ich glaubte, daß jeglicher

Antisemitismus – ein Erzübel des Jahrhunderts – im blutigen Strome so vieler Opfer ertränkt worden sei. Ich hörte von der totalen Zerstörung der Stadt Glogau und dachte mit Sorge an Deutschland, seine Geschichte, seine Dichter und Denker und seine Zukunft.

Ich weiß nicht mehr, wann die Vereinigung »Das Andere Deutschland« gegründet wurde. In scharfem Gegensatz zu einer bestehenden, rechtsgerichteten und sehr einflußreichen deutschen Organisation (es gab damals noch einen linksgerichteten Verein, »Freie Deutsche« genannt) hatten wir »Das Andere Deutschland« ins Leben gerufen. Unsere Gruppe bestand aus Flüchtlingen, die aus verschiedenartigen Gründen in Bolivien Zuflucht gefunden hatten. Etwa ein Drittel der Mitglieder waren deutsche Juden. Wir veranstalteten Vorträge und Diskussionen, meist mit hohem intellektuellen Gehalt. Wenngleich sich unsere politischen Meinungen nicht immer deckten und sogar häufig in krassem Gegensatz zueinander standen, waren wir uns doch alle einig in der Opposition zum Hitler-Regime. Wir überlegten uns, wie man Haß und Mißgunst durch Liebe und Vertrauen ersetzen könne. Ich glaube, daß es eine nicht zu unterschätzende Leistung war, daß es zu einer Zeit, als mit dem deutschen Namen Schindluder getrieben wurde, in Bolivien eine Organisation mutiger Männer und Frauen gegeben hat, die unter großen persönlichen Opfern dafür sorgten, daß es ein »Anderes Deutschland« gab, in welchem humanistische und fortschrittliche Ideale mit deutschem Geist identifiziert werden konnten.

Es kamen die Nachrichten von der bedingungslosen Kapitulation in dem kleinen Schulhaus in Reims, dem Hauptquartier von General Eisenhower, am achten Mai, und am nächsten Tage, am neunten Mai 1945, bestätigte Keitel im sowjetischen Hauptquartier in Berlin-Karlshorst das endgültige Dokument. Wie am ersten September 1939 heulte die schrille Sirene der »Razón«, diesmal aber, um das Ende des Krieges anzuzeigen. In die Jubelstimmung über den Sieg der alliierten Mächte und das Ende der Hitler-Herrschaft, die so unsagbar viel Unheil angerichtet hatte, klangen die optimistischen Botschaften der Vertreter der Nationen. Das waren Momente der Erleichterung und der Genugtuung. Jetzt war das Element der steten Unsicherheit verschwunden. Man konnte wieder frei atmen und an die Zukunft denken. Flaggen wurden gehißt. Ich aber fand es nicht möglich, bei dem sich anlassenden volkstümlichen Festefeiern mitzumachen. Denn ich stellte die bange Frage: Wie wird es weitergehen? Was für Nachrichten werden jetzt aus Europa kommen, wo endlich die Karten auf den Tisch gelegt werden müssen? Welche Nachrichten von den Eltern und der Tante? Wie wird die Zukunft beschaffen sein, die Zukunft der Welt und die Zukunft Deutschlands? Ich war froh und traurig zur gleichen Zeit.

Ich war an jenem achten Mai ins Stadtzentrum gegangen. Auf dem Wege betrat ich das Postgebäude in der Calle Ayacucho, um das Schließfach nach Briefen zu untersuchen. Ich habe immer wieder und wieder nach Briefen, nach Nachrichten Ausschau gehalten. Von der Post führte mich der Weg über die historische Plaza Murillo in mein Büro. Da warteten schon meine Freunde, und noch mehr kamen hinzu. Bald waren wir in lebhafte Debatten verwickelt. Jeder wollte mitteilen, was er gehört hatte, die neuesten Nachrichten wurden ausgetauscht über die Dinge, die sich ereignet hatten, und wohl auch über einige Dinge, die sich nicht ereignet hatten und nur Gerüchte waren. Wie sehr waren wir an diesem Tage beseelt von dem Gedanken, mittun zu dürfen an dem sich anlassenden und notwendigen Wiederaufbau. Wir sprachen von den Zukunftsplänen des einzelnen. Einige saßen buchstäblich auf gepackten Koffern, aber es war wohl klar, daß manche Hoffnungen verfrüht waren.

Ich erinnere mich an die Dringlichkeit, die wir an diesem Tage einer gutfunktionierenden und mit den notwendigen Machtmitteln ausgestatteten Liga der Nationen beimaßen. Unsinniger Ehrgeiz hatte die Welt ins Unheil gestürzt. Warum sollte es nicht möglich sein, daß die Länder anstatt von den Ehrgeizigsten von den Fähigsten regiert würden? Nicht nur sollte diktatorischen Willkürregierungen ein Ende gesetzt werden und demokratische Ordnung etabliert sein, wir fragten uns auch, inwieweit die Rolle des Staates überhaupt reduziert werden könne. Hatte nicht schon Platon gesagt, daß der Staat wie ein Mensch sei, nur im großen, und daß seine wichtigste Aufgabe darin bestehe, die Bürger zur Tugend zu führen?

Und dann gingen die guten Freunde wieder – einer nach dem anderen. Ich versuchte, die Bedeutung dieses Tages zu erfassen. Zwar war da noch der Krieg mit Japan, aber ich war mir bewußt, daß eine tiefgreifende Zäsur in der Geschichte der Menschheit an diesem Tage eingetreten war, eine Zäsur von historischen Dimensionen, und daß diese Möglichkeiten eröffne zum Guten und zum Bösen, zur Harmonie und zur Konfrontation.

Ich bin noch stundenlang durch die Straßen der Stadt gewandert, allein, aber begleitet von so vielen Gedanken, von so vielen Hoffnungen und von so viel Erleichterung und Zuversicht, aber auch von soviel Traurigkeit. Und diese Traurigkeit hat mich seither nicht mehr verlassen bis auf den heutigen Tag.

PETER LUDWIG
## Wehe den Besiegten

Als Neunzehnjähriger erlebte ich den Tag der bedingungslosen Kapitulation im Lazarett in Bad Nauheim. Der malerisch gelegene, unversehrt gebliebene Ort war sogenannte »Offene Stadt«, wurde also nicht verteidigt. Viele Dächer zeigten große Rote Kreuze. Alles war überfüllt. Für unsere Sanitätseinheit war hier Schlußstation des Rückzuges durch Westerwald und Taunus. Schrecklich die Bilder des Endes mit an Bäumen aufgehängten sogenannten Verrätern, Zivilisten und Soldaten mit roh bemalten Hinweisschildern auf Feigheit. Vereinzelt sahen wir weiße Fahnen an Ortseingängen, und unauslöschlich dröhnt das Sturmglockengeläut in mir nach, das von den Kirchtürmen über der Landschaft erklang und das Anrücken jenes amerikanischen Feindes kündete, der von vielen als Befreier begrüßt wurde. Die Deutsche Wehrmacht, in Blitzsiegen Herr über Europa geworden, war in Auflösung, kaum bewaffnete Volkssturmeinheiten standen eher verlegen an Straßenkreuzungen. Wegen der zahllosen gegnerischen Tiefflieger, die auf jede Bewegung eines Fahrzeuges oder Menschen tödliche Jagd machten, vollzog der Rückzug sich nur nachts, während wir tags in Wäldern Schutz suchten. Wenige Stunden nach unserer Aufnahme in Nauheim rückten die Amerikaner ein. Auch dann blieb die Lazarettverwaltung in deutscher Hand. Bis zu meiner Entlassung vier Wochen später sah ich keinen Sieger.

Die ungeheure Freude bei der Nachricht vom Kriegsende ist meine beherrschende Erinnerung. Ich weiß nicht, welches Wetter war, ich weiß nicht, was ich gegessen oder getan habe, ich weiß nur, wie glücklich-erleichtert ich war. All das Grauenvolle, all das Entsetzliche hatte ein Ende. Nur dieses Gefühl füllte mich aus. Mit der Furchtbarkeit dessen, was da mit der »bedingungslosen Kapitulation« geschah, verband ich noch keine Vorstellungen. Endlich war Schluß mit diesem langen Krieg. Schluß auch mit der Schande, die ich so bitter für die Heimat empfand wegen all des Schrecklichen, das in unserem Namen geschehen war.

Als am ersten September 1939 der Krieg begann, hatte ich mich als Vierzehnjähriger sofort zu jedem nur möglichen freiwilligen Einsatz gemeldet. Glühenden Herzens wollte ich alles tun, damit Deutschland siegt. Meine Eltern waren entsetzt und sahen nur die Katastrophe. Ich widersprach leidenschaftlich und habe in den folgenden Jahren als Hitlerjugendführer meine Kräfte für die böse Sache eingesetzt. Daß sie wirklich böse war, erfuhr ich vor meiner Einberufung 1943 auf zweifache Weise. Ein mir befreundeter hoher Hitlerjugendführer schilderte in tiefster Betroffenheit den Besuch eines Konzentrationslagers. Er war sichtlich aufgewühlt. So könne man mit Menschen – auch mit Feinden – nicht umgehen. Schlimmes habe er gesehen. Einzelheiten erfuhr ich nicht.

Und das zweite Erlebnis: Als Kulturfunktionär der Hitlerjugend, gerade siebzehn Jahre alt, war ich zu einer Tagung in Berlin.

Brutal wurde dort von nach dem Sieg geplanten Zwangsmaßnahmen berichtet. Mit allen Gegnern im Reich, besonders aus Kreisen der Intellektuellen, würde man in den ersten Tagen des Siegesrausches kurzen Prozeß machen. Auch wurde erklärt: Die damals laufenden Büchersammlungen aus Privathaushaltungen für die Soldaten dienten wesentlich dazu, deutsche Bibliotheken von Schandliteratur zu reinigen. Dabei genannte Autorennamen waren mehrheitlich jene, die ich besonders liebte.

So begeistert ich mich für die Politik Hitlers als Junge engagiert hatte, noch bevor ich Soldat wurde, war ich innerlich geheilt. Mein Vater war überglücklich. Ich haßte das Regime, dem ich jahrelang ergeben war. Auch und gerade als Soldat wollte ich nichts mehr für eine Sache tun, deren Untergang ich wünschte. Meine Wehrmachtskarriere ließ mich nicht einmal Gefreiter werden. Ich brauchte die Heimat nicht zu verlassen, auch dort holte der Krieg uns ein.

Die Erleichterung und Freude am Tag der Kapitulation waren so übermächtig, daß sie blind machten für das Furchtbare dieses Geschehens. »Wehe den Besiegten«, sagten die Römer. Und was dann die Alliierten mit Deutschland taten, überstieg jede vernünftige Vorstellung. Sie zerrissen das aus tausend Wunden blutende Land und zerstörten jedes staatliche Gefüge. Nach dem erbarmungslosen Terror des Luftkrieges, jenem ungesühnt gebliebenen Kriegs- und Kulturverbrechen, dem auch meine Mutter am 19. Juli 1944 beim Volltreffer in den Luftschutzkeller unseres Hauses in Koblenz am Rhein zum Opfer fiel, wurden Millionen und Millionen Landsleute aus der östlichen Heimat vertrieben und zahllose umgebracht. Des Amerikaners Morgenthau finstere Pläne, die das hochindustrialisierte Deutschland in seinen neuen engen Grenzen zu einer primitiven Agrarwirtschaft zurückführen sollten, wurden diskutiert. All das habe ich an jenem achten Mai 1945 verdrängt. Es wurde erst fühlbare Wirklichkeit, als ich einige Monate später in jenes berüchtigte Kriegsgefangenenlager in Kreuznach gelangte, in dem die Sieger auf blankem Feld Rache zur Richtschnur und Unmenschlichkeit zum Alltag machten.

An jenem Tag der bedingungslosen Kapitulation gab es für mich nur Glück und Hoffnung. Das vor uns liegende düstere Tal der Demütigungen, des Hungers, der Kälte und großer Not habe ich nicht gesehen. Ich sah nur in erträumter Weite die hohen Züge deutschen Wiederaufstiegs: gleichsam blaue Berge einer wieder guten Zukunft. Und daß dann schließlich unser zerstückeltes, erniedrigtes und von aller Welt mit Füßen getretenes Land tatsächlich in nur wenigen Jahren wiederauferstand als Frucht unendlichen Fleißes und alles überwindenden Aufbauwillens – allerdings auch als Folge der West-Ost-Konfrontation, die im Streit der Sieger untereinander die Restländer in der Mitte wieder begehrt sein ließen –, war an jenem achten Mai 1945 noch fern.

ULRICH DE MAIZIÈRE
## Aufgewühlt und erleichtert zugleich

Den achten Mai 1945 habe ich als einen Tag tiefbewegender und zugleich zwiespältiger Gefühle empfunden. Er beendete einen fast sechsjährigen Krieg, der Millionen von Menschen Tod und Verwundung gebracht und unzählige deutsche Städte in Trümmer gelegt hatte. Er befreite Deutschland von einer Diktatur, deren Verbrechen in ihrem vollen Umfang manchem erst nach dem Krieg bewußt geworden sind. Er besiegelte eine politische, militärische und moralische Niederlage, wie sie in der deutschen Geschichte ohne Beispiel ist. Und doch löste das Bewußtsein, überlebt zu haben, ein Gefühl der Erleichterung und der Befreiung von einem fast unerträglich gewordenen Druck aus.

Für mich hielt dieser Tag aber noch eine besondere Aufgabe, eine der menschlich schwersten in meinem Leben, bereit.

Im Februar 1945 war ich nach Genesung von einer Verwundung in die Operationsabteilung des Generalstabs des Heeres versetzt worden. Ende April wurde diese mit der vergleichbaren Abteilung des Oberkommandos der Wehrmacht (OKW) zusammengelegt. Das OKW war in den letzten Tagen des April mit seinen wichtigsten Teilen nach Flensburg ausgewichen. Im Norden der Rußlandfront kämpfte weit abgesetzt, eingeschlossen von sowjetischen Truppen und mit dem Rücken zur Ostsee, in hoffnungsloser Lage, die Heeresgruppe Kurland unter dem Oberbefehl von Generaloberst Hilpert. Hitler hatte seit Wochen trotz intensiver Gegenvorstellungen des Chefs des Generalstabes des Heeres den rechtzeitigen Rückzug oder Abtransport der Heeresgruppe – selbst nur von Teilen – immer wieder verweigert. Nun war es zu spät. Schon am dritten Mai 1945 war ich nach Kurland entsandt worden, um Generaloberst Hilpert die Lagebeurteilung des OKW und gleichzeitig die Vollmacht zu übermitteln, in der bis zum nahen Kriegsende noch verbleibenden Zeit unter Einsatz aller verfügbaren Transportmittel zur See und zur Luft so viele Menschen wie möglich dem Zugriff der russischen Armee zu entziehen. Hierbei sollten besonders gefährdete Personen und die Väter kinderreicher Familien bevorzugt werden.

Kurz darauf wurde die Kapitulation vereinbart, die am neunten Mai 1945, null Uhr, in Kraft treten sollte. Da das OKW wegen der nicht mehr zuverlässigen Funkverbindungen nicht sicher war, ob der Kapitulationsbefehl die Heeresgruppe Kurland wirklich erreicht hatte, wurde ich am achten Mai ein weiteres Mal in einem Sonderflugzeug nach Kurland geschickt. Ich sollte die durch Funk übermittelten Weisungen bestätigen und ergänzen und zugleich die Abschiedsgrüße des OKW überbringen. Ich erhielt den Befehl, nach Erledigung dieses Auftrages noch am gleichen Tag nach Flensburg zurückzukehren. Jeder Soldat wird nachfühlen können, welch schwere innere Belastung ein solcher Auftrag für einen jungen Offizier – ich war erst dreiunddreißig Jahre alt – bedeutete.

Ich hatte damit gerechnet, mit berechtigten Vorwürfen gegen die Oberste Führung empfangen zu werden. Waren es doch deren auch von mir als sinnlos empfundenen Entscheidungen gewesen, die jetzt dazu führten, daß mehr als 200 000 Soldaten ohne jede Chance des Entkommens der russischen Kriegsgefangenschaft ausgeliefert wurden. Es erfüllte mich mit hohem Respekt, daß ich statt dessen eine nüchterne, gefaßte, tiefernste, zuweilen auch bittere, aber menschlich saubere Haltung bei allen Angehörigen des Heeresgruppenstabes vorfand. Man hatte das Ende vorausgesehen und sich innerlich darauf eingestellt. Der Generaloberst und sein Stab sahen ihre Aufgabe nur noch darin, allen Betroffenen das bevorstehende ungewisse Schicksal zu erleichtern. In der Truppe war die Disziplin ungebrochen. Die Heeresgruppe Kurland war an diesem Tage wahrscheinlich der einzige große Kommandobereich des deutschen Feldheeres, der noch voll intakt war.

Die Russen hatten am achten Mai alle im baltischen Raum verfügbaren Flugzeuge zu Tiefangriffen auf Flugplätze und Häfen eingesetzt, um einen Abtransport von Soldaten in letzter Minute zu verhindern. Schon während meines Vortrages beim Chef des Stabes, Generalleutnant Friedrich Foertsch, dem späteren Zweiten Generalinspekteur der Bundeswehr, wurde gemeldet, daß mein Flugzeug am Boden zerstört worden sei. Damit schien sich meine Sorge, am letzten Tag des Krieges nur wegen dieses ohnehin so undankbaren Auftrages in Kurland festgehalten zu werden und in Gefangenschaft zu geraten, zu erfüllen. Aber man gab mir die Chance, mit einem kleinen Flugzeug, einem »Fieseler Storch«, zum Flugplatz Windau zu fliegen, um Platz in einer der dort noch zum Start bereitstehenden Transportmaschinen zu finden.

Beladen mit einem Packen von Abschiedsbriefen an die Familien der Zurückbleibenden – und natürlich auch ein wenig beneidet – flog ich im Tiefflug nach Windau. Es war Nachmittag geworden. Der Flugplatz – ohne feste Piste – war durch lang dauernden Regen in ein Schlammfeld verwandelt. Ein Tiefangriff russischer Flugzeuge folgte dem anderen. Eine Transportmaschine nach der anderen wurde vor unseren Augen beschädigt oder zerstört. Erst am frühen Abend fand ich Platz in der letzten noch flugfähigen Maschine, überladen mit Menschen, viele Verwundete darunter. In einer kurzen Pause zwischen zwei Tieffliegerangriffen startete das Flugzeug mit dem Wind und nur mühsam sich vom weichen Boden erhebend, in westlicher Richtung auf die nahe gelegene Ostsee zu. Wir blieben unbehelligt; aber erst nach einer Stunde löste sich die Spannung.

Und doch waren wir noch nicht in Sicherheit. Wegen des späten Startens konnte das Flugzeug erst bei Dunkelheit in Flensburg eintreffen. Der Flugplatz war bereits unter britischer Kontrolle. Technische Landehilfen gab es nicht. Würde der Pilot den Flugplatz überhaupt finden? Wie würden die Briten auf ein unangemeldetes Flugzeug bei Dunkelheit reagieren? Es war ein Glück, daß die meisten Mitfliegenden von diesen Schwierigkeiten nichts wußten. So blieb es an Bord ruhig, auch wenn Erwartungen und Hoffnungen sich in einer spürbaren Nervosität niederschlugen. Der Besatzung gelang eine bruchlose Landung. Die Briten hatten die Landung zugelassen. So konnte ich mich gegen Mitternacht mit erfülltem Auftrag – tief aufgewühlt und erleichtert zugleich – zurückmelden. Die mitgenommenen Briefe haben ihre dankbaren Empfänger, wenn auch oft erst nach Wochen, fast ausnahmslos erreicht.

<br>

### Hans Marsalek
## Die Tage davor

Woran alles soll man sich erinnern, wenn man die Befreiungstage vom dritten bis zum achten Mai 1945 im Konzentrationslager Mauthausen nach vier Jahrzehnten beschreiben soll? Soll es die Hoffnung aller Häftlinge sein, die Befreiung doch zu erleben, oder die im Gesicht vieler Gefangenen tief eingegrabene Sorge, die SS-Bewachungsorgane könnten zuletzt noch alle Inhaftierten liquidieren? Soll man die Tausenden und Tausenden aus Haut und Knochen bestehenden, hin und her schwankenden – manchmal auch nur noch kriechenden – Elendsgestalten beschreiben, die, ohne ein Wort zu sagen, allein mit ihren tief-liegenden großen Augen immer wieder die Frage stellten: Werde ich vorher sterben?

Für alle war es eine Zeit des Wartens wie des Hoffens. In wechselndem Rhythmus stiegen und sanken die Hoffnungen. Die SS-Folterknechte und ihre Opfer wußten, daß die kommenden Tage für beide Teile schicksalhaft würden. Das Lager zeigte sichtbare Anzeichen einer beginnenden Veränderung: Es waren die Strukturen der Macht, die sich zugunsten der Unterdrückten ändern sollten. Bereits anfangs Mai 1945 machte sich diese Unruhe bemerkbar. – Eine fast fieberhafte Nervosität.

Am zweiten Mai wurden von der SS die letzten »Geheimnisträger«-Häftlinge erschossen. In der Nacht vom zweiten auf den dritten Mai waren vom Westen her die Einschüsse schwerer Artilleriegeschosse der vorrückenden US-Armee deutlich hörbar. In dieser Nacht verließen einzelne SS-Angehörige, manche in Uniform, manche in Zivilkleidung, manche mit gefälschten Personalpapieren, das Lagergebiet.

Am dritten Mai, um 6.30 Uhr früh, fand in Mauthausen der letzte Häftlingsappell statt. Die Zählung nahmen die bekannten SS-Führer ab. Jedoch wenige Minuten nach dem Appell, beim Ausmarschieren der Arbeitskommandos, traten beim Haupttor, im Jourhaus, auf den Türmen und als Begleitmannschaften der Arbeitskommandos den Häftlingen völlig fremde waffentragende Uniformträger als Bewachungsorgane entgegen. Die Neuen trugen die Uniform der Wiener Feuerschutzpolizei und erweckten den Anschein, stramme Nachfolger der SS zu sein. Als Häftlingsfunktionär, sogenannter Lagerschreiber 2, konnte ich sofort wahrnehmen, daß die aus Wien nach Mauthausen evakuierten Feuerwehrmänner Angst hatten. Angst vor ihrer neuen Aufgabe, Angst vor den Häftlingen, Angst vor ihrer ungewissen Zukunft.

Nun verließen die SS-Peiniger als »Waffen-SS, Regiment Mauthausen« mit 260 ehemaligen Häftlingen, die vor zwei Monaten zu den SS-Einheiten zwangsrekrutiert wurden, das Lager. Bereits zeitig früh erhielten die ehemaligen Häftlinge (in den Baracken drei und vier untergebracht), für ihre Uniform

militärische Abzeichen der Waffen-SS, weiter jeder ein Sold-
buch und zu seinem Gewehr sechzig Stück Munition. Außerhalb des Gefangenenlagers, auf den Straßen zwischen den SS-
Baracken, wurden die Häftlinge zu je fünfzehn Mann aufge-
teilt, dem Kommando eines SS-Unterscharführers unterstellt
und einer SS-Hundertschaft zugeteilt. Dann begaben sich die
geschlossenen militärischen Formationen auf den unmittelbar
unterhalb des Häftlingslagers befindlichen SS-Sportplatz. Dort
wurden vom Lagerkommandanten, SS-Standartenführer Franz
Ziereis, zehn ehemalige Häftlinge zu einem Exekutionskom-
mando bestimmt. Diese Häftlinge haben dort bei der Böschung
einen am Vortage festgenommenen und an einen Pfosten ange-
bundenen Zivilisten erschossen. Den Gnadenschuß gab Ziereis
ab. Das war die letzte Hinrichtung im Konzentrationslager
Mauthausen. Nun begaben sich die SS-Organe in die vorher
von Häftlingen östlich von Mauthausen angelegte Graben- und
Bunkerstellung. Diese sogenannte Auffangstellung befand sich
östlich von Mauthausen, und hier wollten sie »gegen die Russen
kämpfen«. Die Rote Armee stand damals etwa hundert Kilometer entfernt, die vom Westen vorrückenden US-Truppen befanden sich etwa in 26 Kilometer Entfernung von Mauthausen.

Begreiflicherweise wurde der Abmarsch der SS-Bewacher
von den Häftlingen sofort wahrgenommen. Blitzartig änderte
sich die Stimmung. Nun war es allen klar: Wenn die SS nicht
zurückkehre, würden sie nicht getötet werden, und die Befreiung werde bald erfolgen. Es gab keinen SS-Zwang, und es gab
auch keine Arbeitsleistung mehr. Die Bewegung der gesamten
Lagerverwaltungsmaschinerie wurde fast schlagartig unterbrochen. Warum auch sollten die hungernden, ausgelaugten, von
jahrelangen Schmerzen und Entsetzen gequälten KZler in den
Steinbrüchen, im Baukommando, in den Messerschmitt-Hal-
len weiterschuften? Doch die Einstellung jedweder Tätigkeit
in den Häftlingsküchen, zum Teil in den Sanitätsbaracken, innerhalb der Lagerverwaltung, so zum Beispiel bei der Wasser-
versorgung, in den Magazinen, führte nicht nur zu chaotischen
Zuständen, sondern auch zu Verhältnissen, die alle Häftlinge

gefährden konnten. Im Mauthausener Hauptlager befanden sich zu diesem Zeitpunkt etwa 23000 völlig unterernährte Kinder (ab sechs Jahren), Frauen und Männer, darunter mindestens 12000 Kranke. Außer den Steckrüben gab es nichts.

Auf dem Appellplatz, in den Baracken, in den Lagerstraßen und in den Arbeitsstätten bildeten sich Menschentrauben. Es wurde über die persönliche Lage, die qualvollen Jahre der Verfolgung und über die Befreiung, über die eigene Familie, die Heimat, die militärische Lage sowie die politische Zukunft diskutiert. Alle nahmen an, daß der Krieg in Europa in wenigen Wochen oder sogar Tagen beendet sein würde. Nach der Abnormalität des barbarischen Nationalsozialismus wurde eine andere Welt erwartet: besser, friedlich, ohne Konzentrationslager, ohne Angst, ohne Verfolgungen. Es gab viele, viele schwärmerische Gedanken und Illusionen. Die anderen, aber Hunderte von »Muselmännern«, die infolge ihres körperlichen Zustandes weder gehen noch stehen konnten, saßen kraftlos in irgendeiner Ecke oder lehnten sich an die Barackenwand. Der Wille, die Niederlage ihrer SS-Peiniger zu erleben, gab ihnen die Kraft, auf die Befreiung zu warten. Manche stellten leise Fragen oder bewegten ihre Lippen, und nicht wenige verlöschten plötzlich wie ein Kerzenlicht.

Es war ein sonderbarer, zugleich tragischer wie auch freudiger Zustand. Man hatte den Eindruck, als löse sich das Lager auf. Nur die Bewachung der Wiener Feuerschutzpolizei funktionierte halbwegs. Dieser Zustand eines allgemeinen Aufbruches und zugleich einer Lethargie – eine Periode zwischen rabiatem SS-Zwang und der eintretenden Freiheit – dauerte zwei Tage lang. Es waren nur wenige Aktive, die versuchten, zumindest notdürftig den Küchenbetrieb und das Sanitätswesen in Gang zu halten. Auch ein Ordnungsdienst mußte provisorisch eingerichtet werden, weil einige Inhaftierte – vor allem Kinder und Jugendliche – die Magazine und Küche zu stürmen versuchten. Außerdem begannen spontane gewaltsame Umsiedlungsaktionen, die zu heftigen Auseinandersetzungen führten. Das alles schaffte eine lynchartige Situation gegen die geringfügige Minderheit der deutschsprachigen Häftlinge, die viele Häftlings-funktionäre stellten. Es gab Verletzte, aber auch Tote.

Der fünfte Mai 1945 war ein sonniger Frühlingstag. Dichter Nebelschleier bedeckte die Tiefen der Mühlvierteler Täler und den Donaustrom. Im Süden, in weiter Ferne, vom Nebel abge-schnitten, sah man die weißbedeckten Gipfel der Ennstaler Al-pen. Die Hügel rund um das Lager glänzten im Frühlingsgrün. Es war ein herrlicher Tag. Etwa um zwölf Uhr hörte man zuerst von der von Nebelschwaden verdeckten Zufahrtstraße ein Mo-torengeräusch und dann . . . dann kamen langsam in das Son-nenlicht ein weißer Personenwagen mit einem Delegierten des Internationalen Roten Kreuzes und zwei amerikanische Pan-zerspähwagen hervor.

Unweit des Krankenlagers blieben die Fahrzeuge zuerst ste-hen. Im gleichen Augenblick wurden die Torflügel des Sanitäts-lagers von den Kranken weit aufgerissen. Hunderte und Hun-derte von Männern, Frauen und Kindern strömten in wilden Scharen zu den Fahrzeugen. Die meisten waren halb nackt, nur mit Lumpen bedeckt, manche ohne jede Bekleidung. Alle ver-hungerte Geschöpfe, lebende Skelette. Es war, als hätte sich ein Massengrab geöffnet. Manche waren ohne Beine, andere kamen auf einem Bein hüpfend, manche schleppten sich, auf allen vieren kriechend oder robbend, heran; sie alle versuchten, die Tanks und die lebensrettenden Soldaten zu berühren, ihnen zu danken. Die anderen, völlig Entkräfteten oder kaum Bewegungsfähigen wälzten sich im Staub und Schlamm der Lagerstraßen, versuch-ten, die Hände oder zumindest den Kopf in Richtung der Panzer-fahrzeuge zu strecken. Alle wollten die Retter begrüßen. Die meisten Befreiten weinten, manche tanzten oder hüpften vor Freude um die Fahrzeuge, schrien in einem freudig-hysterischen Anfall. Andere wieder wurden ohnmächtig, und viele, ja unzäh-lige sind gerade in diesen Minuten der so sehnsüchtig erwarteten und endlich erfolgten Befreiung gestorben.

Oberhalb des Krankenlagers warteten die Häftlinge am Ap-pellplatz, viele kletterten bereits auf die Mauer. Als die Panzer-fahrzeuge herankamen, gab es ein großes Freudengeschrei. Die

Wache der Wiener Feuerschutzpolizei öffnete das Haupttor, und ein US-Panzerspähwagen kam hereingefahren. Dem Fahrzeug entstieg ein Unteroffizier. Er veranlaßte vorerst, daß die Lagerwache auf der Zufahrtstraße vor dem Häftlingslager antreten solle. Die Wiener Feuerwehrmänner kamen vom Jourhaus, aus den SS-Baracken und von den Wachtürmen und stellten sich in einer geschlossenen Formation auf. Während das vor sich ging, konnte man beobachten, wie einzelne Hälftlinge, vorwiegend republikanische Spanier, an den Amerikanern vorbei durch das Tor beim Jourhaus hinausgingen, wie sie die weggeworfenen Waffen der Lagerwache an sich nahmen und auf einige der Wachtürme stiegen. Von diesem Augenblick an war das Lager ohne Bewachung.

Die Panzerbesatzung traf Anstalten, wegzufahren; und trotz der Intervention eines österreichischen Häftlings, im Lager zu verbleiben und den Schutz der befreiten Häftlinge zu übernehmen, fuhr die Besatzung ab, weil sie fernmündlich den Auftrag erhielt, ihre unterbrochene militärische Ausspähung fortzusetzen. Somit verließen nach etwa dreistündigem Aufenthalt die US-Panzerfahrzeuge das Lagergebiet. Schon vorher waren die Organe der Wiener Feuerschutzpolizei in geschlossener Formation als Kriegsgefangene abmarschiert.

Nach der Abfahrt der Panzerbesatzungen rechneten die befreiten Häftlinge – über den Frontverlauf und die militärische Lage in der nahen Umgebung nicht informiert – mit der möglichen Gefahr einer Rückkehr von SS-Einheiten. Aus diesem Grunde und weil überall Waffen leicht zu besorgen waren, haben sich viele Häftlinge bewaffnet. Nun bildeten sich geschlossene militärische Formationen der befreiten Häftlinge. Es waren vor allem die bereits vorher organisatorisch erfaßten Spanier, in der Folge jedoch stellten in ihrer absoluten Mehrzahl die Sowjetbürger bewaffnete militärische Einheiten auf. Diese bewaffneten Häftlinge besetzten im Laufe des fünften bis siebten Mai in der Ortschaft Mauthausen die Post, das Gemeindeamt, die Gendarmerie und bildeten bei der Eisenbahnbrücke am linken Donauufer einen Brückenkopf.

Am fünften Mai übernahm ein österreichischer Oberst die Leitung der militärischen Häftlingseinheiten. Jedoch in der folgenden Nacht mußte die Leitung einem sowjetischen Major übergeben werden. Dieser Zustand der Sicherung des Lagers durch die bewaffneten Häftlinge dauerte bis zum Eintreffen der US-Soldaten am siebten Mai 1945. In den Vormittagsstunden dieses Tages wurde das Lager Mauthausen von Einheiten der 11. Panzerdivision der dritten US-Armee besetzt. An diesem Tag wurden alle ehemaligen deutschsprachigen Häftlinge aus dem Nebenlager Gusen in das Hauptlager Mauthausen überstellt, weil sie von den ausländischen Häftlingen bedroht waren.

Unmittelbar nach dem Einzug der US-Truppen gab es das ungemein komplizierte Problem der Häftlingsentwaffnung. In den Tagen der Befreiung konnte nicht verhindert werden, daß Waffen in unbefugte Hände gelangten. Es haben sich Gruppen von rachedurstigen und ausgehungerten Häftlingen gebildet, die in der Umgebung von Mauthausen mit Gewalt Lebensmittel sowie Kleidung »beschlagnahmten«. Ab achten Mai versorgten die US-Soldaten die Häftlinge mit Lebensmitteln, mit Medikamenten, und die Lage normalisierte sich.

Wir alle wußten: Jetzt sind wir endgültig frei. Daß irgendwo in Norddeutschland oder in Berlin die obersten Herren der deutschen Kriegsmaschinerie kapitulierten, hatten nur wenige der befreiten Häftlinge zur Kenntnis genommen. Für sie war die Abnormalität und Brutalität des Nationalsozialismus bereits am fünften Mai 1945 beseitigt und die SS-Peiniger am siebten Mai 1945 endgültig besiegt.

HANS MATTHÖFER
## Zwischen Wittenberge und Eldena

Wo ich am achten Mai 1945 tagsüber war, das weiß ich ganz genau: auf der Flucht in einem Waldstück zwischen Wittenberge und Eldena, schlafend, dösend oder tagträumend, zugedeckt mit einer großen, unheimlich praktischen italienischen Zeltbahn, die ich aus einem geräumten Feldlazarett in Fehrbellin entwendet hatte, mit Sträuchern getarnt, ein entsichertes Sturmgewehr griffbereit, mit halbem Ohr auf fremde Geräusche achtend, die vielleicht von Soldaten der Roten Armee hätten kommen können und – wie in den kommenden Monaten – nachdenkend darüber, was das alles eigentlich bedeutete.

In den ersten Maitagen hatte ich mit anderen Angehörigen der sich auflösenden Wehrmacht versucht, über die Elbe zu kommen. Ich wollte mich dann allein zu meinen Eltern nach Bochum durchschlagen, aber die Amerikaner beschossen unser mühselig konstruiertes Behelfsfloß von der Westseite her. Bei der Rückkehr an das Ostufer überraschten uns die Russen, die sich geschickt auf die Lauer gelegt hatten.

Nach langer und wohlüberlegter Abwägung des Risikos entschloß ich mich, bei der ersten günstigen Gelegenheit zu fliehen und mich von den Russen nicht wieder gefangennehmen zu lassen. Daß ich dieses – wie sich herausstellen sollte – richtige Kalkül anstellen konnte, verdanke ich ausgerechnet Edwin Erich Dwinger. Dessen Bücher über das Schicksal deutscher Soldaten, die im Ersten Weltkrieg in russische Kriegsgefangenschaft gerieten, hatte ich im Deutschunterricht meiner Volksschule an der Bochumer Feldsieperstraße stundenlang laut vorgelesen, weil ich angeblich eine so klare Aussprache hatte und meiner Deutschlehrerin sonst nicht viel einfiel. Deutschen Soldaten würde es dieses Mal bei den Russen nicht besser ergehen, davon ging ich aus.

Gleich in der ersten Nacht überredete ich einen Fallschirmjägerleutnant aus Wattenscheid, gemeinsam mit mir aus der Scheune auszubrechen, in die sie uns mit etwa sechzig anderen gesperrt hatten. Wir hatten Gerüchte gehört, die Amerikaner seien in Mecklenburg eingerückt. Ohne Kompaß und Karte marschierten wir nachts nach Norden, was bei Regen oder bewölktem Himmel so einfach nicht ist. Wir hatten Glück, weil es meist klar war. Mehr als zehn oder zwölf Kilometer pro Nacht schafften wir aber nicht. Vom Morgengrauen bis zum

Dunkelwerden verkrochen wir uns in den Wäldern. Wir hatten großen Hunger und wahnsinnigen Durst. Statt Verpflegung fanden wir in der ersten Nacht einen Haufen Sturmgewehre mit Munition und nahmen uns jeder eines mit, für alle Fälle. Zu essen und trinken fanden wir wenig, denn wir trauten uns nicht in menschliche Siedlungen.

Es entstand eine gewisse Spannung, weil wir unterschiedliche Auffassungen von der Bedeutung militärischer Rangunterschiede in Grenzsituationen hatten. Ständig in Angst, von den Russen entdeckt und angeschossen zu werden, schien es unseren überreizt-kritischen Sinnen, daß der andere lärmend durch die Nacht tölpelte, aber es gab immer wieder Situationen, die uns zeigten, daß wir unabweisbar aufeinander angewiesen waren. Nach fünf, sechs Tagen haßten wir uns wie die Pest.

Einmal auf dem Rückzug in der Ukraine hatte ich geholfen, ein Vorratslager der Organisation Todt aufzubrechen. Wir fanden riesige Mengen von Pfirsichkonserven, die wir mit dem Seitengewehr aufstachen, um den Saft trinken zu können. Die Erinnerung an diesen Pfirsichsaft ging mir zwanghaft Tag und Nacht immer wieder durch den Kopf. Der Hunger plagte mich. Am linken Oberschenkel hatte ich seit Wochen eine eiternde Streifschußwunde, die so juckte, daß ich sie im Halbschlaf immer wieder aufkratzte. Ich war also mit eigenen Problemen voll beschäftigt. Es hätte mich wenig beeindruckt, wäre mir bewußt gewesen, daß an diesem Tage einige Generäle die endgültige Kapitulation des Deutschen Reiches unterschrieben.

Zieht man die damaligen Umstände in Betracht, ging auf dieser Flucht eigentlich alles recht gut. Nur einmal kamen mir drei oder vier Russen ziemlich nahe. Aber sie waren lediglich in den Wald gegangen, um mit großem Lärm und offenbarem Wohlbehagen ihre Notdurft zu verrichten. Mein Kumpel schlief aus Sicherheitsgründen und weil wir uns – im wahrsten Sinne des Wortes – nicht mehr riechen konnten, etwa hundert Meter weit von mir entfernt. Sofort hellwach, als ich die Russen kommen hörte, lag ich aufgeregt und schußbereit lauernd und konnte nichts anderes denken als: Lieber Gott, hilf mir jetzt bloß, sonst trifft die der Blitz beim Scheißen.

Ich hatte wahrhaftig nichts gegen sie. Im Gegenteil, ich mochte Russen, hatte mir Mühe gegeben, ihre Sprache zu lernen, und kam mit jedem einzelnen von ihnen gut aus. Der liebe Gott, den man eigentlich in solche Dinge nicht hineinziehen sollte, zu dem ich damals aber ein enges persönliches Vertrauensverhältnis hatte und den ich immer wieder mit Erfolg bemühte, war mir und ihnen jedenfalls gnädig. Sie trollten sich nach vollendeter Verrichtung. Wenn es der verdammte Zufall gewollt hätte, die Bundesrepublik hätte sich 1978 wohl einen anderen Finanzminister suchen müssen.

Der Fallschirmjäger und ich gingen noch gemeinsam über die Elbe und trennten uns dann. In Eldena ergab ich mich den Amerikanern. Sie überstellten uns nach einigen Wochen den Briten, die für mich nach der Besatzungszone zuständig waren. In einem Wald gegenüber Fehmarn grub ich mir mein eigenes Loch, spannte die große Zeltbahn darüber und machte mir meine Gedanken. Neunzehn Jahre war ich alt und zuletzt Unteroffizier bei den Panzergrenadieren gewesen. Mich beschäftigte der Krieg, der mich zweieinhalb Jahre meines Lebens gekostet hatte, seine Ursachen, Kosten und Folgen. Daß die Freundschaft zwischen den Vereinigten Staaten und der Sowjetunion schnell zu Ende gehen und neue Kriegsgefahren entstehen würden, erschien mir ganz selbstverständlich und eigentlich unabwendbar. Meine Schlußfolgerung: Ich wollte mit allen Kräften dazu beitragen, diesen drohenden nächsten Krieg zu verhindern, und war mir darüber im klaren, daß ich zuerst herausfinden mußte, wo seine Ursachen lagen. An meinem 20. Geburtstag war ich wieder zu Hause, ließ meine Uniform blau färben, machte mich an die Arbeit und wurde bald Sozialdemokrat.

# Kriegsende in der Heiligen Stadt

Es war schwül an jenem Dienstag in Jerusalem, ungewöhnlich für die Jahreszeit, ungewöhnlich für die Stadt, die mit ihrer idealen Höhenlage auch in der Glut der heißen Jahreszeit ihren Bewohnern erfrischende Brisen zu bieten pflegt; jedenfalls hatten wir dem Kalender nach Anspruch, von hochsommerlichen Bedingungen noch weit entfernt zu sein.

Ich arbeitete im Auftrag der Hagana in einer kriegsbezogenen Behörde der britischen Mandatsregierung. Die Arbeit war subjektiv alles andere als befriedigend, aber für den Nachrichtendienst der Hagana, für die Analysen der vorstaatlichen jüdischen Stellen in Palästina war sie nicht ohne Wert: Die Behörde war ein Umschlagplatz für wirtschafts- und verkehrspolitisches Geschehen im gesamten Mittleren Osten, und vieles, was auf meinem nicht sehr »gehobenen« Schreibtisch landete oder was ich auf ihm zum Landen brachte, gewährte aufschlußreichen Einblick auch in die politische Stimmung im näheren und weiteren Umfeld.

Seit Monaten war das militärische Ende des Krieges in Europa in Sicht; seit Hitlers Tod war es täglich, stündlich zu erwarten. Das spannende tägliche Nachziehen des Vormarsches der Alliierten auf den Landkarten hatte schon fast aufgehört. Man wußte, die Schlacht war geschlagen, gewonnen; was übrigblieb, war eine Formsache. Man durfte die Siegesfreude nähren. Die Meldungen der letzten Tage hatten vor allem von Hunderttausenden von neuen Gefangenen berichtet. Auch bei den Juden hätte die jahrelange Spannung eigentlich vorfreudiger Erwartung weichen sollen. Wir schienen dazu nicht weniger Grund als andere zu haben.

Vor nicht langer Zeit hatten wir fürchten müssen, in dem wallenden Meer arabischer Begeisterung für Nazideutschland unterzugehen; im Irak hatte Rashid Ali einen Aufstand gegen die Briten geführt, dem viele Juden im Zweistromland zum

Opfer gefallen waren; Syrien und Libanon waren unter der Herrschaft Vichys gewesen; der Mufti von Jerusalem, religiöses Oberhaupt der Moslems in Palästina und Prediger des Terrors gegen die Juden des Landes, war von Hitler als Verbündeter empfangen worden und war dessen Unterstützung versichert worden; und vor allem – unter erwartungsvollem Jubel und den ihn begleitenden Freudenfeuern in arabischen Städten und Dörfern – hatte Rommel vor den Toren Alexandrias gestanden, Palästina mit Eroberung und seiner jüdischen Bevölkerung mit Vernichtung gedroht.

All dies war fast vergessene Vergangenheit. Die Gefahr eines Aufrollens des Nahen Ostens durch die Wehrmacht war gebannt; der letzte deutsche Soldat auf afrikanischem Boden war in die Gefangenschaft gegangen; Italien war befreit; Amerikaner und Russen hatten sich an der Elbe getroffen; der Apostel des Schreckens war tot. Die Juden Palästinas – in der Stadt und auf dem Lande, am Fließband und hinter dem Pflug, die Zehntausende in den britischen Streitkräften –, die die einzigen Bundesgenossen im Überlebenskampf für Freiheit zwischen dem Atlantischen Ozean und der Grenze Indiens inmitten einer Flut der Hoffnung auf Hitlers Sieg gewesen waren, schienen aufatmen zu dürfen. Die ersten Opfer der unbeschreiblichen Unmenschlichkeit hatten Anspruch, auch unter den ersten der auf die Zukunft Hoffenden zu sein.

So schien es. Aber schon im Herbst 1942 hatten uns auf Umwegen die ersten Gerüchte erreicht. Nie gekannte Namen wurden mit noch ungläubigem Schrecken vernommen; zunehmend eindringlichere Schilderungen des Grauens wurden mit Vorbehalten der Unvorstellbarkeit von Mund zu Ohr geflüstert. Dann wurden die Vernichtungslager entdeckt, »befreit«, erst im Osten, dann im Westen, und was bis dahin bezweifelte Meldung, erhoffte Ausgeburt der Phantasie gewesen war, wurde zu unfaßbarer Wirklichkeit.

Das volle Ausmaß war noch nicht bekannt; in dem unerschöpflichen »Optimismus« eines über die Jahrtausende geprüften Volkes rechneten wir noch nicht in Millionen. Als sich die Schlachten ihrem Ende näherten, wußten wir um das Schlachten – aber noch immer hofften wir auf »Übertreibungen«.

Die BBC, die Armeestationen und der Sender Jerusalem meldeten endlich die Unterzeichnung der bedingungslosen Kapitulation. Auf dem Korridor des dem Franziskanerorden gehörenden Gebäudes, das die Behörde zu Anfang des Krieges gepachtet hatte, liefen die Beamten zusammen. Der schottische Abteilungsleiter gesellte sich auf einen Augenblick zu uns. Ich habe seine Worte noch im Ohr: »Well, that's that. Good show. Now let's all do some work.« Damit verschwand er.

Was mir alles in den nächsten Minuten durch den Kopf ging, weiß ich nicht mehr, wohl aber, was mich sprachlos an meinen Schreibtisch zurücktrieb. Ein arabischer Kollege, mit dem ich über die Jahre ein zwar nicht intimes, aber durchaus freundliches Verhältnis gehabt und ein gelegentliches Glas Bier getrunken hatte, kam lächelnd auf mich zu. »Marcuse« – das war damals noch mein Name –, »I am so glad for you. Now you will soon be able to go home.« Das war weder ironisch noch hämisch gemeint. Er wußte, daß ich in Deutschland geboren war; daß ich nicht beabsichtigte, dorthin zurückzugehen, kam ihm nicht in den Sinn.

Die Beauftragten der Hagana in einer Anzahl von Regierungsämtern wurden noch am späten Nachmittag zu einer Besprechung bestellt. Die Hitze war noch drückender geworden. Aus vielen Hunderten weitgeöffneten Fenstern sendeten die von jahrelanger Zurückhaltung befreiten Rundfunkanstalten in den drei Landessprachen lautstark und ohne Unterbrechung Schilderungen aus Eisenhowers Hauptquartier, Kommentare, Kommuniqués der Alliierten und erste öffentliche Stellungnahmen der arabischen und jüdischen Führungen.

Kleinere und größere Einheiten der in Jerusalem stationierten britischen und verbündeten Etappen- und Verwaltungstruppen zogen in alkoholischer, von Minute zu Minute zunehmender Ausgelassenheit ans Jaffator und auf den Zionsplatz. Die trotz des Krieges nicht sehr zahlreichen Bars und Cafés, bescheiden und konservativ in Anpassung an den Charakter der Heiligen Stadt, füllten sich in kurzer Zeit, und wohl zum erstenmal seit Bestehen mußten sie Gäste abweisen; die geringen Vorräte von Spirituosen, die normalerweise dem spärlichen Alkoholkonsum von Arabern und Juden mehr als gerecht wurden, waren schnell vertrunken. Auch die Soldaten mußten schließlich ihren Durst mit Limonade stillen.

Auf dem Weg zur Besprechung fielen mir wieder die Worte des Kollegen ein. Ich hatte Berlin im Frühsommer 1933 als Dreizehnjähriger verlassen – jung genug, um in der neuen Heimat ohne Schwierigkeiten Fuß zu fassen; reif genug, um mir zu geloben, den Boden der alten, vermeintlichen Heimat, die uns ausgespien hatte, nie wieder zu betreten. Ich brach das Versprechen, das ich mir gegeben hatte, aber die Umstände ließen mich weder Reue noch Scham empfinden. Als ich wieder nach Deutschland kam, war ich kein geduldeter Fremdling; ich war der Vertreter des jüdischen Volkes in freier Eigenständigkeit. Doch das lag an jenem heißen Spätnachmittag in weiter Ferne.

Die Besprechung war kurz. Ihresgleichen fanden viele an anderen Orten statt. Das Kriegsende brachte die Prioritäten wieder in Ordnung. Der Kampf um Unabhängigkeit – die Entschlossenheit, endlich unseres Schicksals Meister zu sein –, der, solange der Krieg gegen Hitlers Dämonenreich nicht gewonnen war, zumindest in der Praxis vorübergehend zweite Geige zu spielen hatte, würde wieder an erster Stelle stehen. Die Auseinandersetzung mit London würde mit aller Bestimmtheit wiederaufgenommen werden. Doch diese Priorität stand nicht mehr allein; eine andere mußte sich mit ihr als untrennbar und unteilbar verbinden: die Suche nach denen, die die Hölle überlebt hatten; die Verpflichtung, sie in die Heimat zu führen und am Ringen um jüdische Freiheit teilhaben zu lassen.

Das war unser Auftrag am achten Mai 1945. Beide Teile würden vollzogen werden; doch wir ahnten nicht an jenem Dienstag, wie wenige von den Millionen Verschleppten uns für den Weg in die Zukunft geblieben waren. Am folgenden Morgen begann das Zählen der Ermordeten. Es ist noch nicht abgeschlossen.

## Johann Baptist Metz
# Streuungen

Die letzten Stunden des Hitler-Reiches waren für mich die ersten Stunden auf USA-Boden. Das klingt einschneidend, verlockt zu »großen« Überlegungen. Sie wären jedoch alle nachträglich ersonnen, denn auch an diesem Tag spielte sich für mich alles unterhalb dessen ab, was man gern mit großen Begriffen beschreibt. Meine persönliche End-Erfahrung hatte ich an diesem Tag schon ein paar Wochen hinter mir. Von ihr muß ich zunächst reden – und dies nicht nur, weil sie sich mir weit tiefer eingrub und mich auch heute noch bei meinen theologisch-politischen Überlegungen heimsucht, sondern weil nur sie die Atmosphäre und die Umgebung verdeutlicht, in der ich diesen achten Mai 1945 erlebte.

Gegen Kriegsende wurde ich sechzehnjährig aus der Schule herausgerissen und zum Militär gepreßt. Nach flüchtiger Ausbildung in einer Würzburger Kaserne kam ich schnell an die Front, die damals schon über den Rhein tief ins Land gerückt war. Die Kompanie bestand nahezu ausschließlich aus jungen Leuten. Eines Abends schickte mich der Kompanieführer mit einer Meldung zum Bataillonsgefechtsstand. Ich irrte die Nacht über durch zerschossene, brennende Dörfer und Gehöfte, und als ich gegen Morgen zu meiner Kompanie zurückkam, fand ich nur noch Tote, lauter Tote. Sie alle waren kaum ein Jahr älter als ich, und nun waren sie, mit denen ich tags zuvor noch Kinderängste und Jungenlachen geteilt hatte, von einem kombinierten Jagdbomber- und Panzerangriff überrollt worden. Ich konnte ihnen nur noch ins erloschene tote Antlitz sehen. Ich erinnere nichts als einen lautlosen Schrei. Verstört irrte ich noch stundenlang allein im nahen Wald umher; krampfhaft hielt ich, um nicht als Überläufer verdächtigt und aufgeknüpft zu werden – das hatte man mir, dem Buben, eingeschärft – meine Knarre umklammert, ehe sie mir ein riesiger GI aus der Hand schlug und mir so ein betäubtes Leben rettete.

In dieser Erfahrung sind meine Kindheitsträume zerbrochen, und die Fühllosigkeit, die sie in mir erzeugte, durchstimmte auch noch jenen achten Mai. An diesem Tag gab es keine großen Empfindungen mehr. Das Land meiner Kindheit oder was immer ich mit meinem viel zu großen Stahlhelm verteidigen wollte, war schon an jenem Aprilmorgen zerfallen, und die Vision von einem »Großdeutschen Reich« hatte in mir nie so geblüht, daß sie auch nur mit meiner kindhaften Neugierde, mit meiner Lust am Lernen (und sei es denn aus Mathematik- und Physikbüchern) hätte konkurrieren können. Ich war wohl eine jener Memmen, die an der Kanone der Schule nachtrauerten. Als letzten Proviant hatte ich denn auch in meinem Brotbeutel – ein Buch verpackt, ein harmlos-trockenes Nachschlagebuch mit allerlei tabellarischen Übersichten. Dieses Buch gehört schließlich in meine Erinnerungen an diesen achten Mai.

Ich war nach wenigen Gefangenschaftstagen in Marseille – wahrlich aus Versehen – noch auf ein Schiff verfrachtet worden, das mit einem letzten Kriegskonvoi deutsche Kriegsgefangene in die USA brachte. Am Kapitulationstag wurden wir in Richmond, Virginia, an Land gebracht. Im nahen Lager begegnete ich dann an diesem Tag noch einmal dem Gespenst jenes Reiches, das inzwischen in Schutt und Asche gefallen war. Die Mehrzahl der deutschen Soldaten, die dort schon über längere Zeit – übrigens recht komfortabel – untergebracht waren, zumeist Kriegsgefangene aus dem Afrikafeldzug, hielt nämlich die Kapitulation für bare amerikanische Propaganda. Hinter der Lagermauer hatten sie sich eine unsichtbare Mauer gegen die Niederlage gebaut, ein unzerstörtes, sieghaftes Deutschland, das sie gegen die Amerikaner und gegen »diese defätistischen Deutschen« verteidigten. »Feiglinge« und »Verräter« wurden wir geschimpft, als wir versuchten, ihre Träume mit Verweis auf unsere Erfahrungen zu dementieren.

Ich selbst, immer noch betäubt von meiner eigenen End-Erfahrung und auch sonst als Jüngster eher unsicher und scheu, hatte mich an diesem gespenstischen Nachhutgefecht kaum beteilig. Am Abend kam dann einer der alteingesessenen PoWs, der sich besonders verächtlich über den »unsoldatischen Fatalismus« der Newcomer geäußert hatte, zu mir. »Na, Kleiner, dir sollen sie ja sogar ein Buch gelassen haben. Kann ich auch mal drin blättern?« Natürlich konnte er. Und er schob mir dafür noch eine Scheibe golden getoastetes Brot zu.

## EDMUND NEUDECK
## Tromsö – es gab keine Witze

Für mich und meine Mitarbeiter auf der damals nördlichsten deutschen Wetterwarte in Tromsö (Seefliegerhorst) kam die totale Kapitulation nicht wie ein plötzliches Ereignis. Für niemanden konnte das damals gelten. Die Teilkapitulationen in Oberitalien und in Nordwestdeutschland und nicht zuletzt die dank guter Empfangsgeräte so bequem zu hörenden »Feindsender« hatten uns auf diesen Kriegsschluß vorbereitet. Aber es gab auch die bange Frage: Werden vielleicht einige Verrückte angesichts der noch vorhandenen Vorräte an Munition und Verpflegung auf den Gedanken kommen, den Widerstand in Norwegen – von Oslo über Bergen und Narvik bis Tromsö – trotz allgemeiner Kapitulation fortzusetzen? Es verdichtete sich das Gerücht, daß einige hohe Herren hofften, bessere Bedingungen für die Truppen in Norwegen zu erreichen. Ob es diese naiven Bestrebungen angesichts der totalen Luftherrschaft der Anglo-Amerikaner wirklich gegeben hat, weiß ich nicht. Aber auch falsche Gerüchte wirken auf das Bewußtsein.

Die Anordnungen, die uns dann am achten Mai erreichten, befreiten uns von der Befürchtung eines Gegenbefehls: Vor dem Termin, an dem die Waffen schweigen, sind alle Unterlagen, die den Stempel Geheim oder Geheime Kommandosache aufweisen, zu vernichten. Das taten wir dann: Alle Chiffrier- und Dechiffriertafeln für Wetterdaten, die über Funk vermittelt wurden, und die anderen Vorschriften, die im Geheimschrank lagen, wurden in einer tiefen Felsspalte verbrannt, einige nachgeworfene Handgranaten halfen dabei.

Meine Leute machten es zu gründlich, sie warfen auch das Handbuch der Deutschen Seewarte Hamburg mit den Daten über Ebbe und Flut ins Feuer – schon bald sollte mir dieses Buch sehr fehlen. Natürlich stiegen nicht nur in der Nähe meiner Dienststelle Flammen auf – andere hatten mehr zu verbrennen. Aus einigen Unterkünften hörten wir Schüsse. Wie wir erfuhren, waren die Hauptziele Hitler- und Göring-Bilder. Am nächsten Tag erreichte mich die Meldung, daß einer meiner Außenposten Selbstmord begangen hatte.

Eine gewisse Erleichterung trat natürlich dadurch ein, daß es nun keinen Fliegeralarm mehr geben würde und daß die Verdunkelung überflüssig war, das heißt, daß die Waffen schwiegen. Wobei die Frage auftauchte: Wie ist es mit den norwegischen Untergrundkämpfern? Noch am selben Tage kam die Mitteilung, daß auch für die Partisanen der Waffenstillstand gelte.

Immer wieder kam es zu Gesprächen über den Krieg und seinen Verlauf. »Mußten wir Polen überfallen?« fragte ein junger Obergefreiter und gab damit den Anstoß zu der Frage nach den Gründen des Krieges und damit der Niederlage. Der Zusammenbruch hatte sich schon längst abgezeichnet: »Warum wurde nicht früher kapituliert?« Keiner von meinen Gesprächskameraden behauptete, daß dieser Krieg durch Verrat, Sabotage verlorengegangen wäre. Die andern waren stärker und besaßen die besseren Waffen. »Was wird nun aus uns?« war eine der häufigsten Fragen. Müssen wir vielleicht die Kriegsschäden in Norwegen als zwangsverpflichtete Arbeiter beseitigen? Werden wir auswandern können? Aber wer wird uns das nach der totalen Kapitulation erlauben? Was wird aus dem Deutschen Reich? Nicht wenige verdrängten diese Fragen durch Alkoholkonsum. Vielleicht läßt sich die Situation am besten durch den Satz kennzeichnen: Es gab keine Witze.

Mehrere von uns waren aus dem Osten Deutschlands. Seit Herbst 1944 hatte ich keine Nachricht von meiner Familie und meinen Eltern aus Danzig. Werde ich sie wiedersehen? Wenn ja, wann und wo? Hoffentlich ist es ihnen gelungen, vor dem Einmarsch der Roten Armee in den Westen zu gelangen, das heißt in den Bereich der Anglo-Amerikaner. Über die beabsichtigten Besatzungszonen waren wir durch den Hinweis auf die Elbe als Besatzungsgrenze informiert worden. Die Greueltaten der Sowjetsoldaten an der Zivilbevölkerung waren uns bekannt. Auch wer der NS-Propaganda skeptisch gegenüberstand, konnte die Fülle der mitgeteilten Tatsachen nicht übersehen.

Was wir nicht erfahren hatten, war die Abmachung, daß sich die Dienststellen der Deutschen Wehrmacht und damit auch die Wetterwarten der Luftwaffe weiterhin dienstbereit zu halten hatten – nun für die Norweger und Engländer. Und so war ich nach kurzem Schlaf höchst überrascht, als am nächsten Morgen ein Anruf in englischer Sprache eine Wetterberatung für einen Flug nach Tromsö verlangte. Ich mußte meine Dienststelle wieder in Gang bringen, allerdings ohne die Chiffrierer und Dechiffrierer.

### GERTRUD NEUDECK
## Ob ich Erleichterung empfand?

Seit dem 28. März 1945, als die Rote Armee über uns hinweggerollt war, hatten wir keinerlei Nachrichten mehr über das Geschehen in der Welt. Man hatte uns sofort aus unseren Häusern vertrieben. Nun lebten wir am Rande von Danzig-Oliva in kleinen, teils beschädigten Häusern, immer soviel Personen als möglich in einem Raum. Das machte die Nacht manchmal etwas sicherer. Immer wieder fielen mir die Worte meines Schwiegervaters ein: »Mein Gott, jetzt müssen die Verantwortlichen doch die Schleusen im Westen öffnen und die Westmächte durchlassen, damit sie helfen, die rote Flut aufzuhalten.« Auch er war wie fast alle Männer festgenommen worden. Wir sahen ihn nie wieder. Wir Frauen waren nur bestrebt, im

Wald und Feld etwas Eßbares für uns und unsere Kinder zu finden und möglichst keinem Russen zu begegnen.

Eines Abends hörten wir von fern her lautes Schießen. Verstört kamen viele aus den Häusern gelaufen. Einige meinten, die Front käme wieder zurück. Eine andere Erklärung fanden wir nicht. Da aber nichts anderes geschah, gingen wir verängstigt in unsere Unterkünfte zurück und beteten gemeinsam. Nach einiger Zeit hörte das Schießen auf.

Am nächsten Morgen erfuhren wir es dann: Der Krieg ist zu Ende! Die Sowjets hatten über der Ostsee ein Freudenfeuerwerk abgebrannt, und einige in der Danziger Bucht liegende Schiffe schossen aus Anlaß des Sieges Salut.

Ob ich Erleichterung empfand oder Freude? Ich weiß es nicht mehr. Zu groß war damals die Sorge um die Zukunft.

RUPERT NEUDECK
## Ein schrecklich-schöner Tag

Ich war in diesen Tagen in kindlicher Vorfreude auf meinen sechsten Geburtstag: Am 14. Mai 1939 in Danzig geboren, hatte ich alle deutsch-polnischen Symbiosen und Konflikte in mich hineingesogen. Da ich ein Kind war, habe ich nur mit Mühe begreifen können, welches gottverdammte Bedürfnis die Menschen dazu trieb, sich gegeneinander abzuschießen, sich den »Lebensraum« streitig zu machen und das Recht auf Leben. Als drei- und vierjähriger Junge war ich in den Sommerferien auf einem Gutshof in Westpreußen, wo mir die starken polnischen Landarbeiter imponierten, so stark, daß ich mich an meinen ersten Berufswunsch sehr deutlich erinnere: Ich wollte »Pole werden« – der schönste Berufswunsch, den ein Kind haben kann, das so weit die politische Realität begriffen hatte, daß Polen diejenigen waren, von denen sich die eigenen Leute absetzten. Polen waren die Arbeiter, die abseits in schlechteren Unterkünften nachts die betörende Musik machten, die mit ihren Mädels zusammenwohnten und deren freies ausschweifendes Betragen bei den Preußen auf Mißbehagen und Naserümpfen traf, bei uns Kindern auf heimliche Begeisterung.

Die Russen marschierten ein, nachdem wir tagelang und nächtelang die Nervosität unserer Eltern und der anderen Erwachsenen zu spüren bekommen hatten. Eltern waren es meist gar nicht mehr, sondern nur noch Mütter, Großmütter, Tanten, alles Frauen, die jetzt in um so größerer Panik und Angst waren, weil sie wie alle hier von der Welle der Grausamkeit und Brutalität erfahren hatten, die eingesetzt hatte bei Soldaten, die wie losgelassen schienen und sich auf die deutschen Frauen warfen mit einer Gier und vergewaltigenden Lust, daß wir als Kinder durch diese Erlebnisse traumatisch wurden.

Wir waren ja immer dabei: Die Mütter und Großmütter nahmen uns ja überall mit, und wir waren auch, so spürten wir damals sehr deutlich, auch kleine Stoppschilder gegen die Vergewaltigungsorgie, die damals losbrach, weil man mit uns niedlichen kleinen Kinderchen die kinderliebenden sowjetischen Soldaten zu besänftigen oder abzulenken hoffte. Das klappte schon mal; dann strich einer von den Soldaten mir liebevoll über den Kopf oder brachte mir ein Stück Brot mit, bei dem ich dann nur die angstvolle Nebenüberlegung hatte: Ob ich das wertvolle Brot in meiner Hand bei dem Hunger, der mich allein plagte, wohl mit meinen drei Geschwistern werde teilen müssen oder nicht? Schließlich wird der Mensch schon als Kind dem Menschen ein Wolf, wenn er kreatürlichen Hunger hat: Er kann nur noch an seinen eigenen leeren und knurrenden Magen denken, nicht an den seiner größeren Schwester, nicht an den des jüngeren Bruders, noch weniger an den des ganz kleinen Geschwisterchens, das da im Kinderwagen lag, noch nicht einmal zwei Jahre war.

Der achte Mai war ein schrecklich-schöner Tag: Es war wieder einmal wie wüst geschossen worden, in der Nähe der Westernplatte muß es gewesen sein. Angst brach aus wie bei jeder neuen Schießerei, Nervosität. Wir waren aus dem Stadtkern an die Peripherie geflohen vor der plündernden, vergewaltigenden

Soldateska, die besoffen Türen einschlug und sich sofort an die einzige Sache heranmachte, nämlich die möglichst jüngeren Frauen. Wie oft sind mir diese fast archetypischen Bilder auf der »Cap Anamur« hochgekommen, wenn mir Vietnamesinnen erzählten, daß sie versucht hatten, ihre älteren Töchter durch Haarschnitt und andere Kleidung zu Jugendlichen männlichen Geschlechts zu machen – aus Angst vor vergewaltigenden Piraten!

Wir waren innerhalb des Stadtgebiets der mehr und mehr zerstörten Stadt Danzig von dem vornehmen Oliva, wohin wir aus dem zuerst gefährlich umkämpften Langfuhr in das Wohnhaus unserer Großeltern geflüchtet waren, nach Ludolfine gezogen. Dort waren wir wie viele andere, die auf die erste Gelegenheit zur Flucht warteten, in zwei winzigen Räumen untergekommen.

Der achte Mai war ein Tag mit guter Organisier-Ausbeute. Zunächst kam ich auf der Straße nach Danzig an dem Muttergottesbild vorbei und sah im Vorübergehen, daß genau vor dem Heiligenbild ein Butterbrot lag. Ich entdeckte, daß dies nicht nur eine Scheibe Brot, sondern daß es dazu eine Doppelschnitte mit ganz viel Butter in der Mitte war. Als gläubig aufgewachsenes Kind kam mir das geheimnisvoll wie ein Wunder vor, wie das der wunderbaren Brotvermehrung, obwohl ich damals schon theologisch wohl so weit war, daß es mir komisch vorkam, ob ich allein dieses dicke nahrhafte Brot würde aufessen können oder ob ich es mit anderen teilen müßte. Ich wagte also nicht, es gleich hinunterzuschlingen, sondern nahm es mit nach Hause. Dort wußte ich nicht, ob ich es meiner Mutter sagen konnte, daß ich das vor dem Muttergottesbild gefunden hatte. Vielleicht würde sie mir befehlen, das Brot dort wieder zurückzubringen. Ich entschloß mich schlechten Gewissens, das Brot allein zu verdrücken. Der allwissende und alles sehende Gott hat es zugelassen.

Dann gingen wir auf den Hof der nahe gelegenen Schule, wo die Russen ihr Quartier hatten, auf den Lieblingsplatz, wo wir stundenlang am Zaun uns die Beine in den Bauch stehen konnten, wobei uns so oft das Wasser im Munde zusammenlief, daß es gar keinen Speichel mehr gab. Zwischendurch ergab sich immer mal wieder die Gelegenheit, den Moment, da der oder die Köche gerade in den Lagerraum gingen, zum Klau eines oder mehrerer Klöpse auszunutzen. Klöpse sagten wir in Ost- und Westpreußen, nicht Frikadellen oder Buletten.

Die Mutter und meine Schwester, die große vernünftige, die zeit ihres Lebens nicht mehr die verlorengegangene Kindheit einholte, standen an einem Feuerherd und rösteten das wenige Brot, das wir noch hatten. Es sollte ja in den nächsten Tagen losgehen, wir wollten fliehen, denn in dieser Hölle von Willkür, Gewalt und bevorstehender Ausweisung wollte unsere Mutter nicht bleiben.

Doch war dieser Tag ein einziger Glückstag. Gegen Abend kam der Pater Haas von der nahe gelegenen Kirche und hatte unter seiner großen Soutane ein großes, langes, gut durchgebackenes Brot. Fromm, wie wir in dieser Hungersituation auch als Kinder geworden waren, kam ich, nachdem der Pater gegangen war, zu meiner Mutter und fragte sie ernst: »War das der heilige Antonius?« Was Hunger ist, kann derjenige, der ihn sich nur hat vorstellen müssen, nie richtig begreifen. Welches furchtbare Gefühl für eine Mutter, die die Schnitten Brot am Morgen für ihre hungrigen Kinder rationieren muß, die die luchsaufmerksamen Augen ihrer Kinder auf ihrer Hand spürt, wenn sie nicht garantieren kann, daß sie die eine Scheibe Brot dünner schneidet als die nächste . . .

Aber, wie gesagt, der achte Mai war ein Glückstag: Zusätzlich zu den rationierten Scheiben Brot gab es für mich heimlich das Brot, das wahrscheinlich irgendein Opferfetischist der Madonna hingelegt hatte. Es gab die geklauten Klöpse aus der Gulaschküche der russischen Köche. Dann gab es den Besuch des »heiligen Antonius«, der uns in der Not noch ein Brot brachte. Meine Mutter erfuhr dann im Laufe des Tages, weshalb es in der Nacht und am Tage so ausdauernd und wild wieder gebumst hatte: Es war der Tag der deutschen Kapitulation. Wo wohl unser Papa sein würde? Das letztemal war er vom hohen skandinavischen Norden zum Urlaub gekommen, von Kirkenes. Jetzt gab es nicht einen Strohhalm von Nachricht. Wir würden uns bei den an jeder Ecke lauernden Gefahren, zumal für die drei Frauen in unserem Troß – die eigene Mutter, die Tante und die Großmutter, deren Mann kurz vorher gestorben war –, in den nächsten Tagen auf den Weg machen müssen.

An diesem Tage auch sah ich wieder ein totes Kind. Einer Mutter war dieses Kind vom Leiterwagen gefallen. Erschöpft, keines Gefühls, keines Gedankens, keiner Aufmerksamkeit mehr fähig, war sie apathisch mit aufgerissenen Augen weitergegangen. Das Kind war tot. Wir sind durchgekommen, der ganz kleine Veit, den wir schon aufgegeben hatten, kam ebenfalls durch. Wir hatten wenig Hilfe. Die Menschen waren so total von der Anstrengung absorbiert, zu überleben, ihr Überleben zu sichern. Wir müssen jetzt, da es uns so gut geht, anderen helfen, die in ähnlicher Verzweiflung in der Wüste, in ausgedörrten Regionen Afrikas, auf dem Meere in Fluchtbooten, in Flüchtlingslagern, in Gefängnissen überleben müssen.

LEONID OLSCHWANG
## Zur Kapitulation eine Flasche Hennessy

Am achten Mai 1945 hatte die Reichsregierung kapituliert, doch die deutschen Truppen, die uns gegenüber am Frischen Haff lagen, ergaben sich nicht. Sie hatten die Dämme gesprengt und sich im Schutze des Wassers eingeigelt. Im Morgengrauen dieses Tages hatte ein Hauptmann mit einigen Soldaten von der Aufklärungsabteilung in einem Boot eine Erkundung vorgenommen, sie wurden jedoch bemerkt und beschossen. Der Hauptmann und zwei Soldaten wurden als Tote im Boot zurückgebracht. Unser General war darüber erbost, daß der tapfere, mit mehreren Orden und Medaillen ausgezeichnete Hauptmann, den er persönlich kannte, jetzt noch sterben mußte.

In einer ehemaligen deutschen Schule, wo er bald darauf die

Offiziere des Stabes um sich versammelte, sagte Generalleutnant Kalganow mit zorniger Stimme: »Berlin hat kapituliert, die aber wollen weiterkämpfen! Ich werde zu den Deutschen Parlamentäre schicken, und sie sollen ihnen sagen, daß, wenn sie sich nicht noch heute ergeben, dann werden wir ein solches Feuer eröffnen, das sie noch nicht erlebt haben. Das Wasser wird uns keineswegs daran hindern, sie vernichtend zu schlagen.«

Major Skobkin, der neben mir stand und mein Vorgesetzter war, rief: »Oberleutnant Olschwang kann Deutsch, er könnte gehen!« »Gut!« erwiderte der General, »auch Sie, Major, gehen mit!«

Skobkin war darüber nicht glücklich; denn es war bekannt, daß bei Budapest sowjetische Parlamentäre erschossen worden waren.

In einem Jeep, an dem eine hohe Stange mit einer weißen Fahne befestigt war, fuhren wir an einer wasserfreien Stelle in die deutschen Stellungen hinein. Im Jeep befanden sich außer Major Skobkin und mir auch Hauptmann Kusnezow von der operativen Abteilung und ein Sergeant als Fahrer.

Wir wurden von einem Gefechtsstand zum anderen geleitet, bis wir im Gefechtsstand des Divisionskommandeurs, Generalleutnant von Rappard, ankamen.

Wir wurden als Parlamentäre der 48. Armee bei ihm gemeldet (wir waren keine Abgesandten des Armeestabes, aber so war es uns befohlen worden). »Ich habe keine Vollmachten zum Verhandeln«, sagte Generalleutnant von Rappard zu den uns begleitenden deutschen Offizieren, »bringen Sie die Herren Offiziere zum Kommandierenden General!« befahl er.

Eingekeilt zwischen zwei deutschen Fahrzeugen mit Offizieren begaben wir uns in unserem Jeep zum Kommandierenden General. Im tiefen Sand der Dünen mußten wir auf die bewaldete Anhöhe hinaufsteigen, wo sich der Unterstand des Kommandierenden Generals befand. Der Unterstand war tief in die Erde eingelassen und mehrfach mit dicken Baumstämmen gedeckt. Aus der Luft war er kaum auszumachen. Wir gingen in einen großen Raum hinunter. Die Wände bestanden aus

Birkenholz, alles sah sehr gut eingerichtet aus. Ein Offizier in Generalsuniform, von hagerer Statur mit ergrauten Schläfen, ungefähr 55 Jahre alt, empfing uns. Er war Kommandeur des XVIII. Armeekorps, General der Infanterie Hochbaum. Wir richteten ihm aus, was uns von unserem General aufgetragen worden war. Wir wiesen ihn auch auf die ausweglose Lage hin, in der sich die von ihm befehligten Truppen befanden. Er zog darauf seinen Stabschef, Oberst Schmidt, hinzu, und sie beschlossen, die Kapitulation anzunehmen.

Auf einem runden Tisch wurden Karten ausgebreitet, und Major Skobkin zeichnete die Wege ein, auf denen sich die Truppen in die Gefangenschaft begeben sollten. Die Munitionslager und die Geschütze in ihren Feuerstellungen mußten unversehrt übergeben werden. Nur die Verpflegung durfte mitgenommen werden. Der General bat darum, den Offizieren zu gestatten, wenn auch ohne Munition, ihre Revolver tragen zu dürfen. Dies wurde genehmigt. Der General ließ eine Flasche Hennessy bringen, die wir im Stehen am Kartentisch geleert haben. Beim Weggehen reichte der General Major Skobkin die Hand, Skobkin nahm sie jedoch nicht an.

Noch am gleichen Tag wurde mir befohlen, den Kommandeur der 7. Infanteriedivision, Generalleutnant von Rappard, mitsamt Stab in die Gefangenschaft zu begleiten. Neben dem General im Fond des großen und eleganten Horch-Wagens sitzend, der von seinem Fahrer gelenkt wurde, begaben wir uns zum Stab unserer Einheit, der sich bei Tiegenhof befand.

In mehreren Autos und Mannschaftswagen folgten uns Offiziere und Mannschaften seines Stabes. In dieser 7. Division, im 19. Regiment, hatte im Ersten Weltkrieg Adolf Hitler als Gefreiter gedient. Der Kommandeur des 19. Regiments war damals Oberst List. Zu Ehren Hitlers nannte man das 19. Regiment »Regiment List«. Soldaten und Offiziere dieses Regiments trugen einen grünen Streifen am Ärmel.

Unser Horch und die Wagenkolonne hinter uns mußten des öfteren anhalten. In unmittelbarer Nähe befand sich das berüchtigte Konzentrations- und Vernichtungslager Stutthof.

Die an diesem Tage aus dem Lager befreiten Menschen, die noch die Kraft zum Gehen aufbrachten, füllten die Straßen. Ich mußte immer wieder aussteigen und den Weg für uns durch die gegen ihre Peiniger aufgebrachte Menge frei machen.

Im Gepäck des Generals, das bei der Ankunft in unserem Stab von seinen Soldaten ins Haus gebracht wurde, befanden sich unter anderem auch vierzig Flaschen Hennessy. Es war ein verlassenes Gutshaus. Generalleutnant von Rappard bat, ihm einen Raum zuzuweisen, wo er mit seinen Offizieren ungestört sprechen könnte. Wie später einer der Offiziere über das Gespräch berichtete, hatte Generalleutnant von Rappard zu seinen Offizieren gesagt: »Wenn das auch wahr sein sollte, daß der Führer Selbstmord begangen hat, dann müssen wir ihm über seinen Tod hinaus die Treue bewahren.«

Die deutsche Mannschaft des Stabes hat mir beim Abschied ein fast neues Hohner-Akkordeon geschenkt. Dieses lieh sich Major Skobkin zum Üben aus. Trotz mehrfachen Mahnungen hat er es mir nicht zurückgegeben.

ROSALINDE VON OSSIETZKY-PALM
»Nun aber gilt es,
den neuen Geist zu schaffen . . .«

Das Zitat von Carl Ossietzky – ein kurzes pathetisches Emporrecken und dann ein Niedersinken in die Alltäglichkeit – kennzeichnet den achten Mai 1945, den Tag des endlich proklamierten Waffenstillstands, wie wir ihn im Schulkollektiv erlebten.

Natürlich hatten wir in Schweden Monat für Monat, Wochen und Stunden auf die deutsche Kapitulation gewartet. Das Eis begann zu schmelzen. Wir warteten auf die ersten Zeichen des Frühlings. Die harten Winter lagen hinter uns. Wir hatten überlebt! So empfanden wir diesen Tag. Neu geboren. Auch die Verschonten besaßen ein legitimes Recht auf Freude. Denn auch sie wurden befreit. Wir hatten Jahre in deprimierender

Kontaktlosigkeit gelebt. In einer Trennung von Europa, die uns beeinflußte und traurig gemacht hatte. Noch stiller als sonst.

Die Neutralität hatte ihre Opfer von allen gefordert, vor allem Geduld, Rücksicht und Anpassung nach allen Seiten. Ich erinnere mich: Division Engelbrecht durch Schweden auf dem Weg nach Finnland, die operativen deutschen Verbände durch Schweden nach Norwegen, die Züge auf dem Bahnhof Krylbo. Zufällig stand auch unser Zug da. Ich sah die Gesichter deutscher Soldaten. Viele verbissene darunter, aber auch junge hübsche – vielleicht Studenten –, wie konnten sie nur? . . . Ich saß da mit Mann und Kind. Voller Angst, mit ohnmächtigem Haß.

Ich versuche – durch diese Skizze –, mich in das Gefühl zu versetzen, das ich am achten Mai besaß. Chaotisch war es, gespalten zwischen ungeheurer Freude, Erleichterung und nie überwundener Trauer, weil mein Vater nicht mehr lebte . . . und ich nicht zu ihm konnte. Ich lebte als Frau eines Lehrers in dem bekannten Internat Viggbyholmsskolan und hatte einen kleinen Jungen. Um zwölf Uhr läutete die Schulglocke. Alle liefen zur Aula. Der Rektor sprach. Wir hockten um Radioapparate. Die Grüße von Geretteten flogen durch den Äther. Die Stimme meiner Mutter erreichte mich. Sie war gesund und heil. Wir würden uns wiedersehen.

Die Schule beherbergte in den letzten Monaten einige deutsche Soldaten, die über die Grenze von Norwegen – durch Eis und Schnee – bei uns gelandet waren. Auch Jugoslawen wohnten bei uns. Sie sangen und tanzten. Die Schule war kurz vor Kriegsende zeitweise Quartier für Geflüchtete, die nur auf den Sprung zurück in ihre Heimat warteten. Ein kleines jüdisches Mädchen, das jahrelang versteckt in einem Berliner Keller gesessen hatte und beinahe blind war, wurde in der Schule betreut. Sie durfte selten ans Licht. Ich sah sie an diesem Tag: kränklich und blaß, mit dicken Brillengläsern, aber strahlend.

Viggbyholmsskolan lag ungefähr fünfundzwanzig Kilometer von Stockholm entfernt. Etwas mußte von uns unternommen werden. Deshalb begaben wir uns mit dem Vorortzug weg

von der vertrauten, sich eng anfühlenden, doch abseits gelegenen schützenden Umgebung. Wir fuhren in die Stadt.

Schwer, sich heute von der Gegenwart zu befreien und wieder den achten Mai zu erleben: Alle waren wie berauscht. Bei
meiner Ankunft in Schweden war ich eine von wenigen Flüchtlingen gewesen. Mein Flüchtlingsleben rollte sich auf an diesem
achten Mai. Jetzt – beim Zurückdenken – vergleiche ich es mit
der Gegenwart. Man sucht in Strömen die schwedische Küste.
Heute Libanesen und Palästinenser! Sie zerstören ihre Pässe,
werfen die einzige und wichtigste Identifizierungsmöglichkeit
weg. Meine Gedanken suchen – während ich diese Zeilen
schreibe – die Oldenburger Studentin Elke Suhr, die sich in einem Aufsatz »Weg zu Ossietzky« an den 27. Juni 1975 erinnert:

»An diesem Tage wurde unter dem Schutz von 200 mit Schlag-
stöcken bewaffneten Polizisten und Zivilpolizei der Schriftzug
›Carl-von-Ossietzky-Universität‹ vom Universitätsgebäude
entfernt, und das auf Anweisung unseres sozialdemokratischen
Kultusministers. Ohnmächtig, in ungläubigem Schrecken,
standen wir herum und sahen zu. Nur einige wenige Hochschulangehörige gingen auf die Polizisten zu und versuchten,
mit ihnen zu diskutieren. Einer von ihnen, ein Student, wurde
festgenommen und später wegen Widerstandes gegen Voll-
streckungsbeamte zu einer Geldstrafe verurteilt. Er gilt seitdem
als vorbestraft.

Ich glaube, wir alle fühlten damals das gleiche: Zorn und den
unbedingten Willen, etwas gegen diesen Akt willkürlicher
Staatsgewalt zu unternehmen. Wie viele mögen an die Leiden
Carl von Ossietzkys im nahen Esterwegen gedacht, was mögen
sie empfunden haben? Innerhalb der Hochschule gaben Hochschullehrer, Mitarbeiter und Studenten einhellige Protesterklä-
rungen heraus, und noch in derselben Nacht wurden über
30000 Flugblätter in fast alle Oldenburger Haushalte verteilt.
Selten habe ich in der Universität eine solche Einmütigkeit aller
politischen Gruppen und eine solche Bereitschaft zur aktiven
Gegenwehr ohne Wenn und Aber erlebt.

Über Nacht wurde auch der Schriftzug wieder von Studenten an gleicher Stelle angebracht und auf einer großen Kundgebung enthüllt. Universitätsleitung und Hochschulangehörige stellten sich offen hinter diese Wiederanbringung und bekräftigten erneut die Forderung nach dem Namen Carl von Ossietzkys.«

Am Tag des Waffenstillstands, des Friedens, begann schon der kalte Krieg. Vorbereitet. Dann kamen Hiroshima und Nagasaki. Wir waren am achten Mai 1945 froh und naiv. Glaubten optimistisch an die Zukunft. Ich hätte mir an diesem Tag niemals vorstellen können, daß Carl von Ossietzky noch einmal »geschlagen« wird. Es kommt der Tag der Gerechtigkeit: Helmut Gollwitzer, auch von Elke Suhr zitiert, zum Kampf, welchen Namen die deutsche Universität der deutschen Stadt Oldenburg tragen soll: »Kasernen, nach Hitler-Generälen benannt, und Polizeieinsatz gegen Ossietzkys Namen. Dieses Bild unseres Staates ist unerträglich.«

Man kann immer noch von ihm als dem Hochverräter hören. Schnell schwinden die Illusionen, daß mit dem Frieden auch neue Menschen heranwachsen würden, herangelassen mit neuen Gesetzen in der Hand, mit neuem Recht!

Am achten Mai 1945 mußte ich fünf Kilometer laufen, dann in den Vorortzug, dann ins Zentrum der Stadt. Ich kreuzte eine Straße, wo einmal ein Nazi gestanden hatte und Flugblätter verteilte gegen Ossietzky. Einige Schritte weiter, und ich war in der Kungsgatan. Da war was los! Ich sehe alles wieder. Sämtliche Schüler schienen in dieser Straße zu sein. Damals die größte und lebhafteste Straße in Stockholm. Aus den Fenstern der Büros wurden Papierkörbe geleert. Alles, was flattern konnte, flog durch die Luft. Tausende von Menschen schrien, sangen, lachten, tanzten. Wir aus Viggbyholm hielten uns an den Händen, wurden vom Strom mitgerissen, gerieten auseinander, um irgendwann, irgendwie nach Viggbyholm zurückzukehren. Für mich war dieser Tag der Anfang eines jahrelangen Konfliktes. Eigentlich hätte er das Ende meines Emigrantendaseins bedeuten sollen, das Ende eines wurzellosen Gefühls. Die schwedische Staatsbürgerschaft war eben nur eine Eintrittskarte für einen Stehplatz. Einige schwindelnde Minuten lang versank ich in Phantasien, um gleich das Unrealistische und Unmögliche einzusehen. Später hörte ich von jungen Deutschen, die zurückgingen. Ich stand am Kai und weinte.

Wir alle haben verdrängt. Auch ich habe gelernt, meine Sehnsucht zu verdrängen, lernte, mich anzupassen. Langsam gelang es. Ich wurde kühler, beherrschter, konnte studieren, arbeiten, wollte etwas für Menschen ausrichten, mußte meine Lust zu Theater, Tanz und Gesang runterschlucken. Das Leben auf der anderen Seite der Künste mußte gelebt werden. Und der achte Mai hatte einen definitiven Punkt gesetzt. Weil wir uns alle in Europa in einer Situation befinden, die Leben oder Tod bedeutet, möchte ich an Worte von Carl von Ossietzky erinnern. Ich entnehme einige Gedanken und Zitate aus einer kleinen Biographie von Kurt Singer und Felix Bürger:

»Der große Krieg ist nicht die einzige Katastrophe, die im vergangenen Jahrtausend die mitteleuropäische Gesittung in ihren Grundbedingungen erschüttert hat. Wir denken an zwei Ereignisse, die an sich durchaus verschiedenartig, doch mit gleicher eruptiver Kraft auftraten und riesenhafte kulturelle Trümmerfelder hinterließen. Das waren der Schwarze Tod, die große Pest von 1348, und der Dreißigjährige Krieg.

Als das große Sterben längst vorüber war, da schrieb, rückblickend auf die grause Zeit, ein guter Chronikenschreiber: Da die Not vorüber gewesen, habe die Welt wieder angefangen, fröhlich zu sein.

Nach dem Dreißigjährigen Krieg aber seufzte ein Künstler: Es sei gar traurig bestellt um das arme Deutschland; Gewerbe und Künste lägen danieder, und wer etwas könne, ziehe nach Flandern oder Welschland, denn in der Heimat müsse er verhungern.

Auf den Schwarzen Tod folgte das große Blühen der Renaissance, ein langer, heller Tag.

Auf den Krieg der dreißig Jahre aber Verfall, Zerrüttung, unendliche Nacht. Unheimlich zeitgemäß sind für uns die Worte des guten Chronisten und des armen Künstlers. Denn auch wir stehen am Ende einer Entwicklung. In unsern Händen liegt das neue Werden.

Was für ein Urteil wird dereinst der Geschichtsschreiber unserer Zeit über unsere Entscheidung fällen?«

Und lese weiter:

»Das arme Deutschland! Diesmal ist es nicht wie in versunkenen Jahrhunderten an seiner Bescheidenheit verkümmert, es ist zugrunde gegangen wie ein Parvenü, der zu hoch spekuliert und über Nacht Bettler wird. Es ist zugrunde gegangen an der Überspannung des Machtgedankens, an dem blinden Vertrauen, daß Gewalt und blankes Eisen allein maßgeblich seien, und Recht und Wahrheit läppische Phrasen, bestenfalls gut genug, Dumme damit einzuseifen. Wir müssen den plumpen Glauben an die Macht niederringen. Wir müssen der Macht vertrauen lernen, die im Geiste wurzelt, der die Tochter der Gerechtigkeit ist. Was zusammengebrochen ist, war schlecht fundiert, war nicht Wahrheit, sondern Kulisse.

Wir hatten eine wunderbar entwickelte Technik, eine aller irdischen Gebundenheit spottende Wissenschaft.

Wissenschaft und Technik aber – es ist das nicht allein unsere Schuld, wir folgen einer schlimmen internationalen Tendenz – waren nicht in erster Linie da, zu helfen. Sie schufen Werkzeuge der Vernichtung, Werkzeuge gräßlichsten Mordes.

Wir müssen die Wissenschaft wieder menschlich machen.«


LEONIE OSSOWSKI
## Die letzten Tage des Zweiten Weltkrieges

Für mich sind nur ein paar Bilder vom Kriegsende in meinem Gedächtnis geblieben, Erinnerungen an Angst, Wut und Haß, an Tränen und an den Satz eines amerikanischen Soldaten. Alles andere ist ausgelöscht und vergessen.

Nach der Flucht hatte ich mit meinem damaligen Mann in einem Gasthaus mit Landwirtschaft in der Nähe von Bad Salzungen (Thüringen) Unterkunft gefunden. Das Anwesen gehörte zu einem in der Stadt gelegenen Hotel, von dessen Leitung uns die Bewirtschaftung von Land und Vieh übertragen worden war. Wir richteten uns in einer Stube bei den freundlichen Wirtsleuten ein, die froh waren, die Arbeit nicht mehr allein machen zu müssen. Ich entsinne mich noch genau an die Landschaft, an die Tiere, vor allem aber an die Stille. Für den Krieg interessierte ich mich nicht mehr. Mit dem Verlust der Heimat hatte er für mich schon im Januar 1945 sein Ende gefunden. Ich lebte in einem Vakuum ländlicher Ruhe zwischen Vergangenheit und Zukunft, nicht fähig, mich mit etwas anderem zu beschäftigen als mit den Hühnern, Schweinen und Kühen, auf dem Feld zu arbeiten, zu essen und zu schlafen.

Eines Nachmittags im April fuhr ein Bus auf den Hof, aus dem mehr als fünfzig Menschen ausstiegen. Sie lärmten und redeten durcheinander, türmten ihr Gepäck an die Stallwände, liefen durchs Haus, durch die Scheune und nahmen von jedem Raum Besitz, der ihnen zweckmäßig erschien. Die Frauen und Männer waren Angestellte der Deutschen Reichspost, Wiesbaden, die aus unerfindlichen Gründen auf der Flucht vor den Amerikanern bis ins Thüringische evakuiert und nun bei uns einquartiert worden waren. Tagtäglich, so sagten sie, sei mit dem Einmarsch der Amis zu rechnen.

Kaum angekommen, begannen sich die Wiesbadener Postler zu streiten. Da ging's um den Schlafraum, um Betten, Geschirr und um Decken, auch um Eier, die ich verteilte, und die Milch, die ich ausschenkte. Die schöpft den Rahm vorher ab, sagten sie, und von den Eiern behält sie auch mehr, als ihr zustehen. Selbst in den Ställen machten sich die Postler zu schaffen und forderten: Die Schweine sollten geschlachtet und nicht gefüttert werden. Die Idylle war dahin, der Krieg hatte mich eingeholt.

Als die feindlichen Tieffliger uns tagsüber beschossen, die Deutsche Wehrmacht die Brücke über die Werra gesprengt hatte, als sich die ersten Deserteure auf dem Gehöft versteckten, da schlug Mißtrauen in Feindschaft um, und Drohungen wurden laut: Wer Deserteure versteckt, wird angezeigt. Also brachten der Gastwirt und ich den Soldaten Brot und Suppe heimlich und meistens nachts in die Scheune.

Das nächste, was mir einfällt, ist das Schwein, das ausgesucht und geschlachtet werden sollte. Der Hunger und die durch die Brückensprengung verursachte Tatsache, von der Welt abgeschnitten zu sein, löste zwischen den Postlern und uns plötzliche Einigkeit aus. Und während das Schwein, statt fachmännisch geschlachtet zu werden, nun jämmerlich unter den Händen eines der Postbeamten starb, schlichen der Gastwirt, mein Mann und ich zur Straße hinunter und sägten das einladende, zwei Meter lange Gasthausschild von den Pfählen. Wir wußten warum, denn langsam zogen die ersten feindlichen Truppen die Straße entlang. Wir rannten zurück, und ich schrie, so laut ich konnte, über den Hof: Die Amis sind da!

Ohne das Schild, sagten die Postler zufrieden, werden sie das einsam gelegene Anwesen nicht finden, vorerst sind wir sicher. Eine kaum vorstellbare Emsigkeit brach aus. Bald lag das erste Wellfleisch in den Töpfen und wurde Stück für Stück hastig und mit Salz bestreut zwischen die Zähne geschoben. Nie wieder in meinem Leben habe ich so viele Menschen so viel und so schnell und so ausgiebig Wellfleisch essen sehen.

Als der Morgen heraufzog, war nichts mehr von unserem Schlachtfest zu sehen, Schüsseln und Töpfe waren gespült, und jeder suchte sich für seine Portion klammheimlich ein gutes Versteck. Aus war's mit der nächtlichen Gemeinschaft. Als Tag für Tag Kolonnen von amerikanischen Soldaten die Landstraße unterhalb unseres Gehöfts entlangzogen, kroch einer der Postler durchs Gebüsch bis zum Straßenrand, kam zurück und sagte: Zigaretten haben die, aber nichts zu trinken, und wir haben Bier, aber keine Zigaretten.

Mein Bier? schrie der Gastwirt, ohne daß sein Protest zur Kenntnis genommen wurde. Wir rannten, in jeder Hand zwei Literkrüge, hinunter zur Straße und kamen mit Schokolade und Zigaretten zurück. Ein einträgliches Geschäft, an dem schließlich auch der Gastwirt Gefallen fand und das so lange dauerte, bis der erste Jeep auf den Hof rollte. Die Postler und wir hatten in Reih und Glied anzutreten. Der amerikanische Sergeant fragte nach deutschen Soldaten, wir schwiegen. Na gut, sagte der Ami und schnappte sich zwei Postler, dann nehm ich eben euch mit.

Da zeigte eine der Frauen auf mich, durchbrach das Schweigen und schrie: Die da, die versteckt welche und bringt ihnen Essen. Ohrfeigen, dachte ich, ich müßte sie ohrfeigen, sie bespucken, ihr irgend etwas antun, aber ich tat ihr nichts. Statt dessen ging ich zum Stall, hinter mir der Sergeant mit seiner geladenen MP. Ich hörte die Schweine, die Hühner und nahm plötzlich die ländliche Stille wieder wahr, die hier vor dem Eintreffen der Postler geherrscht hatte.

Wieviel? fragte der Sergeant. Soviel wie kamen, antwortete ich. Und wo sind sie? Ich zeigte zum geöffneten Stallfenster. Da nahm der Sergeant seine MP und schoß ohne Ziel aus dem Stall, ging zurück an den vor Schreck starren Postlern vorbei, setzte sich in seinen Jeep und verschwand.

An die folgenden Wochen kann ich mich nicht mehr erinnern, nur noch an einen Tag, den neunten Mai. Da saß ein deutschsprechender Amerikaner in unserer Gaststube. Er trank sein Bier, zahlte in Zigaretten und sagte dann langsam und deutlich: Der Krieg mit den Deutschen ist aus, wißt ihr das nicht?

Wir wußten es nicht, und einer der Postler wollte wissen, seit wann. Seit gestern, sagte der Amerikaner, legte seinen Mittelfinger über den Zeigefinger und fügte hinzu: Und jetzt marschieren wir gemeinsam gegen die Russen.

CHARLOTTE PETERSEN
## Es begann mit »Anneliese«

Mein Tagebuch aus dem Jahre 1945 ist verlorengegangen, wie manches andere damals. Ich kann das Datum nicht mehr genau sagen, es mag Anfang April 1945 gewesen sein, als Anneliese vor unserer Haustür stand mit der behördlichen Anweisung in der Hand, bei uns zu wohnen: eine junge Angestellte des Fernmeldeamtes Köln. Anfang und Einschnitt. Mit der Tatsache, daß das Fernmeldeamt von Köln zu uns in den Westerwald verlegt wurde, war erwiesen, was offiziell in den Nachrichten immer noch geleugnet wurde und nur als Gerücht umlief: Die Front war zurückgewichen. Es wurde auf deutschem Boden gekämpft. Ich kann mich nicht erinnern, daß Anneliese ihren Dienst in Dillenburg überhaupt noch aufgenommen hätte. Es war eine turbulente Zeit. Jeder Tag brachte Neues, und eine geordnete Fernmeldeversorgung gab es auch im Hinterland der Front nicht mehr. Anneliese suchte sich durch freundliche Hilfe im Haushalt dafür erkenntlich zu zeigen, daß sie mit uns zusammen diese Tage leben durfte.

Der nächste Schritt – auf den achten Mai zu – war der Tag, an dem plötzlich auf den Straßen unserer Stadt fliehende deutsche Einheiten zu sehen waren: abgehetzte, müde Männer, beileibe keine Helden oder Herrenmenschen. Bei einem Fliegerangriff lenkten Soldaten ihren Lastwagen in unseren Hof und nahmen unter ihm Deckung. Sie taten uns leid. Sie konnten nichts dafür, was Schreckliches im deutschen Namen geschehen war. Als der Angriff vorbei war, brachten wir ihnen Kaffee – oder das, was damals Kaffee genannt wurde.

Am nächsten Tag waren die Amerikaner da. Wir waren überrascht und durch die allgemeine Nachrichtensperre absolut nicht darauf vorbereitet. Als wenige Stunden später unser Haus beschlagnahmt wurde und wir uns auf Küche und Kellerräume beschränken mußten, waren wir so ahnungslos, daß wir nicht daran dachten, irgend etwas in Sicherheit zu bringen.

So trat der groteske Fall ein, daß ein amerikanischer Offizier alle Schränke und Kommoden verschließen ließ und uns die Schlüssel brachte. Hinterher erfuhren wir allerdings, daß er unser Eigentum erst gesichert hatte, nachdem bereits einiges geschehen war. Seine Leute hatten sich schon bedient. Unsere Fotoapparate, der Feldstecher, Schmuck und manches andere waren verschwunden.

Aus der ersten Zeit der Besatzung erinnere ich mich besonders an jenen Tag, an dem einer der amerikanischen Offiziere zu uns kam und sagte, wir sollten im Keller bleiben, es würde gekämpft werden. Bombenangriffe und Tiefflieger, das waren wir gewohnt, aber daß in unserer Landschaft gekämpft wurde, daß die Front nun hier verlief, war für uns neu und noch nicht erlebt. Wir saßen im Keller, hörten die Einschläge und waren bei aller Erregung über die Gegenwart dankbar, daß dies nun ein weiterer Schritt dem Ende zu sein mußte. Es ist bei dem einen Tag geblieben. Die Kämpfe vollzogen sich im Inneren des Landes, soweit überhaupt noch gekämpft wurde.

Und dann kam der achte Mai. Das Ende. Ich erlebte es mit großem Aufatmen. Wenige verstanden das. Die Menschen waren erschöpft. Jeder hatte seine Last zu tragen. In vielen Familien wurden Söhne vermißt. Wir alle waren arm geworden. Aber trotz allem: die Hitler-Zeit, die große Schande Deutschlands, war vorbei. Viele empfanden das nicht. Sie klagten nur über die augenblickliche Notlage. Manche schimpften auf die Besatzer. Nun ja, Hitler hatte ihnen persönlich nichts getan, während die amerikanischen Soldaten sie nun schikanierten. Ich erinnere mich, daß ich mit einer Freundin, einem Menschen, der mir nahestand und von dem ich glaubte, daß er genauso empfinden würde wie ich, in den ersten Tagen nach der Kapitulation eine kleine Wanderung machte. Wir saßen am Waldrand. Sie sagte: »Ach, das ist doch herrlich, daß man jetzt so etwas wieder machen kann und nicht dauernd Angst haben muß, daß Flieger kommen . . .« Ich war betroffen, daß sie nur daran dachte. In mir läuteten alle Glocken, daß der Nationalsozialismus endlich zerschlagen war. Es gab Frauen unter meinen Bekannten, die in diesen Tagen Trauer anlegten »für Deutschland«. Das war mir fremd. Aber wenige verstanden, was ich meinte, wenn ich vorsichtig versuchte, ihnen zu erklären, daß wir gerade »um Deutschlands willen« trotz allem Schweren, was wir nun durchzustehen haben würden, dankbar sein müßten, daß wir wieder anfangen dürften, freie Menschen zu sein, daß nicht mehr in unserem Namen Unschuldige gemartert und ermordet würden.

Zurückblickend glaube ich, daß man barmherzig sein muß: Die Menschen waren müde, am Ende ihrer Kraft. Sie sahen nur noch den gegenwärtigen Tag, nur die Plage, die ihnen jetzt aufgebürdet war. Wer war ich, daß ich sie deshalb hätte schelten dürfen?

PIERRE PETIT
## Schutzhäftling Nr. 2201

Achter Mai 1945, 14.40 Uhr
*Waffenstillstand!*
Ich hatte immer geglaubt, daß ich
froher wäre an diesem Tag. Der
Krieg ist zu Ende, aber es ist mir eigentlich gleichgültig.

Im nachhinein muten diese Zeilen sonderbar an. Aber als ich sie vor vierzig Jahren niederschrieb, stand ich noch völlig unter dem Schock meiner Erlebnisse in Bergen-Belsen. Am 25. April 1942 war ich als 17jähriger »wegen Gefährdung des Bestandes und der Sicherheit des Volkes und Staates und Betätigung für den Aufbau einer bewaffneten Widerstandsbewegung in Luxemburg« von der Schulbank weg verhaftet worden, überstand dann Verhöre, Prügel, Einzelhaft und Dunkelarrest, ein halbes Dutzend Gefängnisse und die Lager Hinzert und Dachau leidlich gut und wurde am 21. Juni 1944 schließlich nach Bergen-Belsen überstellt.

In dem »Erholungslager für nicht mehr arbeitseinsatzfähige KZ-Häftlinge« herrschten schon damals unmenschliche Zustände: Der Oberpfleger Karl Rothe spritzte – auf Befehl der Lagerführung – die »Unheilbaren« reihenweise ab. Kapos und Blockälteste, von der SS mit Vorliebe aus den Reihen der Kriminellen und der moralisch Labilsten rekrutiert und mit Privilegien bedacht, knüppelten ihre Mitgefangenen nieder und machten ihnen das Leben zur Hölle. Von Kameradschaft, der vielgerühmten »Solidarität der Lagerstraße«, war hier nichts zu spüren. Statt dessen gab es Korruption, Diebstahl und Mord, Angst und Verzweiflung, Hunger, Krankheit und Tod.

In Marcel Servet, einem jungen Franzosen, fand ich einen guten Freund. Zu zweit ließen sich die Schrecken des Lagers etwas leichter ertragen. Zuerst redeten wir noch oft von zu Hause, machten Pläne »für später«. Dann wurden wir immer stiller. Das Überleben kostete all unsere Kraft.

Ende 1944 stellten Bad und Desinfektion ihre Arbeit ein. Auch litten wir an Durchfall und konnten unser verdrecktes Zeug nicht mehr wechseln. Das Waschen wurde zu einem riskanten Unternehmen: Während der eine sich wusch, mußte der andere die Kleider bewachen, damit sie nicht gleich gestohlen wurden. Im Februar 1945 brach eine Typhusepidemie aus, die sich in unsern verlausten Baracken mit rasender Geschwindigkeit ausbreitete. Die Zahl der Toten stieg von Tag zu Tag. Allein im März zählten wir in Bergen-Belsen 18168 Tote: 13867 im »Erholungslager«, 3980 im Frauenlager und 321 in den verschiedenen Lagern der »Austauschjuden«.

Die Verhältnisse wurden immer chaotischer. Ständig neue Transporte brachten Unmengen von Kranken und Invaliden in das ohnehin schon heillos überfüllte Lager. Wir lagen zu zweit, dann zu dritt, schließlich zu viert und zu fünft auf einer einzigen Pritsche. Im Häftlingslager II mit durchschnittlich 8000 bis 10 000 Kranken gab es keinen einzigen Wasserhahn und kein Klosett. In einzelnen Baracken »lebten« bis zu 1500 Menschen auf einem Raum, der kaum für 150 Platz bot. Hier gab es keine Pritschen und keine Strohschütte. Die Menschen schliefen auf dem nackten Boden – wenn sie dazu Platz fanden.

Die Lebensmittelversorgung brach zusammen. Der Hunger machte uns wahnsinnig. Tausende stritten sich mit kraftlosen Händen um das wenige Essen, das ins Lager gebracht wurde. Nur die Stärksten konnten sich bis zu den Suppenkübeln durchkämpfen. Die andern gingen leer aus. Im März wurde tagelang überhaupt kein Essen mehr ausgegeben, weder Brot noch Suppe. Trinkwasser gab es nur noch aus verschmutzten

Zisternen. Ende Februar kamen die ersten Fälle von Kannibalismus vor, die im März dann immer häufiger wurden. Doch während ein paar hundert auf diese verzweifelte Weise versuchten, ihr Leben zu retten, verhungerten Tausende und aber Tausende, die zu schwach waren, sich auch nur von der Stelle zu rühren.

Mitte Februar fiel auch das Krematorium aus. Die ständig wachsenden Leichenhaufen wurden nun im Freien verbrannt. Eine Lage Holz, eine Lage Leichen wurden zu hohen Stößen aufgeschichtet, mit Dieselöl übergossen und in Brand gesetzt. Es bedrückte uns nicht mehr. Wir standen dabei und starrten in die Flammen. Wir suchten nur noch etwas Wärme. Ende März mußte die Leichenverbrennung im Freien wieder eingestellt werden. Es gab kein Holz mehr. Von nun an blieben die Toten eben liegen, wo sie gestorben waren. Die einen lagen in den Baracken selbst, zwischen Lebenden und Sterbenden, die zu schwach waren, um die Toten auch nur ins Freie zu schaffen; die andern wurden vor den Baracken aufgestapelt oder an einigen Stellen des Lagers zu Haufen getürmt. Als am neunten April die Lagerschreibstube ihre Arbeit einstellte, gab es insgesamt 5700 unbeerdigte Leichen, die in allen Stadien der Verwesung im Lager umherlagen. Und Tag für Tag kamen 1000 weitere Tote hinzu.

Als Himmler am elften April die Übergabe des Lagers an die britischen Truppen anordnete, unternahm die SS einen letzten Versuch, das Gelände von den Tausenden von Leichen zu säubern: Vom frühen Morgen bis zum späten Abend mußten wir nun Leichen zu den hastig aufgeworfenen Massengräbern schleppen. Dabei hagelte es Prügel und Fußtritte von Kapos und SS-Leuten. Aber alle Anstrengungen waren vergebens. Als Bergen-Belsen am 15. April befreit wurde, lagen immer noch mehr als 10 000 Tote im Lager umher.

Wir waren nun frei – nach Jahren unsäglichen Elendes endlich wieder frei! Wir lachten und weinten vor Freude, rannten sinnlos hin und her, schrien und gestikulierten. Ich versuchte, an zu Hause zu denken, aber es gelang mir nicht recht. Seit acht

Monaten war ich ohne jede Nachricht. Ich betete, daß meine Eltern noch leben sollten. Dann konzentrierte ich mich wieder auf mein eigenes Überleben.

Der »Waffenstillstand von Bergen-Belsen« hatte uns die Freiheit wiedergegeben. Für uns war der Krieg zu Ende. Ein neues Leben konnte beginnen, aber zunächst ging das Massensterben unvermindert weiter. Der Typhus wütete nach wie vor. Noch immer gingen Tausende an Hunger und Erschöpfung zugrunde, hilflos und verlassen, ohne auch nur wahrzunehmen, daß das Lager befreit war. Und während die einen verhungerten, starben viele andere an ungewohntem, allzu schwerem Essen. Bereits in der ersten Nacht nach der Befreiung waren die Küchen, die Lebensmittelmagazine, die Kartoffel- und die Rübenmieten in einem wilden Aufruhr gestürmt und restlos ausgeraubt worden. Überall loderten Feuer, wurden Fleischstücke halb roh hinuntergewürgt.

Die britischen Truppen waren in keiner Weise darauf vorbereitet, ein Lager mit Zehntausenden von halbverhungerten, durchfallkranken Menschen zu übernehmen. Ihre Truppenverpflegung war eine denkbar ungeeignete Kost für Todkranke, die dieses schwere Essen nicht verdauen konnten und in wilder Gier trotzdem alles hinunterschlangen, was ihnen vor die Hände kam. 14000 starben noch in den ersten Wochen nach der Befreiung.

Nur allmählich kam es zu einer wirksamen Hilfe und etwas Ordnung in dem stürmischen Durcheinander, das unserer Befreiung gefolgt war. Nach und nach wurde das Lager evakuiert, die Überlebenden kamen in die Kasernen des früheren Truppenübungsplatzes – zuerst die Kranken, dann die »Gesunden«. Am vierten Mai war die Reihe an uns. Zusammen mit meinem Freund Marcel und einigen hundert Franzosen bezogen wir Quartier in einem ehemaligen Pferdestall. Auch hier gab es keine Betten, aber eine saubere Strohschütte und eine warme Decke. Wir versuchten, Freunde und Bekannte ausfindig zu machen, die in einem anderen Bau dieser weiträumigen Anlage untergebracht waren – und warteten. Wir wußten nicht, wie und wann wir nach Hause gelangen sollten, und konnten uns auch nicht vorstellen, wie es weitergehen sollte. Essen war noch immer das einzige, an das wir wirklich denken konnten.

Am sechsten Mai wagten Marcel und ich uns zum erstenmal aus dem Lager, um nach Bergen zu gehen. Wir trotteten gemächlich die Straße entlang, blieben stehen, gingen nach links, gingen nach rechts – und genossen es, daß niemand hinter uns herschrie. Kein »Schnell, schnell!« und kein »Marsch, marsch!« Ein herrliches Gefühl! In Bergen waren nur wenige Menschen auf der Straße. Sie hatten bedrückte Gesichter und hasteten stumm an uns vorbei. Als ich vor elf Monaten auf dem Weg nach Bergen-Belsen hier durchgekommen war, hatte eine Horde Hitlerjungen Steine nach uns geworfen. Jetzt gaben alle sich Mühe, möglichst unauffällig an uns vorbeizusehen. Es ging gegen Mittag, und wir waren heißhungrig. So klingelten wir kurz entschlossen an einem netten, freundlichen Haus und baten um Essen. Die Leute waren zutiefst erschrocken und beruhigten sich erst allmählich, als sie endlich merkten, daß wir geläufig deutsch redeten. Die Frau brachte uns einen Teller Suppe, die wir in einem Zug hinunterschlürften. Dann briet sie uns eine Pfanne Kartoffeln – und noch eine zweite und noch eine dritte. Wir wußten, daß wir die gebratenen Kartoffeln nicht vertragen würden, aber wir konnten nicht widerstehen. Es roch und schmeckte allzu verlockend! Nach und nach wurden unsere »Gastgeber« immer gesprächiger. Von »all dem« hatten sie natürlich nichts gewußt und waren »schon immer« gegen die Partei und gegen den Krieg gewesen. Zum Nachtisch hätten sie uns am liebsten ihre halbflügge Tochter auf einem silbernen Tablett angeboten. Ihre Unterwürfigkeit war fast noch schwerer zu ertragen als ihre frühere Herrenmenschenarroganz.

Siebter Mai 1945: Wir mußten uns von diesem ersten Ausflug in die Freiheit erholen. Den Weg zurück ins Lager haben wir kaum noch geschafft. Die Nacht über wurden wir von Magenkrämpfen geschüttelt und waren völlig erschöpft. Wir lagen auf unserer Strohschütte und dösten vor uns hin – wenn wir nicht gerade zu den Latrinen rennen mußten. Wir warteten, warteten voller Sehnsucht darauf, daß endlich wieder Essen ausgegeben würde. Gutes, kräftiges Essen, das unser kranker Magen wieder nicht vertragen würde. Achter Mai 1945: Deutschland hatte kapituliert. Der Krieg war zu Ende. Es herrschte wieder Friede. Wir sollten glücklich sein, aber erst einmal mußten wir leben. Brot war jetzt wichtiger.

ANISE POSTEL-VINAY
## Dunkelheit des Schmerzes

An jenem Maianfang 1945 befand ich mich in Malmö, in Schweden, wo mich das Schwedische Rote Kreuz untergebracht hatte, zusammen mit meinen überlebenden Gefährtinnen aus dem Konzentrationslager Ravensbrück, nachdem wir den Klauen Himmlers am 23. April entkommen waren.

Mit einigen Gefährtinnen war ich im Museum für Naturgeschichte in Malmö einquartiert, wo ich auf Papiermatten unter den Füßen einer ausgestopften Giraffe schlief.

Die Tage vergingen: fünfter, sechster, siebter Mai. Es gelang uns nicht, genau zu erfahren, was in Berlin und bei den Alliierten vor sich ging. Seit Monaten wollte der Krieg kein Ende nehmen. Wir haben geglaubt, daß die Deutschen schon am siebten Mai endlich kapituliert hätten, und erst bei meiner Rückkehr nach Frankreich habe ich erfahren, daß die Kapitulation am achten Mai stattgefunden hatte! Zu Tode erschöpft, lebte ich in Niedergeschlagenheit, Kummer und Angst.

Niedergeschlagen, weil mich die Bilder aus Ravensbrück verfolgten und besonders die letzte Szene, die ich sah, als ich zu Fuß die Schranken des Lagers überschritt, um zu den weißen Bussen des Schwedischen Roten Kreuzes, die etwas entfernt standen, zu gelangen: Unsere Kolonne von befreiten Französinnen kreuzte sich mit einer Kolonne von deutschen »Asozialen« (Frauen), erschöpft, in Lumpen, aschfahl, mit verstörtem Blick, die man in Richtung Gaskammer und Krematorium führte. Erst später, als ich die Geschichte von Ravensbrück studierte, habe ich erfahren, daß der 23. April der letzte Tag war, an dem in Ravensbrück vergast wurde.

Ich war tief bekümmert, weil meine »Lagermutter«, Germaine Tillion, die seit zwei Jahren jeden Tag über mich wachte (ich war zwanzig Jahre alt und sie fünfunddreißig) und die noch in Schweden bei mir blieb, miterleben mußte, wie ihre Mutter im Lager verschwand.

An einem Tag, an dem Germaine sehr krank war, war ich damit beauftragt, sie zu beschützen. Es ist mir nicht gelungen, sie der Selektion zu entziehen. Sie ist am zweiten März vergast worden. Mein Kummer wuchs ins Unermeßliche, als ich von einer schwedischen Klassenkameradin aus Paris, die in Schweden lebte, erfuhr, daß meine Schwester von den Deutschen am 27. August 1944 bei Paris getötet worden war – dreiundzwanzig Jahre alt. Seit acht Monaten war sie also schon tot, und ich wußte nichts davon! Oh, meine arme Mutter!

Außerdem quälten mich die Sorgen, denn noch am achten Mai 1945 hatte ich keinerlei Nachrichten von meinem Vater, der eine Zeitlang in Buchenwald war, noch von meinem Bruder, der im August 1944 deportiert worden war, ich wußte nicht, in welches Lager.

So fand sich die junge Deutschstudentin an der Sorbonne, die 1942 mitten im Kampf für eine helle Zukunft in Freiheit von der Gestapo verhaftet worden war, am Tage der Befreiung derartig tief in die Dunkelheiten des Schmerzes getaucht wieder, daß sie weder den gegenwärtigen Tag noch jene »Tage danach, die singen sollten«, wahrnahm. Sie hat deshalb keinerlei genaue Erinnerung an den Tag des achten Mai.

EDWARD PYŚ

## Nr. 379

Am Tag der deutschen Kapitulation war ich in einem Hotel in Linz, Grabenstraße 30. Seit längerer Zeit spürte man, daß der

Krieg zu Ende geht. Wann das geschehen würde, konnte niemand wissen. Seitdem Hitler Selbstmord begangen hatte, zählten wir eigentlich nur Tage oder Stunden. Endlich kam der Tag. Mein Kamerad, mit dem ich im Hotel wohnte, war in die Stadt gegangen, um Essen zu »organisieren«. Ich nähte an einem Zivilanzug und konnte mit dieser Arbeit nicht fertig werden. Er stand mir nicht gut. Die Aufgabe war nicht leicht, weil ich nur 42 Kilogramm wog. Bei dieser langweiligen Beschäftigung dachte ich an meine Familie. Vater hat doch am achten Mai seinen Namenstag! Ich wußte nicht, ob er noch lebte. Seit elf Monaten hatte ich keine Nachrichten.

Rzeszów, meine Heimatstadt, lag jenseits der Frontlinie. Im Hotel war es ruhig. Wir – ich und noch drei Kameraden – waren die einzigen Gäste. Plötzlich hörte ich Lärm und Schießerei in der Stadt. Beunruhigt lief ich auf die Straße und traf meinen zurückkehrenden Kameraden. Er war sehr erregt und strahlte vor Freude. »Ende mit dem Krieg!« rief er. »Die Deutschen haben kapituliert!«

Obwohl wir auf diese Nachricht schon seit längerer Zeit gewartet hatten, verursachte sie heftiges Herzklopfen und eine unbändige Freude. Auf den Straßen sah man amerikanische Soldaten in Jeeps. Sie sangen und schossen in die Luft. Überall Freude. Man sah keine Einwohner auf den Straßen. Endlich war Schluß mit dem blutigsten und grausamsten Krieg, den die Menschheit erlebt hatte. »Bedingungslose Kapitulation.« Diese Wörter riefen bei mir verschiedene Gefühle hervor.

Zum erstenmal habe ich sie in einer deutschen Zeitung gelesen, und zwar im September 1939. Damals stand in großen Buchstaben: »Warschau kapituliert bedingungslos.« Diese Worte haben damals Verzweiflung und Schmerz ausgelöst. Was wird weiter geschehen? dachte ich. Unsere Zukunft sah ich schwarz. Wir hatten keinen Zweifel darüber, daß für uns grausame Zeiten kommen würden. Jetzt aber, am achten Mai 1945, war es ganz anders. Der Zukunft konnte ich beruhigt entgegensehen. Das Leben lag vor mir. Ich war doch erst dreiundzwanzig Jahre alt – und das Wichtigste: Ich war frei! Erst jetzt fühlte ich das! Bisher, obwohl ich schon drei Tage frei war, hatte ich wie betäubt gelebt. Ich war mir darüber nicht klar, daß das Grausamste schon hinter mir lag. Ich dachte an vergangene Zeiten.

Am ersten Mai 1940 hat alles für mich angefangen. Ich wurde in meiner Heimatstadt verhaftet. Folterungen beim Verhör, dann Gefängnis in Rzeszów und Tarnów, zum Schluß die Überstellung ins Konzentrationslager Auschwitz. Ich kam dorthin mit dem ersten Transport, verlor meinen Namen und wurde Nr. 379 »getauft«. Ich war achtzehn Jahre alt. Damals wußte ich nicht, daß ich auf die Freiheit fünf lange Jahre warten mußte. Ich glaubte nicht, daß ich überhaupt irgendwann noch frei würde. Konnte nicht vermuten, daß ich in Gefängnissen und Konzentrationslagern insgesamt 1.863 Tage, das heißt 44712 Stunden verbringen müßte. Jede Stunde konnte meine letzte sein. Viele dauerten eine Ewigkeit, besonders jene, in welchen man dem Tod ins Gesicht schauen mußte. Solange man lebt, solange aber das Herz klopft, solange hat man die Hoffnung. Manchmal dem gesunden Menschenverstand zuwider! Am Lagertor stand: »Arbeit macht frei.« Wir gaben dazu: Durch den Schornstein / des Krematoriums / eins, zwei, drei! Schon besser paßte eine andere Aufschrift: »Lasciate ogni speranza.«

Freiheit! Was für einen Wert sie hat, weiß man erst, wenn man sie verloren hat. Jeder von uns träumte davon am Tage und in der Nacht. Meistens in der Nacht, weil am Tage angesichts der brutalen Wirklichkeit solche Träume ganz widersinnig schienen. Mit aller Kraft bemühte sich doch die Lagerkommandantur, uns zu beweisen, daß wir »Untermenschen« waren und als solche kein Recht zum Leben haben. Jeder konnte uns – ohne sich verantworten zu müssen – ums Leben bringen. Mit aller Kraft versuchte man, uns das Gefühl der Menschenwürde zu entziehen, wollte uns zur Erniedrigung und Verzweiflung bringen. Man mußte wirklich Seelenstärke haben, um das alles auszuhalten und trotz Schlägerei, Hunger und Tod seine Würde zu behalten. Ich habe das alles miterlebt. Kein Wunder, daß in mir immer stärkerer Haß und Rachedurst wuchsen!

Endlich war der erste Tag der Freiheit gekommen. Am fünften Mai 1945, ungefähr um siebzehn Uhr. Ich war damals in einem Nebenlager des KZs Mauthausen, und zwar im Gusen I. Die Freiheit kam mit einem einzigen Panzer mit weißem Stern. Im Lager brach große Freude aus. Die Laternen auf den Lagerstraßen und Baracken wurden mit den Fahnen der verschiedenen Nationen geschmückt. Häftlinge umarmten einander und weinten vor Freude. Merkwürdig, ich war ganz stumpf! An dieser spontanen Freude konnte ich nicht teilnehmen. Ich war leer und sehr müde. Anscheinend hatte ich zu lange auf die Freiheit gewartet. Am dritten Tag verließ ich das Lager. Ich konnte nicht mehr hinter dem Stacheldraht bleiben, obwohl er nicht mehr unter Hochspannung stand und auf den Türmen keine Posten mit Maschinengewehren wachten. Es schien mir, daß ich so lange nicht frei werden könnte, wie ich im Lager bliebe. Zu Fuß bin ich mit meinen drei Kameraden nach Linz gegangen. Vorher nahmen wir noch den SSlern, die im SS-Revier als Kranke lagen, ihre Waffen ab. Kein Haar wurde ihnen dabei gekrümmt. Wir konnten nicht auf die im Bett Liegenden schießen. Trotz aller Erlebnisse und Gemeinheiten! Trotz ihrer Widerwärtigkeit konnten sie uns unsere Menschlichkeit nicht nehmen.

So haben wir uns in dem Hotel einquartiert, wo wir den Tag der Kapitulation erlebten. Man mußte sich jetzt an das Leben in der Freiheit gewöhnen. Das war nicht leicht. Der Krieg und das Lager hatten fünf Jahre aus meinem Leben gerissen. Jetzt wollte ich alles nachholen. Daß es nicht leicht werden würde, wußte ich. Ich habe es aber geschafft, habe das Abitur gemacht und die Hochschule beendet. Es sind schon vierzig Jahre vergangen, aber das, was ich im Lager erlebt habe, kommt sehr oft in quälenden Träumen zurück. Ich habe Glück, wenn mich jemand weckt. Lange Zeit kann ich mich dann nicht beruhigen.

# Nun ist es zu Ende

In der Nacht zum ersten Mai 1945 setzte sich der Treck von siebenundzwanzig Wagen, mit Treckern und Pferden bespannt, vom Hof des mecklenburgischen Gutes in Bewegung. Die Betten, von den Bewohnern und vielen flüchtenden Gästen des Gutshauses verlassen, wurden von den Soldaten der nahe gekommenen Front belegt. Aus den Unterkünften der russischen Kriegsgefangenen, deren Wachmannschaft bereits den Rückzug angetreten hatte, ertönte lauter Gesang. Das Ende des Krieges war nur noch eine Frage von Stunden oder Tagen. Meine Familie, die von Stettin aus die Flucht begonnen hatte, befand sich mitten in einem riesigen Knäuel von flüchtenden Zivilisten und Soldaten Richtung Westen. Das beherrschende Gefühl war Angst, wie sollte es anders sein. Die Nachricht vom Selbstmord Hitlers, die sich wie ein Lauffeuer verbreitete, wurde nur noch als Bestätigung für den herrschenden Eindruck aufgenommen: Nun ist es zu Ende.

Zwei Erlebnisse im Zusammenhang mit dem Kriegsende haben sich mir, dem damals Vierzehnjährigen, unauslöschlich eingeprägt und im Rückblick symbolhafte Bedeutung gewonnen. Für uns war der Krieg endgültig aus, als die amerikanischen Panzer da waren. Der Gutstreck, in dem wir mitfuhren, war in einem riesigen Strom von flüchtenden Soldaten steckengeblieben. Und dann kamen sie, die Sieger: amerikanische Panzer, auf denen in lässiger Haltung und mit spaßhaften Reden die US-Soldaten hockten. Gekämpft wurde nicht mehr. Die ersten Worte flogen hin und her. Mit Faszination, vor allem aber mit einem Gefühl unendlicher Erleichterung bestaunte ich das Bild. Bombenangriffe, Flucht, die Angst vor den russischen Truppen, alles war vorbei. Und die Amis waren genauso, wie man das erwartet hatte. Ich drehte mich um zu meinem Vater, der auf dem Treckwagen dasselbe Bild anschaute. Aber über sein Gesicht liefen Tränen. Verständnislos fragte ihn der Vierzehnjährige: »Warum weinst du?« Die Antwort: »Junge, das verstehst du nicht! Es ist das zweite Mal, daß wir besiegt werden.« – Dasselbe historische Ereignis, dieselbe Situation, und doch wurde sie ganz verschieden erfahren und erlebt. Für mich war es nur das erfreuliche Ende einer im ganzen fürchterlichen Zeit. Endlich war der Krieg aus und die Angst und Bedrückung vorbei. Und die »richtigen« Sieger waren da. Alles andere zählte nicht: das Schicksal der Nation, die Lage Deutschlands. Der Grundton war: Es kann nur besser werden. Das Kriegsende, so habe ich es erfahren, war gut, neuer Anfang, echte Befreiung.

Das zweite Erlebnis schloß sich einige Tage oder Wochen später an. Unser Flüchtlingstreck war zum Stillstand gekommen mitten in einem großen Lager von deutschen Soldaten, die als Kriegsgefangene in einem großen Gutsareal lagerten. Das ganze Gebiet war von englischen Soldaten bewacht, die das Gebiet inzwischen von den Amerikanern übernommen hatten. An einem Sonntag beschlossen wir, in das nahe gelegene Städtchen zum Gottesdienst zu gehen: meine zwei Schwestern und ich, Jugendliche im Alter von siebzehn, fünfzehn und vierzehn Jahren. Als wir uns den Posten näherten, die die Straße rund um das Areal der Kriegsgefangenen bewachten, wurden wir von einem jungen englischen Soldaten mit Gewehr und aufgepflanztem Bajonett angehalten. Wir sagten nur in dem bißchen Englisch, das wir konnten: We want to go to service! In dem vollen Gefühl, daß er dies respektieren würde, schoben wir sein Gewehr beiseite und gingen weiter. Es klappte. Er ließ uns gehen. Genauso hatten wir es erwartet: Die Absicht, einen Gottesdienst zu besuchen, öffnete die Grenze.

Wir, Kinder eines Pfarrers der Bekennenden Kirche, wußten, was es heißt, wenn der Staat Kirche und Religion zu unterdrücken sucht. Aber wir waren ebenso fest davon überzeugt, daß das jetzt vorbei sei, daß die neuen Machthaber die Kirche nicht mehr bekämpfen würden, sondern achten. Indem der junge Soldat uns ziehen ließ, bestätigte er diese Erwartung: Das Recht auf freie Religionsausübung, das Recht auf Religionsfrei heit – hier war es, unmittelbar, direkt und uneingeschränkt. So wurde für uns diese kleine Szene zum Schlüsselerlebnis der Freiheit auf einer Dorfstraße in Mecklenburg.

Wie habe ich das Kriegsende erlebt? Es war die Erfahrung der Befreiung vom Krieg, von den Ängsten und Bedrohungen des Krieges. Und es war die Erfahrung der Freiheit, das Ende der Nazis, der Unterdrückung der Kirche, des Glaubens. Diese doppelte Erfahrung von Befreiung und Freiheit ließ alles andere zurücktreten und formte die Perspektive, in der alle anderen Ereignisse und Erfahrungen einen bestimmten Richtungssinn erhielten. Diese Erlebnisse begründeten deswegen, etwas hochtrabend ausgedrückt, eine »Hermeneutik der Freiheit«, die, biographisch verwurzelt, für mich normativen Rang gewonnen hat.

### ANNEMARIE RENGER
## Wenn man besiegt ist

Hitler bedeutet Krieg. Dies war für mich, die ich in einem sozialdemokratischen Elternhaus aufgewachsen bin, eine stets angstvolle Gewißheit schon lange vor dem Machtantritt der Nazis. Voll innerer Zerrissenheit war mir auch klar, daß Deutschland den von ihm losgetretenen Zweiten Weltkrieg nicht gewinnen konnte und auch unbedingt verlieren mußte, damit Deutschland die Nazidiktatur wieder loswerden konnte.

Ein Gefühl der widerstreitenden Gefühle kennzeichnete denn auch meine innere Verfassung angesichts der endgültigen militärischen Niederlage Deutschlands.

Hin und her gerissen war ich zwischen der erkannten Notwendigkeit der Niederlage und der tiefen Trauer über den Tod so vieler Soldaten – mein Mann und meine Brüder waren darunter – in einem wahnsinnigen Eroberungskrieg und über die schwere Last der Niederlage, die jetzt auf das ganze deutsche Volk zukam.

Überlagert wurden solche Empfindungen und Erwartungen aber von dem grellen Tagesgeschehen, in dem wir die Ankunft der Alliierten im Mai 1945 erwarteten und gleichzeitig fürchteten. Diesen Monat erlebte ich bei Verwandten in der Lüneburger Heide. Mein Vater hatte dafür gesorgt, daß meine Schwester mit ihren beiden Kindern und ich mit meinem Sohn Berlin verließen. Dieser Abschied fiel mir im April 1945 schwer. Schließlich stand das Kriegsende bevor, und es gab keine Vorstellungen dazu, was später dann gerade in Berlin passieren sollte.

In Visselhövede in der Heide hatte ich zunächst bei einer Tante Unterkunft gefunden und arbeitete in der Küche des dortigen Reservelazaretts. Wegen meiner fast ständig angebrannten Milchsuppe muß ich mich noch heute bei den Soldaten entschuldigen.

Ständige Tieffliegerangriffe, denen schließlich auch das Haus meiner Tante zum Opfer fiel, bestimmten das Tagesgeschehen. Wir lebten im Lazarett, das uns mit seinem Rote-Kreuz-Zeichen auf dem Dach Sicherheit gab, aber bei Fliegerangriffen duckten wir uns doch mit unseren Kindern in der Küche unter einen großen Holztisch. Gegenseitige Panzer- und Infanterieangriffe – bei den Briten von ihrer Luftwaffe unterstützt – rollten immer stärker über uns hinweg. Zuletzt suchten wir in dem Luftschutzkeller eines Arztes Zuflucht, der gegenüber dem Lazarett lag. Wir rannten über die Straße – und ich erinnere mich, wie mein Sohn einen seiner kostbaren Schuhe verlor. Mit der Angst im Nacken, von den Schüssen eines Tieffliegers getroffen zu werden, rannte ich noch einmal zurück, um diesen Schuh zu retten.

Angst herrschte aber auch im Keller. Ich erinnere mich besonders gut an einen jungen, vielleicht sechzehnjährigen verwundeten Soldaten der Wlassow-Armee. In einer geradezu animalischen Angst und Panik, die drohte, auch alle anderen anzustecken, wollte er aus dem Keller heraus, weil er fürchtete, gefangengenommen und erschossen zu werden. Nur mit großer Mühe konnten wir ihn beruhigen.

Über uns tobten die letzten Kämpfe. An einem Tag hatten

die Briten bereits den Ort erobert. Zu unserem Entsetzen hatten sich über uns in dem Haus des Arztes SS-Leute verschanzt, die aus allen Rohren schossen. Die kleine Stadt wechselte noch einmal den Besitzer. Erst am nächsten Tag erfolgte dann die Einnahme durch die Briten.

Am Tage der endgültigen Einnahme der Stadt durch die Engländer sehe ich mich noch in der Küche an der Tür stehen, als die ersten britischen Soldaten vorbeikamen. In angespannter Haltung, das Gewehr mit dem Finger am Abzug in der Hand, über dem flachen Helm ein Tarnnetz. Irgendwie mußte ich wohl eine Geste gemacht haben. Brüsk sprach mich ein Soldat auf deutsch an: »Geh weg, ins Haus!« Meine Reaktion war: »Ach, so ist das jetzt, nun werden wir einfach mit du angesprochen – so ist das eben, wenn man besiegt ist.«

In unserer Lazarettküche hatte sich nicht viel geändert. Vorräte waren genug da, vor allen Dingen Unmengen Alkohol. Am Abend des neunten Mai wurde sogar in dem Kessel, in dem sonst die Milchsuppe brodelte, Punsch zubereitet und an die Soldaten ausgeschenkt. Man kann sich wohl vorstellen, was für eine Atmosphäre entstand. Eine Stimmung von Bangen und Hoffen, von Wut und Verzweiflung. Wahrscheinlich hatten wir alle keine klaren Gedanken, was uns die Zukunft bringen würde.

Ein Mensch wurde mit dieser Tragödie nicht fertig: unser Koch Robert. Er war in die Küche geschlichen und hatte sich mit beiden Händen alle verfügbaren riesigen Küchenmesser gegriffen und schrie, dem Delirium nahe, die unflätigsten Flüche gegen die britischen Soldaten, die unser Gebäude bewachten. Meine Angst, daß uns und unseren Kindern, aber auch den verwundeten Soldaten etwas passieren konnte, war größer als die Angst vor Roberts Messern. Ich kletterte also durch das Küchenfenster zu Robert hinein, redete ihm gut zu, bis er in einen Weinkrampf verfiel und die Küchenmesser fallen ließ. Es berührt mich noch heute tief, wenn ich an den grenzenlosen Schmerz dieses Mannes denke.

Am nächsten Morgen mußten alle hierzu fähigen Soldaten

antreten. Für sie ging es nicht nach Hause, sondern in die Gefangenschaft. Niemand wußte, wohin. Die Gerüchte, daß man nach mehr als vier Jahren Krieg noch in die entferntesten Länder verschickt werden sollte, weit entfernt von den Familien, die ja schon so nahe schienen, um dort als Gefangene zu arbeiten, belastete die Soldaten. Der ganze Irrsinn des Krieges und seine tragischen Folgen wurden an diesem Tag ebenso überdeutlich wie der abgrundtiefe menschenverachtende Zynismus der Nazis, die ein ganzes Volk zugrunde gehen ließen, um ihr jämmerliches Leben zu verlängern. Zu einer Einstellung gegen Krieg und Unrecht in meinem Elternhaus erzogen, war es auch dieses Erleben des Mißbrauchs der Menschen durch eine Clique, die ihre Interessen als Interessen des deutschen Volkes ausgab, das meinen politischen Weg bestimmte, überall in der Welt gegen ideologische Demagogie, gegen Unmenschlichkeit und Entrechtung anzukämpfen.

HELMUT RIDDER
## Ach ja, wir Deutschen!

Mehr als ein Jahr kam er – nach meinen an sich nicht so unvernünftigen, aber von der Geschichte doch falsifizierten Berechnungen – zu spät, dieser auch von mir mit dem vollen ihm von den Siegermächten beigemessenen Gewicht herbeigesehnte Tag. Daß es nicht nur der Entmachtung der Nazis und einer »bedingungslosen Kapitulation« der Wehrmacht, sondern einer »bedingungslosen Kapitulation« aller staatlichen Institutionen und der Herstellung eines wirklichen »Tages Null« bedurfte, sollte eine auch mit dem monarchisch-obrigkeitsstaatlichen Halbdunkel von Weimar radikal aufräumende deutsche Republik eine Chance haben, war mir schon in den Oberschul- und Studentenjahren im Dritten Reich klargeworden. Dank nicht zuletzt dem geistlichen Rektor und Religionslehrer, der – zuvor in Weimar schon am »Rande der Legalität«; »Politik«

in der Schule war natürlich verpönt – von den Religionsstunden immer wieder etwas abzuzweigen verstand, um mit spürbarer Erregung von Demokratie, Volkssouveränität und Reichsverfassung sprechen zu können. Ein »schlechter Pädagoge«, hieß es. Sozialdemokratischer Politiker hätte er sein mögen, gestand er im vertrauten Kreis, wäre ihm das als katholischem Kleriker nicht verwehrt gewesen. Einer aus dem heute völlig unbekannten Münsterland, wo Wiedertäufergeist immer noch sensible Antennen anweht, wo zwar keine Reformation, daher denn aber auch keine Gegenreformation gewesen, wo die Droste, angeblich eine bigotte Jungfer, mit visionärer Kraft im Dom zu Köln das Handelsstift der deutschen Bourgeoisie zu erkennen vermochte, wo Preußen und Berlin ferne Schemen, Frankreich und die Republik nah, wo die Nazis es mit den Bodenständigen genauso schwer hatten wie nachmalig Adenauers CDU mit dem Weichklopfen der Beichtväter und der Zerstörung der wiedergegründeten Zentrumspartei . . . Heimat.

Der Berechnungsfehler bestand in der Fehleinschätzung der Westalliierten, deren zeitigere und zügigere Invasion ein termingerechtes Kriegsende zur Folge gehabt hätte, von deren Doppelstrategie gegen das Dritte Reich und die Sowjets mein noch ziemlich schlichtes politisches Gemüt aber noch keine Ahnung hatte. Sehr wohl begriffen hatte ich hingegen Motivation und Zielvorstellung der meisten Akteure vom 20. Juli 1944, mit deren Restaurationsplänen ich so wenig im Sinne haben konnte, wie ich mit den Trägern der Friedensresolution von 1917 im Sinne gehabt hätte. Als ein somit in dieser Richtung ganz und gar »Unschuldiger« aus einer OKH-Dienststelle entfernt und an die Südwestfront abkommandiert, hatte ich dem Tag weiter entgegengehofft – nichts von Heldentum, nichts von Widerstand, mal à la Schwejk ein Schippchen Sand ins Getriebe (Brecht irrt übrigens: Auch ein paar Millionen Schwejks hätten nicht genügt!).

Da nun – ich muß hier fast alles von dem randvollen persönlichen Erleben des Zugehens auf den Tag beiseite lassen – hat es mich ereilt, just am achten Mai 1945: An diesem Tage der

Befreiung wurde ich im Österreichischen Kriegsgefangener einer marokkanischen Infanteriedivision (sie war immer hinten gewesen, und der General konnte zum erstenmal Kriegsgefangene melden). Es war maßlos deprimierend. Nicht sosehr wegen des Filzens und der sonstigen bei solcher Gelegenheit üblichen Unfreundlichkeiten. Der schlimmste Stachel war dieser: Der Gefangennehmende war ein Elsässer. Und er erzählte kühl – und gern und genüßlich auf deutsch –, während er sich die passenden Stücke aneignete, wie er zunächst bei des Führers Waffen-SS gedient, dann aber eben rechtzeitig die rechte Wende zu den Truppen des »freien Frankreichs« vollzogen habe. Was da bei mir schmerzlich getroffen (und auch erst durch schmerzendes Lernen überwunden) wurde, war ein jugendlich-naiver Glaube an die dem einzelnen geschuldete Gerechtigkeit. Da ist man beleidigt von der Geschichte, an deren Gerechtigkeit man glaubt, ohne von ihrer Gerechtigkeit zu wissen, die individuelle Schuld und politische Verantwortung auseinanderhält, und möchte aus ihr »aussteigen«, wohin auch immer, mit Hermann Hesse den »Weg nach Innen« weitergehen oder Schafe züchten in Australien . . . oder – das hatte dann die besten Konditionen –, den Blick nach vorn und nie zurück, nach dem Zusammenbruch (was war da eigentlich noch zusammengebrochen?) an den Wiederaufbau gehen (»Wir Deutschen haben immer gut gearbeitet«).

Dahinter bin ich denn doch ziemlich früh und arg zurückgeblieben, hinter der Lebenslüge schon von Trizonesien und der daraus entstehenden Bundesrepublik Deutschland, die den achten Mai 1945 rückwirkend aufgehoben hat, die Schuld und Verantwortung in unbewertbare »Verstrickung« zusammenfließen ließ, die wegen ihrer eingebildeten »Identität« mit dem trotz Nichtexistierens »fortexistierenden« Deutschen Reich heute lauter denn je Wiedergutmachung der dem Reich seit dem achten Mai 1945 zugefügten Kränkungen erheischt und deren herrschendem politischen Infantilismus jede Widerrede »so dumm, so ungerecht und so abwegig« erscheint, daß sie nur aus »bestimmten Giftküchen in Moskau« kommen kann. Ob sie angesichts ihrer jetzt mit kompromißloser Zielstrebigkeit wiederhergestellten glanzlosen Isolierung noch fähig ist, am achten Mai 1985 aus einem wüsten vierzigjährigen Traum zu erwachen und die Realitäten zu erkennen, die denen des achten Mai 1945 so ähnlich, wenn auch weitaus gefährlicher sind? Ach ja, »wir Deutschen«!

LUISE RINSER

## Das also war das Ende

Auf diesen Tag hatten wir gewartet. Er war vorauszusehen seit 1942, seit der entscheidenden Niederlage bei Stalingrad. Ich hatte auf ihn gewartet in den Monaten meiner Gefängnishaft. Wir hatten von diesem Tag geträumt. Ein großer Tag würde das sein: die letzten Takte des Walkürenritts würden ertönen, dann ein Paukenschlag, dann der Freudenschrei, der Menschheitschor: Brüder, zur Sonne, zur Freiheit. Oder doch wenigstens so: Nach der Katastrophe senkt sich der Vorhang über die Bühne voller Leichen, und wenn er sich wieder hebt, sieht man eine Maiwiese mit Kindern, die singen: Alles neu macht der Mai.

Und wie war's dann wirklich? Kein Freudenschrei, kein Triumphmarsch. Die neue Zeit, die schlich heran bei Nacht und Nebel im Gefolge eines Zuges von Hungerskeletten in grau und schwarz gestreifter Häftlingskleidung, die noch Anfang Mai an meinem Haus an der Salzach vorbeigetrieben wurden bei der Verlegung eines KZs aus dem Nordosten nach Tirol. Ich wachte nachts auf von einem kurzen Scharfschießen. Die Bauern erzählten, die SS habe auf Flüchtende geschossen.

Die neue Zeit, die brachte den Siegern eine fadenscheinige weiße Fahne entgegen, die nichts andres war als das herausgeschnittene weiße Stück aus der Hakenkreuzfahne. Ich fand in den Wäldern ringsum viele Fetzen Fahnentuch und auf den Misthaufen zerfetzte Bilder von Hitler und Göring und Blechschilder mit der Aufschrift »Adolf-Hitler-Straße« und Achsel-

stücke von Offizieren und NS-Armbinden und Hakenkreuzabzeichen.

Ich hatte am 30. April (meinem Geburtstag, dem ersten in
der neuen Freiheit) schon die weiße Fahne gehißt: ein altes
Bettuch. Eines Morgens wurden Löcher hineingeschossen:
vorbeiflüchtende versprengte SS. Um den Obersalzberg, Hitlers Burg, wurde noch gekämpft. Hitler selbst, er war tot. Als
wir's hörten, nahm ich den Spielzeug-Pappmaché-Hitler, den
meine Kinder einmal geschenkt bekommen hatten, machte ihm
einen Galgen, hängte ihn dran und tanzte mit meinen Kindern
um den papierenen Gehenkten: »Der böse Wolf ist tot, der Hitler ist tot.« Tagsüber zogen die Resttruppen der Deutschen
Wehrmacht von Südosten an meinem Haus vorbei, waffenlos,
die Rangabzeichen abgerissen, erschöpft. Sie flohen vor den
Russen in die Hände der Amis.

War der Krieg wirklich zu Ende? War es zu glauben?

Zu viele sich widersprechende Nachrichten hatten wir gehört in diesen Tagen: Hitler tot, nein, geflüchtet, doch tot, die
Amis vor München, nein, noch lange nicht, doch, die Russen
bei Passau. Alles nicht wahr, doch wahr, München hat sich ergeben, die SS kämpft weiter . . .

Aber eines Abends rollte ein Panzer vorbei, die Scheinwerfer
aufgeblendet, der weiße Stern deutlich sichtbar: die Amis!
Dann war's wieder dunkel und still. Das also war das Ende.
Das also sollte der Neubeginn sein: der achte Mai 1945. War
es ein Freudentag? Oder ein Tag tiefster Trauer über die Niederlage, über das Ende eines großen Traumes?

Wir waren alle zu müde, zu verhungert, zu arm, um uns noch
freuen oder auch trauern zu können.

Nichts als dies: kein Krieg mehr.

Aber wo war der Friede? Daß dieser achte Mai 1945 nur den
Waffenstillstand brachte, war uns zunächst ganz und gar
gleichgültig. Nur keine Toten mehr, keine Luftangriffe, keine
Schreckensnachrichten von den Fronten. Alles andre würde
sich finden. Es fand sich: Wir warten immer noch auf den Frie-
densvertrag. Wir warten auf den Frieden.

# Mein wichtigster Tag?

Es stank gemein, als wir unsere Wohnzimmertür öffneten. Flach lag unter dem Kronleuchter der Auszichtisch mit nach innen geknickten Beinen. Als Tischdecke dekorativ darüber gespreizt, leuchtete unsere große schwarzweißrote Fahne: In das Hakenkreuz, mitten hinein, hatte ein amerikanischer Soldat gewaltig abgeladen, hatte in der Glasvitrine Adolf Hitlers Buch »Mein Kampf« gefunden, die blaue Prachtausgabe, 1939 erschienen zum 50. Geburtstag des Führers, hatte jeweils zwanzig, dreißig Seiten zweimal durchgerissen und es dann dachkantig auf die braune Scheiße gedrückt.

Das war am achten Mai 1945, als meine Mutter und ich aus der »Evakuierung« nach Gelsenkirchen zurückkamen. Ich war gerade fünfzehn damals. Ich ekelte mich. Meine Mutter rollte das Siegesdenkmal des unbekannten Amis zu einem Bündel zusammen, trug es in den Garten, wo ich alles hinter den Rhabarberstauden vergrub. Dabei stand meine Mutter und war glücklich. Nicht darüber, daß die Nazis geschlagen waren, nein, nur darüber, daß der Krieg zu Ende war, daß die Lauferei zum Luftschutzbunker vorbei war, daß die Todesangst vorbei war, daß nun ihr vermißter Sohn von der Front zurückkehren würde.

Sie hatte es nicht mit den Nazis. Auch nichts gegen sie. Sie hatten die Hakenkreuzfahne aus dem Fenster gehängt, wenn es verlangt wurde. Und sie hatte mit derselben Selbstverständlichkeit den Hausaltar aufgebaut und die Straße mit Blumenmustern geschmückt, wenn die Fronleichnamsprozession vorbeikam. »Mein Kampf« hatten sie irgendwann gekauft, aber niemals eine Seite gelesen. Ein Bergmann wie mein Vater hat überhaupt nie ein Buch gelesen, zeit seines Lebens nicht. Und meine Mutter auch nicht.

Sie hatten die Dreizimmerwohnung mit Wasser auf dem Flur, das Plumpsklosett daneben, ein Schwein im Stall und Ka-

ninchen, die Brieftauben, den Schrebergarten und das Grabe-
land. Ja, und dann die Kinder. Die sollten ordentlich gekleidet
sein, wurden zur Schule und zur Konfirmation geschickt, und
als sie dann zum »Jungvolk« wollten und diese Braunhemden
brauchten und die schwarzen Cordhosen dazu und das Fahr-
tenmesser mit »Blut und Ehre« auf der Klinge, dann wurde
auch das gekauft, selbst wenn das schwerfiel. Es ging ihnen
auch nicht schlecht im Nazireich bis 1939. Allerdings war das
Wort »Lebensstandard« für Arbeiter noch nicht erfunden. Bis
eben der Krieg, der Bombenkrieg begann. Und gehungert haben sie erst nach dem Ende des Krieges.

Sie waren nicht in der Hitler-Partei, in keiner Naziorganisa-
tion. Sie waren sehr unpolitisch. Eigenartigerweise aber duldeten sie nicht, daß man mich zur »Adolf-Hitler-Schule« holte
oder meinen Bruder mit fünfzehn zur »Unteroffiziersvor-
schule«. Das nicht. Nur so. Ohne Begründung. Das war ihnen
nicht geheuer. Mitläufer also? Weniger. Aufgetriebene. Zwei
aus einer Herde. Mitgenommene, Nutznießer und Benutzte,
Wasser in der Welle, Steine hinter der Fassade, »Menschenma-
terial« in der Hand aller Despoten und Verführer. Sie lebten
ihr einfaches, menschliches Leben, solange man es ihnen gestat-
tete, arbeiteten, gebaren, aßen und tranken, bis man sie zwang
zum Töten oder zum Sterben, zum Zerstören oder zum Auf-
bauen. Die Freiheiten, die sie meinten, die da oben, die hatten
sie nie und brauchten sie nicht. Unter der beschriebenen Geschichte leben sie sich hindurch. Zum Beispiel als Bergmann –
in Gelsenkirchen so wie in Kattowitz. Unter Hitler oder Stalin.

Mit mir war das schon etwas anderes. Ich wurde gebildet –
nach ihrem braunen Bilde. Ich hatte Glück. Ich bin ihnen entkommen. Und ich brauchte nicht zu töten. Dafür bin ich meinem Schicksal dankbar. Ein glücklicher Zufall – die Gnade, die
mir zuteil wurde, nicht auf Menschen schießen zu müssen. Der
achte Mai 1945 hat mich davor bewahrt.

Was wäre aus mir geworden, wohin hätten sie mich geführt,
meine Führer? Soweit wie Eichmann, soweit wie Schubert vom
KZ Sachsenhausen oder soweit wie Rudolf Höss? Wäre ich Ge-

neral geworden oder Stadtkommandant? (Wie weit kann man Kinder von Eltern führen, die seit 1933 von den Nazis indoktriniert wurden und anschließend in die kommunistische Mangel kamen, die seit mehr als fünfzig Jahren in den Dünsten der Diktaturen atmen?)

Mich hatten sie gut in den Klauen. Ich konnte schießen, das hatten sie mir beigebracht. Und ich hätte geschossen – auf die Feinde meines Führers und meines Vaterlandes. Und hätte man mir eine Panzerfaust gegeben wie den Jungen der Realschulklasse über mir, ich hätte auch die abgedrückt und getroffen.

Die hätten mich vielleicht zu einem Fanatiker gemacht. Und nie hätte ich erfahren, was ich heute weiß: daß jede Art von Fanatismus eine Erscheinungsform des Schwachsinns ist.

Im April 1945 erhielt ich, der gerade Fünfzehnjährige, noch den Einberufungsbefehl zum »Volkssturm«. Ich wollte zu den Waffen. Doch das ließ meine Mutter nicht mehr zu. Köln und München waren schon erobert, und auch mir dämmerte es, daß der »Endsieg« trotz der erwarteten Wunderwaffen den anderen gehören würde. So riskierte ich das Bündnis mit meiner Mutter, die mich in einer Scheune versteckte. Zwei Tage später fuhren die amerikanischen Panzer in unser Dorf ein. Aber ich hatte schreckliche Angst, daß man mich mit Hunden suchen würde. Irgendein todeswürdiges Verbrechen war das ja, was ich da beging, Fahnenflucht oder Schlimmeres. Ich wäre »zu den Waffen geeilt« wie mein Bruder mit siebzehn Jahren, der das mit fünf Jahren russischer Gefangenschaft büßte.

Der achte Mai 1945 ist der wichtigste Tag meines Lebens. Was wäre aus mir geworden? Mag sein, daß ich eines Tages wach geworden wäre und mich aus der Naziumklammerung freigedacht hätte. Sicher bin ich mir dessen nicht. Und sicher sollte sich niemand fühlen. Denken ist durch nichts zu ersetzen.

Mir waren Scheuklappen angeheftet, eine Philosophie war vorbereitet. Ich kam aus so kleinen Verhältnissen, daß mir die Herrenmenschenpositur wahrscheinlich gefallen haben würde, blond war ich auch und arisch (vermutlich), und Hitler war mein Führer, und die Glaubensbekenntnisse kamen mir flott über die Lippen: »Jungvolkjungen sind hart, schweigsam und treu. Jungvolkjungen sind Kameraden. Des Jungvolkjungen Höchstes ist die Ehre.« Und noch heute erschreckt mich, wie viele Texte ich aus dem Naziliederbuch »Uns geht die Sonne nicht unter« mit allen Strophen auswendig weiß. Learned by heart – ins Herz gelernt.

Die kleine rotweiße Kordel des Jungenschaftsführers hatte ich mit elf. Mit zwölf Jahren schon – voller Stolz als einer der Jüngsten überhaupt! – die grüne Jungzugführerkordel vom Schulterknopf bis unter die rechte Brusttasche baumeln, die »Affenschaukel«. Anführer von dreißig Mann! Das wäre vermutlich so weitergegangen: grünweiß als Fähnleinführer, weiße Kordel als Stammführer, die berühmte »Rote« als Bannführer.

Und niemand hat mich jemals vor den Nazis gewarnt? Die Eltern nicht? Die Verwandten nicht? Der Pastor bei der Konfirmation auch nicht? Nein, der trug eine Hauptmannsuniform unter dem Talar – der auch nicht. Nie hat ein Freund zu mir gesagt: »Das sind Verbrecher, Menschenschlächter!« Kein Lehrer hat jemals eine abwertende Meinung über das Regime angedeutet? Nein. Niemand. Niemand. Niemand.

Bleibt nachzutragen, daß zwei Brüder meines Vaters in Konzentrationslagern gestorben sind. Doch das erfuhren wir auch erst nach dem achten Mai 1945.

KURT SCHARF
## Ungewöhnliche Hörbereitschaft

Am Montag, dem 23. April 1945, war ich mit einer Gruppe meiner Kompanie, die zu einer sächsischen Infanteriedivision gehörte, in der italienischen Poebene in Gefangenschaft geraten. Amerikanische Panzer hatten uns überrollt. Italienische Partisanen – kostümiert in Uniformen wie in einer Verdi-Oper, dazu martialisch-modern mit Maschinenpistolen bewaffnet –

führten uns ab in ein amerikanisches Sammellager. Nach Transporten auf Lastkraftwagen waren wir – vorläufig – gelandet in einem Pinienwaldlager am Hafen zwischen Pisa und Livorno. Aus der amerikanischen Armeezeitung hatten wir am dritten Mai erfahren, daß die Südarmee kapituliert hatte. Wir wußten auch von Hitlers Tod und der Nachfolge im Oberbefehl durch Dönitz. Am Sonntagabend, dem sechsten Mai, stieß ich in einer Ecke des Lagers zu einer Gruppe von Kameraden, denen ein Missionarssohn eine Andacht hielt. Das Losungsbuch der Brüdergemeine und meine Bibel hatte ich bei mehrfachen Registrierungen und Filzungen behalten dürfen.

Ich las während dieser Tage in den Samuelis- und Königsbüchern des Alten Testamentes. Am Dienstag, dem achten Mai, erhielten wir neue Nachrichten über den Zusammenbruch in Deutschland. Das letzte Jahr und alle Phasen der Gefangennahme hatte ich in einer Schicksalsgemeinschaft mit einem gebildeten, christlich denkenden Juristen aus Meißen erlebt. Mit ihm überlegte ich, wie wir für den bevorstehenden Himmelfahrtstag, den zehnten Mai, zu einem Lagergottesdienst kommen könnten. Unser Vorstoß beim deutschen Lagerkommandanten – neben dem amerikanischen Lagerleiter gab es in den ersten Wochen der Gefangenschaft einen solchen – war vergeblich.

Am neunten Mai erfuhren wir von der Befreiung Martin Niemöllers durch die Amerikaner und seiner Internierung und Überführung nach Gaëta. Wir sprachen erneut bei dem deutschen Obersten vor, um mit Niemöller in Kontakt zu kommen und um dem Kommandanten doch noch die Erlaubnis für einen Gottesdienst abzuringen. Wir erfuhren ironische Ablehnung. Zu einer möglichen Kontaktaufnahme mit Niemöller meinte er spöttisch, wir sähen ja, wohin Niemöllers antinationalsozialistische Haltung ihn gebracht habe: aus Argwohn zur Internierung durch die Amerikaner. Am Himmelfahrtstag – ohne Andacht und Gottesdienst – traf dann die Nachricht ein, daß die Waffen auf den europäischen Kriegsschauplätzen endgültig schweigen.

In der Nacht zum Freitag, früh um drei Uhr, wurden wir zum Appell befohlen. Wir sollten in das endgültige Großlager – Pisa im Rücken – in die größere Nähe zu Livorno marschieren. Wir standen vier bis fünf Stunden, ehe der Abmarsch begann. Er erfolgte dann von acht Uhr an bis etwa fünfzehn Uhr nachmittags bei zunehmend glühender Sonne. Zwei jüngere Kameraden erlitten einen Hitzschlag, an dem sie zwei Tage später im Lazarett starben. Im neuen Lager für 40000 deutsche Kriegsgefangene konnten wir – eine große Gruppe von Pfarrern und kirchlichen Mitarbeitern – täglich Konvente halten. Abends boten wir Vorträge an, und einmal in der Woche sowie regelmäßig sonntags hielten wir Gottesdienste, und zwar in allen zehn Teilen des Gesamtlagers. Wir erhielten von der nun rein amerikanischen Lagerleitung und dem zuständigen Feldgeistlichen auch Oblaten und Wein für Sakramentsfeiern und zur Nutzung eine gute Bibliothek klassischer und religiöser deutscher Literatur. Es war die Zeit der größten und aufmerksamsten Männergemeinde in meinem Pfarrdienst.

Was ich in jenen Tagen und Wochen empfunden habe? Der Kamerad und Freund jener Zeit, den ich erwähnte, und ich haben viele kirchliche Arbeits- und allgemeinere Beschäftigungsvorhaben für die große fremde deutsche Bürgergemeinde überlegt, in der wir uns vorfanden. Wir wurden dabei überholt, überrascht und unterstützt von einer erstaunlich großen Zahl von Wissenschaftlern der verschiedensten Disziplinen, Schriftstellern, jungen Männern mit großer dichterischer Begabung sowie Künstlern, Malern und Bildhauern, aber auch Sportlern und Sportlehrern. Sie wollten dem Stumpfwerden im Lagerdasein begegnen, der Melancholie, dem Sichzerstören über das, was daheim den Angehörigen geschehen sei, geschehen könnte, oder auch dem, was einem selbst noch drohen mochte: Arbeitseinsatz in Frankreich, Auslieferung in die Sowjetunion, Armut im zerstörten Deutschland. Wir alle – auch die christliche Verkündigung – fanden eine in der Situation begründete ungewöhnliche Hörbereitschaft vor dieser Männergemeinde aus allen Berufszweigen und Bildungsschichten.

Wie die große Mehrheit der Pfarrer der Bekennenden Kirche und ihrer Gemeindeglieder hatte ich während des Krieges mich in dem quälenden Dilemma befunden, nicht zu wissen, worum ich zu Gott beten sollte: nicht für den Sieg des deutschen Heeres, in dem ich diente; denn der Sieg Hitlers hätte Europa in ein einziges großes Konzentrationslager verwandelt und die Institution Kirche ausgetilgt: Konnte ich um die Niederlage beten? Mit schrecklichsten Folgen, die sie für Deutschland haben mußte? Am 20. Juli 1944 hatten ich und Freunde – nachts beim Abhören der BBC bei der Truppe in Italien – einen Augenblick lang gehofft, das Attentat sei gelungen, es biete sich die Gelegenheit zu einem erträglichen Friedensschluß für uns Deutsche. Am nächsten Tag war die Hoffnung zerschlagen. Jetzt wußten wir wieder, worum wir beten konnten: um Vergebung für die Schuld des ganzen Volkes, unverdiente Vergebung, um Errettung aus dem totalen Untergang nach dem Gebetsbeispiel Abrahams für Sodom »wegen der wenigen Gerechten«, zu denen ich die Verschwörer des 20. Juli rechnete. Wir durften beten für die eigenen Angehörigen daheim, ihre Verschonung, für die eigene Gemeinde, ihren Fortbestand, für einen Neuanfang kirchlicher Arbeit und Ordnung und christlicher Existenz im eigenen Land und für ökumenische Verbundenheit über die Erde hin, die Beispiel werden könnte für gegenseitige Hilfe unter den Völkern, und mehr Gerechtigkeit, Freiheit und Frieden auf Erden.

Wir lernten, der Hörergemeinde im Lager die gute Nachricht des Evangeliums zu Schuld und Gnade unter dem Gebet zu sagen, daß sie Einsicht wecke und zugleich Zuversicht und Halt biete. Dies lernten wir in Gesprächen mit ratsuchenden Mitgefangenen und in offenen Auseinandersetzungen mit einer Anzahl unter ihnen, die unsere Deutung des Zeitgeschehens, die christlich-prophetische Deutung nicht annehmen mochten oder konnten.

Später habe ich das Zitat vom Mitverschwörergeneral Henning von Tresckow gelesen: »Wenn einst Gott Abraham verheißen hat, er werde Sodom nicht verderben, wenn auch nur zehn Gerechte darin seien, so hoffe ich, daß Gott auch Deutschland um unseretwillen nicht verderben wird. Niemand von uns kann über seinen Tod Klage führen.« Das waren die Gedanken, die wir im Konvent der Kirchenleute miteinander erörterten, und die Empfindungen, die mich um den achten Mai 1945 bewegten, sehr persönlich bewegten.

## MARGARETE SCHÖPKE
## Lüneburger Erwachen

Nachdem wir im heutigen West-Berlin im November 1943 unsere Apotheke und Privatwohnung durch Bomben verloren hatten, zogen wir am ersten Februar 1944 nach Seelow (Mark), wo wir uns mit viel Mühe wieder ein bescheidenes Heim einrichten konnten. Als ein Jahr später die Russen die Oder überquerten, flüchtete ich mit meinen beiden Kindern und einem kleinen Koffer, der die nötigsten Sachen enthielt, zu meinen Eltern nach Lüneburg. Mein Elternhaus war besetzt mit Flüchtlingen aus Hamburg und geflüchteten Verwandten. Aber ich war froh und dankbar, mit meinen Kindern einen Unterschlupf zu finden. Dort erlebte ich den Tag der bedingungslosen Kapitulation.

Bestimmend für die Erinnerungen an diesen Tag sind für mich die Erlebnisse in den Tagen vorher und nachher und ganz besonders an dem Tag, als die Engländer einzogen. Als ich am ersten Februar 1945 nach Lüneburg kam, war ich besonders in den ersten Tagen beeindruckt von der Meinung vieler Lüneburger, die noch an den endgültigen Sieg glaubten und feste Hitler-Anhänger waren. Es waren nur während des Krieges zwei Bomben in Lüneburg gefallen, die kaum Schaden angerichtet hatten. Die meisten Menschen hatten nichts verloren. Weder Hab und Gut noch nahe Angehörige. Sie hatten nicht wie ich die endlosen Flüchtlingstrecks gesehen, die im kalten Januar 1945 bei Eis und Schnee durch Seelow gezogen waren.

Um so schlimmer war das Lüneburger Erwachen, als sich am

achten Mai alle Illusionen und Zukunftsträume unabwendbar als nichtig erwiesen. Wir machten uns alle große Sorgen, wie es überhaupt weitergehen sollte, was aus unserer Zukunft und der unserer Kinder werden sollte. Beeindruckend für mich waren die langen Züge deutscher Gefangener, die in unsagbar elendem Zustand an unserem Haus vorbeizogen, sowie die provisorisch am Rande der Stadt eingerichteten Gefangenenlager, in denen unsere deutschen Soldaten hungernd und frierend untergebracht waren. Trotz allem verlor ich nicht die Hoffnung, daß auch ich eines Tages wieder eine Existenz und ein Heim für meine Familie finden würde. Ich spürte eine gewisse Erleichterung bei dem Gedanken, daß die schrecklichen Ereignisse der letzten Jahre nun ein Ende hatten, die zahlreichen Berliner Bombennächte, die Flucht, der Verlust jeglichen Besitzes und vor allem das sinnlose Morden. Zu diesem Zeitpunkt konnte ich mir noch keine Vorstellung machen von der unwiderruflichen Abtrennung der Ostgebiete; ahnte nichts von der für mich schlimmsten Folge dieses Krieges, der Teilung des verbleibenden Restes unseres Vaterlandes in zwei Staaten mit gegensätzlichen Anschauungen und Systemen; ahnte nichts von einer fast unüberwindlichen Mauer, die später Familien voneinander trennte.

Beeindruckend für mich waren in diesen Tagen die Nachrichten, die wir über die Konzentrationslager, die Massenvernichtung der Juden und die damit verbundenen Greueltaten hörten. Davon hatte man in Lüneburg kaum eine Ahnung. Es gab sogar Leute, die einen Teil dieser Meldungen für Lügenpropaganda der Feinde hielten. Als Erretter und Freunde konnten wir allerdings die bei uns einziehenden Engländer nicht betrachten. Dazu trugen auch Ereignisse bei wie die Besetzung unseres Hauses, das wir nach einigen Tagen räumen mußten. Als wir zurückkamen, waren die Soldaten zwar ausgezogen. Wir fanden aber eine große Wüstenei vor. Besonders erinnere ich mich an das gute Tafelservice meiner Eltern und anderes wertvolles Porzellan, das die Kellertreppe hinuntergeschmissen worden war, so daß der Keller voller Scherben lag.

Dieses sind einige Eindrücke, an die ich mich noch gut erinnern kann. Sicher haben mich damals andere, meist gegensätzliche Gefühle beherrscht, die im Laufe der Jahre verwischt worden sind.

EUGEN SEIBOLD
## Geschämt

Recht unbeweglich, in einem Lazarettbett in Brixen, erlebte ich den achten Mai. Ein Sandsack hing über einer Rolle an meinem eingegipsten rechten Bein und streckte es. Im April hatte unser Werferregiment, eines der beiden in Italien, auf dem Rückmarsch die schweren Waffen und Zugfahrzeuge beim Übergang über Po und Etsch verloren. Wir hatten dies vorausgesehen und einige Fahrzeuge nördlich davon in Reserve gehalten. Auf diesen fuhren die Reste unserer Einheiten eng gedrängt nach Norden. Da und dort beschossen uns Partisanen. So auch in der Nähe von Schio am Alpenrand nordöstlich von Verona. Als Regimentsadjutant stand ich im vordersten Fahrzeug und wurde beim Beschuß herausgeschleudert. Dabei wurde das rechte Kniegelenk hart mitgenommen. Nach einer unerfreulichen Fahrt durch Südtirol wurde ich am 30. April 1945 in dieses Lazarett eingeliefert. Mein Regiment wurde dann durch den an der Südfront vorgezogenen Waffenstillstand am Gardasee interniert.

Es klingt nach Jägerlatein, doch war es tatsächlich unseren Nachrichtenleuten gelungen, einen Apparat unter mein Bett zu schmuggeln. Sie zapften verschiedene Telefonleitungen an, so daß ich über die mehr als 150 Kilometer hinweg Verbindung halten konnte.

Was bewegte uns bei diesen Gesprächen? Die neue Lage des Regiments, das noch immer fest zusammenhielt. Das Schicksal des einen oder anderen Abgesprengten. Vor allem aber die Zukunft und dabei die Chancen, wann, wo und besonders wie wir zu unseren Angehörigen daheim kommen würden. Ich wurde zum Beispiel aufgeschreckt durch das Gerücht, daß Offizieren eine Gefangenschaft in Ägypten drohe. Deshalb hatte ich mir Fluchtkleidung besorgt und unter der Matratze versteckt. Freilich, ein Humpelnder auf dem Weg über den Brenner wäre sicher nicht weit gekommen.

Der achte Mai selbst? Ich weiß es nicht mehr. Gefühle der Befreiung, der Erleichterung, der Leere, der Hoffnung? Ich weiß es nicht mehr. Der Einschnitt in die aktiven Tage rund um die Uhr in Schio steht heute viel lebendiger vor mir als die Reihe der passiven Tage und endlosen Nächte im Lazarett.

Erwähnt sei jedoch etwas Unvergessenes danach: Ich wurde am 24. Mai in das Kurhaus von Meran verlegt. Es war damals gleichfalls ein Lazarett, und dort erst, im Kreise von vielen anderen, überfiel mich eine ganze Flut von Nachrichten, die uns bis dahin nicht erreicht oder die wir einfach nicht geglaubt hatten. Ich habe mich dabei mit vielen von uns, die seit 1939 als Soldat an der Front gewesen waren, darüber geschämt, was alles im deutschen Namen hatte geschehen können. Wir suchten Trost, wo wir ihn finden konnten. Von irgendwoher war ein Plattenspieler gekommen und von irgendwoher die 3. Sinfonie von Beethoven. Stundenlang saßen wir davor, zwischen tiefer Betroffenheit über den Trauermarsch und Trost aus dem Hauptthema der Celli im ersten Satz, Trost, daß zu den Deutschen auch ein Beethoven gehört. Daneben gab es auch zynische Bemerkungen, daß uns ausgerechnet die »Eroica« in die Hände gefallen war.

Das aber kam, wie gesagt, erst Wochen nach dem achten Mai, und ich weiß es noch, weil ich es nicht nur erlebt habe, sondern weil es zum Erlebnis geworden ist.


OTA ŠIK
# Nummer 3127


Zwei Jahre vor dem »Prager Frühling« hatte ich die Gelegenheit, meiner Familie das Konzentrationslager Mauthausen zu zeigen. Es war ein sonniger Sommertag, und was man sehen konnte, hatte über das hier einst Geschehene wenig auszusagen. Die Zeit hat die meisten Spuren verwischt.

Nicht in mir. Meine Erinnerungen wurden wach, obwohl ich über 20 Jahre dieses Thema in mir verdrängt hatte. Einzelheiten traten spontan hervor und mit ihnen die sie begleitenden Gefühle. Nur mit Mühe konnte ich meine Worte in logische Sätze formen.

Auch damals war ein sonniger Frühlingstag, als zwei amerikanische Panzerwagen am fünften Mai 1945 ins KZ hereinfuhren. Es war eine Vorhut der amerikanischen Armee. Unsere Befreiung begann so einige Tage vor der deutschen Kapitulation. Zu unserem damaligen Erstaunen sind die amerikanischen Panzer wieder weggefahren und haben damit eine nicht vorauszusehende Situation ausgelöst. Die SS war schon in der Nacht vom zweiten auf den dritten Mai geflüchtet. Vor ihrer Flucht hat sie alles Archivmaterial im Krematorium verbrannt und die Bewachung des Lagers einer Polizeiformation der Wiener Feuerwehr übergeben.

Nach Abzug der amerikanischen Panzer und Gefangennahme der Polizeiformation blieb das Lager sich selbst überlassen. Um das ausbrechende Chaos zu überwinden, hat ein internationales Komitee der Häftlinge (im Lager befanden sich an die 66 000 Häftlinge, Angehörige von ungefähr dreißig Nationen) die Lagerleitung übernommen. Aber niemand konnte den Hunger der Menschenmassen stillen und das Schicksal der ausgemerzten und kranken Häftlinge erleichtern, so daß auch nach der Befreiung die Menschen noch zu Hunderten starben.

Am siebten Mai besetzten amerikanische Truppen das Lager, von dessen Existenz sie früher nicht gewußt hatten, und übernahmen seine Verwaltung. Am Tag der Kapitulation war also das KZ Mauthausen bereits definitiv befreit.

Als Häftling ohne Namen, unter der Nummer 3127 und mit einem roten Winkel (politische Häftlinge) versehen, hatte ich das Ende des Krieges und der Haft doch noch erlebt. Daß es zu Ende geht, wußte ich seit den letzten Apriltagen auch ohne Informationsquelle. Manches hatte sich herumgesprochen, und während der letzten Woche war es auch hörbar. Die Kanonade kam immer näher – von wo und von wem sie stammte, wußte allerdings niemand genau.

In mir war beides gestaut – die Hoffnung und die Angst. Ein ungemein starker Lebenswille nach so vielen Jahren kümmerlichsten Dahinvegetierens am Rande des Todes und die Angst, daß im letzten Moment doch noch alles schiefgehen könnte. Diese Paarung von Hoffnung und Angst beherrschte mich seit meiner Verhaftung im Herbst 1940, nur gab es Jahre und Monate, in welchen das Überleben fast unerträglich wurde.

Damals, als ich wegen illegaler Widerstandstätigkeit gegen die deutsche Okkupation verhaftet wurde und nach halbjährigen Verhören durch die Gestapo ohne Gerichtsurteil ins KZ überführt wurde, war meine Hoffnung auf ein Minimum geschrumpft. Die Zeit im Mauthausener Steinbruch überlebte ich als einer der wenigen von Tausenden, die ich Tag für Tag neben mir sterben sah. Der Tod kam für die meisten qualvoll, und mein Überleben schien mir selbst unglaublich und ständig in Frage gestellt. Jede Stunde habe ich das Ende erwartet, und doch konnte ich es mir nicht vorstellen und wollte es nicht wahrhaben. Die ganzen fünf Jahre habe ich mit jedem Gedanken und jeder Bewegung gelernt abzuwägen, was zum Tode oder zum Leben führt. Der Wille zum Leben war also innerhalb der grauenvollen Trostlosigkeit nie ganz verschwunden.

Auch am Tag der Befreiung saß die Angst in der Hoffnung. Die SS konnte zurückkommen und uns alle liquidieren oder – viele andere Möglichkeiten drängten sich ins Bewußtsein. Zum Glück ist die beste wahr geworden. Die endgültige und lange erhoffte Freiheit war gekommen. Ich bin am Leben geblieben. Neu geboren mit sechsundzwanzig Jahren. Eine neue Zukunft öffnete sich, ein neues Schicksal begann.

SHMUEL SPEKTOR
# Eine lang ersehnte Antwort

Der Sieg über Nazideutschland fand für mich nicht am achten Mai 1945, sondern früher statt. Wenige Menschen hatten es 1941 doch noch geschafft, in die Sowjetunion zu fliehen, um der deutschen Okkupation zu entkommen. Auch ich gehörte zu diesen wenigen.

Zwischen Wolga und Ural verbrachte ich die Zeit mit verschiedenen Jobs. Am Neujahrstag 1945 befand ich mich in Kuibyschew. Der Roten Armee war es in den letzten zwei Jahren gelungen, die deutschen Truppen immer weiter zurückzudrängen und an der ehemaligen deutsch-polnischen Grenze Position zu beziehen. Jeder sah das Ende des Krieges herannahen, doch mein Herz konnte sich daran nicht erfreuen.

Als ich 1941 – im jugendlichen Alter – das Haus verlassen hatte, waren meine Eltern und alle meine Verwandten zurückgeblieben. Nun wurden im März 1944 die deutschen Besatzer auch aus meinem Geburtsort vertrieben. Verjagt. Obwohl ich zu diesem Zeitpunkt von der fortgesetzten Massenvernichtung der jüdischen Bevölkerung bereits wußte, lehnten mein Herz und mein Verstand den Gedanken ab, daß alle Juden umgebracht worden seien. »Vielleicht lebt doch noch jemand«, war meine große Hoffnung. In einem Brief an die Stadtverwaltung meines Geburtsortes bat ich um Auskunft über den Verbleib meiner Familie. Gedämpft-optimistisch hoffte ich auf eine positive Antwort.

Einige Monate waren seitdem ins Land gegangen, und eines Tages im Herbst 1944 erhielt ich in der Tat die lang ersehnte Antwort. Geschrieben hatte sie der Vater eines meiner Freunde, der bei der Stadtverwaltung arbeitete. Mit zitternden Händen öffnete ich den Umschlag. Das Lesen wollte nicht gelingen. Zeilen und Buchstaben begannen sich vor meinen Augen zu bewegen, wurden immer undeutlicher, verschwommener, verwischter. Ich brauchte lange Zeit, den Brief zu Ende zu lesen, viel mehr aber, um zu begreifen, was tatsächlich in dem Brief stand.

Aus einer großen Familie mit zahlreichen Angehörigen, die seit Jahrhunderten gelebt und geschafft hatten, war ich der einzige Überlebende.

In der Zwischenzeit wurde auch bekannt, daß es zwischen der Sowjetunion und Polen zu einem Abkommen gekommen war. Jedem, der bis 1939 polnischer Staatsangehöriger war, wurde die Rückkehr in die Polnische Republik gestattet, und da es für mich ab nun »Zukunft« im wörtlichen Sinne nicht mehr gab, entschied ich mich, zurückzugehen, also in Richtung Westen.

Am Tag des großen Sieges begann für mich ein langer Irrweg ins Unbekannte und Ungewisse. Zunächst kam ich in meinem Geburtsort an, einem kleinen Städtchen in der Westukraine. Mit gemischten Gefühlen näherte ich mich der Stadt. Bleiben konnte ich hier aber nur einige Stunden, denn bewaffnete einheimische Banditen kontrollierten bei Nacht das Gebiet und vervollständigten das, was die Deutschen bereits getan hatten: Sie brachten die wenigen noch überlebenden Juden um. Straßen und Häuser wirkten fremd. Überall unbekannte Gesichter. Nirgendwo eine Spur vom so vertrauten jüdischen Leben. Augen voller Haß verfolgten mich überall, als bekannt wurde, wer ich war. Unsere ehemaligen Nachbarn, die während der deutschen Okkupation bei der Vernichtung der Juden freudig mitgeholfen hatten, waren glücklich, uns losgeworden zu sein, um sich unseren seit Jahrhunderten schwer erarbeiteten und angesammelten Besitz anzueignen.

Die meisten Tage habe ich in einer benachbarten Stadt verbracht, in der ich früher das Gymnasium besucht hatte. Auch diese Stadt wirkte fremd. Auch hier waren ganze Straßen völlig zerstört. Wie weggewischt. Meine Schule, in der ich wunderbare Jahre verbracht hatte, stand verlassen da wie in einer Wüste. Eine geringe Zahl von jüdischen Überlebenden, die es wagten, aus ihren Verstecken herauszukommen, fand sich erneut versammelt in einigen Häusern am Rande der Stadt. Sie alle

warteten auf ihre Rückführung in die polnische Heimat. Alle
waren fest entschlossen, Plätze, die verwüsteten Friedhöfen äh-
nelten, für immer zu verlassen. Sie beseelte eine einzige Sehnsucht: ihr eigenes Leben in neuer Umgebung wiederaufzu-
bauen. So dauerte es nicht lange, bis auch ich in einem Zug saß,
der nach dem damals von Polen besetzten Schlesien fuhr.

Aber auch diese Station bedeutete für die meisten von uns
nur einen vorübergehenden Aufenthalt, eigentlich den Beginn
eines neuen Trecks für jüdische Flüchtlinge in Richtung Palästina. Es dauerte noch ein halbes Jahr, bis wir dann sicher und
wohlauf die Küste Palästinas erreichten.

KARL STEINBUCH
## Eine Lehre, die ich zog . . .

Als am achten Mai 1945 das Radio die bedingungslose Kapitulation meldete, saß ich im Ratskeller zu Eckernförde und hatte
vor mir ein »Stammgericht« aus Rüben. Da kam also die Nachricht, das Deutsche Reich habe bedingungslos kapituliert. Danach wurde – noch einmal, zum letztenmal für lange Zeit – das
Deutschlandlied gespielt. Alle Gäste standen auf, alle sangen
mit, manche tief bewegt mit Tränen in den Augen.

Allen war klar, daß in diesem Augenblick die Weltgeschichte
eine scharfe Grenze gezogen hatte: Danach war alles anders als
vorher. Was vorher geboten, war nachher verboten – was vorher gut, war nachher schlecht. Das begann schon damit, daß
man vorher beim Deutschlandlied aufstehen mußte – es jetzt
aber freiwillig tat. Vorher mußte man jede Nacht wegen der
Luftangriffe in den Keller, nachher konnte man ungestört
schlafen. Unverändert blieb nur, daß die Deutschen vorher und
nachher hungerten.

Aber die Dimension dieser historischen Zäsur zeigte sich in
diesem Augenblick des achten Mai 1945 noch gar nicht. Sie er-
schloß sich erst im Rückblick. Man spricht von jenem Datum

oft als »Stunde Null«. Aber es war eher eine Stunde X – eine Linie ging abwärts und eine aufwärts –, und alles war unbekannt.

Ich gehörte damals – erstaunlicherweise – zur Zivilbevölkerung, nachdem ich vorher beinahe acht Jahre Soldat gewesen war, die meiste Zeit davon in Rußland an der Front. Durch Zufall wurde ich – als Diplomingenieur – Anfang 1944 von der Front nach Berlin abkommandiert, um dort an der Entwicklung von »Wunderwaffen« mitzuwirken, von denen man noch den »Endsieg« erhoffte, und zwar an der Entwicklung von Peilgeräten für Einmanntorpedos.

Vorher war ich Batteriechef in einer Raketenabteilung, das hieß bei uns »Nebelwerferabteilung«.

Es ist hier nicht der Ort, über Erlebnisse in Rußland zu berichten – aber dies sei immerhin gesagt: Die Deutsche Wehrmacht hatte Übermenschliches geleistet. Ihre Niederlage war nicht das Ergebnis der soldatischen Überlegenheit ihrer Gegner, sondern deren vielfacher zahlenmäßiger Überlegenheit und unseres Mangels an Munition. Aber die Menschenopfer waren ungeheuer!

Vom Krieg in Rußland fällt mir immer wieder eine einzelne glänzende Situation ein: Im Sommer 1942 waren wir auf raschem Vormarsch durch die Ukraine. Da gab es noch nicht die Katastrophe von Stalingrad, da war Feldmarschall Rommel noch auf seinem Siegeszug durch Nordafrika nach El Alamein. Da wir damals noch die Luftüberlegenheit besaßen, konnten wir in der Nacht Lagerfeuer anzünden. So weit das Auge reichte – bis an den Horizont –, Lagerfeuer deutscher Soldaten und darüber ein dunkler Sternenhimmel. Da stand einer der Soldaten auf – er war Sänger von Beruf – und sang das Lied »Freunde, das Leben ist lebenswert!« Diese eine Situation war wie ein Brillant in einem Morast von Blut und Schmerzen, Hitze und Kälte, Hunger und Durst.

Eine ganz andere Situation verbindet sich in meiner Erinnerung mit dem achten Mai 1945: Wie wir – drei Ingenieure der AEG, die an der Entwicklung der Einmanntorpedos in Eckernförde gearbeitet hatten – im Herbst 1945 zum Obersten britischen Militärgericht geführt wurden – mit Anklagen, die damals für ein Todesurteil gereicht hätten. Da trotteten wir drei – Hosenträger und Krawatten waren abgenommen worden – zwischen vier deutschen Polizisten, umgeben von einem Dutzend britischer Militärpolizisten, Maschinenpistolen schußbereit im Anschlag, durch Eckernförde zum Militärgericht.

Gleich zu Beginn wurde uns eröffnet, daß dieses Gericht die Kompetenz habe, Todesurteile zu fällen, und hiergegen kein Einspruch möglich sei. Wie korrekt dieses Verfahren war, zeigte beispielsweise die Tatsache, daß während des ganzen Prozesses die falsche Identität eines der Zeugen nicht korrigiert werden konnte. Mein dahin zielender Versuch führte zu einem scharfen Verweis. Irgendein schriftliches Urteil erhielt keiner von uns. Ich konnte lediglich ein Schreiben beschaffen, daß kein Delikt gegen deutsche Gesetze Gegenstand des Prozesses gewesen war.

Rückblickend auf den achten Mai 1945 empfinde ich Trauer und Zorn: Trauer über das unendliche menschliche Unglück, das eine verrückte Politik angerichtet hatte – die vielen Millionen Toten, Zivilisten und Soldaten, Deutsche und Ausländer, das zerstörte Vaterland, die verlorenen Jahre. Zorn über unsere Dummheit, die Verführbarkeit unseres Volkes, das die Machtübernahme durch Verrückte weder verhindert hatte, noch ihnen rechtzeitig in die Arme fiel. Zorn auch über das leichtfertige Geschwätz, die bedingungslose Kapitulation des Deutschen Reiches habe uns Freiheit und Glück gebracht. Hier ist viel Ignoranz und Opportunismus am Werk: Unser Volk wurde nicht nur durch die russische Soldateska übel geplagt, Franzosen, Engländer und Amerikaner waren auch nicht gerade zimperlich.

Aus jenem Gefühl der Trauer und des Zornes heraus habe ich mir geschworen, nie wieder zu ideologischen Verrücktheiten zu schweigen. Beispielsweise schrieb ich 1972 – auf dem Höhepunkt der »Kulturrevolution des Westens« – mehrere offene Briefe, die vielfach veröffentlicht wurden, an den damali-

gen Bundeskanzler Brandt, er möge sich doch um die Rechts-
staatlichkeit und Rationalität an unseren Universitäten kümmern. Beispielsweise widerspreche ich Bölls verantwortungs-
losem Treiben, der in unserem freien Land zur »Zersetzung«
aufruft. Unser freiheitlicher Staat, der nach schwersten politischen Irrtümern von verantwortungsbewußten Männern wie
Konrad Adenauer, Theodor Heuss, Carlo Schmid und Ludwig
Erhard aufgebaut worden ist, seinen Bürgern viel Freiheit und
Wohlstand geschaffen hat und keinen Vergleich mit anderen
Systemen in Ost oder West zu scheuen braucht, ist es wert, von
seinen Bürgern entschlossen verteidigt zu werden.

Dies halte ich für die Lehre aus den Erfahrungen während
und nach dem schrecklichen Krieg – daran denke ich im Zusammenhang mit dem achten Mai 1945.

CAROLA STERN
Erschöpft, verlaust, verdreckt

Am zweiten Mai 1945 zogen wir in Wismar ein: Mutter, bis
vor wenigen Tagen Frauenschaftsleiterin in unserem Dorf,
Hänschen, mein vierzehnjähriger Vetter, bis vor wenigen Wochen Jungmann einer Nationalpolitischen Erziehungsanstalt,
und ich, die Ahlbecker Jungmädelführerin. Bis auf einen Rucksack war unser Gepäck im Bremserhäuschen eines Güterzugs
geblieben, den wir in Rostock unter russischem Beschuß
fluchtartig verlassen hatten. Zu Fuß hatten wir uns in Richtung
Westen aufgemacht. Wir waren erschöpft, verlaust, verdreckt,
aber doch noch immer Nazis.

Wismar hatten am gleichen Morgen die Engländer besetzt.
Da uns nun die Russenangst nicht länger trieb, ruhten wir uns
zusammen mit anderen Flüchtlingen erst mal unter einem
Baum an einer Straße aus. Nach wenigen Minuten kam ein britischer Panzer angefahren. Erschrocken erhoben wir uns wieder und folgten furchtsam dem geflüsterten Kommando einer

alten Frau, die Arme hochzuheben und ein weißes Taschentuch zu schwenken. Dies war der Augenblick, in dem ich aufgab – mich dem Feind ergab. Jedenfalls so empfand ich es. Sahen die Insassen dieses Panzers den Trupp mit den hocherhobenen Händen und den verängstigten Gesichtern gar nicht, oder scherten sie sich einfach nicht um ihn?

In dem gleichen Augenblick, in dem der Panzer da an uns vorüberrollte, wurde mir bewußt, daß der Feind zu unserer Unterwerfungsgeste gar nicht aufgefordert, sie nicht einmal beachtet hatte, und die widersprüchlichsten Gedanken fuhren mir durch den Kopf. Hatte ich mich nicht gedemütigt? War nicht mein Stolz verletzt? Doch wer hatte ihn verletzt? Statt eines tragisch-schicksalschweren Augenblicks, wie ich ihn eben noch zu erleben meinte, mußte ich mir eingestehen, daß die Szene etwas Lächerliches hatte und ungeeignet für großartige Gefühle war. Kurzum, die ganz persönliche Kapitulation in der alten Hansestadt mißlang.

Auf dem Heuboden einer verlassenen Schweinemästerei fanden wir eine Schlafgelegenheit. Auf dem Hof sausten zwischen Flüchtlingstrecks betrunkene Soldaten mit einem Jeep herum, unter uns schrien die hungrigen Schweine, und nachts stiegen manchmal befreite amerikanische Kriegsgefangene bei uns ein und vergewaltigten die nah der Luke liegenden Frauen. Von den Flüchtlingsfrauen auf dem Hof borgten wir uns Töpfe und wuschen darin unsere schmutzige Kleidung. Während sie irgendwo zum Trocknen hing, lagen wir halb nackt unter gestohlenen Decken oben im Heu und fragten uns, wie es zu einem solchen Ende hatte kommen können. Für meine Mutter waren schlechte Berater in der Umgebung des Führers schuld, Männer wie der versoffene Ley und dieser Streicher, der alles übertreiben mußte. Sie blieb dabei, daß Hitler viel von dem, was nicht gut gewesen sei, überhaupt nicht wußte. Der Vetter lag meist stumm dabei.

Mir schwirrten wieder die widersprüchlichsten Gedanken durch den Kopf. In Erinnerung an die preußischen Tugenden, die mir so viel bedeuteten, auch in Erinnerung an die vielen

Treuelieder, die wir gesungen hatten, wollte ich jetzt, im Unglück, doch nicht untreu werden und anders denken als bisher. Doch hatte unser Führer uns nicht selbst im Stich gelassen, sich einfach so davongemacht? So hatten wir doch nicht gespielt!

Dann wieder schien alles gleichgültig, wichtig nur das Nächstliegende zu sein: was zu essen finden, irgendwo auch ein Paar heile Strümpfe, sich durchschlagen und überleben. Der Gedanke an Mitschuld kam nicht auf, näher lag Zynismus: Man müßte einen englischen Soldaten angeln und mit ihm nach England gehen . . . Abenteuerlust. Die Vorstellung, endlich von der kleinen Insel an der Odermündung, und sei es auch auf diese Weise, von zu Hause weg und in »die Welt« zu kommen, erleichterte die Situation. Inmitten des Schlamassels war ich neugierig auf das Leben, wie es neunzehnjährige Mädchen sind.

Manchmal versuchte ich, mir auf unserem Heuboden vorzustellen, wie wohl Frieden sei. Dann träumte ich davon, in einem türkisfarbenen Abendkleid am Arm eines befrackten Kavaliers zum Opernball zu gehen. Darf ich bitten, gnädige Frau! sagt der Kavalier, und die beiden wiegen sich im Walzertakt, wandeln, Sekt schlürfend und charmant parlierend, zwischen rotem Samt, vorbei an vergoldeten Balustraden und unter funkelnden Lüstern aus Kristall, und alle Ballbesucher schauen bewundernd auf die türkisfarbene Robe und ihre Trägerin.

Solche Träume darf man nicht zerstören; auf einem Ball bin ich noch nie gewesen.

Es mag am sechsten oder siebten Mai gewesen sein, da fanden wir eine bessere Bleibe. Zusammen mit dem Vetter war ich stundenlang von Haus zu Haus gegangen und hatte an jeder Wohnungstür nach einer Unterkunft gefragt. Ein großer hagerer Mann so um die Vierzig nahm uns mit Mutter schließlich auf. Er erwies sich als hilfsbereit und sehr penibel.

Inmitten der deutschen Katastrophe bestand unser Gastgeber darauf, zur Vermeidung von Wasserstein den Wasserkessel bis zum Rand zu füllen, und hielt uns an, Schuhe zu putzen, durch dreißigmaliges Wichsen unserer abgewetzten Fußbekleidung Hochglanz zu verleihen. Auf dem Flur, vor der Etagentür, stand eine große Axt, die die Gäste nicht berühren durften.

Von morgens bis abends waren wir darauf aus, uns bei dem Herrn nützlich zu machen. Während der Vetter und ich einzukaufen versuchten, denn unser Gönner ging zunächst nie aus, kümmerte sich Mutter um den Haushalt und kam sofort auf den Gedanken, im Balkonkasten Petersilie zu säen. Dabei fand sie, in der Blumenerde grabend, Uniformspiegel und Achselstücke. »Mensch, SS!« murmelte der Vetter.

Unser Gastgeber, stellte sich heraus, war einer der leitenden Gestapoleute in der Stadt gewesen. Da er damit rechnen mußte, abgeholt zu werden, sollten wir danach die Wohnung hüten.

Während andere am achten Mai endlich befreit von der Gestapo waren, hatten wir, die Nazis, sie nun erstmals auf dem Hals. Innerhalb von wenigen Minuten verwandelte sich unsere Dankbarkeit in Furcht, mitverantwortlich gemacht, womöglich auch noch mitgenommen zu werden, und wir beschlossen, uns so schnell wie möglich aus dem Staub zu machen.

Den achten Mai erlebten wir mit dem Gestapo-Mann. War es direkt an diesem Tag oder kurz danach? In Wismar fand unter der Beteiligung britischer, kanadischer und sowjetischer Truppen eine große Siegesparade statt, denn in der alten Hansestadt begann jene Linie, die bis Wittenberge führte und an der die Einheiten der siegreichen Alliierten sich getroffen hatten. Wenn wir auch der Meinung waren, nun müsse jeder an sich selbst denken, und Verbrechen hätten wir, die kleinen Nazis, im Unterschied zu unserem Wirt ja nicht begangen, an diesem Tag lebten wir in Kumpanei mit ihm. Ein guter Deutscher, so befanden wir, hält sich der Parade fern und trauert um die Niederlage.

Sowohl an diesem Tag wie auch an den nächsten mußten alle Leute in der Stadt, die ins Rathaus wollten, um sich Papiere und Lebensmittelkarten zu besorgen, über auf den Rathaustreppen ausgelegte und mit Stahlhelmen befestigte Hakenkreuzfahnen gehen. In langen Sätzen sprangen ich und Hänschen um die Fahnen herum und waren sehr enttäuscht, daß niemand uns bestrafte. Abends in der Wohnung erzählten wir von unserer Heldentat und freuten uns, als Mutter und der Wirt wohlgefällig nickten.

Bevor wir auf einem Gutshof außerhalb der Stadt Unterkunft und Arbeit fanden, bat uns unser Gastgeber noch mehrmals um eine besondere Gefälligkeit. Abends während der Dämmerung schlichen Hänschen und ich mit ihm zusammen aus dem Haus und liefen zum einstigen Amtssitz der Gestapo. Dort standen wir eine Weile schweigend vor dem Haus und gingen dann wieder heim. Einmal wagten wir uns sogar bis in den unteren Flur und hörten zitternd in den oberen Räumen Menschen sprechen. Den Täter zog es immer wieder an den Ort der Tat.

Erst spät begann ich, nach der eigenen Schuld zu fragen. Meine Einsicht finde ich am genauesten im Lebensbericht Jewgenia Ginsburgs formuliert, einer Jüdin aus Kasan, die achtzehn Jahre im Archipel Gulag leben mußte. Über die Jahre davor, da sie eine gläubige Kommunistin war, schrieb sie jene Sätze, die von so vielen einst gläubigen Nationalsozialisten bis heute nicht gesagt worden sind: »In schlaflosen Nächten tröstet das Bewußtsein nicht, daß man nicht unmittelbar an Mord und Verrat beteiligt war. Denn nicht nur der hat getötet, der zugeschlagen hat, sondern auch jene, die das Böse zugelassen haben, ganz gleich wodurch: durch das gedankenlose Wiederholen gefährlicher Theorien; das wortlose Heben der rechten Hand, das halbherzige Schreiben von Halbwahrheiten. Mea culpa . . .«

JOSEF STINGL
## Flucht

Am achten Mai 1945 war ich mit einem Nachkommando der 5. Flakdivision in dem Ort Heisternest auf der Halbinsel Hela. Die Führung dieses Nachkommandos – ich war Oberleutnant – hatte man mir wohl deshalb gegeben, weil ich nicht zum gestandenen Stab der 5. Flakdivision gehörte und schon vorher auch nur »gastweise« mit einem Luftwaffenkommando in Ostpreußen eingesetzt war. Zuvor nämlich hatte ich mit einer Einheit »Fieseler Störche« Luftaufklärung betreiben sollen. Weil aber diese Flugzeuge nicht für Kampfeinsätze gedacht waren, bekam ich Ende März den Befehl, die Flugzeuge in Narmeln zu verbrennen. Die Soldaten meiner Einheit wurden zu einer Luftwaffendivision versetzt, ich selbst zum Stab des Luftwaffenkommandos Ostpreußen in Pillau-Neutief abgeordnet.

In ständigem Wechsel verschob sich mein Einsatz eben dahin, daß ich am achten Mai besagtes Nachkommando führte. Ich erinnere mich daran sehr genau, daß mich die Hast des Rückzugs und die Flucht der Zivilbevölkerung bis ins Innerste berührt hatten. Auch in Heisternest warteten noch viele Zivilisten auf den Abtransport nach dem Westen. Jede Art von Schiffen, die überhaupt in den Hafen kamen, wurde nahezu gestürmt. Ich erreichte es mit meinem Nachkommando, daß wir ein Minensuchboot besteigen konnten, das mit Zivilisten und Soldaten vollgestopft war. Daß wir als Einheit auf das Schiff kamen, verdanke ich wohl dem Umstand, daß der Kapitän des Schiffes ein Oberleutnant war und ich selbst ebenfalls diesen Dienstgrad trug. Wir wußten, daß der Krieg zu Ende war, und alle fieberten jetzt danach, auf irgendeine Weise dem Vordringen der Sowjetsoldaten zu entkommen. Wir hatten alle von den Befehlen über die schlechte Behandlung der Zivilbevölkerung und der Gefangenen gehört. Außerdem waren wir der Meinung, daß es den Angehörigen der Luftwaffe in der Gefangenschaft besonders schlecht ergehen würde.

Von meiner Familie wußte ich nur, daß meine Frau in meiner Heimat war, unser Kind inzwischen ein Jahr alt war und meine Frau ein zweites Kind im Herbst erwartete. Ich hatte also auch sehr große Angst davor, in russische Gefangenschaft zu kommen. Um so beglückter war ich, daß wir auf dem Schiff untergekommen waren, das heißt, daß man einfach einen Platz zum Stehen, Sitzen und Liegen hatte. Bewegen konnten wir uns kaum. Trotzdem kamen zwischen den Menschen an Bord Gespräche auf. Man konnte es kaum fassen, daß man auf dem Schiff war. Und war glücklich.

Am achten Mai um neunzehn Uhr fuhren wir aus dem Hafen von Heisternest. Noch vor dem Waffenstillstand um Mitternacht flogen russische Jäger Angriffe auf unser Schiff, trafen aber nicht. Natürlich war die Verzweiflung, daß nun auch noch diese Angriffe kamen, sehr groß. Als die Angriffe abgebrochen waren und wir nun auch schon ein ganzes Stück zurückgelegt hatten und zudem der Beginn des Waffenstillstandes uns die Hoffnung brachte, daß wir auch keine weiteren Angriffe mehr befürchten müßten, trat eine verhältnismäßig große Befriedigung bei allen auf dem Schiff ein, die insbesondere auch dann später noch bestärkt wurde, als bekannt wurde, daß wir nach Schleswig-Holstein und nicht nach Dänemark oder Schweden kommen würden.

Tatsächlich landeten wir am 14. Mai in Neustadt in Holstein. Wir kamen in englische Gefangenschaft und hatten uns selbst in der sogenannten Korpsgruppe Stockhausen zu verwalten. Den Offizieren beließen oder gaben die Engländer sogar noch Pistolen. Natürlich begann sofort eine fieberhafte Suche nach den Anschriften der Familien. Am sechsten Dezember 1945 war ich dann auf verschlungenen Wegen wieder bei meiner Familie in Maria-Kulm in Böhmen.

MICHAEL THOMAS
## Unwürdig und unklug

Drei Tage vor Kriegsausbruch war ich, beinahe zufällig, in England angekommen. Da es keine »Free German Forces« wie de Gaulles »Free French Forces« gab, meldete ich mich zur britischen Armee, um die Nazis zu bekämpfen. Nun, am 30. April 1945, stand ich, britischer Oberleutnant deutscher Staatsangehörigkeit, als Verbindungsoffizier bei der 1. Polnischen Panzerdivision in heftigem Gefecht nordwestlich von Bad Zwischenahn. Am Abend hörten wir in den Nachrichten, daß Hitler tot sei. Meine Stimmung hielt zwischen Triumph und Lähmung die Waage. Der Mann, der mir mein Vaterland nehmen wollte, war tot. Lebt meine Mutter? Leben meine Freunde?

Am dritten Mai schrieb ich an meine Schwester in London: »Die übelste Clique, die jemals ein Land regiert und die Welt bedroht hatte, ist vollständig zusammengebrochen. Die Freude kann nur gedämpft werden durch das Wissen, daß neue Gefahren drohen: von den Sowjets – und wir sind sehr müde . . .« Am neunten Mai schrieb ich wieder:

»Am vierten Mai erreichte uns in einem Dorf mit dem skurrilen Namen ›Neu England‹ die Nachricht eines Treffens der deutschen Führung mit Montgomery. Kein Zweifel, es ist vorbei. Einige Stunden später erhielten wir den Befehl, daß am fünften Mai, acht Uhr, das Feuer einzustellen sei.«

Unser Divisionskommandeur General Maczek wurde ins kanadische Hauptquartier gerufen, wo General Straube, Befehlshaber der Heeresgruppe Weser-Ems, die Kapitulationsbedingungen stehend entgegennehmen mußte. Zum erstenmal in der Geschichte besetzten Polen deutsches Gebiet, und General Maczek spürt den Schock der deutschen Offiziere, als den Polen Wilhelmshaven als Teil ihrer Zone zugewiesen wird. Am Eingang zum Hafen entdeckten sie den polnischen Doppeladler, den die Deutschen sechs Jahre zuvor in Gdingen erbeutet hatten. Aber was bedeuten diese kleinen Triumphe? Durch die halbe Welt hatten sich die Polen nach England durchgeschlagen, um ihr Land von den Deutschen zu befreien, und ihre Heimat gehörte nun den Russen!

Der große Waffenstillstand vom achten Mai bestätigt nur, was an unserer Front schon am vierten geschehen war. Am fünften besichtige ich Wilhelmshaven.

Ich schreibe:

»Die Stadt ist gänzlich zerstört. Zwei Marineoffiziere salutieren, ich erwidere, und wir kommen ins Gespräch. Am Ende strecken sie die Hand zum Gruß aus. Ich darf nicht akzeptieren: Wir haben unseren Nonfraternisierungsbefehl, demzufolge wir nicht als Befreier, sondern als Sieger auftreten sollen. Es ist ein sehr peinlicher Augenblick für mich, und ich versuche, den Befehl zu erklären. Die beiden Deutschen fühlen sich zutiefst erniedrigt, in ihren Augen flammt Haß auf. Es ist ein Befehl, gegen den Herz und Vernunft sich aufbäumen und den ich nur mit schlechtem Gewissen ausführe. Ich werde das wohl nicht lange durchhalten. In diesem Fall ist es ein kleiner Trost, daß die beiden eher unsympathische ›Etappenhengste‹ waren . . . Wieder spreche ich mit einigen deutschen Soldaten. Sie fragen, ob der Krieg mit Rußland schon angefangen hat. Sie hätten das gehört. Als ich ihnen sage, daß dem nicht so sei, wundern sie sich, warum sie dann nicht nach Hause gehen können. Mein Gott! Immer nehmen die Deutschen Haltung an, immerfort. Wenn die britischen Soldaten verkleidete Zivilisten sind, dann sind die deutschen Zivilisten verkleidete Soldaten. Dennoch, das Volk ist sehr sympathisch, gut aussehend die Jungen und Mädchen, ein hervorragender Menschenschlag. Ist dieses Land wirklich schlecht? Ich glaube es nicht. Sie sind nur verbogen, aber sie können geradegerichtet werden.«

In diesen Tagen brachte ein neuer Befehl Eisenhowers eine Verschärfung der Non-Fraternization. Jetzt durfte auch der militärische Gruß deutscher Offiziere nicht mehr erwidert werden. Ich haderte mit dem Verhalten der Alliierten. Schon in England hatte ich die Politik der bedingungslosen Kapitulation nicht nur für unwürdig, sondern auch für unklug gehalten. Jetzt wurde ich mit ihren Konsequenzen konfrontiert. Wütend erklärte ich meinem Vorgesetzten, einem netten schottischen Major, ich würde noch am selben Abend den deutschen Kommandeur aufsuchen und ihm raten, seinen Offizieren ebenfalls das Grüßen zu verbieten. Als ich mich auf den Weg machte, stand am Ausgang des Dorfes barhaupt mein Kommandeur, Oberst Sheppard: »Michael, ich höre, Sie wollen den deutschen Befehlshaber aufsuchen. Hören Sie, Sie sind britischer Offizier; Sie müssen sich entsprechend verhalten. Eisenhowers Befehl ist töricht, und ich persönlich werde ihn nicht befolgen. Ich werde, wo nötig, den Gruß erwidern. Sie können dasselbe tun, aber Sie können nicht zum deutschen Kommandeur gehen.« Natürlich hatte er recht. Aber bald sollte ich meine Vorstellungen über die deutsch-englische Verständigung auf andere Weise verwirklichen können: als Verbindungsoffizier des stellvertretenden Militärgouverneurs für die britische Zone, General Templer, zu den Ministerpräsidenten und Oberpräsidenten sowie den Parteiführern Adenauer, Schumacher und Blücher.

## GASTON E. THORN
# Schlußstrich

Der achte Mai 1945 ist in meiner Erinnerung der Schlußstrich, der das Ende einer Epoche besiegelte, die für Luxemburg seit der Befreiung im September 1944 mehr und mehr der Vergangenheit angehörte. Ein unvermeidliches Ende, das immer selbstverständlicher wurde, je weiter die alliierten Truppen vorrückten. Die Würfel waren gefallen.

Die letzten Tage vor der Kapitulation – nach Hitlers Ende: die Regierung Dönitz – empfand ich wie die Schlußabschnitte eines Kriminalromans, in denen nichts Sensationelles mehr geschieht. Das Ereignis selbst wurde ohne Überraschung aufgenommen.

Seine Bedeutung trat zurück gegenüber der unmittelbaren Erfahrung der Befreiung, mit der wir am dritten September 1944 – meinem Geburtstag – rechneten. Die Deutschen hatten begonnen, sich aus der Stadt Luxemburg zurückzuziehen. Nur muß irgendwo der amerikanische Vormarsch ins Stocken geraten sein, jedenfalls sind die Amerikaner nicht an diesem Tage, sondern erst am zehnten September eingerückt, ohne größere Kämpfe. Ein großer Teil des Landes fiel leider bei der Ardennenoffensive noch einmal in deutsche Hand. Die Front verlief zehn Kilometer vor Luxemburg, wo sich bereits der amerikanische Generalstab befand; danach war das Großherzogtum endgültig frei.

Ich habe die Ereignisse der Befreiung besonders intensiv erlebt. Meine Mutter war im Widerstand, mein Vater heimlich aus Deutschland zurückgekehrt, wohin man ihn strafversetzt hatte. Ich selbst war im Jahr zuvor wegen »politischer Sabotage und Vorbereitung zum Hochverrat« verurteilt, nach einigen Monaten Straflager jedoch begnadigt worden.

Der Druck, der jahrelang auf Land und Volk gelastet hatte, wich einer ungeheuren Erleichterung, einem wahren Freudentaumel . . .

Vor allem für die Schuljugend brach eine herrliche Zeit an. Das Schuljahr begann im September, nach der Befreiung. Ich war gerade sechzehn Jahre geworden und saß nun als Klassenjüngster in der vorletzten Klasse des Großherzoglichen Gymnasiums. An einen regelmäßigen Schulbetrieb war nicht zu denken. In den Schulen hatten sich die Amerikaner eingerichtet. Der Unterricht fiel ungefähr jeden zweiten Tag aus. Wir genossen unser Leben, und als endlich die Nachricht vom Ende des »tausendjährigen« Reiches kam, war dies willkommener Anlaß, nicht zu arbeiten, sondern einen Umzug durch die Stadt zu veranstalten bis zum Großherzoglichen Palais, um dort der wenige Wochen vorher aus dem Exil zurückgekehrten Großherzogin zuzujubeln. Ein spontanes Fest. Den Abend verbrachten wir in einem Café-Restaurant, wo zu improvisiertem Klavierspiel alle möglichen englischen und amerikanischen Lieder gesungen wurden, und schließlich haben wir im Hause von Freunden bis spät in die Nacht getanzt.

Doch war all die Ausgelassenheit noch von einem Gefühl der Trauer und Angst überschattet. Viele meiner Landsleute waren noch nicht heimgekehrt.

1942 hatte die deutsche Besatzungsmacht die Luxemburger wie auch Elsässer und Lothringer zu »Volksdeutschen« erklärt, ungeachtet des eindeutigen Ergebnisses einer Volksabstimmung, in der sich nahezu die Gesamtheit der Bevölkerung als luxemburgisch und nicht als deutsch bezeichnet hatte. Die Männer wurden zur Wehrmacht eingezogen und größtenteils an den gefährlichsten Frontabschnitten in Rußland eingesetzt, was versuchtem Völkermord gleichkam. Wer floh oder in den Widerstand ging, riskierte die Todesstrafe. Darüber hinaus war ein Teil der Bevölkerung nach Deutschland verschleppt worden und befand sich in Umsiedlung in Schlesien.

Wahre Freude konnte nicht aufkommen, solange nicht Klarheit herrschte über das Los der Verschollenen, ob sie nun in Konzentrationslagern saßen, verschleppt oder kriegsgefangen waren oder im Widerstand kämpften. Nahezu jede Familie wartete auf die Rückkehr vermißter Angehöriger, oft genug vergebens. Ein Beispiel aus meiner Schule: Zu Beginn des Schuljahres zählten die vier Klassen der Sekunda insgesamt nur knapp zwanzig Schüler. Die anderen kamen nach und nach wieder aus dem Krieg oder von der »Heimatflak« auf die Schulbank zurück: Schüler, die im Kriege verwundet waren, in ihren Armen Freunde hatten sterben sehen oder die vielleicht selbst Menschen getötet hatten.

In anderer Hinsicht brachten schon die ersten Monate nach der Befreiung eine Enttäuschung mit sich. Im Widerstand hatten viele von einem völligen Neubeginn geträumt. Nun mußten wir erleben, wie die aus dem Exil zurückkehrenden Politiker die Geschicke des Landes wieder in die Hand nahmen. Der Konflikt zwischen denjenigen, die in den Jahren der Besetzung im Widerstand auf die Erneuerung hingearbeitet hatten, und den Repräsentanten der hergebrachten Ordnung, die 1940 das Land verlassen hatten, ließ nicht auf sich warten. Auch die Streitigkeiten zwischen den verschiedenen politischen und weltanschaulichen Lagern setzten schnell wieder ein. Die Jugend machte da keine Ausnahme. Ich entsinne mich, wie es ausgerechnet bei unserem Umzug vor dem Großherzoglichen Palais aus Anlaß der Kapitulation Hitler-Deutschlands zu einem Zwischenfall kam, als eine Pfadfindergruppe aus Protest aus dem Zug ausscherte, nachdem sie weiter hinten im Zug eine rivalisierende Gruppe entdeckt hatte . . .

Jenseits der Freude über das Ende von Krieg und Besetzung, der Trauer über die Opfer und der Enttäuschung über die Rückkehr in den politischen Alltag waren zwei Erfahrungen mit der Befreiung verbunden: Zum einen waren wir uns unserer Ohnmacht bewußt. Unsere Befreiung verdankten wir den

großen Schlachten im fernen Rußland und dem Eingreifen der
Vereinigten Staaten, ohne daß wir selbst viel dazu hätten beitragen können. Zum anderen ist festzuhalten, daß Gefühle von
Rache oder Haß so gut wie nicht vorhanden waren, wenn wir
auch an eine Aussöhnung damals noch nicht gedacht haben, dafür waren die Wunden noch viel zu frisch. Jedoch waren wir
von dem Gefühl durchdrungen, daß sich so ein Krieg in Europa
niemals mehr wiederholen dürfe.


Georg Stefan Troller
# Heimkehr


Als Soldat des letzten Weltkrieges führte ich, der »historischen
Ereignisse« eingedenk, ein Kriegstagebuch, was streng verboten
war, denn bei Gefangennahme konnte ja die Information dem
Feind in die Hände fallen. Der Feind, das waren in diesem Fall
die Deutschen. Ich war nach langen Jahren der Emigration nun-
mehr amerikanischer Soldat mit zwei Streifen am Ärmel, etwa
dem Grad entsprechend, den Hitler im Ersten Weltkrieg erreicht hatte: Obergefreiter. Meine Aufgabe bestand darin, deutsche Kriegsgefangene zu verhören. Diese Aufgabe endete allerdings mit dem ersten Mai 1945, als unsere Division, die »Don-
nervögel«, in München einmarschierte und wir erfuhren, daß
Hitler tot sei. Am zweiten Mai fuhr ich im Jeep hinaus nach Dachau. Die Fotos, die ich dort aufnahm, besitze ich noch heute –
ich erwähne das nur, weil es ja Leute geben soll, die meinen, der
Holocaust hätte nie stattgefunden. Für den achten Mai verzeich-
net mein Tagebuch stichwortartig auf englisch: »Friedensschluß, bedingungslose Übergabe heute fällig. Deutsche lesen
Proklamationen ausdruckslos an Plakatwänden. Sind Arsch-
kriecher, bewundern uns als Stärkere. Hackenzusammenschla-
gen, jawohl, Herr Offizier. Keine Spur von Gewissen. Wir waren ehrliche Gegner, gebt uns Waffen, gehen mit euch gegen
Russen. Wir gehören doch alle gleicher Rasse an, wissen nicht,

warum ihr gegen uns gekämpft habt. Wir sind Idealisten, sind das Volk Goethes, ihr Amis habt keine Ideale, nur Geld.«

Die Kapitulation erlebte ich hauptsächlich als Triumphgefühl, ohne großes Mitleid mit den geschlagenen Deutschen. Eigentlich tat es mir mehr um die zerstörten Städte leid als ihre Bewohner. Einen aufrechten Antinazi hatte ich während meiner ganzen Kriegsjahre nicht getroffen, dafür Mengen von Opportunisten. Zu differenzieren lernte ich erst einige Zeit später, als ich deutsche Freunde gewann und mich mit ihnen auseinandersetzen mußte. Am achten Mai aber war ich noch ganz Amerikaner. Ich hatte die Nachricht über einen Volksempfänger gehört, der in dem von mir »befreiten« Quartier in München-Bogenhausen stand, und kurz darauf die Details in der Armeezeitung »Stars and Stripes« nachgelesen. Sie kam für uns nicht überraschend, denn wir waren ja in ein paar Wochen durch ganz Bayern gebraust. Komplette Divisionen hatten sich dabei mit erhobenen Armen ergeben, hoch erfreut, bei den »Blutsbrüdern« und nicht »dem Iwan« gelandet zu sein. Wir machten uns nicht einmal mehr die Mühe, sie gefangenzunehmen, sondern winkten sie bloß nachlässig nach hinten. Der achte Mai war für uns nur der Höhepunkt dieses Siegesrausches.

An ein Rachegefühl kann ich mich nicht erinnern. Es war eher so etwas wie eine tief genossene Wiederherstellung der Gerechtigkeit. Es war das Ende des letzten Aktes der Tragödie, die Weltgeschichte hatte sich wieder eingependelt, nun würde gesühnt werden. Von keinem eigenen Schuldgefühl beleckt – ich war allerdings erst dreiundzwanzig –, sah ich mich erhaben auf der Seite des »Guten« – das Böse hatte nichts mit mir zu tun, hatte auf einem fremden Stern stattgefunden, in dem man nur zufällig meine Sprache redete. Es gab »uns«, und es gab »sie« – und daß letzten Endes sie auch ich waren, erreichte nur einen kleinen Teil meines Bewußtseins.

Außerdem hatte ich überlebt, und der Überlebende fühlt sich immer irgendwie im Recht. Eine Art Euphorie muß mich an diesem Tag beseelt haben wie jemand, der nach vielen Rückschlägen einen langen Prozeß gewinnt und sein Schmerzensgeld einheimst. Aber gleichzeitig kam auch der »letdown« (damals dachte ich noch auf amerikanisch), die Enttäuschung. Denn an diesem Tag tat sich, soweit ich mich entsinne, nichts auf den deutschen Straßen. Keine Kirchenglocken läuteten, man sank sich nicht in die Arme, und schon gar nicht ging man in Sack und Asche, wie ich doch eigentlich im Hintergrund meines Schädels erwartet hatte. Kein Sühnezeichen wurde gesetzt. Es ging um Kartoffeln und Kaffee und die dumpfe Angst, daß man jetzt als Sklavenarbeiter zum Wiederaufbau nach Frankreich verschickt würde. Jemand beklagte sich bei mir, daß Marodeure seinen Mickymauswagen – ich hatte keine Ahnung was das war – gestohlen hätten, Kinder bettelten um Schokolade und »Tschungum«. Ich half einer alten Frau, ihren Hausrat über die Straße zu tragen, und bekam dafür später, weil mich ein Offizier gesehen hatte, wegen »Fraternisierens« die Hälfte meines Monatssolds gestrichen. Und ich hörte, daß unsere Division jetzt zum japanischen Kriegsschauplatz abkommandiert würde.

Eine Unruhe ergriff mich, weniger um mein Leben – aber wer will schon nach einem Waffenstillstand an eine neue Front? – als vor der Entscheidung, die ich lang vor mir hergeschoben hatte und die jetzt fällig war. Fühlte ich mich als Amerikaner, so mußte ich mit der Division nach Japan. Fühlte ich mich als Europäer, so mußte ich auf diese oder jene Art hierzubleiben suchen. Am nächsten Tag reichte ich um einen Job bei der Militärregierung ein. Es war der erste Schritt meiner – nie abgeschlossenen – Heimkehr.

HERMANN ULRICHS
## Mäuse haben wir gehabt . . .

Als Verwundeter im Kriegslazarett 581 in der Kopenhagener Wittenbergsgade lag ich im Bett. Erschöpft dachte ich an die Stationen meiner Kriegsodyssee der letzten drei Monate. Vierte Verwundung im Heiligenbeiler Kessel. Hauptverbandsplätze.

Sammelstellen. Unter den Messern der Chirurgen. In papierne Leichensäcke eingeschnürt, über das Eis des Frischen Haffs mit russischen Panjekutschern nach Pillau. Im Hilfskreuzer nach Danzig. Dort Geburtstag in der Langfuhrer Landesfrauenklinik, wo ich vor achtundzwanzig Jahren zur Welt gekommen war. Transport über die Ostsee mit dem schnellen Südamerikafahrer »General Sankt Martin« mit 5000 Verwundeten an Bord ohne Geleitschutz. U-Boot-Alarm bei der Stolper Bank, wo die »Gustloff« versenkt wurde. Nun glücklich in Kopenhagen, wo ich auf einer Stube mit zwölf Mann liege, darunter zwei Offiziere der lettischen SS-Division und ein belgischer SS-Mann der Division Flandern, von Beruf Frisör.

Der fünfte Mai 1945 ist ein sonniger Frühlingstag in Kopenhagen. Doch was ist das? Durch das Fenster sehe ich, wie zwei russische Hilfswillige des Lazarettpersonals die Reichskriegsflagge einholen! »Da stimmt was nicht«, sage ich zu meinen Stubenkameraden, »die Iwans holen die Fahne runter!« Gemurmel setzt ein. Dann überstürzen sich die Ereignisse. Ein Lastwagen fährt vor das Schulhoftor an der Wittenbergsgade. Zwei Schwerbewaffnete in blauen Overalls und Feuerwehrhelmen springen ab, legen sich auf den Asphalt und richten ihre Waffen auf das Lazarett. Zunächst passiert nichts. Dann kommt der Zahlmeister vorbei, auf den sie nun ihre MPs richten. Sie fragen: »Bist du Chef?« Er verneint, bewahrt Ruhe und bringt den Führer des Kommandos, einen Oberleutnant der aufgelösten dänischen Armee, zu unserem Oberstabsarzt, der mit viel diplomatischem Geschick die Übergabe unseres Lazaretts an die dänischen »Freiheitskämpfer« nach den Regeln der Genfer Konvention vollzieht.

Es gibt vier verschiedene Gruppen von Freiheitskämpfern – die Landser sagen: Freizeitbekämpfer –, und zwar monarchistische, sozialdemokratische, kommunistische und parteilose. Ihr vordringlichstes Ziel ist nicht die Gefangennahme wehrloser Verwundeter und einiger Etappenhengste, sondern das schnelle Erbeuten von Kaffee, Tee, Schokolade, Zigaretten und Alkohol aus Wehrmachtsbeständen. Unsere Besatzer sind

monarchistisch. Am Nachmittag greifen kommunistische Freiheitskämpfer an, um den Königstreuen unser Lazarett abzuja-
gen. Doch die Unseren bekommen Verstärkung. Es knallt wie
in alten Tagen in Rußland. Die Kommunisten werden verjagt.

Generaloberst Lindemann, Wehrmachtsbefehlshaber Dänemark, hat für den fünften Mai 1945 die Kapitulation seines Be-
fehlsbereichs erklärt. Aber niemand ist da, die Kapitulation
entgegenzunehmen. Da schweben am Nachmittag zwei Transportmaschinen in Kastrup ein. Sie bringen einen englischen General mit seinem Stab. Die Kapitulationsurkunde wird unterzeichnet. Die englischen Landtruppen sind erst bei Lübeck.
Der sechste Mai vergeht mit Schießereien im Stadtgebiet wie
gehabt.

Der siebte Mai wird heiß! Die Dänen wollen vollendete Tatsachen schaffen, ehe die Engländer da sind. Sie versuchen, mit
etwa dreihundert Mann die im Hafen liegenden, letzten intak-
ten deutschen Kriegsschiffe zu kapern, den schweren Kreuzer
»Prinz Eugen«, den Kreuzer »Nürnberg« sowie etliche Zerstörer und Torpedoboote. Das Kommando hat der Kommandant
der »Prinz Eugen«. Er läßt den Angriff mit Feuer aus MGs und
20-mm-Flak stoppen. Tote säumen die Pier. Die Dänen bringen nun rund tausend Mann für einen erneuten Angriff heran.
Da schickt der Kommandant einen Parlamentär von Bord und
läßt erklären, daß man vor den Engländern und nicht vor den
Dänen kapituliert habe. Wenn sie nicht sofort abzögen, ließe
er die 28-cm-Türme der »Prinz Eugen« rumdrehen und halb
Kopenhagen zusammenschießen! Das hilft.

Ich sitze mit entblößtem Oberkörper im Bett und werde von
einer Schwester neu verbunden. Eine Granate schlägt ins Fenster. Die Schwester fällt, am Kopf getroffen, über meine Füße.
Ich bekomme – zum fünftenmal – den Rücken voller Splitter.
Fünfzehn Verwundete zählt unser Lazarett neu an diesem Vormittag des siebten Mai. Nun wäre eigentlich das goldene Ver-
wundetenabzeichen fällig. Doch der Oberstabsarzt erklärt:
»Krieg vorbei – keine Orden mehr!«

Am Nachmittag erscheint in Begleitung unseres Chefarztes

ein Attaché der belgischen Gesandtschaft auf unserer Stube. Er fragt den Soldaten der SS-Division Flandern: »Vous êtes prisonnier de guerre?« Antwort: »Non!« Der Diplomat wird geradezu beschwörend eindringlich in seinem Ton. Als er zum sechstenmal sein »Vous êtes prisonnier de guerre?« gefragt hat, erhält er ein sechstes Mal ein klares »Non!« Abrupt dreht er sich um und verläßt schnellen Schrittes die Stube. Am nächsten Tag wird der Mann verlegt. Wir wissen nicht wohin. Wir bewundern die Haltung dieses einfachen Mannes aus Flandern.

Der achte Mai beginnt zunächst friedlich. Jedoch unsere königstreuen Bewacher werden munter. Kurz nach dem Essen ruft jemand den Flur entlang: »Sie kommen filzen!« »Herr Hauptmann«, heißt es, »Sie sind der Stubenälteste und müssen etwas unternehmen!« Ich ziehe meine Uniformjacke an. Fünf Freiheitskämpfer betreten unsere Stube. Ich sage mit scharfer Stimme: »Halt, Genfer Konvention, wir sind eine Offiziersstube und lassen uns nur von Offizieren durchsuchen!« Sie weichen zurück, tuscheln und verschwinden schließlich. Die Freude über den Erfolg währt nicht lange. Nach etwa dreißig Minuten erscheinen elf Uniformierte mit zwei Zivilisten, die sich als Kriminalpolizisten ausgeben und Dienstmarken vorzeigen. Im Nu ist die Stube voll. Man hört immer nur: »Dänisch Geld? Dänisch Geld?« Dänenkronen und Reichsmark wurden schon vor drei Tagen vom Rechnungsführer eingesammelt. Ich bin ihrer besonderen Aufmerksamkeit teilhaftig. Der Teufel will es – einer der Kerle langt in die Taschen meiner am Bettpfosten hängenden Reithose und fördert zweihundert Dänenkronen zutage. Ein Aufschrei! Nun werden sie wirklich wild. Ich werde in die Mitte der Stube gestoßen. Man zerrt mir die Sachen vom Leibe, während gleichzeitig vier oder fünf Schießeisen mit ihren Mündungen auf mich gerichtet sind. Ich muß die Arme heben, weil sie sehen wollen, ob unter den Achselhöhlen noch weitere Kronen verborgen sind. Wie immer im richtigen Moment kommt ein Fotoreporter zur Stube herein und schießt seine Bilder. Am nächsten Tag erscheine ich in Großaufnahme auf der Titelseite von »Berlinske Tidende« mit der Überschrift: »Dänische Freiheitskämpfer entlarven deutschen Kriegsverbrecher.« So schnell wird man berühmt.

Am Abend hören wir von der Kapitulation in Reims. Am neunten Mai wird die Kapitulation des Ostheeres bekanntgegeben. Was geht in uns allen vor? Was denken wir?

Es ist still geworden auf der Stube. Jeder versucht, all dies zu verdauen. Zum zweitenmal in kurzem Abstand einen Weltkrieg verloren zu haben – das wird schlimm für Deutschland. Versailles war sicher nichts gegen das, was jetzt kommt. In mir ist eine große Leere. Die Phantasie reicht nicht aus, um alle Folgen der Niederlage schon zu erfassen. Die Freude darüber, daß nun das Schießen und die ständige Lebensgefahr aufhören, wiegt gering gegenüber dem unheimlich dräuenden Nichts, das sich Zukunft nennt. Zu sehr hat man sich in sechs Jahren Infanterismus daran gewöhnt, ständig in Lebensgefahr zu sein, hat Instinkte und Verhaltensweisen entwickelt, die einen je nach Lage Jäger oder Gejagter sein ließen.

Immer öfter wandern die Gedanken zu den Angehörigen. Was ist mit ihnen? Sind sie noch am Leben? Nach dem, was wir von den Russen in Ostpreußen gesehen haben, ist nicht mehr damit zu rechnen. Die Gutsbesitzer wurden ausnahmslos erschossen. Aus Danzig hatte ich noch mit meinem Vater telefoniert und ihn gebeten, alles stehen und liegen zu lassen. »Wir können nicht mehr weg«, sagte er, »die Russen sind bei Kolberg schon an der See.« Und dann meine junge Frau! Vor viereinhalb Monaten haben wir geheiratet. Es war eine Hochzeit wie im tiefsten Frieden dort im allerhintersten Hinterpommern. Ob sie in Danzig auf ein Schiff gekommen ist? Wenn nicht – ich mag nicht mehr weiterdenken.

Allmählich kommen Gespräche auf: War wohl nichts mit den Wunderwaffen, alles Verrat wie anno 18. Die kleinen Hitlers haben versagt. Adolf wollte das Beste. An der Person Hitlers wird vorerst kaum Kritik laut, allenfalls: Den Krieg mit Rußland hätte er nicht anfangen sollen, nach Frankreich Schluß machen und so. Reihum werden nun zivile Berufsmöglichkeiten erörtert. Der Leutnant neben mir, Drogist aus Duisburg, wird wieder seinen Seifenhandel betreiben. Ein Leutnant aus Berlin, gelernter Kaufmann, möchte mit irgend etwas handeln. Der Leutnant und Gutsbesitzer aus dem Bergischen Land wird seinen Betrieb vom Verwalter übernehmen. Der Oberleutnant und hauptamtliche SA-Führer aus Schlesien weiß noch nicht, hat aber einflußreiche Verwandte im Rheinland. Man wird sehen! Der Oberleutnant und Lehrer aus Hessen, na ja, hat einen Schwiegervater mit kleinem Bauernhof und ein paar Kühen. Man wird ebenfalls sehen.

Einer wie ich, bar jeglicher Beziehungen zum Westen, könnte sich selbst bedauern. Mein Blick fällt auf die beiden lettischen Offiziere gegenüber. Sie schauen still vor sich hin, beteiligen sich nicht an der Unterhaltung, obwohl sie gut Deutsch können. In unserer Stube sind sie die größten Realisten. Sie machen sich die allerwenigsten Illusionen – genaugenommen gar keine. Zweimal in kurzen Abständen wurde ihr kleines Land von den Bolschewiken überschwemmt. Um dieser Gefahr ein Ende zu machen, hatten sie sich freiwillig zur Wehrmacht gemeldet. Wie die Esten, Norweger, Dänen, Holländer, Flamen und sogar die Siebenbürger Sachsen landeten sie bei Himmlers Waffen-SS. Nazis oder Faschisten waren sie nicht, von Einzelfällen abgesehen. Daß ihnen allen dies nun übel ausgelegt werden wird, ist ihnen klar. Wie klar, hören wir jeden Abend, wenn die Stadt zur Ruhe kommt. Dann vernimmt man im entfernten Tivolipark die Schüsse und Handgranatendetonationen der Männer der SS-Brigade Danmark, die sich dort zum letzten Gefecht verschanzt haben und von ihren Landsleuten keinen Pardon erhalten.

Ihr Schicksal geht mir nahe. Hatten sie doch namhaften Anteil am Aufbrechen des Kessels von Demjansk, in dem wir mit zwölf Divisionen ein Jahr lang eingeschlossen waren. Ihr tapferer Kommandeur, Major von Schalburg, aus der Garde des Königs, war dabei gefallen. Wer kennt sich da noch aus!

Das Essen wird knapp. Jedoch Milch gibt es reichlich. Bis zum fünften Mai konnten wir gegen Kronen alles kaufen wie Brot, Butter, Mettwurst, Schinken, Räucheraal. Inzwischen sind die Engländer im Landmarsch eingetroffen. Sie lassen sich in den immer noch vollen Geschäften einpacken: Torten, Kuchen, Schinken, Wurst und anderes. Sie sagen freundlich: »bye, bye« und gehen davon. Die Dänen rufen: »He, bezahlen!« Die freundlich grinsenden Tommys drehen sich um und sagen: »Wir haben euch doch befreit, wir sind doch eure Gäste!« Die Kopenhagener Kaufleute seufzen und murmeln: »Mäuse haben wir gehabt, aber die Ratten haben wir bekommen!«

Siegfried Unseld

## Waren wir Gefangene, oder waren wir frei?

Am achten Mai 1945 frühmorgens hörten wir in unseren Zelten, die in einem Wäldchen bei Flensburg-Mürwik aufgeschlagen waren, englische Kommandostimmen und einen von Zelt zu Zelt gehenden Befehl zum Aufstehen und Raustreten. Als wir unsere Zelte verließen, sahen wir englische Soldaten mit Maschinengewehren unterm Arm, die unseren Zeltplatz und den Wagenpark umstellt hatten. Der Führer unserer Einheit, Oberleutnant Adler, wurde aus seinem grauen Wohnwagen geholt; er ließ uns antreten. Ein englischer Soldat schaute in jedes unserer kleinen, mit Schutzfarben getarnten Zelte hinein, um sich zu vergewissern, daß sie leer und keine Hinterhalte zu erwarten waren.

Für uns kam das alles nicht überraschend. Wir waren eine kleine Gruppe von Marinenachrichtensoldaten, die eine bewegliche Funkstelle operierten, einen in einem Fünf-Tonner-Citroën eingebauten Sender und Empfänger. Die Funkstation war unmittelbar Großadmiral Dönitz unterstellt. Wir waren einer der wenigen Marinefunktrupps, die im Januar 1945 bei Rathenow im Bezirk Potsdam für das Oberkommando der Kriegsmarine ausgebildet worden waren; unsere Hauptbeschäftigung war freilich der Versuch, den dauernden Bombenangriffen amerikanischer und englischer Flugzeuge zu entkommen; dann siedelten wir nach Plön über, wohin Dönitz am 22. April sein Hauptquartier von Berlin aus verlegte; von hier aus ging es immer nur bei Nacht nach Wilhelmshaven und schließlich am zweiten Mai nach Flensburg; als wir ankamen, waren wir nur noch die einzige mobile Funkstation, die anderen hatten den Bombenhagel nicht überstanden.

Über unseren Sender liefen die entscheidenden Meldungen der letzten Kriegstage. Ich war zwanzig Jahre alt, im Mannschaftsdienstgrad eines Obergefreiten, hatte drei Jahre als Marinefunker an Kriegsfronten gedient und erhielt nun die Aufgabe, für die Funkarbeit neue, bisher nicht verwandte Codes zu benutzen, um die an Dönitz gerichteten oder von ihm ausgehenden Funksprüche zu entschlüsseln oder zu verschlüsseln. Wir waren außer den unmittelbar Beteiligten wohl die ersten, die am 30. April nachmittags den Inhalt eines für Dönitz bestimmten Funkspruches aufnahmen: »Anstelle des bisherigen Reichsmarschalls Göring setzte der Führer Sie, Herr Großadmiral, als seinen Nachfolger ein. Schriftliche Vollmacht unterwegs. Ab sofort sollen Sie sämtliche Maßnahmen verfügen, die sich aus der gegenwärtigen Lage ergeben. Bormann.«

Wir waren damals nicht in der Lage, über die Tragweite dieser Meldung nachzudenken. Auch nicht über den Funkspruch vom ersten Mai, in dem Dönitz einen Selbstmord zum Heldentod stilisieren ließ: ». . . daß unser Führer Adolf Hitler nachmittags in seinem Befehlsstand in der Reichskanzlei, bis zum letzten Atemzug gegen den Bolschewismus kämpfend, für Deutschland gefallen ist.« Wir hatten Tag und Nacht im buchstäblichen Sinn alle (Funk-)Hände voll zu tun, um Meldungen, Botschaften (»An das deutsche Volk«) und Tagesbefehle an all die Orte zu senden, wo noch deutsche Truppen waren oder die Flotte operierte. Es waren erregende Tage mit dem Gefühl, zwischen den Zeiten oder in einer Niemandszeit zu leben, erregend für uns, die ohnmächtigen Handlanger der Mächtigen, deren Macht freilich von Tag zu Tag verfiel; jeder konnte nun das Ende des »Tausendjährigen Reiches« wahrnehmen. Dönitz erkannte die Aussichtslosigkeit der militärischen Lage, er suchte den mit Kapitulation verbundenen Frieden gegenüber dem Westen zu ermöglichen. Tage- und nächtelang war in unserer kleinen Funkstelle Hochbetrieb, dann, am sechsten Mai, plötzlich Funkstille. Nur unsere Station durfte noch senden und empfangen, um mit den Unterhändlern der Kapitulation zu korrespondieren.

An diesem Morgen des achten Mai wußten wir Zaungäste der großen Geschichte mehr als viele andere Deutsche. Seit dem fünften Mai schwiegen im Nordraum nach einer Teilkapitulation, die Generaladmiral Friedeburg bei dem englischen Feldmarschall Montgomery unterzeichnet hatte, die Waffen; Montgomery hatte die Ablieferung aller Waffen und Schiffe gefordert; so schwer gerade Dönitz dies fiel, er mußte es akzeptieren; das Codewort »Regenbogen« für die auf allen U-Booten vorbereitete Selbstversenkung durfte nicht ausgegeben werden, doch viele Kommandanten versenkten aus eigenem Entschluß ihr Boot. Und wir wußten auch, daß am Vortage, am siebten Mai, in Reims, im alliierten Hauptquartier des Generals Eisenhower, von Generaloberst Jodl im Auftrage von Dönitz die Gesamtkapitulation der deutschen Wehrmacht unterzeichnet wurde. Insofern waren wir also über den englischen Besuch nicht überrascht.

Aus der Gruppe der englischen Soldaten löste sich, lässig mit einem Stöckchen unter dem Arm, ganz so, als befinde er sich in einem Kolonialgebiet des britischen Empire, ein englischer Offizier, ein Major, und hielt eine kurze Ansprache. Er sprach zwar deutsch, immerhin, aber so gebrochen, daß es schwer zu verstehen war, und zudem formulierte er alle Fachausdrücke in Englisch, was wir wiederum nicht so recht verstanden. Er sprach von »unconditional surrender«, »the head« des deutschen Staates, Dönitz, würde »maintained«. Die Engländer wünschten »to negotiate with him« – was immer dies bedeutete.

Wir aber hätten bis auf weiteres unsere Funkarbeit zu verrichten, über unsere Sender sollten die Kapitulationsabsprachen verbreitet werden, jedoch dürfe es keine verschlüsselten Funksprüche mehr geben, und wenn immer möglich, sollten die

Texte in englischer Sprache gesendet werden. Er übernehme das Kommando, Oberleutnant Adler habe seinen Weisungen zu folgen. Oberleutnant Adler salutierte – er sollte noch monatelang eine Art militärisches Regime im Wäldchen bei Flensburg-Mürwik ausüben, noch monatelang galt unsere von den Engländern genehmigte Anschrift O.K.M.-M.N.A.-Skl-M.N.K.100 (Mot) Glücksburg.

Spricht jemand von Ihnen Englisch? fragte der Major. Niemand meldete sich. Kann jemand Englisch lesen? – Ich meldete mich schüchtern, meiner hochstaplerischen Kühnheit bewußt (in den zwei Jahren meines englischen Schulunterrichts haben wir mehr gesungen als gelernt, denn Englischlehrer Zoller war auch für Gesang zuständig, er haßte die Engländer, komponierte Lieder im Stile von »Bomben gegen Engeland«, die wir im Englischunterricht singen mußten). Der Major gab Oberleutnant Adler die Anweisung, den Dienst wie gewohnt weiterzuführen, die Waffen mußten wir abgeben. Für uns ging eine Welt zu Ende, eine andere begann.

Der Übergang war nahtlos und geschah doch mit unbekannten Größen, denn die Bedingungen dieser »bedingungslosen Kapitulation« waren unbekannt. Waren wir Gefangene, oder waren wir frei? Dönitz und seine Regierung wurden in der Enklave Flensburg-Mürwik belassen; man wollte mit ihm verhandeln, und doch hatten nur die Sieger das Sagen. Ich sollte Dönitz einen Tag später, am neunten Mai, zum ersten und letzten Mal sehen, als er im Gelände der Marineschule Mürwik eine Ansprache an das verbliebene Offizierskorps hielt, ich sah ihn nur von ferne, seinen bemüht aufrechten Gang, und wenn ich mich recht erinnere, sprach er von der Notwendigkeit, in der Stunde der Niederlage Würde und Disziplin zu wahren; er konnte noch bis zum 23. Mai »regieren«, dann wurden er und seine Minister von einem englischen Kommando gefangengenommen: Das Deutsche Reich war zu Ende, das Schicksal der deutschen Nation offen. Die juristischen Fragen, wer wir seien, ob es einen deutschen Staat oder eine deutsche Staatlichkeit noch gebe, waren unerheblich. Es herrschten die Sieger.

Oberleutnant Adler teilte die Mannschaft zur Arbeit ein. Der englische Major nahm mich zur Seite, bat oder befahl mir, mich anzuziehen und ihm zu folgen. Im Jeep ging es nach Flensburg ins englische Hauptquartier. Ich wurde von Offizieren verhört, nach meiner Dienst- und Kriegszeit ausgefragt und nach den Gründen, wie ich in den Stab von Dönitz gekommen sei.

Schließlich erhielt ich eine Bescheinigung, wonach ich für eine englische Behörde arbeite und mich im Raum Flensburg bewegen dürfe. Der Major empfing mich zum Tee – mein erster englischer Tee. Ich mußte ihm die Geschichte der Einheit Adler erzählen, unser bewegtes Schicksal in Rathenow, Plön und Flensburg. Wir sahen uns in den folgenden Monaten immer wieder, entdeckten bald die gemeinsame Leidenschaft des Schachspiels, es schien, als hegte er väterliche Gefühle für mich. Wie er hieß, weiß ich nicht mehr. Ich bin ihm nie mehr begegnet. Dabei habe ich allen Grund, ihm dankbar zu sein: Von ihm erfuhr ich die erste reale Aufklärung über die Verbrechen der vergangenen Jahre, und wahrscheinlich hat er mein Leben gerettet. Als nämlich auf Drängen der Sowjets jene Reste der deutschen Armee, die die Engländer noch duldeten, aufgelöst wurden, war es auch mit der Einheit Adler zu Ende, wir sollten ins Gefangenenlager Rostock eingeliefert werden. Am Vorabend des Abtransports steckte mir der Major ein Papier zu, nach dem ich vom Bürgermeisteramt Flensburg als Dolmetscher angefordert sei. Mit den Soldaten meiner Einheit betrat ich am Morgen das Gefangenenlager, am Abend wurde ich als einziger entlassen. Am nächsten Morgen oder jedenfalls nur Tage danach wurde die Grenze der sowjetischen Besatzungszone über Rostock vorgezogen, und die Sowjets übernahmen das Lager; ich habe von keinem der damaligen Kameraden irgend etwas mehr gehört.

Dieser achte Mai 1945: Irgendwie war alles widersinnig. Man hatte als Deutscher für einen guten Ausgang des Krieges gekämpft, und nun mußte man das Unvorstellbare, Niederlage und Kapitulation, herbeiwünschen, der Wahnsinn mußte zu Ende sein. Ich sagte nicht die Wahrheit, wenn ich von Erleichterung oder Befreiung spräche. Irgendwie war alles zu Ende, und es war richtig so. Irgendwie mußte es aber weitergehen, aber wie sollte es weitergehen? Nie wieder das, was war, das war sicher! Aber Gefühle von Schuld, Scham und Schande wurden erst später bestimmend. Ohnmacht und Bewußtheitslosigkeit vermischten sich mit dem selbstbewußten Gefühl, Gefahren, oft auf des Messers Schneide, überlebt zu haben und mit dem lebhaften Instinkt des Zwanzigjährigen weiterleben zu wollen. Man hatte Furcht vor der Gefangenschaft und Furcht vor der Freiheit. Für mich war dieser Tag Leere und Lehre zugleich. Es ist gut, sich daran zu erinnern. Wer das Böse vergessen will, läßt es dauern, nur wenn wir erinnern, vermögen wir, uns von ihm zu lösen, zu erlösen.

HANS-JOCHEN VOGEL
## Neunzehn Jahre alt

Dienstag, den achten Mai 1945, den Tag, an dem die bedingungslose deutsche Kapitulation um 23.01 Uhr wirksam wurde, habe ich als neunzehnjähriger Unteroffizier in einem amerikanischen Kriegsgefangenenlager bei Pisa in Italien erlebt. Wahrscheinlich erfuhren wir von dem Ereignis – die Amerikaner nannten den Tag V-E Day (Victory in Europe Day) – aus der Soldatenzeitung »Stars and Stripes«. Da ich den Auftrag hatte, wichtige Meldungen aus dieser Zeitung ins Deutsche zu übersetzen und den Mitgefangenen zur Kenntnis zu bringen, habe ich die Nachricht von der Kapitulation vermutlich sogar selbst am Schwarzen Brett des Lagers angeschlagen.

Für unser Leben in der Gefangenschaft hatte die Kapitulation kaum eine Bedeutung. Unsere Sorge galt der täglichen Verpflegung und der Frage, was aus uns eigentlich werden würde. Dazu gab es eine Menge Gerüchte. So spekulierten einige darüber, daß es zwischen den USA und der Sowjetunion bald zu einem Konflikt kommen würde, bei dem man auch auf uns zu-

rückgreifen müsse. Mehr Glauben fand die Voraussage, daß alle
Kriegsgefangenen für Jahre zum Wiederaufbau nach Rußland
oder nach Frankreich überstellt werden.

Für gründlichere Betrachtungen über die Bedeutung der Kapitulation blieb da wenig Raum. Daß der Krieg so enden würde,
war uns in der Gefangenschaft ohnehin klar. Deshalb verspürte
ich ein Gefühl der Erleichterung darüber, daß nun jedenfalls das
sinnlose Töten und auch die Luftangriffe auf die Zivilbevölkerung vorbei waren. Daneben ging mir aber auch der Gedanke
durch den Kopf, wie rasch die Macht und der äußere Glanz eines
Reiches einer völligen Zerstörung gewichen waren. Immerhin
lag der Frankreichfeldzug ja erst fünf Jahre und die Zeit der An-
fangssiege im Osten erst vier Jahre zurück. Und auch die Frage
nach der ungeheuerlichen Verblendung und der Schuld derer beschäftigte mich, die das alles zu verantworten hatten.

Noch eins ist mir in Erinnerung geblieben: die allgemeine
Überzeugung, daß wir den Rest unseres Lebens in ärmlichen
Verhältnissen zubringen würden. Wer auch nur andeutungs-
weise hätte behaupten wollen, wir würden vierzig Jahre später
so leben, wie wir das heute tun, wäre ausgelacht und für verrückt erklärt worden.

ERNST WALTEMATHE
## Das Ende eines Alptraums

Was ich am achten Mai 1945 gemacht habe, weiß ich nicht. Für
mich war der fünfte Mai das wesentliche Datum. Ich war zehn
Jahre alt und lebte mit meiner jüdischen Mutter und meinem
um vier Jahre älteren Bruder in Amsterdam. Mein Vater war
1938 nach unserer Flucht kurz nach der Reichskristallnacht in
Bremen geblieben; ich war also – wie mein Bruder – Deutscher,
fühlte aber wie ein Niederländer. Das war die Nationalität meiner Mutter und von deren Verwandtschaft, die es aber inzwischen praktisch nicht mehr gab.

1942 – Razzien in Amsterdam, mein Großvater wird aus der Wohnung geholt, kommt über Westerbork und Theresienstadt nach Auschwitz, durch Vergasung ermordet.

1942 – Onkel (Bruder meiner Mutter) und seine Frau haben sich die Haare blond färben lassen und sich einen Paß von Honduras besorgt, kommen aber nicht mehr aus Amsterdam heraus, werden »geschnappt« und nach Bergen-Belsen verbracht. Mein Onkel überlebt das Konzentrationslager nicht: Im März 1945 stirbt er Hungers. Meine Tante kehrt kurz nach Kriegsende nach Amsterdam zurück, als Krüppel.

1942 bis 1943 – Tante (Schwester meiner Mutter, berühmte niederländische Malerin und Graphikerin) taucht auf einem Bauernhof unter. Das Versteck wird 1943 verraten, die Gestapo kommt, meine Tante entgeht dem Auschwitz-Transport dadurch, daß sie Gift schluckt und stirbt – vierzig Jahre alt.

1943 – Weitere Razzia in Amsterdam. Meine Mutter soll mit. Sie trägt Schwarz, weil gerade die Nachricht vom Selbstmord ihrer Schwester auf Wegen des Untergrunds eingetroffen ist. Sie redet in der mir fremden deutschen Sprache mit den beiden Uniformierten (SD). Es dauert unerträglich lange, aber sie vermag zu erklären, daß ihre Söhne (zwölf und acht Jahre alt) einen »arischen« deutschen Vater haben, dem sie auch zugesprochen sind, um die sie sich aber kümmern muß. Nach einer Ewigkeit ziehen die Deutschen ab, ohne meine Mutter mitzunehmen. Wir tanzen auf dem und um den Tisch, meine Mutter weint und weint.

1944/1945 – »Hungerwinter« in Amsterdam. Wir essen Zuckerrüben en masse und gelegentlich Blumenzwiebeln und Tapioka (scheußlich!). Brot: 400 Gramm pro Woche. Warmes Essen pro Tag; ein halber Liter aus der Garküche. Keine Heizmöglichkeiten. Wir haben noch Glück, was auch immer dieser Begriff bedeuten mag: Meine Mutter war bei einer Spielzeugfabrik beschäftigt, die längst dichtgemacht wurde (jüdischer Inhaber). Holz gab es da. Die Spielzeugräder und andere Kleinteile dienen uns zur Verfeuerung im Notofen (fünfzehn Zentimeter Durchmesser, etwa zwanzig Zentimeter hoch: eine

Kochgelegenheit, so man etwas zum Kochen hat). Angelieferte, aber nicht mehr zur Produktion verwendete Balken, Latten, Bretter usw. dienen zum Tausch: Es gibt immer noch betuchte Amsterdamer, die sich Hamstervorräte angelegt haben, aber Heizstoffe brauchen. Die liefern Weizen und ein nicht raffiniertes Öl, sogar einiges an Kartoffeln, meine Mutter liefert Holz. Der Weizen wird in der Kaffeemühle gemahlen, das grobe Mehl mit Wasser vermischt, Öl (schwarzfarbig) kommt in die Bratpfanne, und fertig sind die Pfannkuchen. Es gibt Leute, denen es weitaus schlechter geht.

Fünfter Mai 1945 – Holland ist »befreit«. Nicht anders als eine Befreiung habe ich den Sieg über die verhaßten Deutschen empfunden. Die alliierten Sieger wurden in Amsterdam freudig begrüßt. Es waren Kanadier, die in einem wahren Triumphzug in »meine« Stadt kamen. Ich stand an der »Noorder-Amstellaan«, die kurz nach dem Krieg in »Rooseveltlaan« umgetauft wurde.

Was für eine Freude! Endlich keine Angst vor (diesen) Uniformierten. Ich bekam das erste Kaugummi meines Lebens und durfte mit auf einem »Duck«, einem Amphibienfahrzeug. Wir fuhren mitten durch eine Gracht und dann wieder über von Tausenden von Menschen gesäumte Straßen.

Es war ein Freudentag, ein Tag des wirklichen Glücksgefühls, der Befreiung von tausend Ängsten. Nach Hause rannte ich mehr, als daß ich ging. Ich weiß heute noch, daß ich mir immer wieder einhämmerte: »Jetzt ist Friede, du brauchst keine Angst mehr zu haben, deine Mutter ist zu Hause, sie ist nicht weggeholt, und sie wird auch nicht mehr weggeholt.« Ich dachte an nichts anderes, konnte an nichts anderes denken. Mindestens drei Jahre hatte ich als Kind fast nur Sorgen, Ängste, Gerüchte, Informationen über »gute« und »schlechte« KZs erlebt, erfahren, aufgeschnappt. Schon als Siebenjähriger wußte ich, was Dachau, Bergen-Belsen, Auschwitz, Mauthausen, Theresienstadt, natürlich Westerbork und Vught bedeutete.

Haben wir alles nicht gewußt? Das kann ich heute noch nicht glauben! Wir wußten! Wir mußten die Schnauze halten, weil die Informationen aus dem Untergrund kamen.

Gestapo, SS, »grüne Polizei«: Wir wußten!

Gaskammern, Experimente an lebenden Menschen, Folter: Wir wußten!

Dieses Gefühl, daß das alles ein Ende hatte! Da konnten einem der Hunger und der Zustand der Unterernährung nichts mehr anhaben.

Und dann kamen die ersten Lebensmittelzuteilungen. Armeekekse (ganz trockene, ungesüßte Dinger: eine Delikatesse), Bluebandmargarine (aus Care-Paketen der Schweden), Brot!

Es kamen aber auch die Überlebenden des Holocaust. Die Ausnahmen. Meine Tante aus Bergen-Belsen. Sie heulte und heulte, und meine Mutter heulte mit. Ich konnte es nicht aushalten. Ich durfte mir ein Fahrrad mieten. Ich fuhr immer wieder um unseren Häuserblock. Zwei Stunden lang. Und schielte zur Wohnung, ob meine Tante nicht endlich ging. Diese verdammte Heulerei.

Die Nachricht aus Deutschland: Mein Vater, Eisenbahnschlosser, als Nichtnazi im Kriege vom Eisenbahnausbesserungswerk zum Fahrdienst als Hilfslokheizer strafversetzt, war auf einem der letzten Züge, die von Bremen nach Verden (Aller) fuhren, in Tieffliegerbeschuß geraten: sieben Schüsse in den Rücken und das linke Bein ab. Meine Mutter erzählte mir nur, daß er ein Holzbein bekommen würde. Ich konnte mir meinen Vater ohnehin nicht vorstellen. Und jetzt sogar als Krüppel? (Im Oktober 1948 lernte ich ihn kennen, als wir nach Deutschland zur Wiedervereinigung der Familie zurückkehrten. Da heulte ich, denn Deutscher zu sein, das war so ungefähr das Schlimmste, das ich mir vorstellen konnte. Obwohl ich immer einer gewesen war! Aber ich fühlte mich als Niederländer.)

Amsterdam ist nicht meine Vaterstadt, sondern meine Mutterstadt. Gerade die Zeit der deutschen Besatzung und der Verfolgung war gleichzeitig die Zeit des Freiheitswillens und tausendfach erfahrener Solidarität. Helden habe ich kennengelernt: fast allesamt »kleine« Leute mit einem untrüglichen Sinn für das Richtige.

Amsterdam am fünften Mai 1945: Das war »meine« Stadt,

das wird Symbol bleiben für Freiheit und Toleranz. »Mein«
Amsterdam befreit: Ein Zehnjähriger atmete freie Luft, hatte
keine Angst mehr. Nahm sich vor: Nie wieder darf so etwas
kommen, was Verfolgung und Massenmord bedeutete. Ja,
wirklich: Mein politisches Denken fing damals an, auch wenn
ich noch nicht alles begriff, ich hatte ein Ziel: eine bessere, eine
wirklich freie Welt! Und ich hatte Vorbilder: kleine Leute, die
ungeheuren Mut hatten, ohne berühmt zu werden. Die ihren
eigenen Kopf zum Denken benützten. Das habe ich gelernt,
und das tue ich heute noch. Auch wenn es für mich oder für
andere unbequem ist.

CARL WEISS
## Mein Kapitulationstag

»Beug dich nicht raus!« sagte Tante Milada zum hundertsten-
mal. Das Fenster war im ersten Stock, zweites Haus in der Seitenstraße. Alles, was ich sehen konnte, eng an den Vorhang gepreßt, war ein schmales Tortenstück vom Ringplatz und an der
Ecke, da, wo unsere Straße in die Laubengänge des Platzes
mündete, ein Radiogeschäft. Es war geschlossen. Unser Radio
ging nicht mehr. Es zu klopfen und zu schütteln hatten wir seit
einer Woche aufgegeben.

Wie lange lag ich schon auf dem Sofa, in einem seidenen
Schlafrock, einem roten mit gelben Streifen? Zwölf Tage oder
vierzehn? Tante behauptet, ich hätte nach der Ankunft drei
Tage und Nächte geschlafen. Als ich aufwachte, war die Uniform weg, Stiefel, Pistole, Papiere. Tante Milada hatte alles
Stück für Stück unter ihren Kleidern fortgetragen. Aber an Onkels ausgelagerte Sachen kam sie nicht ran. Alles, was es gab,
war ein seidener Schlafrock.

An Führers Geburtstag waren wir noch einmal zum Einsatz
gerollt. Unter Blätterdächern in Schützenpanzerwagen. Von
Landshut in Bayern nach Osten. Dann wird die Erinnerung

verschwommen wegen Fliegerbomben-Ohrendröhnen und dauernder Schlaflosigkeit. Wo genau war das Barackenlager, in dem es so fürchterlich stank? Hieß es oder hieß es nicht: »Außenstelle Flossenbürg«? Und wie sind wir durch den Stacheldraht hineingeraten? Wieso blieb ich in Gestank und Dunkelheit zwischen dreistöckigen Holzpritschen sitzen, und zu wem gehörten die Stimmen dieser Nacht, die auf slawisch-wienerisch gänzlich unerhörte Metzgerphantasien über Menschenfleisch redeten? Zurückgelassene KZ-Insassen?

Kapos? Aus der Uniform schon ausgestiegene SS?

Jedenfalls habe ich des Morgens meine Kompanie nicht mehr gefunden. Angesichts der Schemenhaftigkeit dieses Lagereindrucks weiß ich bis heute nicht, ob ich sagen dürfte: Ich habe die Kompanie bewußt nicht gesucht. Die folgende Nacht bin ich mit einem der Wienerischen durch den Wald marschiert. Habe später, zackig meldend, Kragenknopf geschlossen, mehrmals die Feldgendarmerie passiert. Tags in Scheunen. Nachts ein Stück in einem Holzvergaser, dann in einem Kübelwagen, wo ein Hauptmann sich per du und ungeniert mit seinem Fahrer übers Abhauen unterhielt. Das wie oft noch? Weitere Gedächtnislücken bis zum Straßenschild České Budějovice. Da wieder präzise einsetzende Kindheitserinnerung an den Ringplatz. Dort nämlich erste Krawatte aus Onkels Wäschegeschäft. Die Wohnung in der Seitenstraße.

Tante Milada hat bloß »Karlíčku!« gesagt und: »Komm rein!« Schon vierzehn Tage oder zwölf im Schlafrock. Beug dich nicht raus! Durch das einsehbare Ringplatzsegment waren mehrfach feldgraue Einheiten gefahren. Im Radio war verkratzt von General Schörner die Rede gewesen. Dann nichts mehr als Rauschen. Nachts unterm Fenster Wehrmachtsstreife, Kettenhunde auf BMW. Angst.

In der Küche standen ein Sack Mehl und ein großes Glas Butterschmalz. Wir aßen abwechselnd geröstete Mehlknödel, salzig, und mehligen Butterschmarren, süß.

Dann – war es am vierten oder fünften Mai? – in aller Morgenfrühe Aufruhr, ein paar Schüsse draußen. Ein Lastwagen und drei Dutzend leichtbewaffnete Zivilisten durchqueren das Stück Außenwelt, das ich sehen kann. Auf dem Wagen eine blauweißrote Fahne. Sie halten vor dem Radiogeschäft und reißen vom Wagen aus über dem Torbogen das Schild Adolf-Hitler-Platz herunter. Es liegt auf dem Pflaster.

Tante ist Tschechin. Onkel ist Deutscher. Er wurde vor drei Monaten mit dem Volkssturm abtransportiert. Wir reden Verwandtschaft. Wir reden keine »Lage«. Wir wissen nicht, was passiert.

Nächsten – oder übernächsten? – Morgen wieder Lärm und Schüsse. Durch das Blickfeld zieht viel Wehrmacht. Ein Wagen rollt übers Adolf-Hitler-Platz-Blech und zerknüllt es. Nachts darauf ratternder Verkehr.

Nächsten Morgen erst mal Stille, dann kommen Zivilisten auf die Straße, sie tragen rote Armbinden, und aus dem Fenster gegenüber schiebt sich eine blauweißrote Zwickelfahne. Der Ringplatz, man kann es besser hören als sehen, füllt sich. Im Radiogeschäft geht der Rolladen hoch.

»Wart noch«, sagte die Tante Milada. »Ich schau' erst mal nach.«

CURT VON WITZENDORFF

# Weichselniederung

Den Tag der bedingungslosen deutschen Kapitulation erlebte ich als Adjutant einer Infanteriedivision in der Weichselniederung, dem sogenannten »Danziger Werder«. Der Verband führte äußerlich noch die Bezeichnung Division, in Wahrheit entsprach die noch vorhandene Kampfkraft bestenfalls der von zwei verstärkten Bataillonen.

Während die Masse der deutschen Zweiten Armee auf die Halbinsel Hela abgedrängt war, sollten wir auf dem Westufer der Weichsel südlich Gottswalde einen etwa zehn bis fünfzehn Kilometer tiefen Brückenkopf halten. In ihm ballten sich zahlreiche Trecks zusammen. Sie kamen aus allen denkbaren Richtungen: aus Ostpommern, aus Danzig, aus West- und vor allem aus Ostpreußen. Da ihnen aufgrund der Lage ein Weiterkommen nach Westen verwehrt war, bemühte sich die Kriegsmarine, möglichst viele Flüchtlinge noch vor der Kapitulation auf dem Seewege in Sicherheit zu bringen.

Mit dem Auftrag, diese Menschen einzuschiffen, bekam »die Verteidigung bis zuletzt« für uns in dem sonst nutzlosen Geschehen noch einen Sinn. Das Aufreißen des Weichseldammes erleichterte den Endkampf. Feindwärts wurden die Ländereien so unter Wasser gesetzt, daß der Russe nur noch im Zuge weniger, höher gelegener Straßen angreifen konnte. Solche Versuche vermochten wir dann mit geringen Kräften abzuwehren.

Hinter diesem so gebildeten Schutzwall zogen damals Tausende von Zivilisten zunächst planlos in der Hoffnung hin und her, vielleicht doch noch irgendwo ein Loch zu finden, um der Einschließung und damit der Vernichtung zu entrinnen. Infolgedessen waren bis zur Küste alle Straßen und Wege hoffnungslos verstopft.

Für einen schnellen und möglichst reibungslosen Abtransport über See war aber erste Voraussetzung, daß es gelang, die Trecks zum Stehen zu bringen, das herrschende Durcheinander zu ordnen und die Menschen in Absprache mit der Marine erst dann zu den Einschiffungsplätzen abzurufen, wenn Schiffsraum zur Verfügung stand. Die Durchführung der hierzu erforderlichen Maßnahmen habe ich als schwierig, aufreibend und unerfreulich in Erinnerung. Sollten die Bemühungen Erfolg haben, mußten die Menschen geduldig bleiben und die gegebenen Anweisungen beachten.

Der Russe erschwerte zudem den Ablauf. Aufgrund alleiniger Luftherrschaft nahm er mit einzelnen Kampfflugzeugen aus niedrigen Höhen alles unter Feuer, was sich zeigte und bewegte, ohne daß wir das unterbinden konnten.

Die allgemein herrschende Angst um das nackte Leben, die im Verlauf der bisherigen Treckzeit gemachten Erfahrungen, die Sorge um das tägliche Brot, der noch nicht vorhandene

Wille, die letzte bewegliche Habe – meist Pferd und Wagen – stehenzulassen, sowie vor allem die Furcht, das Einschiffen zu verpassen, brachte die Flüchtlinge immer wieder dazu, sich selbständig in Bewegung zu setzen. So kam es häufig zu aufgeregten und daher unüberlegten, meist unliebsamen Auseinandersetzungen, sogar zu Tätlichkeiten.

Russische Kriegsgefangene, die bisher der deutschen kämpfenden Truppe treu und zuverlässig als »Hiwis« (Hilfswillige) gedient hatten, wurden hier gleichfalls zusammengezogen. Was sollte aus ihnen werden? Weder für sie noch für uns Soldaten stand Schiffsraum zum Abtransport zur Verfügung. Beiden Gruppen drohte die sichere Gefangenschaft.

Auch aus der Heimat hatten wir schon länger nichts mehr gehört. Es war gut, bis zuletzt genügend beschäftigt zu sein. So brauchte ich mir nicht mehr den Kopf zu zerbrechen über Fragen, auf die ich damals doch keine Antwort fand.

Die Nachricht von der beabsichtigten Kapitulation nahm ich mit Erleichterung auf. Das unsinnige Leiden und Sterben war damit zu Ende. Andererseits quälten die Ungewißheit über das Schicksal der eigenen Familie und die Unsicherheit gegenüber allem, was kommen sollte.

Zunächst wurden die eigenen Fahrzeuge verbrannt und noch vorhandenes, brauchbares Gerät zerstört. Die Truppe sollte am Tag der Kapitulation – nach Zusammenlegen der Waffen – einheitsweise antreten und vom Russen übernommen werden. Alles erfolgte in Ruhe und Ordnung.

Anschließend wurden die deutschen Generäle bei einem russischen Korpsstab nordwestlich Danzig versammelt. Ich sollte den Divisionskommandeur auf dessen Geheiß hin begleiten. Nur widerwillig tat ich das, denn damit wurde ich von den mir bekannten Menschen getrennt. Außerdem war mir der Mann seinem Wesen nach unsympathisch. Aufgrund seiner Gesinnung lehnte ich ihn innerlich als Vorgesetzten ab. Der Hund, von dem er sich auch jetzt noch nicht trennen wollte, war schon oft Stein des Anstoßes gewesen. Die Atmosphäre war gespannt.

Der russische Kommandierende General sprach von seiner

Herkunft – er war Sohn eines Fischers vom Kaspischen Meer – und mit Stolz von den großen Taten der Roten Armee, die nun auch das deutsche Volk vom Naziregime befreit hätte. Er erinnerte an die deutsch-russische Waffenbrüderschaft in den Freiheitskriegen gegen Napoleon und sprach vor allem von unserer baldigen Entlassung in die Heimat.

Einige der Anwesenden waren von dem Gehörten angetan. Etliche blieben skeptisch. In einer anschließenden Diskussion prallten die Meinungen hart aufeinander, und die Frage nach der Schuld am Krieg und dessen Ausgang spaltete die eigenen Reihen. Das sich zu Beginn der Gefangenschaft häufig wiederholende und vom Russen geschickt genutzte Spiel nahm seinen Anfang. Es fand sein vorläufiges Ende, als man uns Quartiere zuwies, die von Posten bewacht wurden. So teilte ich bald mit dem General und dem Fahrer einen kleineren Raum.

Nur noch gelegentlich fielen belanglose Worte. Die Ablehnung meines Vorschlages, die erste empfangene russische Verpflegung zu teilen: Fleisch und Kartoffeln für den General, Kartoffeln für mich und rohe Hirse auf die Hand für den Fahrer (!) sowie die Unmöglichkeit, für den Hund Fressen zu beschaffen, erhöhten die Mißstimmung.

Die Eindrücke des Tages, die Enttäuschung, daß Opfer und Hingabe vermeintlich umsonst waren, die Ungewißheit vor der Zukunft und ein Gefühl absoluter Hilflosigkeit ließen mich lange nicht einschlafen. Als ich an die Luft gehen und hierzu leise den Raum verlassen wollte, fuhr mich der russische Posten scharf an. Erst jetzt begriff ich, die persönliche Freiheit tatsächlich verloren zu haben.

•

RYSZARD WOJNA
## Vivat!

Den nachstehenden Text habe ich vor Jahren aufgezeichnet, um die Erinnerung an jenen Tag festzuhalten.

Die Nachricht erreichte uns am frühen Nachmittag. Zwischen Mons und Charleroi blockierte eine große Gruppe von Menschen die Chaussee. Wir mußten anhalten. Es umgab uns angerauschte Freude: »La guerre est finie!« Jemand drückte mir ein Glas Weißwein in die Hand. Wir hörten die Rufe: »Vive la Pologne!«

Ich leerte das Glas bis auf den Grund. Stanislaw, obwohl Sergeant der Fallschirmtruppen, zierte sich. Mit Gesten erklärte er, daß er Fahrer sei und nüchtern sein müsse. Nach einer Weile aber erlag auch er der fesselnden Stimmung. Über fünf Jahre hatten wir auf diesen Augenblick gewartet und oft gezweifelt, ob wir ihn erleben würden.

Wir wurden in einen Tanz gerissen. Hände haltend, bildeten wir ineinander übergehende, sich bewegende Kreise. Ein in der Mitte stehender breitschultriger Mann spielte Ziehharmonika.

So sieht also das Ende des Krieges aus? Man singt und tanzt. Was würden diejenigen sagen, die es nicht erlebt hatten, wenn sie uns sehen könnten: die bei Kutno getöteten, die im Warschauer Aufstand Erschossenen, die im KZ Auschwitz zu Tode Gemarterten, die in den Gettos vor Entkräftung Gestorbenen? Warum wandten sich unsere Gedanken nicht ihnen zu, sondern blickten in die Zukunft, berauscht von einem irrealen Optimismus?

Es kamen weitere Autos. Eine kleine Verkehrsstockung hatte sich bereits gebildet. Die Menge der Tanzenden wurde immer dichter.

Nur Stanislaw und ich trugen Uniformen. Wir fuhren mit dem Fahrzeug der polnischen Panzerdivision von General Maczek. Ihr Emblem – der Husarenflügel, an den Seitenwänden des Fahrzeuges angebracht – war hier allgemein bekannt. Vor einem halben Jahr hatten die polnischen Soldaten diesem Land Freiheit gebracht. Daher auch wurden wir mit einer Herzlichkeit gefeiert, die das Maß des Verstandes überschritt.

Nach mehreren Gläsern Wein spürte ich, daß ich mehr getrunken hatte, als ich vertragen konnte. Wir sollten uns am Abend noch in Brüssel melden.

Nicht ohne Schwierigkeiten entriß ich Stanislaw den Armen

einer molligen Blondine und schob ihn ins Auto. Wir machten uns auf den Weg und hupten Vivat. Die tanzende Menge blieb hinter uns.

Es wurde still. Der Tag war heiter. Die Chaussee leer. Eine Zeitlang sprachen wir kein Wort. Der Rausch schwand. Erst jetzt begann sich in uns der Sinn für die Welt und für die bahnbrechende Nachricht zu regen. Grundlegendes würde sich von nun an in unserem Leben ändern.

Wir hatten es bereits seit Tagen erwartet, genau von dem Moment an, als auf der Reichstagskuppel die sowjetische Fahne angebracht wurde. Etwas früher hatten die polnischen Soldaten die weißrote Fahne an der Siegessäule im Tiergarten gehißt.

Ich sagte zu Stanislaw, der keine Lust verspürte, ins Gespräch zu kommen: »Vor den Augen habe ich jetzt das Dunajectal in der Nähe von Stary Sącz (Alt-Sandez). Dort begann für mich der Krieg. Es war Sonntag, der dritte September 1939, am Nachmittag. Ich ging mit einer Patrouille, und bei Ząck gerieten wir in deutsches Feuer. Mein Gott, haben wir uns seit dieser Zeit verändert . . . Nichts mehr wird so sein, wie es war.«

Stanislaw schwieg. »Freust du dich nicht, daß der Krieg zu Ende ist?« fragte ich.

»Es kommt drauf an, für wen!«

»Für alle ist er zu Ende!«

»Worüber soll ich mich denn freuen? Mein Polen, das aus der Vorkriegszeit, hat diesen Krieg verloren!«

Ich schwieg. Was sollte ich ihm entgegnen. Ich wollte so schnell wie möglich in mein heimatliches Zakopane zurückkehren, während er, ich wußte das, die Emigration wählte. Ich war mit der Polnischen Sozialistischen Partei verbunden, die zwar zerrissen war, hinsichtlich der Frage der Beziehungen zur Sowjetunion, die aber doch einen Teil des Lagers der polnischen Linken bildete, die in dem befreiten Land die Macht übernahm. Stanislaw hingegen, vor dem Krieg Berufssoldat, war im Antisowjetismus erzogen worden.

Stanislaw: »Wir haben den Krieg verloren, weil der Westen uns verraten und an die Sowjets verkauft hat.«

Ich versuchte, ihm klarzumachen, daß Polen bereits unter verschiedenen Systemen lebte und doch immer es selbst geblieben war. »Denn Polen«, sagte ich, »das ist vor allem das Volk. Überdies kann man die Nachkriegswelt nicht mit Vorkriegsaugen beurteilen.«

Stanislaw sarkastisch: »Ich sehe, du agitierst für das neue Polen. Herzlichen Glückwunsch!«

»Ich agitiere für eine andere Zukunft. Überleg mal, wir erlangen wieder die Freiheit, darüber zu entscheiden, was wir morgen machen werden. Die Menschen werden nicht mehr von Angst beherrscht. Menschliche Grundbegriffe wie Gerechtigkeit, Heim, Familie werden wieder Sinn bekommen.«

Stanislaw lächelte: »Und ich gründe in Frankreich einen Laden«.

Es dämmerte bereits, als wir in Brüssel ankamen. Wir parkten unser Auto am Nordbahnhof. Und wieder lockten unsere Uniformen mit dem Abzeichen »Poland« am Arm die feiernden Belgier. Und wieder wurden wir in Tänze hineingerissen.

Das Ende war nicht gerade fröhlich. Spät in der Nacht versuchte eine kanadische Patrouille, in irgendeinem Café unsere Dokumente zu prüfen. Die polnische Panzerdivision bildete einen Teil der kanadischen Korps. Stanislaw, der schon total betrunken war, weigerte sich, seinen Militärpaß vorzuzeigen. Er drohte den Militärpolizisten mit der Faust und stammelte: »Ihr habt uns verraten . . . Ihr seid alle Hurensöhne . . .«

Sie richteten ihn übel zu. Da ich mich für ihn einsetzen mußte, wachten wir am nächsten Tag früh, am ersten Tag des Friedens, im Militärarrest auf.

BRIGITTE WÜRTZ

Der Anfang

Vierzig Jahre ist es her. Aber nichts hat sich so in die Erinnerung eingegraben wie diese Tage, als der Krieg zu Ende ging.

Ich sitze auf den Eingangsstufen vor der Haustür, die zweijährige Maja im Arm. Sie ist eingeschlafen. Ich beobachte ihre Atemzüge. Die Nachmittagssonne scheint warm. Vor mir im Sand spielt ein kleiner Junge. Er mag ebenso wie Maja zwei Jahre alt sein. Immer wieder sieht er zu uns hin. Er hofft, daß Maja aufwacht und mit ihm im Sand spielt. Seine Mutter, eine Russin, steht in einiger Entfernung und wäscht in einem Waschzuber Kinderhemdchen und bunte Lappen. Zwischen den Bäumen sind Stricke gespannt. Dort hängen einige Kleidungsstücke. Hosen und Jacken mit typischen Streifen, wie sie in Zuchthäusern getragen werden. Diese hier stammen von befreiten KZ-Häftlingen.

Waschen ist jetzt eine mühsame Angelegenheit. Wasser holt man in Eimern vom Brunnen, und der ist hinten im Pferdestall. Man muß dabei über schlafende Russen steigen, die ihre ersten Tage in Freiheit hier verbringen. Weil es kaum Seife gibt, wird die Wäsche kräftig gerieben. Die Frau hängt ihre nassen Stücke auf die Leine. Alles ist fleckig, blutig. Vieles zerrissen. Niemand achtet darauf. Auch meine Wäsche ist voller Löcher. Sauber bekomme ich sie schon lange nicht mehr.

Maja räkelt sich. Als sie den Jungen bemerkt, ist sie hellwach und rutscht mir vom Schoß. Sie läuft zum Sandhaufen, fällt in fertige Sandkuchen. Der kleine Kerl ist nicht ärgerlich. Im Gegenteil, auch er läßt sich fallen, bewirft Maja mit Sand. Sie wirft zurück.

»Njet!« ruft scharf die Russin.

Das Spiel wird ruhig. Mit einer alten Konservendose formen die Kinder Sandkuchen.

Meine Mutter kommt aus dem Haus. »Möchtest du Kaffee?« Sie hat zwei Tassen in den Händen. An einer fehlt der Henkel, die andere hat einen Sprung, aber sie ist dicht. Vorsichtig setzt sie sich neben mich. Der Kaffee ist das, was wir Ersatzkaffee nennen.

»Moje, moje!« schreit der kleine Russe und nimmt Maja die Konservendose weg. »Moje, moje!« schreit Maja und holt sie sich zurück. Am achtzehnten Januar sind wir in Schlesien aufgebrochen. Heute ist der achte Mai, und der Krieg ist immer noch nicht zu Ende. Beim Kaufmann wollte eine Frau ihre

Zuckerration holen, doch die war bereits verfallen. Es gab große Aufregung. Mehrfach deutete der Kaufmann auf den Kalender und sagte, heute wäre doch schon der achte Mai!

Der Zucker hat seine eigene Geschichte. Eine der ersten Anordnungen der Amerikaner betraf die Auflösung aller Vorratslager an die Bevölkerung. Im Nachbarort wurden Schlafanzüge verteilt, fünf Stück pro Kopf. Bei uns gab es Zucker. Einen halben Zentner für jeden. Ein unverhofftes Geschenk.

»Die arme Frau«, sagte meine Mutter, »unvorstellbar, daß sie es nicht gewußt hat!« Ich hole mein Nähzeug und ribbele einen alten Socken auf. Das gibt Stopfgarn. Wir besitzen nur eine Stopfnadel. Hüten sie wie eine Kostbarkeit. Mit den aufgeribbelten Fäden bessert meine Mutter einen Wollstrumpf aus. Ich sehe hoch und blicke über den Hügel. Die Sonne steht schräg. Genau wie vor drei Wochen, als wir dort die ersten amerikanischen Panzer sahen. »Erst drei Wochen ist es her«, sage ich, »was ist seither nicht alles passiert!«

Meine Mutter nickt. Sie weiß, woran ich denke. »Du kamst in den Keller gerannt und warst schneeweiß im Gesicht.«

»Die Panzer sahen so unheimlich aus und kamen direkt auf uns zu.«

»Ein Glück, daß es zu keinen Kampfhandlungen kam!«

»Unvergeßlich, wie die vielen Panzer die Dorfstraße langkamen. Hunderte nagelneuer riesiger Panzer! Die Soldaten standen in den Luken, alle jung und wohlgenährt!«

Das Gegenteil von unseren Soldaten. Die waren entweder alt oder noch Kinder und alle unterernährt. Und der Gauleiter hatte gefordert, sie sollten mit kochendem Wasser und Reißnägeln die Panzer bekämpfen.

Ein älterer Mann kommt in Unterhosen und nimmt den gestreiften Anzug von der Leine. Er zieht sich die Hosen an und hilft der Frau beim Aufhängen der Wäsche. Ein paar Stücke sind runtergefallen. Wäscheklammern sind rar.

Auf dem Hof haben sich kleine Gruppen gebildet. Dort werden die neuesten Nachrichten ausgetauscht. Auch Elard, mein Mann, hat sich dazugestellt. Seine schwere Kriegsverletzung ist

Glück im Unglück. Er wurde vom Wehrdienst entlassen und ist nun bei uns. Eigentlich sollte unsere Flucht aus Schlesien nur bis in die Nähe von Berlin gehen. Aber die Russen stießen im Mittelabschnitt immer weiter vor. So sind wir schließlich in der Magdeburger Börde gelandet. Verwandte haben uns ein Notquartier im Büro einer Baumschule eingerichtet. Wir wohnen zwischen kriegsverschleppten Russen und Polen.

Heute scheint es Neuigkeiten zu geben. Mehrere Männer stehen um einen Polen, der mit den Händen gestikuliert. Wir können nichts verstehen. Er spricht Polnisch. Elard wartet, bis ihm jemand das Wichtigste übersetzt.

»Vorige Woche soll sich Hitler das Leben genommen haben«, sage ich und lasse die Menschen drüben nicht aus den Augen, »glaubst du, daß das stimmt?«

Meine Mutter zuckt die Schultern. Wortlos. Sie fädelt einen neuen Faden in die Nadel.

»Es wäre gut, wenn man mal wieder eine Zeitung zu lesen bekäme. Ohne Zeitung und ohne Radio kommt man sich wie abgeschnitten vor, bekommt alles aus dritter Hand.«

»Trotzdem verbreiten sich die Nachrichten in Windeseile.«

»Ja, wie im Urwald.«

»Bin gespannt, was es heute gibt. Elard scheint was erfahren zu haben!«

Lächelnd kommt er auf uns zu. Unsere Spannung wächst.

»Die sind ja alle ganz aufgeregt, was ist denn passiert?« frage ich.

»Große Neuigkeit! Es ist Waffenstillstand!«

»Was?«

»Es soll vorhin durchs Radio gekommen sein!«

»Weißt du Näheres?«

»Bedingungslose Kapitulation. Jodl hat unterzeichnet. Morgen tritt der Waffenstillstand in Kraft!«

Meine Mutter umarmt uns mit Tränen in den Augen.

»Endlich ist der Krieg zu Ende! Endlich, endlich!«

Mein Vater tritt aus dem Haus und erfährt die freudige Botschaft. Wir alle stehen im Kreis. Jeder spürt die Erleichterung.

Ein unsagbarer Druck ist von uns gewichen. Maja kommt gelaufen. Sie fühlt unsere Freude und lacht auch. Mit einem Schlag scheint unsere Umgebung heller geworden zu sein. Stimmen schwirren durcheinander. Polen und Russen tanzen. Irgendwann sagt Elard: »Es werden sehr schwere Zeiten kommen!«

Mir fällt ein, gestern hat uns ein Amerikaner eine Tafel Schokolade geschenkt. Eine Kostbarkeit. Ich laufe ins Haus und hole sie. Gehe zu der Russin, will sie ihr schenken, aber sie dreht sich um, kehrt mir den Rücken.

Ich sage: »Schokolade, für Kind!« Halte ihr die Schokolade hin, gebe nicht auf. »Waffenstillstand heute!« Nach einer Weile nimmt sie die Tafel. Sagt nichts, kein Lächeln, nichts! Aber sie hat sie genommen. Ein Anfang.


PETER VON ZAHN

## Alle Sinne waren gespannt


»Was mit Kurland geschieht, ist nicht klar.« So lautet der letzte Satz einer Eintragung in mein Tagebuch vom siebten Mai 1945. Ich muß das in einem Erdbunker im Wald von Renda geschrieben haben, nachdem ich spätnachts die Nachricht von der Kapitulation der deutschen Heere in meinem Rundfunkapparat gehört hatte. Ob die in Kurland eingeschlossenen deutschen Truppen weiterkämpfen oder sich ergeben sollten, war nicht klar. In Zweifelsfall mußte man damals immer den sinnloseren Befehl für wahrscheinlicher halten.

Tagebuch: »Achter Mai. Es ist klar, wie ich das Gesicht des LDN am frühen Morgen sehe. N. (der Ic der Armee) verabschiedet sich. Mein Entschluß steht im Augenblick fest. Niemals soviel Energie verspürt. R. (der Kompanieführer) wird überrannt. Zwei Stunden später fahren wir.«

Ich muß hier einschieben, daß der Oberleutnant R., obwohl Parteigenosse, ein räsonabler Mann war. Trotzdem ging ich mit entsicherter Pistole in der Hosentasche zu ihm. Es gab dann noch den Nationalsozialistischen Führungsoffizier, auf den man ein Auge haben mußte. Er ließ sich aber nicht blicken, während wir telefonisch unsere Außenstellen alarmierten. Der Adjutant des Generals war mir wohlgesinnt. Er gab mir einen Marschbefehl »zwecks Auflösung der Außenstelle Windau«. Ohne ein solches Papier konnte man von jeder Streife der Feldgendarmerie angehalten und womöglich an die Wand gestellt werden. Dergleichen war unter Feldmarschall Schörner gang und gäbe gewesen. Wir hatten noch wenige Tage zuvor ein Verfahren erlebt, aufgrund dessen ein Angehöriger der Kompanie wegen Wehrkraftzersetzung zu fünf Jahren Zuchthaus verurteilt wurde. Ein mildes Urteil. Mein Tagebuch vom 30. April enthält dazu den Satz: »Keinerlei Terror – das nicht; die Maschine wurde von sanften, geübten Händen bedient.«

Soviel zur Erläuterung der kleinen Vorsichtsmaßregeln, die acht Tage nach Hitlers Tod im fernen Berlin noch immer angezeigt schienen, wenn man sich aus einem kurländischen Armeehauptquartier französisch empfehlen wollte.

Unterwegs hielt uns keiner an. Wir fuhren zwei Stunden durch Wälder, an deren Saum noch Schnee lag, und durch stille lettische Dörfer. Die Straße war leer – keine Truppen, die zur Küste hasteten. Ein solcher Befehl war nicht erteilt, und Benzin gab es auch nicht.

Mittags in Windau. Tagebuch: »Am Kai die Abwehr (= der Ic-Stab der Armee, der nicht in sowjetrussische Hände fallen sollte und deshalb ausgeflogen wurde). Im allgemeinen Disziplin. Kleine Plünderungsversuche schnell erstickt. So am Marineproviantamt. Luftangriffe. Überspringen auf KTK 03 (= ein zum Minensuchboot umgebauter Fischkutter). Nervensäge des Wartens. Explosionen. Um acht Uhr abends legen wir ab. Um neun Uhr aus Außenhafen, nachdem noch Marinesoldaten zurückgelandet. Übernachte mit Steigner im Backbordnock.«

Das Tagebuch hat mehr nicht zu sagen. Die Erinnerung erzählt mir noch, als ob es darauf ankäme, daß wir unseren Wagen über die Kaimauer ins Wasser plumpsen ließen. Sie erzählt, daß die Männer von zwei oder drei unserer Außenstellen auftauchten und ebenfalls mitkamen. Sie enthält nichts, was auf offene Gespräche, überraschende Gelöbnisse, was auf Jubel, Trauer oder Verzweiflung schließen läßt. Alle unsere Sinne waren gespannt. Es galt, das richtige Schiff zu erwischen. Was uns auf See geschehen konnte, schien harmlos, verglichen mit der Aussicht auf eine endlose Gefangenschaft in Rußland. Als die Stadt Windau im Schein von Bränden und Explosionen hinter unserem Schifflein versank, fühlte ich mich freier als an irgendeinem Tage seit dem Beginn des Krieges.

JÖRG ZINK

## Das Ende der Schizophrenie

Es war eine Landschaft aus Draht, grundlosem Lehm und, so weit das Auge reichte, schwarzen Armeezelten. Hunderttausend oder mehr Menschen in den Käfigen.

Ich habe den Kriegsschluß nicht anders erlebt als Millionen anderer, die ihre jungen Jahre auf den Schauplätzen des Zweiten Weltkrieges zugebracht hatten. Ich hatte den Krieg satt bis über die Ohren und wollte nichts mehr als nach Hause, um zu sehen, wer von den Meinen noch lebte, ob das Haus meiner Kindheit noch stand und ob sich vielleicht irgendeine Chance bot, ein »normales Leben«, das man sich noch kaum vorstellen konnte, anzufangen.

Der Tag, an dem der Krieg endete, hatte aber seine Innenseite. Da wuchs etwas wieder zusammen, das sich rund sieben Jahre zuvor gespalten hatte. Ich sehe mich als Pennäler bei einer Abiturfeier in der Aula unseres Gymnasiums, während der Direktor, ein großer, aufrechter Mann mit kahlem Schädel, darüber redete, wozu ein Mensch heute noch, da Humanismus nicht gefragt sei, die griechische Sprache erlerne.

Man lernt Griechisch, so ähnlich höre ich ihn sagen, damit man an einem entscheidenden Punkt seines Lebens sagen kann, was die Griechen ihren Freiheitskämpfern an den Thermopylen in den Mund gelegt hatten: Wanderer, kommst du nach Sparta, verkündige dorten, du habest uns hier liegen gesehen, wie das Gesetz es befahl.

Das paßte nahtlos in die Vorkriegsatmosphäre dieser Zeit und in die vormilitärische Bewußtseinsbildung, von der die Schulen damals beherrscht waren. Aber ich ahnte, daß der Mann am Pult etwas anderes meinte. Wir wußten alle, daß er ein Gegner der Nazis war, und ich fühlte, hier sei ein anderes Gesetz gemeint, nach dem er selbst, dieser Mann, angetreten sei und dem gehorchend er vielleicht eines Tages daliegen werde.

Damals erfaßte mich – er sagte den Spruch natürlich griechisch – der Sprachklang allein so tief, daß ich ihn von da an unverlierbar im Kopf hatte. Aber er brachte keine Lösung für meine Schulfreunde und mich, sondern eine tiefgehende Spaltung des Bewußtseins zwischen Kriegsbegeisterung und Widerstand.

Ich habe mich im zweiten Kriegsjahr wie alle meine Kameraden freiwillig gemeldet und habe damals als einer der vielen »Helden« das Meine getan, um dem deutschen Vaterland und seinem »Gesetz« zu dienen. Ich habe aber schon im dritten Jahr Briefe nach Hause geschrieben, in denen stand: »Es ist unmöglich. Wir dürfen den Krieg nicht gewinnen. Es wäre ein Unglück für die ganze Menschheit.« Lose Verbindungen zu dem Freundeskreis der Weißen Rose vertieften die Spaltung. Welchem Gesetz, dem des Krieges oder dem des Gewissens, sollte der Gehorsam gelten?

Viele von uns haben so in zwei Welten gelebt. Wir flogen gegen den Feind, wir schossen und ließen uns abschießen und flogen erneut. Wir wußten, daß die Chance, zu überleben, in unserer Staffel wie eins zu hundert stand. An den Abenden aber las ich das Edelste der deutschen Literatur und Dichtung und wußte, daß dies der Krieg des Unmenschen war. Ich las in den Reden Jesu von Nazareth und wußte, daß es für das, was wir taten, so etwas wie einen Segen oder nur eine Erlaubnis Gottes nicht gab, und wünschte mir, dieser Krieg möge baldmöglichst sein verdientes Ende finden.

Der achte Mai war das Ende der Schizophrenie. Ich erlebte

ihn mit dem Entschluß, künftig aus einem Stück zu sein und zwischen dem, was politisch zu tun war, und dem eigenen inneren Maß nicht noch einmal zu trennen. Und so hat mancher in der Enge der Drahtkäfige die Einheit seiner Person wiedergefunden, wie auch sonst mancher seine Identität nur unter Druck entdeckt.

Aber dann kam eine Zeit neuer, unerträglicher Doppelstrukturen. Da verband man alsbald die Freiheit des Christen mit der Freiheit der Wirtschaft. Da verband man christlichen Glauben und militärische Potenzprotzerei so mühelos wie zuvor. Da verband man Gottesliebe und an rabenschwarzen Feindbildern orientierten Haß. Da gingen Kirchen und politische Interessengruppen ihre unheiligen Verbindungen ein, und der Mann, der als Heimkehrer noch geschworen hatte: »Der Arm soll abfallen, der je wieder eine Waffe trägt«, amtierte wenige Jahre später als Verteidigungsminister in Bonn.

Unter Christen bedeutete der achte Mai 1945 für die einen das endgültige Ende jener unseligen Zweireichelehre, mit der im Hinterkopf der bürgerliche Christ sich erlauben durfte, allenthalben mit zweierlei Maß zu messen, für die anderen ihre erneute Rechtfertigung mit der Folge einer allgemeinen »christlichen« Wischiwaschipolitik, als deren Maxime jene Ausgewogenheit gilt, die das gespaltene Bewußtsein zu verklammern hat.

Man war in den Jahren nach dem Krieg sehr rasch politisch einsam, wenn man aus den Lehren der Nazizeit versuchte, Konsequenzen zu ziehen, und es hat fast vierzig Jahre gedauert, bis eine öffentliche Kraft entstand, in der wenigstens einmal die Frage nach Krieg und Frieden in der Einheit von Glauben und politischer Verantwortung bedacht werden konnte. Die Friedensbewegung unserer Tage, die heute getragen wird vornehmlich von jungen Leuten, die so alt sind, wie ich am Ende des Krieges gewesen war, ist für mich die späte Frucht jenes achten Mai, jenes Tages, an dem, für mich jedenfalls, die Schizophrenie endete.

# Die Autoren

WOLFGANG ABENDROTH
geb. 1906 in Wuppertal-Elberfeld. Bis 1972 Professor für öffentliches Recht und politische Wissenschaft, gest. 1985.

HEINRICH ALBERTZ
geb. 1915 in Breslau, Pfarrer. Von 1963 bis 1966 Regierender Bürgermeister in Berlin, gest. 1993.

HELMUT ALLARDT
geb. 1907 in Königsberg. 1968–1972 Botschafter in Moskau.

JEHUDA BACON
geb. in Polen. Hochschullehrer an der Hebräischen Universität in Jerusalem.

ARNULF BARING
geb. 1932 in Dresden. Ordentlicher Professor für Zeitgeschichte an der Freien Universität Berlin.

JITZHAK BEN-ARI
geb. 1924 in Wien. Ehem. Botschafter des Staates Israel in Bonn.

ERNST BENDA
geb. 1925 in Berlin. Bis 1983 Präsident des Bundesverfassungsgerichts.

TONY BENN
geb. 1925 in London. Britischer Politiker der Labour Party.

KURT BIEDENKOPF
geb. 1930 in Ludwigshafen. Jurist und Politiker (CDU).
Ministerpräsident von Sachsen.

ERIK BLUMENFELD
geb. 1915 in Hamburg. Ehem. Mitglied des Europäischen Parlaments
(CDU).

WILLIAM BORN
geb. 1895 in Hamburg. Ehem. Ehrenvorsitzender der FDP, gest. 1989.

SIGISMUND VON BRAUN
geb. 1911 in Berlin. Botschafter a. D.

LEO BRAWAND
geb. 1924 in Hannover. Journalist.

MARTIN BROSZT
geb. 1926 in Leipzig. Direktor des Instituts für Zeitgeschichte in
München, gest. 1989.

GÜNTHER DE BRUYN
geb. 1926 in Berlin. Schriftsteller.

MARGARETE BUBER-NEUMANN
geb. 1901 in Potsdam. Schriftstellerin, gest. 1989.

GERD BUCERIUS
geb. 1906 in Hamm/Westf. »Zeit«-Verleger und Publizist.

HELLMUTH BUDDENBERG
geb. 1924 in Bünde/Westf. Ehem. Vorstandsvorsitzender der
Deutschen BP.

JAMES CALLAGHAN
geb. 1912 in Portsmouth. Britischer Politiker der Labour Party.

WALTER DIRKS
geb. 1901 in Dortmund. Publizist. Mitbegründer der »Frankfurter Hefte«, gest. 1991.

MARIANNE DIRKS
geb. 1913 in Stuttgart. Musiklehrerin.

GÜNTER DÖDING
geb. 1930 in Isenstedt. Ehem. Vorsitzender der Gewerkschaft NGG.

ALFRED DREGGER
geb. 1920 in Münster/Westf. Ehem. Vorsitzender der CDU/CSU-Bundestagsfraktion. Mitglied des Deutschen Bundestages.

INGEBORG DREWITZ
geb. 1923 in Berlin. Schriftstellerin, gest. 1986.

FREIMUT DUVE
geb. 1936 in Würzburg. Verlagslektor und Bundestagsabgeordneter (SPD).

LEO EITINGER
geb. in Polen. Vorstand des Psychiatrischen Instituts an der Universität Oslo.

BERNT ENGELMANN
geb. 1921 in Berlin. Journalist und Schriftsteller, gest. 1994.

DIETER ERTEL
geb. 1927 in Hamburg, Ehem. Fernsehdirektor Südwestfunk.

ERHARD EPPLER
geb. 1926 in Ulm. Ehem. Bundesminister und Mitglied des SPD-Bundesvorstandes.

WERNER FILMER
geb. 1934 in Iserlohn. Kulturchef des WDR-Fernsehens.

MASCHA M. FISCH
geb. 1931 in Winterthur. Journalistin.

OSSIP K. FLECHTHEIM
geb. 1909 in Nikolajew/Rußland. Ehem. Hochschullehrer für
politische Wissenschaften an der Freien Universität Berlin.

RUFUS FLÜGGE
geb. 1914 in Hamburg. Stadtsuperintendent i. R.

JOCKEL FUCHS
geb. 1919 in Hargesheim bei Bad Kreuznach. Ehem.
Oberbürgermeister von Mainz.

LISELLOTTE FUNCKE
geb. 1918 in Hagen. Politikerin (FDP). Ehem. Bundesbeauftragte
für Ausländerfragen.

HEINZ GALINSKI
geb. 1912 in Marienburg/Westpreußen. Ehem. Vorsitzender der
Jüdischen Gemeinde zu Berlin, gest. 1992.

GÜNTER GAUS
geb. 1929 in Braunschweig. Staatssekretär a. D., Publizist.

EUGEN GERSTENMAIER
geb. 1906 in Kirchheim/Teck. Hochschullehrer und Politiker.
Bundestagspräsident a. D., gest. 1986.

JUTTA GIERSCH
Schriftstellerin.

SOPHIE GOLL
geb. 1921 in Erfurt. Schauspielerin. Publizistin.

JOHANN BAPTIST GRADL
geb. 1904 in Berlin. Ehem. Bundestagsabgeordneter und
Minister(CDU), gest. 1988.

MARTIN GREGOR-DELLIN
geb. 1926 in Naumburg. Schriftsteller. Präsident des PEN-Klubs,
gest. 1988.

PIERRE GRÉGOIRE
geb. 1924 in Strassen. Ehem. Minister. Ehrenpräsident des
Luxemburger Parlaments.

ALFRED GROSSER
geb. 1925 in Frankfurt/Main. Franz. Politologe und Publizist.

MAX VON DER GRÜN
geb. 1926 in Bayreuth. Schriftsteller.

HILDEGARD HAMM-BRÜCHER
geb. 1921 in Essen. Staatsminister a. D., Ehem.
Bundestagsabgeordnete (FDP).

LUDWIG FREIHERR VON HAMMERSTEIN
geb. 1919 in Berlin. Journalist. Rias- Intendant a. D.

ADELAIDE HAUTVAL
geb. 1925. Mitglied des »Comité International Des Camps.«

Elisabeth Heisenberg
Witwe des Physikers Werner Heisenberg.

Helmut Heissenbüttel
geb. 1921 in Wilhelmshaven. Schriftsteller.

Wilhelm Hennis
geb. 1923. Ehem. Direktor des Seminars für wissenschaftliche
Politik der Universität Freiburg.

BURKHARD HIRSCH
geb. 1930 in Magdeburg. Bundestagsabgeordneter (FDP).

HANS-EGON HOLTHUSEN
geb. 1913 in Rendsburg/Schleswig. Schriftsteller.

HANS-GÜNTER HOPPE
geb. 1922. Ehem. Bundestagsabgeordneter (FDP).

HEINZ WERNER HÜBNER
geb. 1921 in Potsdam. Ehem. Programmdirektor WDR-Fernsehen.

KARL IBACH
geb. 1915 in Wuppertal-Elberfeld. Ehem. Vorsitzender des
Zentralverbandes demokratischer Widerstandskämpfer- und
Verfolgtenorganisationen (ZDWV).

WERNER KIESSLING
Ehem. Präsident des Verbandes der Heimkehrer, Kriegsgefangenen
und Vermißtenangehörigen Deutschlands.

KARL KLASEN
geb. 1909 in Hamburg. Bundesbankpräsident a. D.

NORBERT KLOTEN
geb. 1926 in Sinzig. Ehem. Präsident der Landeszentralbank Baden-
Württembergs.

SHMUEL KRAKOWSKI
geb. in Polen. Archivdirektor des »Jad Vashem« in Jerusalem.

WERNER KRUSCHE
geb. 1917. Ehem. Bischof von Magdeburg.

HERMANN KUNST
geb. 1907 in Ottersberg. Ehem. Bischof von Bonn.

HERMANN LANGBEIN
geb. 1912 in Wien. Publizist und Sekretär der Arbeitsgemeinschaft
zur Dokumentation »Nationalsozialistischer Massentötungen durch
Giftgas«.

DIETER LATTMANN
geb. 1926 in Potsdam. Schriftsteller und ehem. SPD-MdB.

EUGEN LODERER
geb. 1920 in Heidenheim/Brenz. Ehem. Vorsitzender der IG Metall.

FRANZ D. LUCAS
geb. in Berlin. Generalkonsul a. D., London.

PETER LUDWIG
geb. 1925 in Koblenz. Unternehmer und Kunstmäzen.

ULRICH DE MAIZIÈRE
geb. 1912 in Stade. General a. D.

HANS MARSALEK
geb. in Wien. Vorstandsmitglied der österreichischen
Lagergemeinschaft Mauthausen.

HANS MATTHÖVER
geb. 1925 in Bochum. Ehem. Bundesminister und
Bundestagsabgeordneter (SPD).

YOHANAN MEROZ
geb. 1920 in Berlin. Ehem. Botschafter Israels in der Schweiz und in
Bonn.

JOHANN-BAPTISCH METZ
geb. 1928 in Welluck/Opf. Theologieprofessor in Münster.

EDMUND NEUDECK
geb. 1905 in Danzig. Oberstudienrat a. D.

GERTRUD NEUDECK
geb. 1913 in Danzig. Hausfrau.

RUPERT NEUDECK
geb. 1939 in Danzig. Journalist. Vorsitzender des Komitees
»Notärzte« e. V.

LEONID OLSCHWANG
geb. 1905 in Plonge/Litauen. Oberrevisor i. R., Journalist.

ROSALINDE VON OSSIETZKY-PALM
geb. in Berlin. Sozialarbeiterin in Stockholm.

LEONIE OSSOWSKI
geb. 1925 in Ober-Röhrsdorf/Schlesien. Schriftstellerin.

CHARLOTTE PETERSEN
geb. 1904 in Niederschelden. Journalistin.

PIERRE PETIT
geb. in Luxemburg. Mitglied des »Comité International Des Camps«.

ANISE POSTEL-VINAY
Leitende Mitarbeiterin der Auncale des Anciènnes Déportes de Ravensbrück«, Paris.

EDWARD PYS
geb. in Polen. Mitglied des »Comité International Des Camps«.

TRUTZ RENDTORFF
geb. 1931 in Schwerin. Theologe. Ehem. Professor der Univ. München.

ANNEMARIE RENGER
geb. 1919 in Leipzig. Ehem. Bundestagspräsidentin (SPD).

HELMUT RIDDER
geb. 1919. Jurist, Ehem. Hochschullehrer der Universität Gießen.

LUISE RINSER
geb. 1911 in Pitzling (Obb.), Schriftstellerin.

KURT ROSSA
geb. 1930 in Gelsenkirchen. Ehem. Oberstadtdirektor von Köln.

KURT SCHARF
geb. 1902. Theologe und Kirchenpolitiker, gest. 1990.

EUGEN SEIBOLD
geb. 1918 in Stuttgart. Ehem. Präsident der Deutschen
Forschungsgemeinschaft.

OTA SIK
geb. 1919 in Plzen. Ehem. Tschechischer Politiker und
Wirtschaftswissenschaftler.

SHMUEL SPEKTOR
geb. in Polen. Mitarbeiter von »Jad Vashem«, Jerusalem.

MARGARETE SCHÖPKE
geb. 1907 in Lüneburg. Apothekerin.

KARL STEINBRUCH
geb. 1917 in Bad Cannstatt. Ehem. Professor für
Nachrichtenverarb.

CAROLA STERN
geb. 1925 in Ahlbeck/Seebad. Journalistin.

JOSEF STINGL
geb. 1919 in Maria-Kulm/Böhmen. Ehem. Präsident der
Bundesanstalt für Arbeit.

MICHAEL THOMAS
geb. 1915 in Berlin. Schriftsteller.

GASTON THORN
geb. 1928 in Luxemburg. Ehem. Präsident der EG-Kommission.

GEORG STEFAN TROLLER
geb. 1921 in Wien. Journalist.

HERMANN ULRICHS
geb. 1917 in Danzig. Landwirt.

SIEGFRIED UNSELD
geb. 1924 in Ulm. Verleger.

HANS-JOCHEN VOGEL
geb. 1926 in Göttingen. Ehem. Vorsitzender der SPD-
Bundestagsfraktion.

ERNST WALTEMATHE
geb. 1935 in Bremen. Bundestagsabgeordneter der SPD.

CARL WEISS
geb. 1925 in Zuckmantel/Schlesien. Ehem. ARD-Korrespondent in
Brüssel.

CURT VON WITZENDORFF
geb. 1916 in Erfurt. Ehem. Berufssoldat.

RYSZARD WOJNA
geb. 1920 in Polen. Journalist und ehem. Mitglied des polnischen
Parlaments.

BRIGITTE WÜRTZ
Hausfrau.

PETER VON ZAHN
geb. 1913 in Chemnitz. Journalist.

JÖRG ZINK
geb. 1922 in Elm. Pfarrer und Publizist.